SOFÍA. Brilliant and beautiful, talented and courageous, the mysteries of her past and the poverty of her present compelled her to challenge destiny.

ROBERT. The English Mendoza determined to regain the wealth and power lost by his Spanish cousins, he heard Sofía's entrancing song and knew she would become his salvation . . . or his destruction.

PABLO LUIS. The crippled Mendoza heir, he lived only for the bullfight . . . squandering his life and fortune.

MARIA ORTEGA. Sensuous, seductive, she played three roles . . . two of them false.

CARLOS. The half-Gypsy boy who saved Sofía's life, later the brave matador who risked his own to be worthy of her.

DOÑA CARMEN. The betrayed wife, once lovely, now disfigured by disease, who lusted for vengeance.

HARRY HAWKINS. The saintly man who bore a cruel burden on behalf of the Mendozas.

FRANCISCO DE MAYA. The fanatic who would incite revolution and never count the cost.

ZOCALI. The Gypsy chieftain who held Sofía's life and death in his hands.

Another Bantam Book by
Beverly Byrne

THE MORGAN WOMEN

A Lasting Fire

BEVERLY BYRNE

BANTAM BOOKS
NEW YORK · TORONTO · LONDON · SYDNEY · AUCKLAND

A Lasting Fire

A Bantam Fanfare Book / July 1991

FANFARE and the portrayal of a boxed "ff" are trademarks of Bantam Books, a division of Bantam Doubleday Dell Publishing Group, Inc.

ISBN 0-553-28815-6

Published simultaneously in the United States and Canada

Bantam Books are published by Bantam Books, a division of Bantam Doubleday Dell Publishing Group, Inc. Its trademark, consisting of the words "Bantam Books" and the portrayal of a rooster, is Registered in U.S. Patent and Trademark Office and in other countries. Marca Registrada. Bantam Books, 666 Fifth Avenue, New York, New York 10103.

PRINTED IN THE UNITED STATES OF AMERICA

OPM 0 9 8 7 6 5 4 3 2 1

For H.M., who had a wonderful idea,
and W.F.M., who supported it

⧼ Author's Note ⧽

Spanish surnames are not formed as they are among English-speaking peoples. A woman does not change her last name when she marries; those of a husband and wife remain different, and everyone has two. Children are given the first of the surnames of both father and mother, and retain them all their lives. For example, the child of Juan Gonzalez Rodriguez and Maria Lopez Hernandez will be Carlos Gonzalez Lopez. The first of the two surnames is the one commonly used; the final one is for official identification.

In Spain the titles Don and Doña are honorifics used with the first name. While they are roughly comparable to Lord and Lady, they are not reserved for the aristocracy, but are used in any formal situation and, in former times, always when a person of a lower class addressed a social superior. Further, though señorita designates an unmarried woman and señora one who is married, señorita was, until recently, considered the more polite form.

Certain moves of the bullfighter as described in this story were invented by toreros who lived after the time period in which *A LASTING FIRE* is set. I have allowed myself literary license in using them. I have also taken minor liberties with elements of the history of banking in Spain.

Book One

here was no moon on that night in 1380; the three figures worked by brittle blue starlight and the dull glow of a single lantern. The night was cold, but the bodies of the woman and the two men were drenched in sweat as they heaved on the ropes supporting the huge slab of granite.

"The whole idea is insane." Nathan shot a quick glance at his father. Benhaj was struggling to breathe as he pulled the last line taut. "How often do you think we can do this?" the son demanded.

Benhaj's every muscle trembled with exertion; hot pains shot down his arms and legs and across his chest. "We will do it as often as we have to," he said between grunts.

"It's finished," his wife, Rasha, said when the final straining pull lifted the slab back into position. She sank to her knees, her heart beating wildly, and fanned herself with the hem of her dress.

The strongroom was now as it had been before the three of them began their labors—a small declivity in a naturally occurring granite outcropping in the garden of the Mendoza palace in Córdoba. When they coiled away the ropes there was no sign that anything had been disturbed, that another much larger storeroom existed behind the first.

The sun rose brilliant red that morning, and Benhaj looked at it and knew it was a portent of the fire to come. "It's not finished, Rasha," he told his wife. "It's just beginning."

The cache in the secret cave grew bit by bit as Benhaj and Nathan tithed to it. The Mendozas were moneylenders, had been so since before anyone could remember. Now, after each transaction, they divided their profits. "This to meet our needs and the taxes," Benhaj would say, pushing the largest part of the gold ducats to one side. "And this for the future."

Other things were also hidden away—Rasha's contributions. Her selections were intensely personal, but she assured her husband they were treasures worthy of protection.

The storm Benhaj had anticipated broke on June 17, 1391. A rampaging mob burned to the ground the Jewish section of Córdoba, the Palacio Mendoza along with all the rest. Two thousand Jews died that day and their bodies were left to rot in the streets. But the family Mendoza survived, Benhaj and Nathan lived to return and see that the false wall protecting their secret hoard was unbreached.

Standing in the midst of charred and blackened desolation, swaying to age-old rhythms, the old man cried for vengeance in the words of the ancient psalm. " 'By the waters of Babylon where we sat down, how we wept when we remembered Sion.' " He paused and his voice trembled. " 'If I forget thee O Jerusalem, may my right hand forget her cunning . . .' "

Nathan took up the chant. " 'Babylon, pitiless queen, blessed be the man who deals out of thee the measure thou hast dealt to us; blessed be the man who will catch up thy children and dash them against the rocks.' "

❧ 1 ❧

The synagogue in Bordeaux was cramped and dark, a small single room below ground level. Random shafts of daylight pierced the gloom, finding their way in through slitted openings near the ceiling. The openings were barely noticeable gaps at the bottom of the outside wall of an ancient house in a twisting narrow alley. Within the sanctuary an oil lamp burned beside the ark containing the Torah scrolls. Day and night its red glow suffused the gloom.

Despite the fact that no Jew could legally be a French subject, it had suited the authorities to allow Jews to remain in France. This ark and its sentinel fire had been unmolested for nearly three hundred years, which was one reason that in this year of 1788, in his sixty-third spring, Benjamin Valon was a happy man.

"Imagine, my little Sophie, our people have prayed here since the fifteenth century," the old man repeatedly told his five-year-old granddaughter. "That's a miracle. Remember what I've said about the way it used to be—how in 1492 the Spanish king and queen expelled all the Jews from their kingdom and our ancestors came to Bordeaux. Never forget we are Sephardim, Jews from Spain. We have a wonderful past."

Benjamin Valon was fascinated by the history of his line. He had taught himself Spanish and read with delight of the wonders of sun-drenched Spain, and he dreamed of visiting it one day. When he spoke of these things Sophie would listen and nod, though she couldn't really understand. Her grandfather answered her simple questions with complex explanations; besides, the concept of past and future had little meaning to the child. Still, she tried. "Why did the king make us leave Spain?"

"His name was Ferdinand, and his wife was Queen Isabella, and they wanted everybody in their kingdom to believe in the Christian God."

"But you say there's only one God . . ."

"True, Sophie, true. But . . ." Benjamin began another long discourse she couldn't follow.

The old man knew little Sophie wasn't grasping his words, but it didn't matter. Benjamin adored his only grandchild, and the hours he spent with her were the finest of all the pleasures of these peaceful days at the end of a difficult but successful life.

His father had been a peddler, traveling the streets with a wagon filled with used clothing; today the Valons owned a haberdashery that employed thirty tailors and served the best-dressed gentlemen of southwestern France. Having accomplished all that by 1783, when Sophie was born, Benjamin, a widower for many years, had retired and turned the business over to Sophie's father, his son, León.

"Now you will have time for your prayers and your books, Papa," the young man had said.

"And to be with your beautiful daughter," the old man agreed.

How sweet these past five years had been. The child delighted him; merely to look at her was a joy. Sophie's hair was black and thick and framed her face in a tangle of curls. Her skin was honey-gold, her cheeks pink with health. Her eyes, however, were not the expected brown. Some rogue element of the past had gifted the little girl with enormous eyes of startling aquamarine blue. They flashed with the fire of a diamond. Without such eyes she would have been remarkably pretty; because of them, Sophie Valon was destined to be a beauty.

Rachelle, León's wife, was not a pretty woman, and Benjamin suspected she was jealous of her daughter. Rachelle spent little time with Sophie. She preferred to work every day in the store with her husband. A woman was employed to look after the child, but it was actually Benjamin who took charge of Sophie's upbringing. He watched over her first steps and nursed her childhood illnesses. He taught her to read and to count. When Benjamin went anywhere, the little girl went with him, clinging to his hand.

Thus almost every morning they would walk together through the streets to that alley of ancient houses and down the steep, narrow staircase to the synagogue. Inevitably, just before they arrived, Sophie would ask the same question. "*Grand-père,* can I sit with you today?"

"No. Not today, and not next week, and not next year."

"Why not?"

"Because, as I have told you and told you, women and men mustn't sit together there."

"We sit together at home."

"Yes, but not in the synagogue."

Sophie sighed and stifled her protests, afraid that if she persisted, she'd be left at home. Anyway, it wasn't so bad, her beloved *grand-père* wasn't very far away. The tiny synagogue was too small for the customary balcony separating female and male congregants. It had only a token barrier across one corner, fashioned of wooden strips woven in a lattice pattern, and covered with a dark red curtain secured top and bottom with a polished brass rod. Sophie had discovered early on that if she moved the curtain very cautiously with one finger, she could peek at the men, and neither they, nor any woman around her, would know.

Sophie saw everything—the richly decorated Torah scrolls, the black skullcaps she learned to call yarmulkes, and the tallith, the fringed silk shawls that swayed back and forth as the worshippers moved to ancient rhythms, and on occasions of special ceremony, the curved ram's horn, the shofar, all overlaid with the crosshatched shadow of the wooden screen.

At times during the day at home Benjamin would hear the

little girl singing the chants of the synagogue. "Such a voice," he murmured as he listened transfixed with wonder. "My Sophie, if you were a boy, you would be a cantor. God must have had a reason to put such a voice in a girl's body, but I don't know what it could be."

Usually Sophie was in bed before León and Rachelle returned from the store, so they seldom heard her sing. It was left to Benjamin to tell them about the child's astonishing voice. "We must do something about it. I don't know what, but such a gift is not to be ignored."

"Yes, Papa, yes. But right now there are more important things to think about."

"Like what? What can be more important than your only child?"

"Papa, these are great days. *Liberté, égalité, fraternité,* they're more than words. Look what they've accomplished in America. A revolution, nothing less. Now, right here in France, such things are happening..."

León spoke with enthusiasm of the political upheaval of the past eighteen months. Seduced by the possibilities, he had no way of predicting the firestorm that was to be unleashed. He did not recognize that *la belle France* lay under the lengthening shadow of *la guillotine.* "A new age is coming," he told his father. "It will be marvelous. I promise, Papa, you will live to see things you never dreamed could exist."

"Maybe. If God makes days of ten hours instead of twenty-four, and months that take only two weeks. I'm an old man, my son. The future cannot come fast enough for me. It is for you. And for little Sophie. Maybe in this miraculous future a girl will have a use for such a voice...."

Because Benjamin was not a political man, he did not hear the songs of a different sort being sung in France. But León was right, they were there to be heard. They rose from the rivers and fields of the countryside, and from the stones of the cities. Bread for all, they sang; freedom, they sang; equality, they sang; down with the oppressors, they sang. On Sophie's sixth birthday, the fourteenth of July 1789, they reached a

crescendo. The Bastille was stormed and fell. The French Revolution had begun.

"I told you, Papa, I told you," exulted León. His euphoria
seemed justified when in late January of 1790 the Sephardim
of southern France were declared full citizens of France, children of *la patrie*.

A turbulence swept the nation, a whirlwind. The newly en-
franchised Jews put their hearts and souls and resources into
the battle to insure the success of the revolution. They poured
out their treasures and enlisted in the guard. Rachelle and León
could not bear to sit on the sidelines and watch. "We're going
to Paris, Papa," Leon told his father in September. "Only for a
few weeks. Just to see, to help if we can. You and Sophie will
be fine without us for a short time."

Scholar though he was, Benjamin had never been a reader
of newspapers or a student of current events. That autumn in
Bordeaux was mellow and warm; what he learned came to him
through the gossip and rumors he heard as he strolled the
streets and parks, holding Sophie's hand. In those early days
of the civil war, ideals were yet untarnished by the terrible
excesses to come. The Reign of Terror was no more than a
shadow on the horizon. Believers still spoke of *liberté, égalité,
fraternité,* and the phrase was not a mockery.

Without León to interpret for him, the old man formed his
own evaluation of the situation. He became convinced that all
Europe was now safe for Jews, that an almost messianic age
had arrived.

"The *hamashiah* himself must be coming, Sophie," he said.
"And I have lived to see it, and you were born in time to see
it. . . ." Marveling at these wonders, Benjamin made a plan. He
would take his beloved Sophie across the mountains to Spain.
They would greet the Anointed One in the land of their fore-
fathers.

Two figures moved cautiously along a path that was no more
than a double handspan of solid ground above a sheer precipice.
These were the southern foothills of the massive Pyrenees, the

relatively gentle slopes that drifted down into the Spanish province of Lerida, but just here the swift and icy Noguera River had cut a deep gorge far below.

The pair went slowly. The narrow ribbon of ground was rimed with the season's first real frost, hard and slippery underfoot. They were Gypsies, and Joselito, the elder, led the way. "It gets bad here," he muttered. "Only for a little way. Then it widens again." They had to press their bodies to the wall of the cliff and pull themselves along by the strength of their fingertips. "There's a foothold here," Joselito whispered. "Follow me."

Carlos—fifteen years old, half man, half boy—stepped with confidence. He was taller than Joselito, more sure-footed, more intelligent, but in his short lifetime persecution had been a good teacher. Carlos could have overtaken and outpaced his guide, but he didn't. "How much farther?"

"Not much. The village is around the next bend."

Carlos glanced at the sky. It was just past midday. Even now, approaching its winter nadir, the sun was a bright white glow. He kept his face expressionless, but something in his gray eyes gave him away. "I know," Joselito said gruffly. "But there's a cave we can hide in until it's dark. No one will see us. The villagers are all stupid anyway. Typical *busne*," he added.

The youth didn't wince. In the ancient tongue they had brought with them to Spain, *busne* meant others, all who were not Gypsies. The mother of Carlos was a Gypsy who died when he was born, so the tribe had raised him, but his father was *busne*. To Joselito and the rest he remained an outsider, one of the others, tainted by impure blood and his mother's sin.

Ten minutes more of the slow, treacherous path and they had reached their destination. Some twenty feet below them was a settlement nestled into a declivity in the cliffs, approachable only by this tortuous route or a single dirt road on the far side. Carlos and Joselito stood for a moment in the shadow of the rock face, surveying the village.

What passed for the pueblo of Mujergorda was a jumble of stone huts clustered around a small open square that served as the meeting place and heart of the tiny community. One corner of this makeshift plaza housed a three-walled shed. A few goats and two donkeys were tethered there out of the wind. A short distance from the animals were some sacks of grain and baskets of what looked like dried beans and lentils. "Not much worth taking," Carlos murmured.

"More than we have."

Carlos nodded agreement. They were a band of five at the end of a summer's wandering, heading back the length of the land to their home in the caves near Seville. It had been a pleasant journey until the day before, when one of their donkeys, the one laden with all their food and tools, stumbled and fell over a cliff. There were no women with them to go into a town and tell fortunes in return for a few coins, and now no tools with which the men could repair tin pots and sharpen knives in exchange for food. The choice was clear—they must steal or starve.

All Gypsies knew their wanderings began in ages past, and that they had been in Spain at least three hundred years, and that stealing had always been one manner of livelihood. But it was dangerous; wit and cleverness were better tools. Still, in this situation, they decided that a bit of careful thievery was necessary. So a scout had been dispatched—Joselito. When he returned he reported that the pueblo of Mujergorda was easy prey.

The two climbers came to a shallow cave, just as Joselito had promised. He backed into it. "Come in here and sleep awhile. It will be a long night."

Carlos followed the other man, but he didn't sleep. He lay on his belly, head forward, eyes roving over the scene below.

About three dozen adults and a handful of children moved from house to house. Of that number only three or four seemed to be able-bodied men capable of fighting. Carlos fingered the hilt of the knife tucked into the small of his back. Probably it wouldn't be necessary. Most likely he and Joselito could climb down after everyone was asleep, kill one of the goats, and take as much fresh meat and dried food as they could carry. Probably none of the villagers would wake up, and he and Joselito would be back with the others before morning, the only blood on their knives goats' blood.

Joselito chuckled softly, as if he read the boy's mind. Carlos was squeamish; there were things he didn't like. Everyone knew it. His *busne* blood. "Well?" he asked. "What do you see? What are you watching so carefully? Is there a fat woman? A *mujer gorda,* like the name of the pueblo. Maybe if there is she will pay something for the cock of a blond virgin boy."

Carlos shook his head and ignored the taunt. "Nobody is fat. They are all thin and look half starved. Mostly women and children and old people. Only a few men."

"Good, less trouble for us. Now stop watching and get some sleep."

Carlos started to pull back into the shelter of the cave. "Wait, I see something else."

"What?" Joselito crawled forward and peered over the edge of the cliff. "What do you see?"

"Down there on the right. Someone's coming. Strangers. An old man and a little girl."

Benjamin and Sophie Valon stumbled into the settlement two hours before sundown. Exhausted and hungry, they rode together on the donkey Benjamin had purchased the day before. The animal stopped to drink at the stone trough in the plaza, but when he lowered his head the rest of him followed. The donkey crumpled onto the ground.

"*Grand-père,* what's the matter with him?"

"Nothing. He's old and so he collapsed. Nothing is the matter."

Benjamin took Sophie's hand. Another old man was sitting in a doorway across which fell a shaft of the westering sun. "My granddaughter and I need food and a place to sleep," Benjamin said. "I can pay."

He spoke in French and the peasant looked at him blankly. They'd come too far from the border; the locals no longer knew the language.

Benjamin tried again, this time in the Spanish he had taught himself years before. "The coach we were taking to Madrid broke down yesterday. We were stranded until I bought that poor animal there. Now I want food and a bed. I will pay," he added.

The other man nodded and a deal was made. The Valons would be given some bread and cheese and a straw mattress on the floor of the smallest, most outlying stone hut in return for a single gold coin. Benjamin had a few more such coins, but he was wise enough not to let anyone know about them. The money was secreted in a small velvet bag tied around his waist and hanging inside his trousers. With the coins was a treasure of much greater worth, his tallith and yarmulke and prayer book.

After the money changed hands, Benjamin turned to the little girl. "Come, Sophie, we will rest."

"I'm not tired. I want to walk around."

He started to refuse, then nodded agreement. In this simple place there could be no danger. As long as he could watch her she was safe. "All right, if you want to. But don't leave the village."

There was little to see. She wandered to the edge of the settlement, then ventured a short way along the bank of the river. "Sophie," Benjamin called. "Remember, not too far."

Sophie halted and was about to turn back when a bird darted overhead and attracted her attention. She raised her eyes. And looked into other eyes.

Carlos stared down at the child. She stared up at him. Neither made a sound. The boy was aware of Joselito, snoring softly in the cave behind; the little girl was aware of her grandfather watching her. Seconds later Carlos looked away and slithered back into his cave. Sophie returned to the village.

"What did you see?" Benjamin asked.

"Nothing, a pretty bird with gray eyes." Why? She didn't know. Perhaps because she wasn't sure she'd seen anything else.

"We will rest," Benjamin said.

They huddled together on the straw on the floor. Sophie slept, but Benjamin did not. There was a knot of terror in his belly.

He had made a terrible mistake. A week they'd been traveling and there was no sign of the Messiah, no sign that the miraculous new age had arrived in Spain. God had misled him. No, not God, he had misled himself.

Still, it was sundown, time to pray. He rose, leaving his heavy coat tucked around the child. She was shivering, murmuring in her sleep. He was afraid she had a fever. Tears began to run down his cheeks. He wiped them away and turned to face the east.

He did not don his skullcap and prayer shawl. God did not require a man to commit suicide to keep the law, least of all when he had charge of a child. He would say his prayers, but not in such a manner that this town of sullen mistrusting peasants—campesinos in the Spanish tongue—would know that a Jew was among them. He kept his hand on the hidden velvet bag and swayed ever so slightly while his lips mouthed silent Hebrew words.

Later the few survivors of Mujergorda remembered it as the night of the screams. The two Gypsies thought of it the same way.

Joselito had been right about one thing—the pueblo was easy prey. Whatever fat woman had been the source of the name, the tiny settlement had long forgotten her. The place was poor and filthy, and the inhabitants skin and bones because there wasn't enough to eat. The village was utterly forgotten by the king in Madrid, except once a year when the tax collectors came. Certainly it did not rate protection from the king's troops, or from the duke who claimed to own the land on which the campesinos eked out a subsistence living.

There had always been raids. Outlaws roamed free in these mountains. The event on that October evening in 1790 differed from the rest only in its ferocity. And because the leader of the outlaws was El Hambrero, the Hungry One.

The invaders did not approach from the rear in stealth, like Carlos and Joselito. Just past sundown, when Benjamin Valon had uttered his final amen, the horses· thundered down the single dirt track that was Mujergorda's only street.

There were eleven of them, all with muskets slung over their saddles, and bullwhips, *rebenques,* in their hands. The whips were more lethal than the guns. They were long and specially crafted, and they cracked in the air with the sound of death.

Within seconds a woman and a small boy had been beheaded by the whistling lashes. The old man with whom Benjamin had struck his bargain appeared in another doorway and ran screaming to the side of the already dead child. A horseman roared past him, swinging the deadly weapon, and the man's left leg was severed below the knee. The rawhide thong cut through flesh and bone as if they were lard. Blood and gore spilled into the street faster than the hard earth could absorb it. The stench excited the horses, who reared and whinnied and trampled two more of Mujergorda's citizens. It was a maelstrom of death.

Carlos and Joselito watched from above. "I should have known," Carlos whispered. "Fanta read my palm before we left Seville. She said this journey would end in trouble. . . ."

"Fanta always lies. She makes everything up. If you believe her, you're as gullible as the *busne*. Shut up! We're safe as long as we're not found."

"It's El Hambrero, isn't it?" Carlos's mouth was almost too dry to form the words.

"*Sí,* El Hambrero."

"*Dios mío* . . . It's true—he eats raw human flesh?"

Joselito shrugged. "So they say."

Dark was tumbling down the mountains, but Mujergorda was suddenly ablaze with light. A charcoal brazier in one of the huts was knocked over and set fire to the wooden furniture and straw bedding. The flames escaped through the small window and the narrow door and danced up the street. They forced the cowering people out of their homes and into the arms of the outlaws. Fire licked the bodies of the fallen, and the smell of cooked flesh ascended into the night.

It was easy to pick out the leader of the outlaws. His horse was the biggest, and pure white. Unlike the others, he wore no hat. His hair and his beard were red. They glowed in the firelight and seemed themselves to be ablaze. He galloped forward, and the terrified campesinos were caught between the pounding hooves of the white horse and the flames. "*¡Tengo hambre!*" he roared. "*¡Quiero carne cruda!*" It was his rallying cry, the slogan that gave him his name. *I am hungry. I want raw meat.*

The *rebenque* in the hands of a master could be an instrument of delicacy, a scalpel as well as an ax. With one flick of his wrist El Hambrero cut through the cloak of a woman on his left. With a second motion he had cut off her breast.

The screams began in earnest then. A crescendo of cries of horror and agony and terror. But when the red-haired demon leaned down from his horse and scooped up the severed breast and tore at it with his teeth, there was a time of utter silence. It lasted only a few seconds, until the unthinkable had been accepted as truly happening. Then the screams began again.

El Hambrero tipped back his head and laughed. Blood dripped from his mouth to his chin and trickled down his beard, staining it an even darker red.

Benjamin and Sophie were not outside with the citizens of Mujergorda when the nightmare began. They were still huddled inside the hut at the extreme end of the settlement. The fire had not yet reached them. Benjamin wanted to run, but there was no place to go. The hut had only one door, and that led directly on to the street filled with outlaws. He remained by the window, unable to take his eyes from the scene. He pressed Sophie's face to his chest so that she might not see, but he could feel her sobs of terror and the shuddering of her small body.

"*Carne más joven,*" El Hambrero shouted. Younger meat. His eyes roamed the crowd and fastened on a baby clutched in its mother's arms. In seconds, pieces of the infant were scattered on the earth and the red beard was yet redder.

Benjamin could look no longer. He gagged and retched and began to tremble violently. Sophie wrenched free of him and stared out the window at the diabolical scene her grandfather had tried to keep her from seeing. For a moment Benjamin was too distracted to pull her back into his arms. He could see the leaping tongues of the fire. They were much closer now;

barely the length of a tall man separated the hut from the flames.

"Sophie," he murmured. "Sophie. Come to me, don't look." He embraced her once more, pressing her close to him. She wasn't crying. She was not even trembling anymore. Instead, she was as still and as cold as a piece of ice. "My God, my God, what have I done?" It was a confession of guilt and a plea for mercy. Benjamin whispered the words aloud, but there was no reply.

Outside, the screams went on, and the raping began. For these men, this, too, was an art. They did not permit themselves such distractions until their victims were so thoroughly sickened that even thoughts of resistance were impossible.

Benjamin made himself face the terrible reality. No angel would come and magically take them away. If Sophie was to survive, he must save her. To do that he must get her out of the hut. Perhaps now, while the outlaws were occupied. Yes, now. It was their one chance.

He lifted Sophie into his arms and wrapped his coat around her, then edged a little closer to the door. The fire began licking at the far wall of the hut, forcing him on despite his fear. Keeping his back to the wall, mindful of the scant protection of its shadow, and carrying his precious burden, Benjamin stepped outside.

"Look," Carlos whispered. "The old man, the stranger, he's trying to get away. Down on the left."

Joselito looked. "He has the little girl with him. He won't make it." The words were spoken without emotion. They were safe up there in their aerie, and the doings of this night would make an incredible tale to tell later. If there was a later. They still had no food and Joselito's belly rumbled in protest.

Benjamin remained standing in the lee of the hut, trying to decide what to do. Sophie was a dead weight in his arms; she must have fainted. He couldn't worry about that now. Every part of him strained toward the road; he wanted to run down it, to leave Mujergorda and its unspeakable terrors behind him. But he resisted. The light of fire illumined the dirt track for a long distance. It was insane to believe that carrying his granddaughter—and on his old legs—he could cross that distance and reach the safety of darkness without being spotted by one of the outlaws. But he had to do something. The fire was so close its heat singed the hair on the back of his head.

Seconds later a spark landed on his woolen sleeve. With his one free hand Benjamin slapped it dead. Another landed on his shoulder, and yet another on Sophie's hair. He beat out the pinpricks of fire, then a shower of sparks descended on them and he had to act. In an instant he decided and committed himself. Clutching his beloved Sophie, Benjamin dashed for the hills behind the hut and with a superhuman effort began to ascend the cliffs.

"*Dios mío*," Carlos murmured. "They're coming this way."

"They'll never make it," Joselito said again.

Carlos remembered the little girl's eyes. Such a color. He'd never seen eyes that blue before. He moved forward. Joselito reached out one arm and grasped his shoulder. "Idiot! Where are you going?"

"I'm going to help him. He might be able to climb up here if he didn't have to carry the child."

"Now I know you're a *busne* fool. Those pigs will see you."

Carlos shook his head. "No. Not now. They're too busy enjoying themselves."

"How long do you think it takes to have a woman? A matter of minutes for men like those."

"Long enough," Carlos said. He tore away from Joselito's grasp and started down the cliff. He was as agile as a goat, and faster.

Benjamin had climbed only a short distance. Sophie seemed suddenly so heavy. And his heart was pounding with terror and exertion. He did not see Carlos until the youth was practically on top of them, his lips pressed close to Benjamin's ear. "Shh, don't say anything. Just give me the little girl. I'll carry her up. You follow me."

The Spanish was too fast, too tainted with the accents of the south. Benjamin couldn't follow it. "*Je ne comprend pas . . .*" he murmured, lapsing into French in his exhaustion, and clinging to the unconscious child the boy was trying to pry from his arms.

"You're French," Carlos said. The band had sometimes crossed the border into France, he knew a few words. "*Ami*," he whispered urgently. "I'm a friend. Give me the little girl."

Benjamin could resist no longer. He had to trust. He handed Sophie to the Gypsy boy and sank to his knees in total exhaustion. Seconds later his heart stopped and he was dead.

They called her Sofía. That was as close as the five Gypsies could come to the name the child burbled in the tongue of the *busne* on the far side of the mountains.

During the first few days the little girl ran continuously from one to another, thrusting her small body before them on the path, bobbing a little curtsy and repeating over and over, *je m'appelle Sophie*. She annoyed them, she tripped up their feet and flustered their one remaining donkey. No one understood that her small ritual was a desperate attempt to escape the screaming terror in her mind and create order out of chaos.

For the first few days they remained preoccupied with the need to steal food and they largely ignored her. But they were traveling south to Seville, and as they moved from the hills toward the flat farmlands of Castile, it became easier to glean greens from the roadside and catch the occasional squirrel or hedgehog for stew. Zocali, their leader, began to pay more attention to the child. "She must know more than those few words. Unless she's *loca*. Have you brought us a *niña* with a demon in her head, Carlos?"

The boy didn't answer, but one of the others did. "Even if she's crazy, she's obviously highborn. She should be worth a ransom, Zocali."

The leader nodded. "Yes, and if I knew where her people were, I'd demand it. But you've heard what Carlos and Joselito said. The old man brought her that very afternoon to Mujergorda. And listen to her tongue. They were from the other side of the mountains. It's already snowing in the peaks, we'd never get through the pass. And if we did? Where would we look for the family of this one *niña loca*?"

It was because Zocali was clever and because he knew the Gypsy law that he had been elected chief of his tribe. That was the way of his people. The Spaniards called them *Gitanos*. They knew the word, after more than three centuries Spanish was also their language, but they called themselves the Romany, the husbands. Among them, leadership was never hereditary, nor could any one man claim to speak for all of them everywhere. Scattered across most of the world, they were divided into countless small groups. Each chose its own leader and having done so, obeyed him. Zocali's word was law. The notion of ransoming the child was abandoned.

They neared Madrid, and another of the band suggested selling her as a servant to a wealthy family. Zocali considered that idea, but rejected it as well. "The law of the Rom says that children are a precious gift from God. They belong to the whole tribe. If the holy one has given us another child, our tribe is blessed."

"But she's a *busne* child," another protested.

"A child all the same. Besides, even *busne* can serve a purpose." Zocali glanced at Carlos. The boy's strength and agility were often valuable. Sometimes his courage was in doubt and he had a soft heart, but even that could be useful. As it was now, for instance; Carlos took charge of the little girl. He saw to it that she ate, and when night came he slept beside her, comforting her sobbing dreams with the warmth of his body.

"Look at him, he acts like a woman," Joselito muttered.

They were camped by the side of a road. In the dull glow of the embers of the fire Zocali idly whittled a whistle from an ash twig. He stopped the work and looked at Joselito. "*Si*, perhaps. But thanks to Carlos she isn't bothering the rest of us. So the *busne* in his blood speaks to hers. Why should that concern you?"

Joselito studied the short, stocky figure. He could take Zocali in a fight, no doubt about it. He was twenty years younger and twice as muscular. But Zocali was the chief, chosen to serve for life. If he was killed by another Gypsy, that Gypsy would be executed before there was a new election. Murder could never lead to power within the tribe. Joselito turned away.

Still the issue of Sofía wasn't resolved; the Gypsy hatred of outsiders was too profound. Two others murmured protests. Zocali listened for a moment, continuing his whittling. "Enough," he said finally. "The business is decided. No more talk." He put his knife down and faced the other four. "Listen to me, all of you. The *busne* child stays with us. Someday we'll find a use for her." He waited, but there was no challenge to his authority.

They trekked on, following the sun. The child could not walk as fast or as far as they did, and when she stumbled with exhaustion, Carlos carried her, or held her while she rode on the donkey's back.

Days blended into weeks. Hour after hour Carlos tried to speak to Sofía in his few words of French. Except for repeating her name she never replied, never said anything other than the one parrotlike phrase, *je m'appelle Sophie*. Eventually she stopped saying even that. For many days she was silent, except for the screaming sobs of her nightmares.

"I have been thinking," Zocali said. "Maybe she's not *loca*, maybe words were frightened out of her. The things you told us about, El Hambrero and the rest, what child wouldn't be terrified? Leave her alone, she'll talk when she's ready."

Nonetheless, Carlos longed to speak with Sofía. Her eyes haunted him. She was like no one he'd ever known and it seemed to him that this small girl was a clue to that half of his own blood about which he knew nothing. His French was too limited. He switched to soft, slurred Andalusian Spanish, holding long conversations with her as he carried her along the narrow dusty roads of the country. She never answered and nothing changed.

At last, in the middle of November, the journey drew to an end. They were almost in Seville, a brief day's walk from the caves of the Triana that were home to them and to a large proportion of the *Gitanos* of Spain. That night they lingered a long time around the cooking fire when their meal was finished. "Play for us, Joselito," Zocali said. "We're close enough to home. Music won't attract the demons here."

Joselito dug deep in his knapsack and withdrew a small

tambourine ringed with tiny silver bells. Only one type of song was appropriate to the end of such a long and adventurous journey, a seguidilla, a chorus interspersed with verses made up to suit the occasion. "This is the moment, the time to come home," Joselito sang, tapping the rhythms with his fingertips.

"In my cave my wife is waiting," Zocali added, taking the honor of composing the first verse. "And between my legs I'm waiting too."

The men laughed, then joined together in the chorus. "This is the moment, the time to come home."

Sofía sat beside Carlos, close to the fire. They had all become accustomed to her presence and her silence, and they assumed that she still spoke nothing of their language. But in the few seconds pause while the next man thought up a verse to add and Joselito tapped the tambourine, Sofía opened her mouth and sang exactly what she had heard, the chorus followed by Zocali's bawdy verse, then the chorus again.

Joselito stopped playing, they all stared at the child. "*Otra vez*," Zocali said finally. "Sing it again."

Obviously Sofía understood him. She did as he asked. This time, as if to hear her better, Joselito did not tap the tambourine. There were only the silent hills, the firelight, and the pure soaring notes of Sofía's song.

"*¡Mi madre!* It's incredible. Joselito, play something else. See if she learns it as quickly."

This time it was a *tirana,* one of the classic melodies of Andalusia. Joselito struck the rhythm and Carlos sang two verses that told of a lost love. Sofía listened, then sang the song back to him. She was letter perfect, but more important she was pitch perfect with incomparable purity of tone.

"Wonderful," the Gypsy leader murmured when Sofía was done. "I told you this one was a gift from God. What a voice."

Love of music was bred in the Gypsy's soul. His songs were part of his being, as important to life as food and water. Because of her voice, Sofía had ceased to be the *niña loca*. She had earned a place in Zocali's tribe. There was a reason for her existence and her presence among its members. And with her song she had signaled her acceptance of the Gypsies.

The tragedy had made her mind an empty slate, everything before the night of the screams forgotten. They were all gone; her grandfather, her parents, her home in Bordeaux, even her native language. But she spoke theirs. She had learned it almost automatically from Carlos, and she had adopted their music. For the time being it was enough, for the Gypsies and for Sofía.

❧ 2 ❧

The early morning sun buttered the Plaza de la Corredera in Córdoba. It was September of 1798, the day of the feast of Our Lady of Sorrows, the city's patron saint. Later there would be a corrida, a bullfight. Now the plaza hosted an open market. A huge crowd of people and horses moved in twisting ribbons of color among stalls selling every manner of food and goods. It was utter confusion and the noise was deafening, but the eyes and ears of Fanta, the old Gypsy woman, were sharp. They darted back and forth until she spotted her prey. "Look, there she is."

Fanta pinched Sofía's arm to be sure she had her attention. "See? She's getting out of that carriage across the road. That's Doña Carmen."

Sofía peered at a woman whose mountain of flesh was shrouded in black. From head to foot she was draped in flowing black lace, and she didn't walk, she waddled. She was grotesque. "That's her? But you said she was beautiful."

"I said she used to be beautiful. Years ago before all her troubles. Stupid girl, you never remember what I tell you." Another pinch, this one much harder than the first. "Do you remember what you're supposed to do?"

Sofía pulled her arm away. "Yes, I remember."

"Then go do it. Quickly. She leaves her palace only once a year. Her son was born on this feast and she comes to light a candle to Los Dolores. God knows if we'll ever be in Córdoba at the right time again. We may never get another chance."

Sofía had been in Fanta's charge from the beginning. Zocali had given her to the old woman eight years earlier, when he first brought her into his cave. Sofía had never forgotten his words. "Here, you barren old witch. No child of your own to look after you in your old age, so you can have this one. She's a little crazy, but she sings like an angel. And look at those eyes. Make her into a good Romany woman so someday I'll get a decent bride price for her."

No child of her own. That was Fanta's great sorrow. For a Gypsy woman, Sofía had learned, there was no greater shame than to be barren. Fanta had borne that curse, and been tolerated by her tribe in spite of it because she knew the healing arts and could read the cards. They were real skills, but she did not use them to benefit outsiders. "My gifts are for our own blood," she said. "If I used them for the *busne*, they would be taken away." That didn't stop her from promising miracles to any woman she could inveigle into giving her a few coins in return for useless powders and lying fortunes. This time she had set her sights high—on the wife of the wealthiest man in Spain.

Sofía had learned long before that if she didn't want to be beaten, she had to obey Fanta. Now she ran across the plaza, weaving her way deftly between the horses and the carriages and the pedestrians. In seconds she had put herself between the woman wrapped in black and the steps of the church. "Señora, Doña Carmen . . . please, spare me one moment, I must speak with you."

Sofía flung herself to the ground at the woman's feet. Doña Carmen's bulk did not allow her to sidestep, but she did not deign to answer the girl. Instead, she lifted a black-gloved hand. Instantly one of the footmen jumped from behind her carriage and was beside them. He swung a booted foot and kicked Sofía out of the way.

She gasped with pain, but it didn't distract her. "Doña Carmen, please, I beg you. I must tell you about the dream. It's important. It could change everything." While she spoke she grabbed a handful of the black lace and clung to it.

The footman took a knife from its scabbard at his belt. "Out of the way, Gypsy. Move!"

Sofía's eyes darted from him to his mistress, and to old Fanta, waiting and watching on the other side of the plaza. She twisted her body slightly, so she would present a less easy target to the knife, but she did not let go of the black cloak. She searched the woman's face, speaking as quickly as she could, words tumbling over each other. "Please, listen to me. I had a dream. God told me to come here and find you today. My grandmother can help you. Let us tell you about it, I beg you. For the sake of God, Doña Carmen. For your own sake."

The footman lunged toward the girl, his knife at the ready.

"Leave her be." The woman's voice stopped him just in time. "I will hear what she has to say." She studied the kneeling figure. Filthy, like all Gypsies. She was bedecked with golden ear hoops and chains, although dressed in rags. Yes, but what eyes. They did something to Doña Carmen, made demands she could not refuse. "Wait here. When I come out of church I will speak with you."

An hour later the two Gypsies were sitting in one corner of the great Palacio Mendoza, telling the story of Sofía's dream. "It was my grandmother here who understood, Doña Carmen, for she has the gift of second sight. That is how we knew where to find you to help you in your great trouble."

Maria Carmen Rodriguez Machin, wife of the mighty Domingo Mendoza, knew that all Gypsies were liars and thieves and never to be trusted. The old woman was doubtless a cheat and a charlatan, but the girl was irresistible. Her thick black braids and honeyed skin reminded Carmen that once she, too, had been beautiful, but this Sofía's eyes were unique. They were the deep blue of the ocean, fringed with lashes so long and thick they cast shadows on her cheeks. Seeing her was a kind of wicked stimulant, an evil lure. The girl reinforced Carmen's rage, and with it her desperation. Perhaps this creature who called herself Fanta really could help her.

* * *

"The Gypsy woman is here, Doña Carmen." The maid did not look at her mistress while she spoke. It was a sin, what Doña Carmen did, listening to the old Gypsy *bruja*. Among themselves that's how the servants referred to her, the witch. Such people were in league with the devil.

"Put her in the usual place. I'll be down shortly." Carmen waited until the maid had gone before she got out of bed, and she did not summon anyone to help her dress. These days she could not bear to be seen, much less touched. She could not even tolerate looking at herself. Every mirror in the enormous room had been draped in black, only one candle was kept burning, and the shutters of the balcony doors were never opened.

Carved wooden cupboards lined one entire wall. They were filled with splendid gowns that once had been the talk of Córdoba. Carmen ignored them. She wrapped herself in a length of black velvet and made sure it hid every part of her— the swollen ankles and legs wealed with ugly purple blotches, the bloated stomach that made her seem like a woman about to give birth, the arms so thickened by her affliction that the skin was drawn tight and veined with the barely healed wounds of constant cracking. She wasn't satisfied until the velvet cloth covered everything. Only her dark brown eyes showed, and her swollen fingers in which rings were so deeply embedded she could not remove them.

No shoes would fit her these days. She descended the great marble staircase barefoot. Here, too, she allowed as little light as possible. She knew where she was by habit, and because she could feel first the marble, then the woven Turkey carpet, then the cool tile of the patio floors against her burning soles.

There were fourteen patios inside the walls of the Palacio Mendoza. The one where the Gypsy women waited was known as El Patio de los Naranjos, the Patio of the Orange Trees. It was in the far southwestern corner of the sprawling mansion, but if one knew which little doors to use and which paths to follow, it was possible to walk from one patio to another without ever going inside. Carmen knew each corner of the huge property as well as she knew every painful inch of her disfigured body.

For as long as anyone could remember, the palace of the family Mendoza had been there, in the heart of the ancient city of Córdoba, angled between two streets now called Calle Judios and Calle Averroes. The streets had been created after the palace was built, slowly, over passing centuries in which the destiny of the city unfolded.

Averroes was the name of a celebrated Arab thinker, and during the seven hundred years of Moorish rule, Córdoba had been the seat of the caliphate, capital of what the Moors called Al-Andalus, the land in the South. The second street was called the street of the Jews. It had been the center of the Jewish quarter from the time the Christians retook the city in 1236 until the Jews were expelled in 1492. The Mendozas had been intimately involved in everything that had transpired there, and responsible for much of it. These days they were devout Catholics and no one dared repeat aloud the old rumor that they had first been Jews, then Muslims, then Jews again.

Such calumny was far from Carmen's mind. She was preoccupied with her own bitter memories. Thirty years she had lived there, since she came as the bride of Domingo Mendoza, and thought herself blessed because she had married the master of one of the world's great fortunes. Her husband carried only the minor title of hidalgo, nobleman. The Mendozas weren't dukes—much less one of the hundred nineteen favored nobles known as grandees—but they had more money, and thus more power, than most of those. Carmen understood the bargain her father had made on her behalf. As Domingo's wife she shared in his power and his privilege. In exchange she must give him and his ancient name and his great wealth a son and heir.

Five times she conceived in the first five years of marriage, and each time she was delivered of a dead child. Until in 1776 Pablo Luis was born. This son lived, but with a twisted arm and a humped back, and a soul as tormented as her own had become.

At first Domingo had been so overjoyed he would not recognize that the boy was a cripple. He pretended everything was fine and the child would outgrow his afflictions. When such foolishness was no longer possible, he dragged the boy to doctors all over Spain, until finally he had to accept that not even the mighty Mendozas could buy a cure for the twisted body of Pablo Luis.

The beatings began then. Late at night, when all the servants slept, Domingo would come to his wife's bedchamber like a lover, in silence and stealth. With his own hands he would undress her, admiring her soft, smooth flesh, running his fingers over it. Then the caresses would become pinches, and in minutes blows. First with his open hand, finally with his fists.

He never shouted his curses, he whispered them so the servants would not hear. They came to sound to her more terrible than shouts. "Whore! She-devil! You must have lain with Satan to produce such atrocities. One of the dead sons had cloven feet. They tried to keep it from me, but I found out. And finally you gave me a son marked all over with your sins. Whore! Bride of the devil!" All the while he was beating her Carmen would clamp her lips tight and not make a sound. What she endured was bad enough without everyone knowing how her husband despised her.

In the end he would take her, pumping his hot seed deep into her belly with cries of fury, leaving her the instant his shuddering release was over. Then and only then she would weep, but not for long. Only one treasure was left to her, pride. She would not lose this single consolation by sobbing until her eyes were red and swollen.

Pablo never touched her face. When Carmen rose and dressed in the morning, nothing of the night's agony showed. On the contrary, she looked magnificent. She owned the brightest, most sumptuous gowns imaginable, and each day she dressed as if she were attending a ball at the court of the king in Madrid. She went about the streets of Córdoba inviting all in the city to note that Doña Carmen remained a great beauty. Then, two years ago, even this last pleasure was taken from her. The swelling sickness came. This time it was she who made the rounds of doctors far and near, and found they could offer no relief. Now she was reduced to listening to the promises of the Gypsy woman.

"Doña Carmen! It does my old eyes good to see you. My heart sings because maybe I can do you some small service."

"If you do, it will be the first. The potion you gave me last week didn't help at all." Carmen's tone was petulant but not angry. She could not afford to be angry with this creature who was her one remaining hope. "Come, sit over here with me in the shade. Did you read my cards? Did they tell you how to cure me?"

"Every night this week," Fanta said. "And I'm sure that what has been wrong so far is the moon. Forgive me, I am a stupid old woman. I did not think to allow for the cycle of the moon. I have made a new potion. It is sure to work."

Sofía sat some distance from the two women, in another corner of the patio. She was there not because Fanta needed her but because Doña Carmen insisted on it. Neither woman paid her much attention while they conferred, but she could hear everything they said. No, she thought, this potion wouldn't help Doña Carmen either. Nothing would work because Fanta didn't even try. She wasn't giving the medicines of herbs she made for the tribe, because she didn't want her to get well. She was a *busne* and Fanta despised *busne*. . . .

Carmen turned to Sofía as if she felt her gaze and read her mind. "What do you think of this latest potion? Will it cure me?"

Sofía didn't meet her glance. "Fanta is very wise, the wisest of all the Gypsies. She can help you."

"Yes, so you've said." Carmen turned away. She had come to hate looking at the girl. What right did she have to such beauty? But the voice, ah, the voice and the songs. They soothed her as nothing else did these days. "Sing," she commanded. "You are useless except for your voice."

Sofía knew many songs. Everywhere she traveled with Fanta and the others, she roamed the streets, doing whatever she was bid at the moment. Sometimes it was to read a document or a notice posted near a church. "We should know what they say," Zocali insisted, "even though their laws mean nothing to us."

He had shouted with glee when years before he discovered Sofía could read. No Gypsy, male or female, could do so. Reading was a mystery, a magic thing reserved for highborn *busne* men. All the same, Sofía could read. Apparently she had learned how when she lived with the old man among the *busne* on the other side of the mountains, and it seemed to make no difference that these were words in a different language. Zocali marveled at that, but more often he simply basked in the glow of his wisdom. "I could have left her to starve by the roadside near that cursed village," he reminded the tribe. "Instead, I was charitable and I've been rewarded with my own spy."

The need to read arose seldom. Usually Sofía was sent begging with a baby in her arms. "Food for the child, for the love of God, please . . ." She hated that, but she was quite good at it. On other occasions she inveigled women into allowing Fanta or one of the other Gypsies to prescribe potions or read their cards, as she'd done with Doña Carmen. But always, whatever the role in which they'd cast her, she listened to the music heard in the streets and seeping its way out from behind closed doors and windows and it became part of her.

They had been in Córdoba for two months and she had learned the *alegria*, the *solea*, and the *serrana*, all forms of the classic Spanish fandango, in versions unique to Córdoba. But Sofía knew that Doña Carmen did not wish her to sing a Córdobés song. What she craved were the melodies Sofía had learned in the Gypsy caves in Seville, the songs of the flamenco.

Sofía did not move from her place on the low bench in the far corner of the patio. She sat composed and serene, hands folded beneath the tattered shawl she wore and sang unaccompanied. Her pure, bell-like voice filled the small patio; the notes danced through the overhanging leaves of the orange trees. They shimmered across the still water of the tiny reflecting pool and climbed to the top of the high walls, where they tumbled over into soaring freedom. The words were of love unrequited and a woman's pain, and ultimate triumph. "Someday he will know what he has rejected and beg for my embrace and I will refuse him . . ."

Doña Carmen listened in silence. Her head was bowed, but her chest heaved with sobs. Soon Fanta began to clap in rhythm with the music, one long beat, four short, another long. Her palms were an instrument for making music, as the girl's voice was. The two sounds had been joined in perfect unison since before any Gypsy could remember; together they were a picture of the Romany soul. When the girl sang like this, Fanta could almost forgive her *busne* blood. Sofía sang the songs of the flamenco better than any Gypsy alive.

Then, from somewhere deep in the house the sound of a second pair of clapping hands joined Fanta's. They, too, kept perfect time in the ancient rhythmic patterns and blended with the long, throaty notes Sofía held until it seemed her heart must stop. "My betrayer will know my vengeance and I will know joy." The song ended. The rhythmic clapping stopped.

The three women turned to look toward the interior of the palace. Both Fanta and Sofía half expected another Romany to come through the low, arched door and join them. No one appeared. The old Gypsy woman looked questioningly at Doña Carmen. The women's lips stayed tightly pursed and she offered no explanation. Fanta shrugged. None of this would put more coins in the little bag hanging between her withered breasts. "Doña Carmen, I have another idea to help you. Besides the potion, I mean. It came to me in a dream."

"How convenient that your dreams seem always to concern me. What is it this time?"

"I think there is a ghost in this palace," Fanta said. "An evil spirit that wishes you harm."

Carmen shrugged. "There are many ghosts in the Palacio Mendoza. The family of my husband has lived here for many hundreds of years. Only God knows all its secrets."

"But this ghost is evil. I can send it away," Fanta insisted. "I know I can."

"I see. How do you propose to do it?"

"We will bury some gold and jewels here beneath the orange

trees. The ghost will take them and be satisfied and leave you alone."

Carmen knew she should laugh aloud at such nonsense. But what if it were really so? What if Fanta were a true seer, not just a greedy Gypsy hag? What if sending her away would call down yet more curses? "I'm not sure. I will think about it and let you know," she said finally. She stood up, clutching the black disguise to her body with one hand while she placed three coins on the bench with her other. "Here is your money. Take it and go. Come back to me on Friday and I will tell you my decision."

Fanta and Sofía left the mansion as they always did, through a massive oaken door that led directly from the Patio de los Naranjos to the Calle Judíos. The door was nearly a foot thick and bolted with iron. "If she agrees," Sofía said when they were outside, "how can we get in to dig?"

It was a logical question. What Fanta had proposed to Doña Carmen was merely a variation on the most often used scheme of Gypsy women, the one they called the "great trick." Had Doña Carmen been a woman who needed more money, Fanta would have suggested that if they buried one gold bracelet, they would later find two, thanks to a kind spirit who wished the woman well. In any case, the profit depended on the Gypsy herself returning to the site and digging up whatever had been buried.

Fanta snorted. "It will be easy. I'll send Carlos. He's like a goat. He can climb those walls with no trouble."

Sofía started to say something, but a man appeared, blocking their way. "You two, Gypsy women, I want to speak with you."

He wore a flowing black cape and a broad-brimmed black hat pulled low over his face. Sofía could see little of him, but Fanta seemed to know who he was. She made a deep curtsy. "We are at your honor's service, poor beggars that we are," she said in that whining tone she reserved for the *busne* she despised.

"You're at no one's service but your own," the man said. "I know all your games." He was speaking to Fanta but studying Sofía. His eyes were black and they seemed to see right through her. Sofía couldn't meet his gaze. It made her feel ashamed and naked and she turned away. "I want you to know I won't allow you to play the 'great trick' on Doña Carmen," the man continued. His tone was matter-of-fact, as if there were nothing odd in his knowing what they had proposed, or what they called it among themselves. "Don't try it. The poor woman is suffering enough without being robbed further by you."

"There is no trick," Fanta said. She reached out as if to touch him and the man pulled back. "I swear to you by El Señor Jesus," Fanta pleaded. "I want only to help Doña Carmen."

"Not with the 'great trick,'" the man said again. "I won't allow it." He turned to Sofía once more. "And you, señorita? Do you also swear that there is no trick and you want only Doña Carmen's health and happiness?"

Sofía couldn't answer. Lying to those all-seeing black eyes seemed impossible. Fanta reached out and grabbed the girl's arm, her bony fingers digging into the soft flesh. "Tell him, you stupid girl. Tell him the truth or I'll beat you until you bleed."

She didn't dare to remain silent. "I wish the señora no harm," she said. "I swear it."

The man laughed softly. "A nice escape. So you have brains as well as the face and the voice of an angel." He looked at Fanta again. "Don't beat her. Her answer satisfies me. And don't be afraid to come here again. Doña Carmen takes some comfort from your visits. But do not play the 'great trick.' It is too much and she would hate herself afterward for being so gullible. Adios."

"Who is he?" Sofía asked when his swinging cape had disappeared around the corner.

"Her cursed son." Fanta spat on the ground. "Don Pablo Luis Mendoza, a hunchback with a crippled arm. In all Spain only the hangman still dresses as he does, the *mantela* and the sombrero, even now in the heat of summer. It is to disguise that he has been marked by the devil. Like his mother. I curse them both. Now come, the others are waiting."

They turned the corner into an unnamed alley that skirted one section of the palace walls and Fanta stopped walking and chuckled softly. "Look." Her bony finger indicated a faint mark scratched there years before. It was a cross, the Gypsy symbol for "here they give nothing," left as a warning for Gypsies to come. Quickly Fanta bent down, picked up a sharp-edged stone, and drew a line through the cross. Next to it she marked a dot within a circle. Any Gypsy who passed by in the future would know that the Mendozas were susceptible to Gypsy claims. Fanta thought for a moment, then scratched a triangle next to the circle. "So they'll know that telling fortunes with cards is best," she murmured before they walked on.

During the following weeks Sofía and Fanta returned many times to the Patio de los Naranjos, but when in late October they left Córdoba for the homeward journey to Seville, the "great trick" had not been mentioned again. Whatever Fanta's opinion of Pablo Luis, she obviously feared his anger.

"Thank God," Carlos said when Sofía told him. "I would have hated sneaking into the Palacio Mendoza to steal."

"Do you feel sorry for them? I do. All that money, but look what terrible things have happened to them."

"I'm not a bit sorry for them. And you shouldn't be either. They are bigger thieves than we'll ever be. How else do you think they got to be so enormously wealthy? It's only that if I got caught I would have been hung without even a trial. That's how people so powerful do things. Fanta was aiming too high. The reason she dared to do it was because of you, because the woman liked your singing."

"My singing," Sofía said softly. "It's all I have, isn't it, Carlos?"

They were walking behind the donkeys on the dusty road south. Strict rules governed the behavior of unmarried Romany, but on this journey, though they were watched, they were out of earshot of the others. They could speak freely and still not break the law. "Not all you have," Carlos said. "You're beautiful, Sofía, you're the most beautiful woman in the world."

His voice and his words pleased her; everything about Carlos pleased her. Of all the Gypsies, only he was gentle and sweet. Carlos never made her feel like an outcast. She always tried to hide her feelings, embarrassed that he should know, and frightened that if the others found out, the two of them would be watched with even more vigilance. Sofía shook her head impatiently. "What I look like doesn't answer any of the questions."

"That again," Carlos said. "There are no answers. I keep telling you so, why won't you believe me?"

"There have to be answers. You were there, Carlos. You saw the man who brought me into the village where you rescued me from the outlaws. You must know something about him. *Madre de Dios,* why can't I remember?"

"I don't know anything about him. Or about you before I first saw you. And if you can't remember, then you can't. Forget about it."

"I can't forget. Tell me again about that night," Sofía insisted.

"I've told you what I can. Some outlaws came and set fire to the village and the old man tried to get you to safety. He died and I took you back to Zocali and the others and we brought you to Seville with us. That's all there is to tell."

He'd never remind her of the rest of it, the people cut in half by the murderous whips, the horror of the leader who ate raw human flesh. In his heart Carlos was sure that the reason Sofía could remember so little was because the night had been so terrible her mind had closed it out. Besides, those details he knew which she'd forgotten would not solve the mystery of her origins. So he would never remind her of the full horror. It was a small gift he could give to the woman he hoped would someday be his wife.

Seville was born in the earliest days of commerce, the Phoenicians and the Romans knew her, but her reason for being where she was and as she was remained what it had always been.

The Guadalquivir River was Seville's source of riches and her link to the world. Columbus chose the city for the administrative head of his great enterprise, and for centuries every treasure ship laden with gold from the Indies and Spanish America emptied its cargo onto Sevillano docks. Eventually Cádiz, in the southwest, had a share in that exclusive privilege, but not before the coffers of Seville were swollen with profit.

The wealthy city queened herself on the left bank of the

river; on its right was her stepchild, the district known as the
Triana. It was a clutch of low hills laced with caves carved out
of limestone by that same ebb and flow of oceans which eons
before had created the river. The Gypsies owned the caves;
they claimed them soon after they arrived in Spain, when laws
were passed making it illegal for them to camp in the open in
substantial numbers, but they did not own all of the Triana.
They shared the barrio with the rest of Seville's poor and outcast.

The narrow, fetid streets and alleys were home to thieves
and pickpockets and whores, to the maimed whose only means
of survival was to beg, to artisans whose crafts earned them a
precarious livelihood at the whim of the gentry on the opposite
bank—the Triana was home to all of these, and to the Gypsies,
and to Sofía.

No one knew how many Romany lived in the caves. Many
hundreds surely, perhaps thousands. From a distance the hills
looked empty, bleak, and barren; up close they revealed doors
carved into the soft rock and piles of stones erupting above
ground which were chimneys. Within the labyrinthine maze,
each family had its own cave. Ten or twelve such families made
up a tribe known by the name of their chief. Sofía was grateful
to have been accepted as one of the Zocali tribe, but she never
stopped being afraid of the man himself.

There was no real reason for her fear. Zocali had never
touched her. He left the occasional beating to Fanta, and a
Gypsy leader would never sacrifice the virginity of one of the
women who belonged to him. Without it she would bring him
no decent bride price when the time came to marry her off.
But the way he looked at her was terrifying. It was the way all
men looked at her, even Carlos. But only he didn't frighten
her. The others seemed to carry some evil intent behind their
eyes.

The rest of the girls didn't feel the way she did. They made
lewd jokes about the men's private parts and speculated about
what kind of a husband each would be. Sofía was horrified at
the prospect of marriage, unless it was to Carlos. She knew he
planned to ask for her. She hoped he would be successful. But

Zocali would ask a high price and Carlos had very little. Still, they were both *busne*. Maybe Zocali would prefer that to tainting more Romany blood. He was like the rest in despising outsiders.

Sofía knew how they felt and accepted it, but occasionally she longed for something barely remembered, a kind of affection that had nothing to do with the things men and women did in the dark of the night. Once when she had a high fever she almost remembered what it was. Fanta had given her a potion.

"Drink this, it's the same thing I give to the others. I can't afford to let you die when I've finally trained you to be something less than useless," Fanta had said gruffly. But for a moment the girl had seen emotion in the old woman's eyes, true caring and acceptance. Someone used to look at me like that, she thought. Long ago, before the night of the screams . . . She grasped at the memory, but it disappeared, as always, lost in confusion.

Like the individual notes of a forgotten song, fragments of memory returned to haunt her. Often it was music, poignant and plaintive melodies unlike any she knew, the themes of another world. Sometimes there were scenes, smells, a painfully elusive sense of movement and texture. There was white silk edged with black-embroidered characters she did not know, and shadow and light interwoven in lattice strips, and swaying bodies that seemed always just beyond her ability to see them clearly, to discover who they were, what they were doing. Sometimes she remembered laughter, joy, a sense of abiding peace and security.

Who? Where? No matter how hard she strained to grasp the memory, to hold it and examine it and understand it, she could not tear aside the curtain that shrouded an inexplicable past and an insoluble mystery.

"Sofía, come here."

She had been musing again, trying to remember. She put down the pot she'd been scrubbing with sand for at least half an hour and went to Zocali. He summoned any woman nearby when he wanted something; that wasn't unusual.

"Prepare yourself," he said as calmly as if he were telling her to bring him wine. "You're going to represent our tribe next week at the Vigil of Sara."

That was all, no explanation, no fanfare, simply an announcement that she, the *busne* outcast, had been chosen for the highest honor possible for an unmarried Gypsy girl.

❧ 3 ❧

"Some call her La Macarena. In the tongue of our mothers she is Sara-la-Kali, the black Gypsy." The storyteller was Concha of the Vincento tribe. Twice before, Fanta had brought Sofía to Concha's fire to hear the tales of the old days and the old ways, but this was different. Now she was one of thirty young women being prepared for the vigil.

Concha puffed deeply on an enormous cigar. The smoke rose in a haze around her head. The hair of most Romany women remained black until death; those who were not so fortunate went to Fanta and got special herbs to color the gray, but Concha's hair was white. She wore it piled high, in a topknot pierced by a gold dagger. The full curve of her right earlobe was studded with jewels, from the left hung four gold hoops. She had a cast in one eye, and as the two did not focus together, it made her seem to see everything at once. When she spoke, Sofia noticed that most of her teeth were gone; the few she had left were stained bright yellow by the tobacco.

"Sara-la-Kali lived in a town by the sea and she was a great *drabarni*." Concha paused and looked at her charges. "You young ones speak only the tongue of the *busne*, but do you know what a *drabarni* is?"

For a moment there was no reply. Then a timid voice from the rear said, "A wise woman."

Concha snorted. "Much more. A *drabarni* is a witch. Only a Romany witch—no *busne* can be as we are in magic. But of all of us who have been and will be *drabarni*, no one has ever been the equal of Sara-la-Kali. One day El Señor Jesus spoke to her. He told her to go to the shore and calm the waves so a boat carrying three of his friends could land."

The old woman leaned forward and studied the faces of her listeners. "Understand me, none of you are *drabarni*. To have the gift of magic, to be a witch, your body must have been taken by a demon while you slept. But each of you has been chosen because you have not lost your *lacha*." She fixed her listeners with her small black eyes. The cross-eyed gaze demanded any truth they had to tell.

Sofía shivered. She had an urge to leap to her feet and say something, anything that would turn those eyes away from her, but she had nothing to confess. Of course she was a virgin, she had not lost her *lacha*. So were the others; anything else was unthinkable. Concha waited, but no one spoke. At last she grunted with satisfaction and went on.

"Sara-la-Kali did what El Señor told her to do and the boat brought three holy women to Sara's town. One of them, Maria la Magdalena, went with Sara to her cave and they lived there together. When it came time for Sara to die, her body was taken straight up to heaven. Now she watches over Romany girls, and when they have a husband, she sees to it that they have many babies."

The stories continued until dawn, interspersed with instructions about what they were to do on the sacred night itself. Then the girls were taken to a separate cave and allowed to sleep until it was dark and Concha spoke to them again.

So the days had gone for a full week. Sofía felt dazed and disoriented. Worse, she was terrified that because she was not a true Gypsy, she would make some horrible mistake. "Don't worry," Fanta told her the evening she came to bring Sofía the clothes the women of the Zocali tribe had made for her. "You will do well. Haven't I trained you myself?" She chuckled softly.

"And when the singing starts, you will make them all sound like donkeys braying at the moon."

Two more days passed, then it was time. The procession formed when the sun went down. Whatever they thought of the chief's choice, the Zocali tribe had done well by Sofía. A bright green skirt hugged her hips, then flared out in ten tiers of ruffles edged in white lace; her blouse was red striped with white, the sleeves and the deep-cut neckline yet another profusion of ruffles. Like the others, she was barefoot, and like them she wore a white lace mantilla that covered her hair and trailed down her back. Each girl held a lantern made of clay pierced with intricate patterns. The glow of the interior candle created a complex interplay of light and shadow on each expectant face.

They moved out of the caves. Ahead of them walked seven men carrying flaming torches. The smell of burning pitch hung in the air. Behind the torches were two more men. One bore a long staff topped with a crucifix, the other held high a crescent moon painted with diverse Romany symbols. They were followed by the soul of the procession, its reason for existence. Six men supported on their shoulders a pallet draped in red velvet and woven gold. On it stood the carved wooden image of the black virgin of the Romany, Sara-la-Kali. The statue was seven feet tall and resplendent in a crown and royal robes. After her, in single file, marched the thirty virgins.

With slow, measured paces they wound their way through the Triana. Tradition demanded that all other women hide themselves on this night; the route was lined with men. The *busne* who lived there hung from open windows and crowded onto small balconies. On the streets below, Gypsies pressed three and four deep against the damp, crumbling walls of buildings that had been old before the Moors came. The narrow lanes were so jammed with people there was just enough room for the procession to pass. The onlookers stared. They devoured the marchers with their eyes, but they did not make a sound.

It was like moving through a dream, made real only by the slap of bare feet on cobblestones, the jangle of gold chains and bracelets, and the sighing sound of swaying cotton and lace.

Always, as Sofía's limited memory measured such things, her world had been filled with squabbling women, crying babies, imperious men demanding attention. The caves echoed constantly with sound. When they went among the *busne,* the Gypsies added their noises to that of the outsiders. The men banged metal pots to attract attention to their skills as smiths, the women shouted that they could tell the future. Tonight there was such deep quiet, Sofía could hear her own breathing.

The cobblestones were rough and cold under her feet. She ignored them and concentrated on not stumbling, and on keeping her lantern alight. "If any girl lets the wind put out her candle, she must immediately drop out of the line," Concha had said. "Her tribe will be in shame for a year."

They reached the alley of the glassblowers halfway to their destination, and an insistent percussive sound broke the silence. A single pair of hands began to beat a measured rhythm. Another joined in, then more. In seconds the night rang with the staccato music of Gypsy clapping. It filled the narrow streets, and it seemed to invade her body. Sofía and the others swayed to its demanding call. The whole line twisted and rocked as it snaked its way toward the parish church of Santa Ana.

Throughout the rest of the year this church belonged to the whole of Seville, rich and poor, *busne* and Gypsy alike. Tonight it was reserved for the Romany. Still, the procession did not go in through the main door. It went around to the side to a narrow entrance. The nine carrying torches and staffs melted into the crowd; the men carrying the statue stopped.

Six of the girls set down their lanterns and came forward. One by one they replaced the men, until finally they bore on their young shoulders the entire weight of the sacred burden. Now the dazzling virgin belonged to them alone and they carried her forward into the crypt. For seven hours they would kneel in silent vigil before Sara.

Above the black face of the statue was an elaborate seven-tiered tiara. She was dressed in seven sets of splendid robes and as each hour passed they removed one layer, uncovering another yet more gorgeous and ornate beneath it. The last was the most beautiful of all, woven gold cloth studded with jewels.

The moment it was revealed a great banging started over their heads. This wasn't clapping but the clatter of hundreds of canes and sticks being stamped on the floor of the church above. It was the signal for the final part of the ceremony.

For hours—it seemed for all of the past week—the girls had barely said a word. Now one opened her mouth and began to sing the Lamentations, begging Sara to continue to watch over the Romany, to make them fertile and give them many children that their tribes might increase. There were thirty verses, one for each of them, and they sang in preassigned turns. Sofía was to sing last.

At first she thought her placement was another proof of her lack of status among them. Then her turn came and she understood, and suspected Fanta's hand in the arrangement. Her voice soared through the vaulted space, a stunning culmination of what had gone before. She kept singing, as was her duty, until the sun rose and the door of the crypt was thrown open.

This year it was Zocali who had that honor. He stood with the red sky behind him and called them out into the day. "Daughters of Sara, come forth!"

One by one they left the crypt. When Sofía stepped through the door into the sunlight, Zocali smiled at her. His dark face wore an expression of approval she'd never before seen.

"She does many things well." Zocali nodded toward the corner where Sofía sat weaving a basket of river reeds.

The visitor was built like a barrel, squat and thick through the middle. He had a full black beard, but his head was entirely bald. The combination made him look menacing; there was a rumor that he shaved his scalp. He continued picking his teeth. They had dined well on rice and beans and stewed goat, and they had drunk much wine. He belched loudly. "Sí, so you say. That's why I'm here. She looks all right, but her blood is bad, we both know that."

"Not bad, only *busne*."

"It comes to the same thing."

Zocali shrugged. "As you say, we both know that. If it bothers you, why did you come?"

The visitor concentrated on the embers of the dung fire. "I'm a poor man. Now I'm a widower. I have to look at what I can afford."

"You are the richest man in the caves," Zocali said. "Spare me your lies and moans. You have seen her and you have heard her, you know she's a prize. And there's something else—she can read letters, even whole words. I won't let her go cheaply."

Sofía didn't look up, but her fingers stopped plaiting the reeds. All the while she served them supper she had wondered what was happening. Normally they had few dealings with the Paco tribe. There had to be some important reason for Paco himself to come to Zocali's cave. Now she knew what it was.

Fanta sat by the fire, laying her well-thumbed cards in ever-changing patterns on the room's only table. She made a soft, barely audible clucking sound. Sofía heard it, as she was meant to. She raised her eyes. Fanta shook her head in silent warning.

Zocali had buried three wives; his fourth was called Teresita. She was only a little older than Sofía, but not half as beautiful. Teresita's first child was a healthy son, but that did not make her envy Sofía any less. The baby was sucking avidly at her swollen nipple and her arms were full of him. She reached out a foot and prodded Sofía. "You, lazy one, can't you see their cups are empty?"

Sofía rose to get the jug of wine. Zocali looked angrily at Teresita. She could say what she liked when they were alone, but calling the girl lazy while he was negotiating her bride price was stupid. He turned back to the other chief. "Two hundred reales, Paco. Plus three copper pots and a donkey. And one other thing." He leaned forward and touched the gold ring in Paco's left ear. It was a coiled snake with a ruby like a droplet of blood on the tip of its thrusting tongue. "I want this too."

"Ridiculous," Paco said. Sofía was bending over him to fill his cup. He reached up and put his fingers around her arm. "She's skin and bones."

"Only because she's a virgin. Once she's married she'll fatten up. And her breasts are good. They'll give plenty of milk. You, open your blouse and show him."

Sofí did not hesitate because of modesty. She knew that

among *busne,* women's breasts were kept hidden, but Gypsies found that a ridiculous attitude. A woman's breasts would nourish her children, the most precious gift of the tribe. They were an object of pride. Sofía's were full and firm and she was not ashamed of them. She held back because she didn't want to seem to agree to Zocali's plan. Gypsy girls had some say in the matter of marriage. It was the tradition.

The constant soft slapping sound of the shuffling cards stopped. Fanta cleared her throat loudly.

Zocali and Paco watched and waited. In another few seconds Sofía's reluctance would become open disobedience. She'd be beaten for it. Worse, if Zocali was angry because he'd been made to lose face, he would be harder to reason with. She untied her bodice and freed her breasts.

Her thick black braids hung over them, obscuring the taut pink nipples. Paco reached up a stubby finger and flicked one braid away. Sofía shuddered.

Zocali chuckled. "See, you frighten her because she's a pure virgin. Easy, my friend. You can look but not touch. Not until you pay me her bride price and marry her."

"Two hundred reales, three copper pots, a donkey, and my earring. You're a thief, Zocali. No Rom steals from another, it's our law."

"I know our law. I call it a fair price. Go and think about it. Tell me your answer by Friday. There are others who are interested."

If so, it was an interest newly born. Until this night no one but Carlos had paid any attention to her. That had been Zocali's reason for choosing her to represent his tribe at the Vigil of Sara. Sofía understood now. It had nothing to do with affection. She had gained status which pushed up her price.

She waited until Paco left the small windowless room, then she turned to Zocali. He had put his head back and closed his eyes. She didn't dare disturb his sleep.

Fanta was still watching her. Sofía sent her a pleading glance. The old woman merely shook her head and went back to her cards. Sofía returned to her weaving. A few moments later she felt Fanta's gaze on her again. She looked up. The old woman was staring first at her, then at the cards. "What is it?" Sofía whispered. "What do you see?"

"Nothing." Fanta gathered the cards into a pile with one sweep of her hand. "I see nothing. Why would I waste my time reading the cards of a worthless girl like you?"

"Not worthless," Zocali's voice said. "Sing something, Sofía."

"I thought you were sleeping."

"I was. Now I'm awake. Sing something."

"Please, I want to talk to you . . ."

"I know what you want to say. I don't want to hear it. Do you think I can pick and choose a husband for a *busne*? It won't be easy to find someone who will marry you. I have to take what I can get."

It's not true, she wanted to shout. You wouldn't be asking such a high price for me if it were true. She didn't say that, and she certainly didn't shout. "Carlos wants to marry me," she whispered. "I know he does."

"Everyone knows it," Zocali agreed. "But he has no money. I have supported you for eight years, I took you in when you would have been murdered by outlaws or left to starve. Am I not entitled to a small return now? Stop talking, Sofía. Sing."

She did as he asked. Making him angry would gain nothing. She needed her wits and her wiles. They were her only weapons.

Carlos came the following morning. His gray eyes were dark with rage. "They say you are going to give Sofía to that filthy animal Paco. You can't do it."

"Oh? Why can't I?" Zocali was tying his pack of smithing tools to his back, preparing to go into the town.

"Because she's mine. I found her and brought her to the tribe, didn't I? She belongs to me. I want to marry Sofía."

"*Bueno*, to me it's all the same as long as I don't have to feed and clothe her forever. Two hundred reales, three copper pots, and a donkey, and you can have her. I'll forget about the earring."

"Very well," Carlos said instantly. "I agree."

Zocali narrowed his eyes and stared at the young man. "Show

me the money and she's yours. We'll announce the betrothal tonight."

Sofía's heart was thumping. She didn't take her eyes from Carlos.

"I can't," he said. "Not right now. I've been saving, but I don't have enough yet."

"¡Dios mío! Am I not a reasonable man? A kind man? What other chief has given protection to two busne outcasts all these years? If you're a little short, Carlos, do you think that will matter? A real or two I can wait for. How much do you have?"

Carlos hung his head. "Ten reales. But I know where I can steal the pots and the donkey."

"Ten reales! You have the cheek to come here and tell me to my face that you want to take my virgin lark for the price you'd have to pay for an old hag with no milk left in her breasts? For this I have sheltered you since your cursed mother died? To be insulted and shamed by you?" Zocali's voice got louder with each word.

He was pretending anger, Sofía knew it. He never believed that Carlos could pay the asking price. He had maneuvered the younger man into a position where he looked ungrateful and ridiculous, and now he was shouting about it so the whole tribe would hear.

"Leave him alone," she screamed. "Leave Carlos alone. It's not his fault he's poor. And neither of us are to blame for our blood."

Zocali whirled on her. His open-handed slap was so hard it sent her staggering. Carlos dived at Zocali. He knocked him to the ground and began pummeling him. Each blow was payment for years of insults and rejection. He might have killed him, but two men ran into the room and pulled him off.

Zocali clambered to his feet. His face was covered in blood. He wiped his mouth with the back of his hand and spat, and two teeth flew onto the dirt floor. His rescuers held Carlos, one on each side. Zocali's hand went to the knife at his belt, but only for a moment. He was a tribal chief, not a hotheaded idiot.

"Take him away," he murmured at last. "I don't want to look

at him again." He turned to Sofía. "I want her out of my sight too. Teresita, get her out of here. Beat her well for her impertinence." He picked up a jug of wine but paused before he drank. "See you don't mark her face or break any bones," he called after his wife.

The beating was not so terrible. Sofía had endured worse. By nightfall she felt better and she left the cave carrying a water jug she would fill at the river.

The evening was mild and still. Somewhere an owl hooted and the wind rustled in the trees. This was the finest music of all, even better than hers. She walked quickly, her heart light despite everything that had happened. Carlos had asked for her. He wanted her. Carlos . . .

They had been meeting by the river for many years. It was their secret place, hers and Carlos's. Such trysts were forbidden, but they knew they did nothing wrong. They only talked and sometimes, if she seemed very sad, he touched her hand. "Why do you mourn what you can never have?" he asked her repeatedly. "They are gone, the mother and father who made you. For you they are dead. You must accept it."

"I can't." Sofía always gave him the same answer. "I can't accept it. I do not know who I am, Carlos. I do not know what I am."

"You are Sofía of the Zocali tribe. A beautiful young girl with the voice of an angel. It is enough."

It had never seemed enough to her. But now . . . Now perhaps it would be. Because Carlos wanted to make her his wife. As she approached the bank of the river, Sofía knew exactly what she would say. "We must go now, Carlos. We have talked about running away before. Now it is time. It will not be so impossible. We will find a priest to marry us. We will go far away where no one knows us. You will get what work you can find, and I will tell fortunes. I've listened to Fanta often enough, I know how it's done. . . ."

She was full of the words she would say to him. They trembled on the edge of Sofía's lips, waiting to spill over.

The riverbank was deserted. She waited as long as she dared, but he didn't come. Every night for a week Sofía returned to the meeting place, but Carlos never appeared. Neither did she see him by day. He had disappeared from the caves and from her life.

On Friday Paco came to Zocali's cave and said he would pay the bride price. "Everything except my earring." He fingered the jewel lovingly. "It's my good luck, this earring."

Zocali shrugged. "So, would I steal a man's good luck? Very well, we will forget the earring."

Paco nodded. "And I have one other condition."

"What?"

"We marry within two months. I am too old for a betrothal of two years."

Two years was the customary period. But that presumed that both bride and groom were barely past childhood, as was the usual case. This was different. "Done," Zocali agreed, putting out his hand.

Paco shook it warmly. "Done."

Carlos had one hope. The bulls. They were his only chance of getting money in a short time, and he needed a lot of money. He would have to pay Zocali the two hundred reales plus a bonus, because he was asking him to renounce a bargain already made. Then he'd have to pay Paco the same amount, to compensate him for the loss of a promised wife. But with enough money he could do both these things; such arrangements were not unheard of, they were within the law of the Rom. If he could get the money. There was no place he knew where he could steal such a sum without being caught. The bulls were his only hope.

On Sundays at the great corridas in the plaza in Seville a matador often made more than two hundred reales for a single afternoon's work. That fact was of little use to Carlos. He could not fight in such a spectacle because he was not a matador.

The title and the rewards were reserved for one who started as a torero, a bullfighter, in the minor corridas in the provinces and worked his way up, always fighting bigger and braver bulls.

Eventually, if he avoided being mutilated or killed by the horns and if word of his skills and grace spread, he would be invited to perform in Madrid. This would be the most important appearance of his life, his *alternativa*. Only after he danced his exotic dance of death on the sands of the Plaza Mayor in Madrid, in front of aficionados who knew what they were seeing could a man be called not merely a bullfighter but a matador. Only then could he demand exorbitant prices each time he entered the arena.

"You've been standing there for over an hour. What do you want?" The man who questioned Carlos was almost as big as the bulls he bred and prepared for the ring.

"I want to fight."

The breeder laughed, but it was a sound without humor. "Every boy in Spain wants to fight the bulls. That's why no animal can graze safely in a field at night. Some stupid *muchacho* comes along and torments the poor thing into a frenzy so he can convince his friends that someday he'll be a great matador."

He paused and looked closely at Carlos. Tall and slender, the build of a torero, no doubt about that. Blond hair and gray eyes too. Good looks never hurt—the ladies went to the ring as often as their men. But this young man appeared to be in his twenties. If he had any special skill his name would be known. "You look a little old for that game, *chico*. Where have you been fighting up to now?"

"Nowhere," Carlos said. "I've never fought before."

The breeder laughed again. This time he really was amused. "And you want me to put you in the ring?" He motioned to the corral beside them. "With something like that black killer in there, eh? Why should I end up paying for your funeral?"

"You won't." Carlos fixed the other man with his eyes. "I am going to be the greatest matador you've ever seen."

The breeder started to turn away. "You're *loco, chico*. I have work to do."

"I'm a Gypsy. I have secret powers."

The breeder looked at him once more. "A blond Gypsy with gray eyes? *Loco*," he said again. When he started to walk away,

Carlos jumped over the fence and into the corral. "Hey! Get the hell out of there. *¡Cuño!* That's my best bull. . . ."

He had absolutely no craft. The only thing Carlos knew about bullfighting was what he'd seen on the rare occasion when he and a few other Gypsy boys had sneaked into the plaza during a *corrida.* He knew what a matador looked like while performing his art, but he had no idea of how he achieved his grace. Neither did Carlos have any equipment—no cape with which to inaugurate the preliminary passes, no banderillas to implant in the neck and lower the creature's head for the kill, no sword and *muleta* with which to kill. Carlos had only his desperation.

So big. *¡Dios mío!* he could scarcely believe its size. "Come, *toro,*" he whispered, "look at me . . ."

The bull continued to ignore him. Carlos stood very straight, the way he'd seen the matadors stand, as if his body were the most beautiful thing on earth. The breeder was still screaming at him to get out of the corral, but he paid no attention. He made insistent clucking noises with his tongue and his teeth; he'd seen the matadors do that too. The bull looked up and slowly turned its massive head.

Slowly. Speed was the single advantage a man had against an animal that weighed more than a thousand pounds. The bull was ponderous, completely without agility—of which Carlos had a great deal. "Come," he called softly. "Come get me, *toro.*" The great lidless eyes locked with his. Then the horns lowered.

"Jump! You crazy *chico,* he'll kill you. Jump!"

Carlos did not jump, not until the final fraction of a second. He turned sideways to present a smaller target and stood absolutely still. If he had a cape, he would use it at this moment as an alternative goal for the two-foot horns. He had no red cloth to guide those curved instruments of death past soft human flesh. The bull lunged. When he felt its hot breath on his face, he spun away.

The animal's charge carried it six feet farther before it realized that the man was no longer in its sights. The bull turned its huge bulk and looked for him. Carlos was standing in the same spot as before, just as still and just as tempting.

The breeder had stopped shouting; he was staring in open-mouthed awe. Insane. The *chico* was insane. But brave. *Mi madre,* what *cojones.* Nothing but his body and the bull. He shrugged out of his jacket. "Hey, *chico!* You want this?"

Carlos looked at the "weapon" the man was offering to toss him. He shook his head. That motion was enough. The bull began its second charge.

It seemed to Carlos as if he could count the paces of the creature's legs as they closed the distance, as if they moved in some measured dance outside of time. Two more strides, then the horns would have him. No, they would not. He knew they would not as surely as if an angel rode on his shoulder and told him so. Carlos turned his back to the bull. When he felt the hot wet breath on the nape of his neck, he sprang to safety.

This time he continued his run all the way to the fence of the corral and jumped over it. He wasn't even winded. "Well," he demanded of the breeder. "Can I fight? For money?"

"We'll see," the man said slowly. "We'll see. There's someone I want you to meet."

"Who?"

"Never mind who. It's no one you would know, I promise you that. Come, eat with us now. Later you can sleep in there." He jerked his head toward one of the barns. "I'll send the señor word tonight, maybe he'll come in a few days."

"It is dangerous to love what you can never possess," Domingo Mendoza warned his deformed son in 1783 when the boy was ten. "Forget the bulls, Pablocito. They cannot run for you."

The words changed nothing. He had seen his first corrida when he was eight, and from that moment Pablo Luis Mendoza Rodriguez yearned to take his chance in the arena. A matador with a humped back and a shrunken arm was a joke, but it did not make him laugh.

All during his youth Pablo Luis studied the world of the corrida in every particular. Now he was twenty-six years old and no *gañadero* was unknown to him. He visited every ranch in Spain where prize bulls were raised. Pablo was always there

for the *tentadero*, the first test of courage of a *novillo*, a young
bull. When an *alternativa* took place in Madrid, he was present.
When the program of a corrida in Córdoba seemed less exciting
than one to take place in some other city, Pablo left his home
and journeyed to the better-favored place. When an aspiring
torero could not afford the hundreds of reales for his *traje de
luz*, the elaborate suit of lights that had lately replaced buckskins
as the customary fighting costume, he went to Pablo Mendoza.
If he was a bullfighter of promise, invariably he got what he
needed.

Pablo Luis, the cripple, ate, slept, drank, and loved only the
bullfight. On this January day in 1799 he read the message
from the breeder outside Seville with a frisson of excitement.
"Come if you can, Don Pablo," the note said. "I think you will
see something remarkable."

It took four days to cover the distance between Córdoba and
Seville for a Gypsy band traveling by foot with a donkey or
two; for a man in a carriage pulled by four powerful horses it
was a matter of some sixteen hours. Pablo arrived at the ranch
three days after Carlos had entered the corral and faced his
first bull.

"I don't know if he's just crazy or the bravest man I've ever
seen," the breeder confided. "He's over there. That blond *chico*
trying to pretend he doesn't know we're talking about him."

Pablo looked. The sight of the young man twisted his gut.
It was always so, the ones who looked as if they were born to
be matadors—straight, tall, handsome, broad-shouldered, and
slim-hipped—he hated them, but he loved them too. They
provided whatever he knew of joy in life. He'd learned to hide
the storm of conflicting emotions. "He is fine to look at," he
agreed. "But obviously you're talking about something else."

"Something else," the breeder said slowly. "You might call
it that, Don Pablo." He told him what Carlos had done.

"Very brave," Pablo agreed. He did not sound convinced.

"More than brave," the breeder insisted. "He has looks and
he has *cojones*, but you and I know it takes what you called
'something else' to make a matador. He has that too. When he

was in the corral he was . . . like a god. He was exquisite. I know
no other word. To see him was like watching music come to
life. That is why I think he could become a great matador."

Pablo appraised the breeder with narrowed eyes. "I have
never heard you so poetic, my friend. Perhaps I will react in
the same way. Let us see."

"You understand," the breeder said quickly, "he has never
held a cape before. He has been practicing while we waited for
you, but he is not yet as graceful as he will be someday."

"A cape? No, I want to see what you saw. The *chico* and a
bull. *Sin nada.*"

"Without anything? Don Pablo, forgive me. It is suicidal. He
did it, I swear to you on my mother's soul. He really did it."

"I don't doubt your word, but I want to see for myself."

The breeder paused a moment, then shrugged. "Carlos, come
here."

Carlos approached them. The breeder was mistaken, he
did know this man from Córdoba. Sofía had described him
when she spoke of their meeting in the Calle Judíos. The
man was dressed today as he had been than, in a great black
cape that half concealed the hump on his back and his
deformed arm, with a broad-brimmed black sombrero pulled
low over his face.

Carlos had not told the breeder what he knew of the Mendozas. Now he waited to be introduced, then bowed. "*Buenos
días,* Don Pablo. I am at your service."

"My friend here tells me you're a Gypsy. What tribe?"

Carlos hesitated. Few *busne* knew that the tribes existed; they
thought of all Gypsies as the same. But Sofía had said that this
one seemed to know a great deal, even about the "great trick."
"The Zocali tribe," Carlos said. It didn't seem to matter, and
so much depended on this man's patronage.

"I see. Tell me, is there by chance among you a young woman
with a remarkable voice? I heard her once or twice. Blue eyes,
as I recall."

Carlos shook his head. "I know no such Gypsy, Don Pablo."
Never would he discuss Sofía with the *busne.*

The older man shrugged. "*Bueno,* it's unimportant. Now, I

have heard what you did the other day. Are you prepared to do it again? As before, without a cape or a weapon," he added.

Carlos's eyes flicked to those of the breeder. The man had said that Don Pablo would watch him with a cape. That he was an aficionado who would understand that Carlos was as yet unpracticed with it. The breeder's glance was steady, it gave away nothing. If the Gypsy wished to risk his life, he would do it by his own choice.

Carlos understood. He nodded. "Of course, to please your lordship."

The bull waiting for him in the corral was not the same one he'd faced before. As far as fighting was concerned, he had ruined that bull forever. No *toro* was ever placed in a ring with a man for a second time. After one experience, the bull would have learned all the tricks and he would be unbeatable. The black bull of the first encounter was now fit only for stud and eventually for stew. The one waiting today was a little smaller and a russet-brown color.

"It is a good bull?" Pablo asked while Carlos walked toward the corral.

The breeder didn't look at him. "Of course, a fine bull." Well, maybe not so fine. A little less brave, less straight of charge. *¡Cuño!* He had lost one perfect specimen this week, it was enough.

Pablo grunted. He guessed that the man was lying. He wouldn't sacrifice another prime bull to this mad Gypsy. So be it. It was entirely the young man's choice. If this Carlos wanted the patronage of Pablo Luis Mendoza, he must prove himself worthy of it.

Pablo waited and he watched. The feelings warring inside him were what they always were. Because he hated the Gypsy for doing what he could not do, he wanted the bull to kill him; because he loved the spectacle and the courage, he wanted the torero to triumph.

Carlos sprang over the fence of the corral and took his stance. It was as the breeder had said. Something happened the moment Carlos faced the bull. He changed. He wasn't a mere mortal any longer. Pablo knew it and sensed an invisible link

between him and the bullfighter—all their emotions, their
fears, their hopes, their triumph, their disaster passing along
it. The surge of pleasure he felt now was as it always was at
such moments. No, it was better.

For a brief second Carlos looked back at the man watching
him. Their eyes locked. Then Carlos turned his attention to
the bull. "*Ay, toro,*" he called softly. "I'm over here, come get
me."

In seconds Pablo knew this was a performance he would
never forget. It was better than the breeder had promised.
Carlos took three charges, one head on and two with his back
turned, each time springing away from the horns at the last
possible instant in a movement of surpassing grace. Then he
faced the bull a fourth time. Bellowing its fury, the beast
charged. Carlos waited until it was too late. It had to be too
late. But it wasn't. He did not try to spin away. He leapt into
the air and over the length of the bull.

"*Dios mío,*" Pablo whispered.

"*Olé!*" the breeder shouted. The whole thing was so extraordinary for men who followed the corrida, so remarkable. "Look,
Madre de Dios, he's going to do it again."

Carlos was summoning the bull to him one more time. If
the animal had been of a higher caliber, he would have succeeded and been a hero. But this was not such a fine *toro*. He
didn't charge true. He turned at the last second and hooked his
horn through Carlos's side. The great tusk entered below
the young man's rib cage and exited beside his spine. For a
moment the Gypsy was impaled on the horn. Then the bull,
hating this new frustration, swung his head and hurled him
free.

He was conscious while they carried him to the house. And
strangely, he was very happy. Not such a coward after all. Not
the way they always said. Zocali and Joselito and the others
were wrong. He had bigger *cojones* than they did.

Pablo bent over him. "Carlos, can you hear me?"

The Gypsy nodded.

"*Bueno.* You are incredible. If you live, and if you have the
courage to fight again, I will be your sponsor."

Wait for me, Sofía, Carlos thought. The betrothal will last two years. Don't forget me. I'll get the money and I'll come. . . . He passed out from loss of blood.

Repeatedly Sofía told herself that Carlos would return. There was nothing to worry about. Before she was married to Paco, Carlos would come for her. He had saved her once and he would save her again. Everything would be fine. When Carlos returned.

She kept hoping right up to the morning of her wedding day. Not until the women of the Zocali tribe had dressed her in white, and Fanta had put a high comb in her hair and attached to it a long white lace mantilla, did she realize that she really was going to marry Paco. By then it was too late.

❧ 4 ❧

Sofía became the wife of Paco when almond blossoms spread a lacy pink mantilla over Andalusia, on a February Thursday three days before Carnival began and ushered in the Lenten period, La Cuaresma, of the year of 1799. They had been betrothed a week short of the two months Zocali had agreed to, but the Church would not allow a marriage during the forty days of Lent, and Paco would not wait for the two months to turn into more than three.

The wedding feast lasted two days. There were Gypsies present from as far as Granada in the east and Cádiz in the west. They came because Zocali was a respected chief, and because, having heard the enormous bride price he'd been paid for his *busne*, they expected a fiesta of extraordinary proportions. Zocali did not disappoint them.

The women of his tribe roasted forty baby goats on spits and stewed a hundred hedgehogs. The men stole a pig and slaughtered it, and denuded an entire field of its cabbages and boiled the two together. There were twenty cauldrons of rice cooked with fish from the Guadalquivir, and twenty more filled with a savory porridge of ground maize, the delicacy that came on the treasure ships from the New World, and which the Triana Gypsies had learned to prize. Countless barrels of wine were emptied, innumerable songs sung and dances danced. "You'd think Zocali's favorite daughter was being married," Joselito grumbled. "Not the *busne*."

"But is it true he got two hundred reales for the *busne*?" someone asked. Joselito nodded. "But why did Paco agree to pay so much?"

"Paco's an old fool. He had an itch between his legs, that's all," Joselito said sullenly.

The other man shrugged and said nothing; perhaps it was true, incredible as it seemed. He would have liked to judge for himself if the *busne* woman was worth two hundred reales, or if Paco had perhaps lost his mind, but it was impossible. Neither the bride nor the groom was with the guests.

In the past Sofía would have been alone at the fiesta for the first twenty-four hours, then Paco would have appeared and the wedding ceremony would have been conducted according to ancient Romany custom. Some of the oldest Gypsies remembered such ways, but the younger ones had never seen such a wedding. These days the priests and the Inquisition made Gypsies marry in church, like all Spaniards, and there would be fines and terrible punishments if they followed the Catholic ceremony with one of their own.

Paco and Sofía were married in the crypt of the Church of Santa Ana. The event took place in the morning and lasted only a few minutes. When it was over, Paco took his new wife to his cave. All his tribe were at the fiesta. The newlyweds were alone except for Fanta, who had brought Sofía to the church and accompanied the couple back to the Triana.

Sofía had not spoken a word all morning, not to Paco and not to Fanta. When she had to tell the priest that she married of her own free will and that she accepted Paco as her husband, her voice had been a faint whisper. Now she stared at the entrance to Paco's cave and continued to ignore Fanta. Why should she speak to her? The old woman had not helped her before, and now it was too late. She was married to this man. Her only hope was to do as he bid her. A Gypsy woman who disobeyed her husband could be turned out of the tribe and left to wander the streets.

"This is your home now," Fanta murmured. "May you be happy here and give your husband many children."

Sofía still didn't answer. The entrance to Paco's cave looked much like the one that led to Zocali's, but she suspected that she would find things very different inside. Fanta reached up and undid Sofía's mantilla, then she handed it to Paco. With a broad grin he took it and disappeared through the low entrance.

Sofía started to follow him, but Fanta stopped her. "Wait, you go to your husband as you came into the world." Her rheumatic old fingers began undoing the fastenings of Sofía's wedding dress. In seconds the girl was naked. "Now go in to him. When I hear you scream and he brings me the mantilla stained with blood, then I will know that you have not betrayed our law."

The screaming began very quickly and went on for a long time. It was an hour before Paco reappeared in the doorway and handed the mantilla to Fanta. "Don't look at me like that, old one. I had to hurt her a little. Fear is good for a woman. It teaches her to obey."

Fanta did look at him. His beard dripped rivulets of sweat, his massive chest was heaving, and he stank like an animal. But she knew her duty. There was only one thing she could say. "She was a virgin and she pleased you?"

"Yes."

Fanta nodded and left. Her face was furrowed with worry while she walked to the place of the celebration. The fiesta was being held outside Zocali's cave, in a flat space between two of the Triana hills. Fanta approached it through a cleft in the limestone, and paused for a moment to survey the scene.

The smoke of cooking fires and roasting meat perfumed the air. There was music—dozens of guitars, yet more tambourines, and the fierce clicking of castanets held between expert fingers. The bright red and blue and green of the women's clothing swirled in ever-changing spirals of color. The men wore somber black, but they moved among the women like gods, strong *Gitanos* filled with wine and song.

Fanta felt a surge of pride in her race, until she looked back toward the cave where she'd left the girl. The child's screams still rang in her ears. The old woman permitted herself one moment's regret for the stupidity and greed of men, even Zocali, who was usually wise. Then she lifted her head and shouted in triumph as she ran toward the crowd, waving the bloody trophy. The law was the law and its ways must be respected.

"Welcome, Robert," Domingo Mendoza said. "Welcome to the mother house in the mother country. I'm told you speak excellent Spanish, so I can say it in my own tongue, *mi casa es tu casa.*"

Robert Mendoza embraced his cousin with more formality than warmth, then took the chair he was offered. It was elaborately carved in black walnut and upholstered in red velvet, but it didn't cushion his buttocks or cradle his back the way a chair would at home in London. So far everything in Spain seemed to him to have been planned for the most show and the least comfort. Not this room, however. It was small and unadorned except for shelves crammed with books and ledgers. The only furnishings were the chairs he and his cousin occupied, and the large table between them.

Domingo noted the younger man's appraising eye. "You're thinking everything you've heard about the Palacio Mendoza is a lie, aren't you?" he asked. "But this isn't really part of the palace, it's where we do business. We're in the oldest wing of the property here, this room and a few others were never burned down or rebuilt." He looked around. "It sounds fanciful, I suppose, but sometimes it occurs to me that my ancestors might have been negotiating from this spot since the house was founded."

No one knew exactly when that had been. Robert had heard stories that put the origins of the family in the time of the Phoenicians. Probably posturing rubbish, but one thing was true—the Mendozas aged well. Domingo was over fifty and he still looked like a vigorous man. There was no gray in his dark hair or his small neat beard. Bit of a fop though, Robert thought. He was dressed in the prissy French manner in blue broadcloth frockcoat over an elaborate white silk waistcoat and red knee breeches. He wore white stockings, too, and shoes trimmed with gold buckles. A popinjay, like all continentals. Plenty of Englishmen did the same these days. Damn, a man wasn't a peacock. Robert fingered his somber black coat and high white collar. His cousin was still speaking.

"Later you'll see the palace. I don't think it will disappoint you. For the moment this is better. The servants aren't allowed in here, and what we have to say is best not overheard. First, may I call you Roberto? After all, that's your name in Spanish."

"If you don't mind, I prefer Robert."

Domingo smiled wryly. "Very well. Robert, then. Tell me, how was the journey?"

"Long," Robert admitted. "Thanks to our friend Napoleon, I had to cross the Channel on a fishing vessel and do the rest of the trip overland."

"Ah, yes, Napoleon. A great nuisance," Domingo agreed. "He interferes with shipping and thus with trade. Perhaps someday soon he'll learn that the business of government is business, not military adventures."

"He's your ally," Robert said stiffly.

Domingo looked puzzled. "Mine? I've never met the man. . . . Ah, I see. You mean he's Spain's ally."

"Yes."

"*Muchacho*," Domingo said softly. "Your father tells me you're wise beyond your twenty-four years. That is not a wise statement."

Damn, he'd offended the man. "I only meant . . ."

The Spaniard held up a forestalling hand. "I know what you meant, that six years ago your Mr. Pitt prevailed on Spain to join her in a war against France. Then three years later that idiot Charles IV who, God help us, is the king of Spain, made a separate peace with this upstart Bonaparte and declared war on England." Domingo shrugged. "And how many others are involved? Russia, Austria, Naples . . . ? I suppose God knows, but I've lost track." He chuckled. "What does it matter, *muchacho*? As we speak, they may all be changing sides yet again."

"There are issues," Robert said stiffly. "Important questions of right and wrong."

Domingo's mood changed suddenly and he slammed his fist on the table. "There is the family. That is the only issue for us. I am not Spain, my young cousin, and while you may insist on being called Robert and not Roberto, you are not England. We are Mendozas, and that's a far greater thing, because it will outlast the generals and the kings, and all the fools who do their bidding."

For a time Domingo was silent, then he rose and put his hands on the younger man's shoulders. "Do you understand?"

Robert nodded. He did understand. Not with his head—that was as full of patriotism and pride as any other Englishman's—but with his gut. It was why he hadn't balked when his father sent him on this visit. Spain and England might be at war; the two branches of the mighty Mendoza empire were not. "Yes, Don Domingo. Forgive me."

"There is nothing to forgive, *muchacho*. You are young and entitled to be excited by the exploits of heroes like Nelson. England is enjoying him, no?"

Robert stretched his long legs in front of him. Damn this chair, he wasn't built properly for it. Too tall, too thin. "England is enjoying him, yes. They're ecstatic over Nelson's victories." He broke off. He'd said the wrong thing again. The latest such triumph was a defeat of the Spanish Navy at Santa Cruz in the Spanish Canary Islands.

Domingo waved his hand again. Bedecked with no less than three rings, by God, a ruby and two emeralds, Robert noted. A popinjay for sure, but at least his cousin wasn't going to lecture him a second time.

"Don't look so embarrassed, Robert. As I've said, it needn't concern us." He laughed again. "Besides, the Mendozas are patriotic supporters of the Spanish crown. We lend Charles money to refit the ships your Admiral Nelson blasts holes in. Napoleon borrows from us too. And in England the exchequer also signs an occasional Mendoza note. If one is clever, even war can be good for business." He dismissed the topic with another wave. "Tell me about the family in England. That's much more important."

On safer ground now. Robert breathed easier and almost

relaxed. "My brother is married to a fat and sassy wife due to give him a child in three months time, and Father is very well. Except that Mother plagues him to move out of London. She wants to trade Creechurch Lane for a grand country manor. Father won't hear of it."

"I approve his decision. That's why here, too, we remain in the heart of Córdoba. The country may be refreshing, but business is done in the city, and business comes first." Domingo poured two goblets of the sweet strong wine of Jerez and passed one to the younger man. "A drink before more talk, and welcome to you yet again."

Robert raised his glass. "A toast, in the sherry that unites us. I drink to your continued good health and good fortune, hidalgo."

Domingo paused before drinking. "For the toast I thank you, but it's more than the wine of Jerez that unites us, Robert. It's blood."

"I know, that's why I'm here."

"Good, then we may both drink."

The two men emptied their goblets with a single swallow, Domingo refilled them. "Before you leave you must see the Jerez vineyards and bodegas. I think they'll please you. The harvest has been good for four years running, praise the Virgin and all the saints."

The Englishman did not immediately reply. Certainly he didn't make the sign of the cross as a pious Spaniard would have. "So the old ways persist," Domingo said very softly.

Robert looked unwaveringly into Domingo's eyes. They were the same golden brown as his own, but faded with age. "It's good if this is open between us, hidalgo. My father, my brother, myself—we're none of us religious men. But at some level I can't truly explain, the old ways do persist. I'll be quiet about them while I'm here. I didn't come to set the Inquisition on you."

"It's not just that," Domingo said thoughtfully. "The Inquisition has fewer teeth these days. Mostly the Inquisitors devote themselves to hounding people who read the books on their forbidden list, their Index. Of course they keep an eye out for 'relapsed' Jews, Marranos they call them. It means swine, but they haven't burned any for forty years. Not since fifty-nine."

"Still, I imagine they'd rekindle the auto-do-fé if they found any."

"No doubt," Domingo agreed. "But let me speak plainly, *muchacho*. The Inquisition will find no Marranos in my house. You English Mendozas may pose as Protestants and continue to think of yourselves as Jews. Here that would never be enough, even if we wanted it, which I for one do not. Personally I've never thought much about God, but if He exists, I'm content to find him in the Catholic Church. More important, this is Spain, Robert, the country whose piety sets the standard for all Christendom. In Spain religious practices rival the pursuit of bread, even for the most destitute peasant."

It was evening, and the sun was just setting. Domingo walked to the window facing the street and closed the shutters, then he turned back to his guest. "Let me tell you a little story. In sixty-six there was a revolt in Zaragossa. Hundreds of people took to the streets, looting and burning. At the height of the uprising a religious procession passed through the town, a bishop carrying the Blessed Sacrament. Every one of the rebels stopped what he was doing to kneel until the procession passed. When it was out of sight they resumed their rebellion, but it was too late. By then the Zaragossa authorities had time to organize their soldiers and they slaughtered the rebels. Perhaps that story would be remarkable anywhere else. But not here, not in Spain. Do we understand each other, my young cousin?"

Robert nodded.

"I'm glad of that. Now, the affair of the Mesta—"

Domingo stopped speaking. The blood drained from his face and he clutched his chest. Robert quickly poured him another drink and the older man took it gratefully. "Thank you. It's nothing. Merely that I'm not as young as I was. How much did your father explain?"

"About the Mesta? They're a guild that controls the wool trade."

Domingo looked away, his fingers drumming on the table. "Yes, every sheep shorn from Aragon to Andalusia gives up its coat on behalf of the Mesta, and has done so for centuries. It's not for nothing that the lord chancellor in your Parliament sits on a sack of wool. The stuff's like gold, an elementary part of the wealth of nations."

Robert cleared his throat. "It was like gold, hidalgo. It hasn't been anywhere near so vital for a long time."

The older man jerked his head around and looked sharply at his cousin. "So you don't think I wanted only their wool," he said slowly.

"I don't doubt your word, Don Domingo. It's just—"

"Just that you're not a fool and I was wrong to treat you as such." Domingo leaned forward. "Benjamin told me that you're smarter than many men twice your age. Your father thinks highly of you, *muchacho,* apparently with good cause, so I will tell you what I've told no one else, not even him. There are those in power in Madrid who are eager to be done with the Mesta, but not to appear to oppose them. I was their . . ." He hesitated. "There's an expression in English, I can't remember it."

"Their stalking horse, hidalgo?"

"Exactly. And in return, if I succeeded, they offered a prize." He fixed Robert's gaze. "The right to form a chain of banks backed by the crown. An official Spanish bank to which every private bank must give way."

Robert caught his breath and the sound was audible.

"Yes," Domingo continued, "I thought you would understand. It is, it would have been, beyond dreams. Virtually every gram of silver and gold that comes in from the colonies would have passed through our hands." He poured another drink and swallowed it quickly.

Robert's head was spinning with the glories of the scheme. It would set the Mendozas of Spain on a level with the Bank of England. "There's no breaking the Mesta's hold?"

"*Mi madre,* how I have tried. The amount of resources needed to fight them was enormous, and the reason why I involved your father. If we had won . . . But that's women's talk. We lost, and the Mesta still controls the wool trade."

Domingo leaned back in his seat. He rubbed his left arm

while he spoke, apparently a habitual gesture. "As well as various dukes, there are a dozen monasteries in the guild. The most powerful abbots in Spain make palaces out of their abbeys and support themselves like kings on the proceeds from the Mesta. It was the abbots who defeated me. I could go only so far for fear of seeming to oppose the Church. If your father sent you to Córdoba to find out if I can return the money he put into this catastrophe, the answer is simple. I can't. Not one real."

"I see." He wouldn't lie to the hidalgo. "That's one of the questions Father sent me to ask. I'm sorry I won't have a better answer to take back to him."

"So am I. Now, ask me the other questions. I want whatever divides us done with before we leave this room. England and Spain may go to war as they have countless times, but the house of Mendoza presents a single face to the world."

"Only one other question, Don Domingo. And I wouldn't have to ask it if the answer to the first were different. Since it isn't, will you agree to changing the division of profits from the trade in sack?"

"Reversing them, I presume. Sixty percent to you, forty to us."

Robert shook his head. "Not exactly. My father suggests seventy–thirty. In our favor."

Domingo stared at the Englishman for a moment, then he threw back his head and guffawed. "You cling to the old ways in more than just religion, my young cousin. I don't for a moment believe seventy–thirty was Benjamin's suggestion. He's conservative and cautious, sometimes to a fault. Your father would have said reverse the division, just as I did. You made up your mind to chance the bigger bite in the last few minutes. While we sat here and you decided that I'm old and ill, and not so sharp an opponent as I once was. That's the truth, isn't it?"

It was, Robert thought, and that his only son was a cripple, and according to rumor, was totally uninterested in the affairs of the house. "It's the truth," he admitted.

"Sixty—forty, in your favor," Domingo said. "Not a real more, but I respect you for asking. I'm glad your father had the foresight to hire a Spanish tutor for you back in London, and to send you here now. You're a good son, *muchacho*."

The Spaniard said the last with a hint of something in his voice, envy perhaps, or sadness. Robert didn't probe. If Domingo wished to speak of Pablo Luis, he would.

Domingo stood up, his color was better now, less ashen. Undoubtedly, getting the unpleasant topic of the Mesta behind them had helped. "Come," Domingo said. "I will show you the palace you expected to see."

The passage between the office and the main house was below ground level, cool and dark, lit only by the lantern Domingo carried. "This was once a hiding place for gold, God knows how many years ago," he explained. "Then they moved the gold to a storeroom in what we call the Patio de la Reja, the Patio of the Gate. Later, according to the legends, there was a secret cave, and the gold and the treasures were kept there. No one today remembers the whereabouts of that cave—or if it even existed." He paused. "But I must stop boring you with these tales."

Robert wondered where Domingo stored his gold bullion now, but he didn't think it his place to ask. "I'm not a bit bored. The old stories are fascinating."

"Sometimes," Domingo agreed. "In any event, this tunnel is a convenient way to return to the palace without going into the street."

They reached the door at the end of the long, narrow corridor, but Domingo hesitated before opening it. "One more thing, Robert. My wife, Doña Carmen, is unwell. She won't be able to join us. Since her illness, I have employed a housekeeper, Doña Maria Ortega. She will dine with us later. I'm sure you'll find her company pleasant."

"I'm sure I will," Robert said. And so did the old fox, Robert thought. He could tell from the way Domingo looked when he spoke her name. He'd wager a year's profit Doña Maria warmed his bed, but, godstruth, why shouldn't she? Robert had heard

as many stories about the repulsive Carmen as about the mal-
content Pablo. A man needed some comfort besides money in
this life.

"What's troubling you?" Pablo Luis asked.

Carlos didn't look at him. He hadn't looked directly at his
patron since the man arrived five minutes earlier. "Nothing is
troubling me."

Pablo leaned forward and lit a large black cigar from the flame
of the candle on the table. "The wound hasn't festered, I trust."

"The wound is healed. The doctor said so."

"Yes, he told me. He also told me that your recovery has
been remarkable. He thinks you may have used some Gypsy
magic to supplement his skills."

Carlos shook his head.

"No, I thought not. It's the women among you who know
the potions and cures, isn't it? And the breeder tells me no
Gypsy women have been near you."

"The breeder treats me as if I were a prisoner in a jail."

Pablo shrugged. "I asked him to look after you. To protect
my interests, you might say. But that didn't prevent you from
going into Seville today, did it?"

Now Carlos looked up, and his gray eyes searched the other
man's face. "How did you know that? No one here knew I was
gone."

"Let us understand each other, my young friend." Pablo flicked
a bit of ash into the brass bowl on the floor by his feet. "There
are many eyes watching many things that interest me. You
interest me. You've been at this ranch for fourteen weeks. For
twelve of them you required constant care, not to mention food
and shelter. That was not free. It's not free now."

"I didn't ask you to pay for me."

"Yes," Pablo said, "you did. The gift you displayed that day
in the corral asked me. Understand, I don't care about the
money. It's unimportant to me. I care about making you
the greatest matador this country has ever seen. Are you interested?"

Carlos didn't answer. Yesterday he would have said yes. Eagerly. The prospect and all it meant had filled his mind since the delirium and the fever left him. The thought of his future with Sofía—and because of the bulls and Pablo Luis Mendoza they had a future—was what had cured him. He had embraced a new emotion, hope, and found it good. Now he knew it was a trick.

"I'm waiting for an answer," Pablo said.

"I'm not sure." Carlos studied the extraordinary man who was offering to be his *apoderado,* his manager and sponsor. Don Pablo wore the black cape as always, but he had removed his sombrero. His face was thin, the dark eyes set deep and shadowed by a strong forehead. A handsome man, except that he must carry a hump around like a pack on his back. All his money couldn't relieve him of that burden. "What will fighting the bulls gain for me?" Carlos demanded.

Pablo stared at him. If a man didn't know the answer to that himself, deep in his belly, he wasn't destined to be a matador. He still believed this one was. "Tell me something, what were you thinking of when you came here and jumped into the corral like a madman? What's changed now? Or is it just that having been gored, you've lost your courage?"

"I've lost nothing."

"Yes, I think you have. You came here looking for something. Now you aren't looking for it. Why? Who did you see in Seville today?" He leaned forward and the cape fell open. Carlos could see the twisted stump that passed for a right arm. "Was it a woman?" Pablo demanded.

"No, an old friend."

There was a jug of wine on the table and two goblets. Carlos ignored the goblets and took a long drink from the jug. He couldn't explain that he'd seen Joselito and heard how the pig Paco had refused to wait the customary two years. He'd learned that Zocali had been so greedy for the bride price, he'd given in to him. Sofía had been married for two months. A week ago she and Paco had gone traveling, no one knew where. The story sat like lead in his gut now. It burned in his heart like a

dung fire, hot and stinking. But this Don Pablo would understand nothing. No man made as he could know about loving
a woman.

Carlos set down the wine and wiped his mouth with the
back of his hand. "I saw an old friend."

Pablo poured wine into a goblet. "Here, try drinking like a
gentleman. And did your old friend convince you not to fight
the bulls?"

"We didn't talk about that."

"*Bueno,* so you say. But whatever you did talk about hasn't
put you in a sweet temper." Pablo stood up and took his hat
from the hook on the wall. "Very well, I have no more time
to waste on you. I'll tell the breeder that you'll be leaving
tomorrow."

Carlos waited until Pablo had actually pushed open the door,
then he stood up. "Don Pablo, don't go. I have decided. If you
will sponsor me, I wish to become a torero."

Pablo paused, but didn't turn around. "You're sure?"

"Yes, I'm sure." There was nothing else for him. And he
remembered the way he'd felt. Not when he faced the bulls,
but afterward, when he'd been gored and realized that what
the others had told him all his life was a lie. He was not a
coward. He'd been happy when he thought about it. He wanted
to be happy again. "I'm sure," he repeated.

"Very good," Pablo said softly. "So am I." He hesitated, then
sat down again. "Carlos, listen to me. You must understand
what you propose to do, and that means you must understand
the bull. He is the bravest animal on earth. And the most noble.
With the herd he is tranquil, separated from it he is ready to
fight. And how he will fight. No wounds will deter him, they
rouse him to greater bravery. A bull never crouches and attacks
from behind. He faces his enemy and continues the struggle
to the death. In single combat no other animal has ever defeated
a bull, not a lion or a tiger, only a man. Sometimes."

Pablo stopped speaking. He stared at the wine for a moment,
as if in its red depths he could find the origin of his passion,
and the eternal thwarting of its consummation. Carlos knew
he should say something, but he didn't know what.

Pablo stood up again. "We begin tomorrow." His tone was different now, less devout, less haunted. "You have much to learn and it will take time, but give me absolute obedience and in two years, perhaps less, you will make your *alternativa* in Madrid. The triumph you will know then will repay everything, Carlos. Whatever happens, remember that. Nothing in this life is sweeter than triumph."

"Here, sir, in the bodega is where the grapes are brought after they are picked."

Robert saw a broad terrace outside the low whitewashed building. "What are those for?" He pointed to a stack of what looked like rolls of straw.

"Those are the mats, Don Robert. When the harvest begins, we spread the straw mats here on the terrace and the grapes are laid on them to dry in the sun." The steward conducting the tour paused for effect. "So you might say this is where the unique wine of Jerez begins." He pointed to a series of large square wooden troughs with holes in their bottoms. "When the grapes are dry they are moved into these *lagores,* and the *pisadores* put on their special shoes and begin to tread."

Robert nodded. Here at last was something he knew about. This dainty little man prancing about as if he personally owned the winery would not have to explain about the treading of the grapes by men wearing little beside a beret and shoes with iron spikes. Domingo had already told him about it—how the men sang a song to give them the rhythm, and how the juice flowed until it was a gushing stream. "You put the must into the barrels then, eh?" He was pleased with himself for remembering that the proper name of the juice was must.

"*Sí,* Don Robert," the little man said. "And we leave the barrels in the sun until the fermentation starts." His face broke into a broad smile. "Then we move it to the bodega." He stepped forward and dramatically opened the door of the building.

Robert peered into the gloom, waiting for his eyes to adjust after the sun. It was an impressive sight, a vast expanse of oak barrels stacked three high in whitewashed, arched corridors.

"This is the oldest of our bodegas," the steward said. "It is where our operation began some two hundred years ago." His pride was palpable. Robert could all but feel it as he followed him into the cool, dim, spotlessly clean interior. "Of course," the steward added, "the bodega was much smaller in the old days. Only one room behind the house of a poor man. But he was a genius, no? No one had ever made wine the way he made it. And because of him, and because of your family, Don Robert, all Jerez has prospered."

Robert cocked his head and studied the fellow. "That pleases you, does it?"

"It pleases me very much, señor. I am descended of the family Ruez. We have been here since the enterprise began. We have a small share in the profits. But you know that, of course."

"Of course." Robert did know it, but not why. Some ancient arrangement that had gone on so long it was impossible to change. That annoyed him, but it was the only part of the operation in Jerez of which he didn't approve.

For a time it seemed the visit might be canceled because Domingo was ill and couldn't accompany him. At least they said he was ill. It was an odd kind of sickness. Robert had been in Spain nearly six months. Sometimes he found Domingo lucid, clear, decisive, as he'd been that first day when they talked in the counting room of the palace. But often, too, he found the hidalgo vague and preoccupied, with a vacant look in his eyes. He'd never seen a madman, but when that peculiar look was on Domingo, Robert thought of madness.

There was nothing he could do except report it to his father, but he wanted to report as well on the vineyards. Sack was the foundation of everything the Mendozas had achieved in England. So he'd come alone to the vineyards, except for the retinue of servants Domingo sent with him.

A pox on those servants! They were a plague, more obtrusive and fawning than the English sort, but everything else in Jerez delighted him. The acres of grapes growing on the most favored ground—the compact, chalky soil known as *los albarizas,* the *soleras,* where they conducted the complex threefold decanting and mixing system that made sack unique among all the world's wine and freed it from the vagaries of vintage, and the bodegas like this one, where the sack waited shipment to the docks in Cádiz. Thank God England was the world's largest consumer of the wine of Jerez, and shipped huge quantities of it to her colonies. And thank God he'd gotten Domingo to reverse the split of profits. His father would have been content with fifty–fifty. Robert smiled at the thought.

"Now, sir," the steward said, "luncheon is ready. After the siesta I will show you three more bodegas."

"I think not." Robert had seen enough. He was weary of being shepherded around like a child with a nanny. He turned and led the way out of the cavern filled with wine barrels, the steward following anxiously after.

"Is there something wrong, sir? Have I offended you?"

"Of course not, man. You've done splendidly. I'll tell Don Domingo how well you arranged my tour." He eyed the carriage waiting for him, then, on impulse, turned back to the steward. "Tell me, have you a decent riding animal available?"

"A horse, sir?"

"That's what I had in mind, yes. I don't see myself on one of your donkeys."

"A horse, certainly sir."

The steward held a hasty conference with the coachman. Minutes later Robert was astride a fine stallion. "Tell that gaggle of servants they're to pack my things and go on to Córdoba. I'll meet them there."

Robert came to the Posada of the Four Horses on the second day of his ride. His entourage hadn't stopped there on the westward journey, but he remembered seeing it. He hesitated. Two hours more in the saddle would bring him to Seville and better food and lodging. The devil take Seville, he was tired and thirsty. He tugged on the reins and turned the horse's head toward the inn. There'd be enough of splendor once he returned to the Palacio Mendoza.

The posada was a rectangle of arched colonnades built around an open courtyard. There was a wellhead in the center of the open space. A sign announced that the water was free for men and animals, but there were charges posted for the other services offered. Lodging, drink, and food could all be had for the equivalent of a few English pence. Cheap enough. There was a bell in one corner. Robert tugged impatiently on its cord, and in seconds a man appeared. "*Sí*, señor?"

"Are you the landlord?"

"No, señor."

"Well, is he here?"

"No, señor. The landlord is never here."

"Never? Then how can he make a profit? And how do I get lodging for the night and some food?"

"He makes a profit because I pay him rent, señor. Much rent. I send it to the Palacio Mendoza twice a year. At Christmas and at Easter." Robert hid his grin. "As to lodging and food . . ." The man eyed Robert's clothes. They might be as black as pitch, but they were the clothes of a gentleman. "What we have is very poor and hardly what your lordship is used to, but if you wish—"

"I do wish."

"Very well. I can offer you a place to lie down in there with the others." The innkeeper jerked his head toward a large room in the rear. "Or a bed to yourself upstairs."

"I'll take the bed upstairs. I presume there's a room around it."

"*Sí*, señor," the man said gravely. Apparently humor was beyond him. He led the way up to the balcony and opened one of the doors leading off it.

The room was small but reasonably clean. "It will do," Robert said. "What about a meal?"

"Later, señor. My wife will be cooking sausages tonight."

"I prefer something other than sausages." Time was when simply to refuse pork was to invite the attention of the Inquisition, but Domingo had assured Robert it wasn't like that these days.

"As you wish, señor. I can tell her to prepare a chicken for you. It will take some time to kill the bird and cook it, but it will be ready by eleven, when the others are eating."

He'd never get used to mealtimes in Spain. They supped when every other decent nation had long since put itself to bed. "Very well." He undid his cloak and began pulling off his boots. "Call me when it's ready, and meanwhile see to my horse."

Robert did not need to be called. The smell of sizzling meat wakened him. And the sound of music.

He recognized the song at once. His Spanish tutor had introduced him to the country's music as well as to its language. A Protestant fugitive driven from Madrid by the Inquisition, the tutor had few good things to say about his native country. But among those few were her songs. He had played many of them on the clavichord in Bess Mendoza's drawing room. Robert had found the songs the best part of the lessons and he'd never forgotten them. So he knew that what he was hearing was a fandango. But the voice! In all his life Robert had never heard such a voice.

He pulled on his boots and his shirt, then followed the music to its source. By the time he found the singer she'd changed her song, it was a *soléa* now, a tearful lament about a lost love. Robert stopped bothering to translate the words the minute he saw her.

She sat in a corner, smaller and more frail than the depth and range of her voice had led him to expect. A Gypsy, judging from her long black braids, her layers of multicolored clothes, and the ear hoops and gold chains she wore. He'd seen few Gypsies, and everything he knew about them was bad. This one, however, was beautiful and her voice was exquisite. He was entranced.

Most of the inn's customers paid little attention to the singer, they'd already paid too much attention to the wine. But Robert felt as if her songs were entering his soul. He was thrilled by the clarity of her tone and the way her high notes soared. He remained transfixed by her until summoned to supper.

They'd laid a table for him in a small room off in one corner, removed from where the Gypsy was singing. "Who is the girl?" he asked the woman who brought his food. "Does she sing here often?"

"Never before, señor. She and a man were passing and asked

permission to entertain our guests. I'm told her name is Sofía, and the man with her is called Paco. They're Gypsies. I think he is taking her to sing in all the posadas in these parts."

"*Sí*, my wife sings everywhere," a man said, entering the room.

He had to be twice the girl's age, and a rough brute from the look of him. "You're fortunate to have such a talented wife," Robert said.

"*Sí*, señor. I am. But we are poor. . . ." The man held out a battered hat. Robert opened his purse and dropped two coins in it; on impulse he added a third. "Buy something nice for your wife. Her voice pleased me very much."

"I will, sir. Bless you for your kindness. May heaven smile on you, sir."

The words were accompanied by many bows, but the obsequious manner didn't reach the Gypsy's eyes. A sham covering pure meanness, Robert guessed. He was a fool, a soft-hearted idiot to give the Gypsy extra and imagine he'd spend it on the girl. Not much chance of that from everything he'd heard about Gypsies.

He watched the man back out of the room, as if Robert were some Oriental potentate, then returned to his supper.

There was no rhyme or reason to fate. Had that girl been born to parents who were neither poor nor Gypsies, her face and voice could have made her a nobleman's wife. Instead, she was married to a man old enough to be her father, singing for peasants so drunk they hardly heard her. He shook his head, then put the business out of his mind and attacked his chicken. It was delicious. He didn't allow himself to dwell on the fact that it had probably been fried in lard.

Robert saw the Gypsy girl once more. It was after he'd finished his meal and gone to the stables to check on his horse. The animal had been brushed and fed and was comfortably housed. Satisfied, Robert turned back to the inn, thinking of his bed and an early start in the morning. The Gypsy couple was just leaving.

She had pulled her shawl over her head against the chill of the night. Only her face showed, and those remarkable, unexpected blue eyes. She walked a few paces behind her husband. Robert's path took him between them. "*Perdón*, señor," she murmured, hanging back to let him pass.

"After you, señora——" Robert paused and waved her ahead of him. She smiled a small, shy smile and took a step forward. "Señora," he murmured on impulse. "Thank you for your songs. I enjoyed them greatly."

"You are very kind, señor."

The man heard the interchange and turned back. "Yes, this is the gentleman I told you about. The kindest man in all Andalusia." He bowed repeatedly, as he had in the posada. "Now, come, we mustn't delay his lordship." He spoke in that same subservient whine, but Robert noticed the way he gripped his wife's arm and pulled her after him. Poor little thing, she deserved better.

❧ 5 ❧

June and July were cooler than usual in Andalusia; there was even some rain. Sofía did not much mind the days spent walking the many miles between posadas, singing for hours, then sleeping by the roadside. It was bearable, even though she was expecting a child. Until August brought the stifling heat. Then her life became a torment. It went on for weeks without respite, into the beginning of October.

She did not dare complain. Paco beat her at the least provocation. He enjoyed beating her, she realized. Not the way Teresita had enjoyed it, as a means of purging some of the venom in her soul; for Paco the stinging blows he delivered with his fists or a knotted rope were exciting. Afterward he would throw himself on her like a rutting bull, thrusting himself into her body with groans of pleasure.

Was it always like this between men and women? Was this what the girls had giggled about in the caves? Would it have been the same if she had married Carlos? No, she wouldn't think about that. Carlos had deserted her. He was weak and afraid, just as the others had always said.

"Stop sitting there dreaming." Paco reached for the jug beside him and took a long swallow of wine. Red droplets escaped his lips and dribbled down his beard, like blood. He wiped them away with the back of his hand. "Get all this packed up before you go to sleep so we can start early in the morning."

She began gathering the remains of their meal, stuffing the cheese and bread and the tin plates into the basket that would travel on her back. When they began their journey four months earlier, they'd had a donkey, but Paco had sold him one night when the guests in one of the inns had not been generous. "You can't earn your keep, so you can be our donkey," he'd said.

Sofía had carried many a basket when she traveled with the Zocali tribe; that wasn't unusual. What made these wanderings so strange was that she'd never before been with just one other human being for so many weeks on end. And the singing. She had never heard of a Gypsy singing for money. She suspected it was against the law of the Rom. Lately she'd been thinking a great deal about the law.

"Husband . . ." She looked over at him. He seemed to be asleep. She was wasting her breath. She had little to spare; even now in the dark of the night the heat weighed on her. When the sun came up it would be a million times worse. Sofía wiped the sweat from her face with a corner of her skirt and tried again. "Husband, are you awake?"

"*Sí*. How can I sleep with you chattering?"

"I want to ask you something."

He turned to her and opened his eyes. There was a sliver of moon in the western sky. It made just enough light for her to see the gleam of the ruby on the tongue of the snake coiled in his ear. "I will give birth in two months, I think," she said. "Will we return to the caves before then?"

"Are you afraid? Am I married to a *busne* without the courage to bring my son into the world?"

Sofía shook her head. "I'm not afraid." She took a deep breath before she spoke again, summoning her courage. She mustn't falter now. They were far from Seville, almost in Cádiz. If they didn't begin the homeward journey soon, it would be too late. "I'm not afraid," she repeated. "But I must be with Fanta for the birth. It's the law." She dropped her eyes, terrified to see his reaction.

"A *busne* tells me about the law of the Rom," Paco said softly. He sat up and began untying the rope around his waist. She could see his smile in the light of the moon.

Sofía did not move. "It is also the law that you cannot beat me when I am like this." She put her hands protectively over her swollen belly. The clothes she wore when she sang in the posadas, the layers of skirts and the shawls, hid her condition. Here by the roadside she had on only a shift, and the child was obvious.

Paco stopped smiling, and a wordless roar of rage erupted from his throat. He curled his great hands into fists and lunged for her, then stopped at the last moment. Another great bellow burst out of him, an animal cry of fury. The fists did not land on Sofía's flesh. He dropped to the ground and beat the hard, dry soil. He pummeled the earth over and over, until at last he stumbled to his feet and grabbed the jug of wine and left her.

Sofía was trembling, but not with fear. She felt an emotion she could not name because she had never felt it before. It rose up inside her like a song; it filled her with a strange mixture of calm and excitement. She had stopped Paco from beating her. With nothing but words. For the first time in her life a man had given way to her, done her will rather than his. She hugged herself with the pure joy of it. After a while she lay back on the dry, heat-singed grass and slept.

When she woke he was standing over her, staring at her. She opened her eyes and they looked at each other in silence. Finally he spoke. "You're fat as a pig. No use in the posadas now. Get up. We're starting back to Seville today."

The journey took three weeks. They reached the Triana at the end of October. Paco took her to Zocali's cave. "Here, she's lazy and useless. Her bride price was a robbery."

Zocali looked at Sofía's bulging stomach. "She's not barren. You can't divorce her."

"I never said anything about divorce. She will have my son in a few weeks. In the meantime it's up to you to feed her. Give her back to me after the *niño* is born. If he's not perfect, it will be your fault. That is our law."

Fanta seemed truly glad to see her. For the first time Sofía was made to rest while the others worked. "For the sake of the *niño*," Fanta said. She gave the girl strengthening potions to drink and the best food to eat. Every night the choicest morsels went first to Sofía; the others, even Zocali, had what was left. Teresita was pregnant as well, but not so close to the time of birth. Sofía was queen.

The dreams came back with greater force than ever before. Every night she saw the images of white and black, the strange patterns, the woven strips of light and dark. And she heard the unearthly music that she could not remember when she woke. The dreams made her restless and agitated. "Calm yourself," Fanta said. "What makes you pace like a rat in a cage? It's not good for the *niño*."

Sofía could not explain, would not even if she knew how. "Read my cards," she said instead. "Tell me what the future will be, Fanta."

Fanta started to make the old protest, that she could not use her gifts for a *busne*, but the words died on her lips. She had raised this one. This *busne* was, for better or worse, the only child she would ever have. She moved a candle to the table and picked up the cards, shuffling them expertly through her gnarled fingers.

The first pattern was seven cards faceup and two below them. Fanta looked at them for a moment, moved two from the top rank to the bottom, added two more from the deck in her hand, then nodded. "You will give birth with no demons present. It will go well. The child will be healthy."

"Thank God." Sofía moved to the bench opposite her, placing herself within the circle of yellow light made by the candle's flame. "Is it a son?"

Fanta shook her head. "I can't tell. The cards aren't clear."

Hundreds of times Sofía had heard her tell *busne* women that they would have a son. But she knew Fanta only pretended to read the cards for them. This was real. She accepted the limitation. "Afterward?" she asked. "What will happen after the child is born?"

Fanta shuffled the cards again, laid them in a new pattern,

five above and five below. "Look, there is the fish without a tail. There will be a long journey."

Sofía thought of the months on the road, the many inns. "Like the journey of last summer?"

"I can't tell that either. But here is the snake with one eye. That's your husband." She turned another card over, stared at it for a moment, then gathered the deck together with one swift movement of her fingers.

"What is it? What did you see?" Sofía leaned forward. The candle flame flickered with the motion of her body. "Tell me, Fanta."

"I saw what I told you," the old woman insisted. "A good birth, a fine child. Don't plague me like some stupid *busne* woman who doesn't understand."

Sofía started to say something, then stopped. She felt a peculiar wetness between her legs, and when she looked down, her skirt had a spreading dark stain in the center. Fanta followed the girl's glance, then grunted with satisfaction. "Good, it's time."

The labor was long, because it was her first child, Fanta said, but she bore it because she must. Part of the time she lingered in some peculiar state between sleeping and waking which was induced by the things Fanta gave her to drink. But after many hours there were no more potions. "You must work now," Fanta said. "Push the child out into the world. There is no time for sleep."

Two other women joined Sofía and Fanta in the corner of the cave where the girl squatted and screamed out her agony. A hundred times Sofía had been part of this scene, as the rest of the tribe were part of it now. They went about their own lives, pretending not to notice what was happening a few feet away, pretending not to hear the screams of pain. "Don't pay any attention," Fanta had told her when it was some other woman giving birth. "You mustn't let the demons know what's happening or they'll come and mark the child."

No one invited the demons to Sofía's side. Even Teresita would not dare to give her the evil eye now. Not when her own time was nearing. Sofía wedged her back into the corner,

seeking support from the unyielding rock of the cave. A woman
stood on each side of her, holding her arms. Fanta knelt between her legs, hands forcing open the girl's thighs. "Push!
Push now. I see the head."

Sofía screamed and heaved. Tongues of fire licked her flesh.
She felt as if her body must surely tear apart.

"Again! Push again!"

She bore down, silent now, all her energy concentrated on
the pain. On and on, agony without surcease, continuing for
so long she knew she would die.

"*¡Ayee!*" Fanta's scream of triumph was the last thing Sofía
heard before she passed out.

She came to on the straw mattress on the floor where she had
slept these last weeks while she waited for the child. "A girl,"
Fanta told her, thrusting a swaddled bundle into Sofía's arms.
"I'm sorry, a son next time. But thank God, she's healthy."

Sofía wrapped her arms around the tiny form and held it
close. She made a motion as if to give it her breast, but Fanta
smiled and shook her head. "Not yet. The milk won't come
for some time. Then she'll be starving and you'll be ready." She
adjusted the covering of the straw, keeping busy, not meeting
Sofía's eyes. "What will you call her?"

It was an embarrassing question. If it had been a son, Paco
would name it. The naming of girl children was left to women
because it was a matter of no importance. Sofía was almost too
weary to answer. But she was filled with a strange peace, and
with happiness. Not a boy, so Paco wouldn't be pleased. Good.
She didn't want to please him. She hated him. No, she mustn't
think things like that, he was her husband. But . . . No, it must
be the potions that Fanta had given her to drink. Her mind
was playing tricks. "You name her," she murmured.

Fanta shook her head again. "It's your right, not mine. She's
your child."

"Sara," Sofía said dreamily, still fighting the sleep of exhaustion. "We'll call her Sara and she'll grow up wise and strong
like Sara-la-Kali."

The old woman nodded approval.

There was no approval from Paco. Not when he saw his

daughter for the first time three days after she was born, or two weeks later when Sofía and the child moved back into his cave. That first night he pushed the child away from Sofía's side and rolled on top of her. "Make me a son, you *busne* witch," he whispered as he thrust himself into her. "A son."

She was so sore from the birth she almost screamed aloud with pain. But others of the Paco tribe slept nearby. The thin curtain hanging between them would not stifle such sounds, and their opinion of her would be lower still. Sofía jammed her fist into her mouth and sank her teeth into her own flesh rather than cry out. Finally he was done. A few seconds later Sofía heard his snores and the deep breathing that told her he slept.

So it would be always. Until one of them died, Paco would sleep beside her. Every night of her life his stench would be in her nostrils; whenever he chose, he would use her body for his pleasure.

The only relief she would know was a few weeks before and after the birth of a child, when she would live with Fanta in Zocali's cave. But Fanta was an old woman. She could not live forever. What then? Teresita would refuse to have her, she knew that. Where would she give birth then? Who would ease her labor and cut the cord? And what would Paco do if she had another girl? How could she survive so much hatred and pain? Sofía felt tears on her cheeks. Sara began to whimper with hunger, and she reached for her and gave the child her breast. Sofía found some comfort in the act of comforting her child.

The feast of Navidad came, and in the caves of the Triana, as in all Seville and all Spain, they celebrated the birth of the infant Jesus. The holiday continued until the sixth of January, the commemoration of the coming of the three kings to the manger in Bethlehem. It was on this day of *Los Reyes* that the children were given presents and surprises and a great communal meal took place on the flat ground between the hills. Sara was barely a month old. The law of the Rom said a woman was unclean until six weeks after she gave birth. If she approached another pregnant woman, that one would give birth to a demon. Sofía remained alone while Paco and the rest of his tribe went to the fiesta.

Once she'd hated being alone. Now Sofía welcomed any time spent away from her husband. She loved being with the baby and singing to her. Sara seemed to like her mother's songs. While Sofía sang a *soléa* about the bittersweet joys of autumn, the infant smiled her first toothless smile.

Sofía chuckled with pleasure and hugged the child to her with one arm while she threw another lump of dung on the fire with the other. She could hear the sounds of the fiesta, laughter and music and the voices of happy children. Sara, too, would grow up a happy child. She'd see to it.

Paco was already talking about their going on the road as soon as spring came. He hadn't said it, but she knew he meant her to sing in the posadas again because he'd made a great deal of money from it last year. That's why he didn't take any of the others with him. He didn't want anyone to know that he was selling music, part of the Gypsy soul, or how rich Sofía's voice was making him. She suspected her bride price had already come back to him with interest. Well, if he wasn't good to their daughter, she would refuse to sing. No matter how much he beat her, she wouldn't open her mouth, not if he did anything to make Sara unhappy. The plan had come to her during these last few weeks, and she knew it was a good one and that it would work.

"What are you doing, sitting there grinning like a witch? You're *loca*. I've known it for a long time. I have a crazy wife."

Paco had obviously drunk a great deal of wine. He could barely walk. He had to keep one hand on the wall to stay upright. Sofía rose and put the baby in the little wooden cradle beside the fire. "Sit down. I'll get you some food to soak up all the wine in your belly."

He sprawled at the rickety table and she served him rice and onions from the pot hanging by the hearth, but he didn't eat. "Why are you looking like that?" he asked, pushing the bowl away. "You're giving me the evil eye, I know it."

"Don't say such foolish things. Why would I give you the evil eye? You're my husband."

"Yes. Yes, you *busne* witch, I'm your husband!" He lurched to his feet and his huge thighs overturned the table. The rice spilled all over the floor. His roar of anger woke the baby, and she began to cry.

Sofía made a move toward the cradle. "Leave her," Paco shouted. "Leave your screaming witch-child. Come here, I want you."

"Wait," Sofía whispered. "I'll feed her. It will take only a few minutes. She'll go back to sleep then."

He ignored her words and grabbed her arm, pulling her toward the mattress in the corner. "Wait," Sofía begged again. "Just a moment until—"

His open handed slap cut off her words. Sofía tasted blood, and with it a fury as great as his. "Stop! Leave me alone, you devil! I warn you, I'll never sing again. You won't make another real from me if you don't leave me alone."

The baby was screaming now, and that fueled his anger. Sofía's defiance enraged him further. "Bitch woman, *busne* whore! I'll teach you to threaten me."

Paco forgot about the mattress. He threw her to the bare floor and flung himself on top of her. Sofía fought back. Not for herself—she could survive this time as she'd survived so many times before, but the baby was screaming. The cries sounded to Sofía like pure terror. Her child needed her and this beast was between them.

She thrust her hands against Paco's shoulders and beat his chest with her fists. She couldn't dislodge him. Even drunk and uncoordinated as he was, his bulk was beyond her strength to move, but she managed to squeeze her thighs together and keep them that way. Paco trumpeted his fury in a bellow of wordless frustration. Suddenly he let her go and staggered to his feet.

Sofía thought she'd won. She didn't take the time to stand up; she crawled toward the cradle and the child. But Paco got there first. With one massive hand he picked up the infant and flung her the length of the cave.

"Sara! Oh my God! My baby . . ."

She tried to drag herself across the floor to where the inert little body lay. Paco fell on her before she'd covered half the distance. His teeth sank into her shoulder and the shock made Sofía limp. With a cry of triumph he forced her legs apart and pushed himself into her, moving up and down in a savage rhythm that was as much punishment as passion. Her whole body bounced beneath him on the rock floor of the cave. Sofía ignored the pain and stretched out her arm to try to reach the baby. She strained every muscle to drag herself and the creature on top of her to where Sara lay. Her exertions forced him out of her, but it didn't matter, he'd passed out.

Sobbing and choking, Sofía pushed him off and pulled herself to the far wall. Finally she reached the motionless body of her child. Sara had stopped crying. She would never cry again. The top of her head was crushed where it had struck the wall and the tiny features were obliterated by blood.

Fanta found her two days later. She was huddled in a deserted cave close to the river, one Carlos had shown her years before, when they used to sneak away to be alone and talk.

Sofía still held the lifeless body of her daughter. The cave was cool and dry and the flesh had not yet begun to rot. "Give her to me," Fanta said softly. "I will bury her."

Sofía had spent all her tears. The time of hysterical grief had passed. She released the thing that had once been Sara but was no longer. "How did you know where to find me?"

"The cards told me. A long time ago. I have been waiting for this day, Sofía. I knew it would come. You must leave the Triana. Leave Seville."

"No, not until I get revenge for my child. Not until I kill Paco." Her words were a growl of pure hate.

"You cannot. Paco has told everyone you murdered your own child. If you return, you will be stoned to death."

"They believe him? They think I would do something like that?"

Fanta didn't look at her. "You are *busne,*" she said softly. "Has not many a *busne* woman asked us for a potions that will murder the child in her womb? Would any Romany woman do such a thing? If they would kill the unborn child, why not the living one?"

Sofía stared at the old woman. "Do you believe I did that?"

"No, I know you did not. But I also know you must go, Sofía. You are not Romany and your place is not with us."

"Where will I go? The life of the Gypsies is all I know."

"Anywhere. But far from here. If you are seen by a member of Paco's tribe or Zocali's, you must die." She knelt beside the girl and smoothed her hair back from her forehead. "Don't be afraid. You have a wonderful future waiting. Your cards have said so since I first read them when you were a small thing who barely spoke our tongue."

"I thought you never read my cards."

"I did. Every day, from the moment Zocali brought you to me."

Fanta stood up, covering the tiny corpse with her shawl so Sofía need not see it again. "I must leave you. If I'm gone too long, someone may suspect." She nodded toward a basket she'd left in the corner. "You will find things you can use in there. Wait until it's dark, then take them and go. Tomorrow I will tell Zocali about this cave. I'll tell him I've just remembered that you used to come here. I must. If I continue to break the law of the Rom, my soul won't fly free when I die."

She went to the entrance, bent low to leave, and paused, as if she could not bear to go.

Sofía rose. "Fanta, wait." She went to the old woman and wrapped her arms around the bent frame. The body of the dead child was pressed between them. "Adios," Sofía whispered. "And thank you, *mi madre.*"

"God bless you, my daughter. May Sara-la-Kali protect you."

For the first four days she walked when it was light and slept when it was dark. Fanta had put a flint in the basket, and each evening Sofía gathered twigs and moss and made a small fire to ward off predators and the January chill.

She had lived this way many times, but never before alone. She had been unmolested thus far, but she couldn't rely on such good fortune. Still, she couldn't seem to make a plan. Her heart was dead inside her. Her arms ached for her child. Her dreams were tormented by visions of that tiny head battered beyond recognition. What she did the next day or the next year seemed without importance. The only emotion that touched her was hate, and its offspring was cunning.

Paco had murdered her daughter and someday he would pay, but for her to avenge Sara she must survive. Sofía knew the Gypsies too well to imagine they wouldn't carry out the sentence of stoning if they found her. The thought drove her forward, not because she cherished her own life, but because she mourned Sara's.

Each morning she traveled on, her eyes cast down so that usually she saw nothing but the road beneath her feet. Until the fourth day, when she looked up and saw the cockscomb carved into the willow tree growing beside the river.

Sofía looked at the symbol and shuddered. All Gypsy tribes had a secret mark. The mark of the Zocali was the cockscomb. But this one wasn't fresh. It had been etched into the wood some years before, quite probably when she was with them. So she must know this place.

She stood with her back to the willow and surveyed the scene. Nothing was familiar in any decisive way. There had been too many roads, too many riverbanks. Though she had roamed Andalusia from one end to another, she couldn't say what part of it she was in now. She couldn't even remember which direction she'd taken when she left the Triana.

She pressed her hand to her forehead and tried to think. She'd almost certainly gone north. She remembered crossing the Guadalquivir and entering the heart of Seville through the Jerez Gate. Yes, and she went past the tobacco factory. So where was she now? She still didn't know. She began walking again.

Twenty minutes later she rounded a bend and saw the golden city of Córdoba spread out in front of her. At first she was pleased that at last she knew where she was, then she realized that this was the worst place she could have come. Córdoba was home to a thriving community of Gypsies. Many were friends and relatives of the Zocali tribe. And they knew her;

she and Fanta and the others had lived with them two summers past. If they saw her, they would surely send word to Seville.

Sofía fought the panic and the urge to run. She couldn't flee like a hunted animal, she had to have a plan. She clutched the basket. Fanta had put twenty reales in it, more money than Sofía had ever actually seen. So far she had spent nothing. She'd existed on river water and mouthfuls of the bread and cheese that were also in the basket. Her head began to clear. It was a dull, cloudy winter day. There wouldn't be many Gypsies on the road. But it needed only one to end her life and her dreams of revenge.

She suddenly realized she was putting herself directly in their path, because she was living like a Gypsy. Paco, might he be damned to everlasting hell, had shown her other ways and other lives. There had to be an inn in Córdoba.

She found the Posada del Potro half an hour later. It was in the eastern corner of the town, a two-story structure ringed with a balcony and topped by a thatched roof, and constructed, as most were, around a well. She rang the bell for the innkeeper, just as she'd seen Paco do so many times last summer.

He looked at her the way *busne* usually looked at Gypsies. Sofía ignored the contempt in his eyes. "I want a bed for the night. I can pay."

"You are alone, señorita?"

"Yes," she said with as much defiance as she could muster. He could think what he liked about a woman, even a Gypsy woman, coming alone to an inn. "I can pay," she repeated.

The innkeeper smiled, but without warmth. "Do you come here to give me money or to take it from my customers? In Córdoba the *putas* all walk the streets on the other side of the river."

He thought she was a whore. "I am not a *puta*," Sofía said through clenched teeth.

"No? Forgive me. I apologize most profoundly to your noble ladyship." He made a deep, mocking bow. "What are you, then? I'm a simple man. I don't understand about women who come by themselves to a public inn without the protection of a father or a husband. Perhaps you can educate me."

"I'm a singer." She hadn't planned to say that, it had just come out. "I will pay for my bed. But during supper tonight I will sing for the other guests. If I please them and they give me money, I will give you a third part." It was what Paco had said in every inn they visited, though they had never slept under the inn's roof. They'd had no need to. She did.

The man narrowed his eyes and stared at her. "I heard of a Gypsy singer in some of the posadas south of here, but that was last summer."

"This is winter and here I am. Well, do you agree?"

He shrugged. "Please yourself, as long as I'm paid for lodging. Do you wish to pay two reales or four?"

"Two," Sofía said instantly.

He smiled again and stretched out his arm. "Right this way, señorita."

She followed him to the rear of the courtyard, and he opened a set of tall wooden doors. They were broad enough to allow a carriage to enter, and they led to what looked to her like a huge stable. "A place on the floor in here costs two reales. The straw is clean. I change it once a month."

Sofía saw a half dozen men sprawled on the straw. Most were asleep, but one grizzled old man opened his eyes and stared at her. He and the innkeeper exchanged looks and grins. The man on the floor had only a few teeth, but those few were long and pointed, like fangs.

She backed away hastily. "This won't do. Is there some other place?"

"Sí. A room such as the gentry use. For four reales, as I said."

"Show it to me," she demanded.

He led her up a narrow flight of stairs and opened another door. This room was much smaller than the first. It contained a single brass bedstead. In all that she remembered of her life she had never slept in a real bed. There was also a window looking out to the street and a wall sconce holding a candle. It was a palace. "I'll stay here," Sofía said.

"Very well. If you pay me four reales."

Sofía doled out the money. She sensed the man watching her. Probably he thought she was too ignorant to give him the correct amount. Among all the Gypsy women she knew, she was the only one who could read letters, but every one of them knew how to count coins, and so did she.

Sofía knew it was time when she heard the noise from below. They were the same sounds she had heard when she traveled with Paco. The customers were drinking their fill of wine while they waited for their supper. Sofía took a deep breath and opened the door of her room.

All last summer she had sung in her ordinary clothes, the full skirts and blouses and shawls that were everyday dress for Gypsy women. Tonight she wore a lace mantilla attached to a high comb, and the elaborate ruffled green skirt and red and white blouse that had been made for her when she kept the Vigil of Sara. Fanta had packed the clothes in the basket. Sofía blessed the old woman yet again, and padded across the courtyard on bare feet, following the sound of talk and the smell of wine.

She paused in the doorway. There was a roaring fire in one corner. The flames filled the room with dancing light. In the glow she saw what she had expected to see, *busne* men very like those who lived in the Triana. These were workmen and artisans, all half drunk and making a determined effort to finish the job. No one noticed her. Sofía waited a moment, then she raised her hands over her head and struck her palms together in the musical clapping that was so much a part of Gypsy song.

A few of the men turned and looked at her. Then a few more. Gradually the noise of their chatter died away. Sofía did not sing a note until every one of them was silent. She kept clapping and waited until the rhythmic clatter of her palms was the only sound to be heard. Then she threw back her head and uttered the first piercing notes of a flamenco song. It was the one she had sung a short distance away at the Palacio Mendoza, the one Doña Carmen liked about the vengeance of a woman wronged.

Many hours later, when she returned to the room at the top of the stairs, Sofía was flushed with triumph. She had never enjoyed singing for strangers when Paco was her master, but tonight had been different. She had done everything differently. She hadn't sat in a corner like a shy little mouse, but had looked into their faces, forcing them to pay attention. It made her heart beat faster, it made her feel the way she felt that night on the road when she forced Paco to bend his will to hers.

Sofía had brought a burning coal with her from downstairs, but before she lit the candle she barred and bolted the door to her room. She had seen the men's thoughts in their eyes. Here there was no law of the Rom to protect her from violation.

She felt along the wall until she found the sconce with the candle and put the coal to the wick. The flame sputtered, then flared and lit the room. Sofía caught her breath. She was standing in the middle of chaos. The clothes she'd worn earlier were flung about and her basket was overturned and empty. The remaining eighteen reales were gone.

What a fool she was. Here she'd been congratulating herself on how she'd made the men pay attention; now she realized that she knew nothing of surviving on her own. No man would have left his money where thieves could so easily get it. Paco had always carried his on his person, in a leather pouch hung inside his trousers. But how could she do that? The clothes she wore clung to her body. Where would she have hidden a money pouch if she had one? Sofía put her hand to her bodice. Here, of course, between her breasts. Too late to think of that now.

She sat on the edge of the unfamiliar bed and bit back tears of frustration. She'd earned six reales and had to give the innkeeper two of them. It didn't matter, she told herself finally. Four reales were enough to get her a room at the next posada she came to. There she would earn more.

The plan had been born while she sang. She couldn't stay there. Córdoba was too close to Seville. Tomorrow she would go farther north, but tonight she'd sleep. She would not waste her energy regretting a stupid mistake she couldn't undo.

Despite her good intentions and her tiredness, it was a long time before she could put the loss of the money from her mind. She tossed and turned in the bed. This way of sleeping wasn't so marvelous after all. When it was almost dawn and she heard a cock crow, Sofía took the bed covering and spread it on the floor and lay down.

Finally she was comfortable, and she felt herself drifting into sleep. Her last thought was that the loss of the money was a valuable lesson. It had reminded her she was at the mercy of the *busne* world as well as the Gypsies. She belonged to neither, only to herself.

❧ 6 ❧

A short time after the Englishman had left Córdoba, the wife of Domingo Mendoza was on her knees in the deepest and oldest wine cellar beneath the palace. She was searching frantically, her swollen hands pawing the contents of a leather-covered chest moldy with age. "It has to be here. It has to be here," she kept muttering. But there were only notebooks filled with jottings about vintages long forgotten.

Carmen slammed down the cover in disgust, then thought she heard a footstep and froze. She strained to listen, ready to snuff out the light of the single candle flickering beside her. It was nothing, a rat perhaps. She was alone.

Surely no one had any reason to follow her into the bowels of the earth. But what if the usurper sent the servants down here? Maria Ortega made a great show of giving orders. Clean this, polish that, fix the other. A great show of being the house-keeper, clucking her tongue over all that had been left undone before she came—before Domingo lost all sense of shame and brought his mistress to live under the same roof with his wife. "*Puta, puñetera, pajarilla . . .*" Whispering curses, Carmen resumed her search.

It took enormous effort to shift the heavy barrels of wine, but she moved each one. Still nothing. It had to be here. She'd heard Domingo telling the Englishman about it. "The plaque is mentioned repeatedly in all our old records. Made of brass, they say, the letters carved by a Moorish slave who was the finest engraver the world has ever seen." On and on he had gone about how exquisite the thing was, and how if anything happened to it the house of Mendoza would fall. "But no one's seen it for five hundred years and we're still here."

In the wine cellar Carmen closed her eyes and remembered. She had heard the Englishman's question. "What did it say, hidalgo? What was engraved on this famous plaque?"

In her mind's eye she saw them still—Domingo, the Englishman, and the *puta* who sat at her place at the table, stuffing themselves like pigs, and believing they were unobserved. Carmen permitted herself a soft cackle of triumph. There were many hiding places in this ancient house, and she knew them all. No one guessed that she watched and listened. She had seen her husband shrug and avoid the whore's eyes when he admitted that the words on the plaque were probably in Hebrew, the foul language of the Jews. "So I wouldn't know what it said if I saw it, not that I ever will."

"What about the old records?" the Englishman had asked. "Don't they tell you what was written on the plaque?"

"No. At least I've never been able to find any such reference. I imagine the inscription was so familiar, no one needed to write it down. They knew what it said. It didn't occur to them that later generations might not know."

"A common failing of historians," the Englishman had said. "They always leave out the best bits."

Carmen remembered that Maria Ortega had laughed at the foreigner's words, that she had flirted with him all during the meal, fluttering her fan in his direction whenever she thought Domingo wasn't looking. The *puta* wanted the handsome young one between her legs; she must despise the old man who thought he possessed her. ¡Ay! How she had prayed to the Virgin that the whore would make Domingo cuckold in his own house, and he would find out and throw her into the street.

It hadn't happened, but surely the Virgin was listening to

her prayers. Why else had providence allowed her to hear her husband's story? For thirty-five years Domingo had avoided talking about the history of the Mendozas. She had never heard him admit the shame of their Jewish origins until this Englishman came. Now he had given her the weapon she craved. She would find this cursed plaque and give it to the Inquisition, and tell them Domingo Mendoza was a Marrano, a pig Jew in secret, and they would burn him at the stake and she would have revenge.

Carmen spent four hours in the wine cellar and found nothing. But she would not give up. She had been searching for weeks in each of the forty-six rooms of the palace. This was the last place, and if she didn't find it soon, it would be too late. Domingo was ill. Carmen could smell death on him. But an ordinary death was too good for the man who had caused her so much torment. "Don't let him die," she prayed as she began again to search the places she had searched before. "*Dios mi Señor,* don't let Domingo die before I can be the one to kill him."

It was Robert's mother who demanded he relate in infinite detail what he'd seen in the Mendoza palace. "What about the curtains?" she demanded. "And what kind of cutlery do they use at table?"

"The curtains are wonderful," Robert said, winking at his father. Benjamin Mendoza was enduring all this domestic detail with exaggerated patience, sighing loudly and looking over their heads and tapping his fingers on the table. "Exquisitely embroidered," Robert continued. "The same sort of needlework as on the folding screen in your room, Mother."

"Crewel," Bess supplied. "That's what it's called. So, crewel curtains are everywhere?"

"No. Some of the rooms have damask. From France I imagine. Wonderful colors." He picked up a three-tined fork and waved it teasingly under his mother's nose. "And they eat with solid silver, makes this look as if you bought it from a Gypsy peddler."

The forks at Bess's table were part of a set that had belonged to her mother. They had pistol-butt handles of green Venetian glass and silver ferules. Until this moment she'd loved them. Bess stood up. "I must retire. I have a headache. It's living here in the foul air of London that does it. If I could move to the country like the wives of everyone we know, I'd be a well woman again."

Benjamin and Robert rose politely. Benjamin kissed his wife's cheek. "Rest, my dear. No doubt tomorrow the air of London won't disturb you so much. When you go to the silversmith's to order new cutlery the skies will seem clearer."

Robert watched the little drama with barely concealed amusement. "I think you're going to give in to her sooner or later," he said after Bess had gone.

Benjamin shook his head. "I told her I planned to make an offer for St. James's Palace. If the king will sell it to me, we can move. Otherwise we stay here in Creechurch Lane. It has been good enough for nine generations of Mendozas, and it is good enough for me."

"I used to think ours was a long history," Robert said quietly. "That nearly two hundred and fifty years in England made us true Englishmen. Now I'm not so sure."

Benjamin cocked his head. "And what does that mean? What are you unsure about? Do you fancy yourself a Spaniard after six months in Spain?"

"No, of course not. But Don Domingo talks about five hundred years as if they were nothing. He speaks of the family under the Moors and before them. You have to admit, Father, *that* is a history."

"Perhaps, but it's ours as much as his." Benjamin extracted the kernel of a walnut and dipped it in his wine. "You're as much a Mendoza as Domingo is. A truer descendant, if it comes to that. You're circumcised. I never asked, it hasn't come up in our business correspondence, but I doubt he is."

Robert chuckled. "I never asked either. But circumcised or not, he knows how to use what's between his legs." He told his father about Maria Ortega.

"Not a nice story," Benjamin said with a pout of distaste. "If a man has to have a mistress, she shouldn't be under the same roof with his wife."

"I suppose not, still . . . I never saw Doña Carmen, but the stories I heard were horrific."

"Stories. A whore's a whore and a wife is something else. Speaking of which—"

"Please, Father, I just got home. At least wait until tomorrow to plague me about marrying."

"Very well. We'll talk of other things. Come into my study and give me the real details, not all this nonsense your mother is interested in."

They spoke for over an hour. That is, Robert spoke. Benjamin listened, nodding occasionally, making notes sometimes. He was well pleased. Not that the business with the Mesta and the amount of money lost was pleasing, but that was only money. A son was something else, and this was a son worthy of the name. "Very good," he said when the recital was finished. "You've done well, lad. I'm proud of you."

"Thank you, Father. Now, if you'll excuse me, I am suddenly feeling the burden of the journey. I'm for bed, with your permission."

"Go ahead. Sleep well." Then, before the younger man left the room: "Robert, wait a moment." Benjamin reached into a drawer in his writing table. "I've been keeping this for the right time. I think it has arrived."

He held out a leather-bound book. Robert took it, glanced at the cover, then at his father. "What is it?"

"A record. Written originally in Spanish by the first Mendoza to come to England. It was translated some years later, I'm not sure when."

His father was trying to sound casual, but something in his tone told Robert that what he held was important, and the decision to give it to him momentous. "Has Liam read this?"

Benjamin shook his head. "No, Liam knows no more about it than you did until this minute."

Robert knew he was his father's favorite. Nonetheless, Liam was the eldest and usually his rights were scrupulously re-

spected. Besides, Liam had given the family an heir, little Joseph
Simon Mendoza, born while Robert was away. He'd have
thought . . . Ah, he was too tired now to figure it out. "I'll read
it first thing tomorrow."

"Yes, do that," Benjamin agreed. "I suspect you'll find it
fascinating. In any case, I am eager to know what you think."

Robert carried the book to his room and laid it unopened
on a chest. Tomorrow was time enough. God, it was good to
be home, in his own room, soon to be in his own bed. He
undressed, lay down, and waited. Sleep wouldn't come. The
book called to him, tempted him awake despite his exhaustion.
"Damn!" he said finally. He'd have to read a page or two.

"What is this thing?" The head of the house of Mendoza in the
year 1575 was Don Miguel Antonio and today was his name
day, the feast of St. Michael the Archangel, and incidentally his
fiftieth birthday. His eyesight was not what it had been, and
he peered closely at the yellowed document the younger man
had passed across his writing table.

"It is a credit with your house. For a thousand gold ducats."

The speaker was named Felix Ruex Zaban. His family, too,
had been in Córdoba for centuries. They were not wealthy like
the Mendozas. The Ruez patrimony was only a few vineyards
and a small winery. These Felix had recently inherited, along
with their debts. But he had also been gifted with brains and
a taste for ferreting out information.

"I found the document in a chest in the oldest wine cellar,"
he explained. "I'm afraid my ancestors have been good vintners
and poor clerks, the records are badly kept. Sometimes not
kept at all."

"Were you looking for this?" Miguel asked. "How could you
know . . ."

"I knew nothing. I was searching for a history of our grapes,
their yields in past times. The credit was a—" He hesitated.
"A happy accident."

Miguel Antonio Mendoza was thinking that it was not so
happy for him. A thousand ducats was a great deal of money,
even for a Mendoza. He looked again. "It is very faded."

"Yes, but readable." Felix leaned forward and traced the words with his finger. "I, Benhaj ben Simon Mendoza, grant to Gilberto Ruez Tracito, the winemaker, a credit of one thousand gold ducats, to be paid on demand," he read aloud. "It also says, 'In payment for inestimable services.' And it is signed."

Miguel nodded. "Someone signed it, yes."

"Your ancestor."

"Perhaps. How can that be proved now? Benhaj . . . I don't know the name."

"There's a date under the signature. The seventeenth of June, 1391."

"So? Whoever signed also marked a date. That does not make it a true credit issued by a legitimate ruler of the house."

The younger man leaned back in his chair. "Don Miguel, I am a reader of history, are you?"

One finger drummed impatiently on the thick black wood of the writing table. "Come to the point."

"In June of 1391 there was a great riot in Córdoba. The entire Juderia was burned to the ground."

It was spoken. This impertinent young man was reminding him of the distasteful past, the Jewish blood of the Mendozas. There was no point in denying it, the truth was well known. "I suppose that would have been important to my ancestors, yes," Miguel admitted.

"Perhaps this Gilberto Ruez sheltered them. They survived, did they not?"

The old man shrugged. "I do not know the details. Certainly some Mendozas survived, the house continued."

Felix hesitated, then he put his hand into the pouch he carried and withdrew something else. "This was with the papers."

Don Miguel looked at the pendant the young man had put on his table. He fingered it gingerly, then tested a corner between his teeth. "It's certainly gold, but what does it have to do with me?"

"I don't know," Felix admitted. "But it was carefully wrapped, and with the letter of credit as I said. I think there is writing on it."

"Yes, of course," Miguel said impatiently. "I can see that. But I can't read what it says."

"Neither can I. But I think . . . forgive me . . . I think it is written in Hebrew."

Miguel started and drew back. Heretical writing. In his house, beneath his very hand. The Inquisition was a hundred years old in Spain and less virulent than it had been. Still, given the background of the family . . . "I know nothing of Hebrew writing," he said loudly.

"No, of course not. Only I think this is a Mendoza thing," Felix insisted. "Something that is supposed to prove that the letter of credit is authentic."

It was a not unlikely suggestion, and for a long moment there was silence while Don Miguel considered it. The pause weighed on Felix. He did not have the older man's experience and skill at negotiation, and he broke first. "I ask payment of the debt, Don Miguel. It is my right."

"If there is a debt, you have a right to collect, yes." Miguel stood up and rested his hand lightly on the paper. "I would like to study this and search through our own records. Will you permit me to keep it a day or two?"

This time Felix did not hesitate. In matters such as this it was a truism that the Mendozas were as trustworthy as almighty God. They were also almost as clever. They did not cheat because they did not need to, and because cheating would eventually be detrimental to their business. "You may keep the document and the pendant, of course. I will return the day after tomorrow."

Miguel Antonio remained standing after the young man left. A thousand gold ducats. In normal times an unexpected debt of such an amount would be merely an expensive annoyance. Today it was entirely different. He was facing a crisis, and this claim was the final stroke of the lash, the one that could kill. And God chose to make this last cruel joke on his name day.

In an agony of rage and frustration Miguel shook his fist at heaven. Then he hastily made the sign of the cross. His wife was in church praying, importuning the Holy Virgin for aid. It was not a moment to shout defiance at God.

The years after Ferdinand and Isabella had been a time of expansion and excitement, but also of chaos. The discovery of the Americas had led to new dreams of glory and wealth, but also to imprudent risks. And as luck would have it, the Mendozas had been led by visionaries for two generations, men inclined to gamble.

Miguel Antonio's grandfather had a fatal weakness for colonial adventures. It need only be said that the money was going to be invested in one of the colonies and he opened the coffers without thought. All because he was devoted to the memory of El Colón; there was even a painting of the discoverer of the New World hanging in the main reception room of the house. Why? God perhaps knew, Miguel did not.

Nor did he know why his father was so intemperate in the loans he made. In his case there was not even an obsession to justify it. He simply made unwise choices. When in 1542 it was already clear that the liberals were going to prevail and the sale of Indians sold as slaves in Spain would be prohibited by law, Miguel's father was still financing slave ships headed for Hispaniola and Panama.

When his turn came, Miguel had tried to counter the imprudence of his forbears, but if he was cautious he was also unlucky. There were now over a hundred thousand Spanish settlers in the American colonies, and they required every necessity to be sent to them from the motherland. Surely financing such cargoes should be a safe investment? Not when God was laughing at a man. Three ships backed by the house of Mendoza had been lost at sea in the past nine months. In each case the owners were ruined and unable to make good their debt.

Now this—a demand out of an unsavory past for a thousand gold ducats. It was too much in every sense. Perhaps there were a thousand ducats in the storeroom in the garden; but if there were, they were the last coins he possessed. The Mendoza holdings were vast and worth countless times that amount, but of hard gold there was almost nothing.

But it was not of all these things that Don Miguel Antonio thought as he sat with his head in his hands on the afternoon of his birthday. It was of his son, Ramón. In almost a century and a half of Christianity the Mendozas had not produced a priest. Not until Ramón. Then the prayers of Ana, Miguel Antonio's wife, were answered and the youngest boy expressed a desire to go to the Dominicans. Both parents were pleased. Ana because of her devotion, Miguel because a connection to the Church could prove useful in business. Both were now distraught.

Yesterday Ramón unexpectedly came home. He had decided not to take Holy Orders. Why? For a reason so terrible Miguel had difficulty thinking of it. *Dios mío,* how can such a thing be true? How can my son wish to become a Jew?

"Because of all the books," Ana had said last night when neither could sleep and they talked until dawn. "I told you he should go to the Franciscans. The Dominicans are mad. Study, study, study, that's all they do. They teach them Hebrew and give them terrible things to read."

"I know," her husband had countered. "I know. But now it is too late to say, 'I told you.' Be quiet, let me think."

But he'd thought of nothing then, he could think of nothing now. And it was growing dark. Ana must be back from church. Ramón was doubtless still upstairs in his room, perhaps praying to his heretical God. *Dios mío,* what was a man to do?

Later there was a special birthday dinner. It took place in the great dining hall in the west wing of the house. It was Miguel's obsessed grandfather who had built the west wing as a kind of celebration of the Spanish expansion into America. He'd employed *mudejares,* Christian Moors, to decorate it and spared no expense. The walls were covered in brilliant gilt and mosaics, and the floor intricately laid with different colored marbles. It was a setting splendid enough for a sultan, and that night the meal was its equal.

The table groaned with food. Three goats had turned on a spit for hours, pheasants stuffed with raisins nestled under domes of pastry, rice was scented with cinnamon and cloves and colored deep yellow with saffron. There was a great bowl full of the new fruit called tomatoes which the *conquistadores* had brought back from the New World, and another heaped with their second edible discovery, the mealy tubers called potatoes. Miguel shuddered inwardly at the cost of this feast, but when he looked around the room he understood why his wife had authorized such extravagance.

The entire family was present. Fifty-two faces beamed at Don Miguel. A brother, two sisters, all their families, his own seven children, the spouses of six of them, his seventeen grandchildren—even Ramón had left his room and was managing to act as if he'd come home only to celebrate his father's feast day. Ana was right not to skimp on a meal which all Córdoba would hear about.

Don Miguel tried to be as jovial and good humored as was expected, but when he looked at the assembled clan he saw only burdens. Every one of them depended on the house of Mendoza for the roof over his head and the food in his belly. Each of them relied on Miguel to provide incomes for their sons, dowries for their daughters, and comfort for their old age. And he alone knew that the house was close to collapsing under the weight of their combined demands.

At last the celebration ended. The daughters left and went to the houses of their husbands, the married sons of Miguel and Ana said good night and disappeared to their separate apartments under the single roof. The house had grown countless times over the centuries, it was thirty-four rooms now, and the people of Córdoba referred to it as the Palacio Mendoza.

This night Don Miguel did not feel as a man should who lived in a palace. He looked at Ramón and at Ana, and from them to the servants clearing the table. "Come, we will go to my study. I wish to speak with you privately."

Ana was white-faced and trembling. All day she'd alternated between praying and weeping. It had drained the last of her strength to welcome the family this evening. Now her husband had summoned her to a meeting that by rights should have involved only him and his son. *Ay, mi madre, da la fuerza . . .*

Miguel took up his usual place behind the table and looked at his wife and son. "Sit down, woman. And don't faint. I want you here and listening, not senseless on the floor. Ramón, what have you decided?"

The boy hung his head. It grieved him to be a source of such misery to his parents. "I have no decision to make. It is made for me."

"By whom?" Miguel roared. His face was red and the veins in his necks bulged. "Who decides that you should become an apostate, an outcast, a heretic? Who decides that you should expose every man, woman, and child who was here this night to the attention of the Inquisitors? Who? Tell me, and with my bare hands I will ring his neck."

"You cannot, Father," the boy whispered. "It is God who dictates what I must do. The God of our fathers, of Moses and Abraham and Isaac."

"I, too, worship that God." Miguel lowered his voice and fixed his son's eyes with his own. "Jesus Christ is that God. The Father and the Son and the Holy Spirit. And his Church is the Holy Catholic Church, and you are a heretic and if you do not repent, you will burn forever."

Ana was weeping; she could not help it. Ramón looked not at his father but at her. "Mama, please . . ." She did not answer, and he turned to Don Miguel.

"Before heaven I swear to you that if I could still believe as you do, I would. In this world there is nothing that could make me cause both of you such grief. But this matter is not of this world and I have no choice."

Ramón leaned forward, his eyes burning, his body trembling as he tried to explain. "If only I could make you see the beauty of Judaism, the purity. It is so complete, Papa, so rounded and whole. All things are accounted for, transformed, made of God. In Judaism there is no conflict between life and religion, they are integrated—" He stopped speaking when Don Miguel raised his hand.

The older man had slumped, all the fire gone out of him. Now he sat heavily in his chair. "Very well. What you say is insane, but I see that you are sincere. If that is your belief, then nothing I can say will change it. But know well what you do, Ramón. As a Jew, you are forbidden to remain in Spain. If you stay despite the law, you will be brought before the Inquisition and first tortured then burned alive.

"They are very fancy these days with the auto-de-fé. The people demand circuses. The night before your death they will march through the streets carrying a green cross. They will put it on the high altar of the cathedral for all to see. In the morning, while they build the pyre for you in the Plaza de la Corredera, they will publicly confiscate every holding of this family. By then your mother and I will also have been tortured, probably we shall be dead. Your cousins and nieces and nephews, your brothers and sisters, everyone whom you saw here tonight will be destitute, lucky to escape with their lives."

He paused. There was not a sound in the room. Even Ana's weeping was stilled by such terrible words. "Is this what your God demands that you do, Ramón my son?"

The young man's head hung over his chest. His hands gripped the carved arms of the chair. "I must be a Jew," he whispered. "I must atone for the apostasy of our ancestors. We are all rightly Jews."

Now Don Miguel did a strange thing. He straightened his clothes and wiped his face with a square of linen and stood up and went to the chest in the corner and withdrew a decanter of wine and poured three cups. He seemed peaceful, almost matter-of-fact. It was as if all his excitement, all the dramatic pronouncements, had been a show. "Here, drink. Calm yourselves. I have a plan."

Ramón raised his head. "You will not turn me over to the Inquisition?"

"Me? Now I know you are mad. Do you think I believe their swearings and threats? I am not going to be condemned to hell for protecting my own son and all my kin, whatever they say. And you, do you have a crazy desire to be a martyr, or do you wish to live like a Jew, not simply die like one?"

"To live, certainly," Ramón said eagerly. "In the Talmud it says—"

Ana's shriek cut off his words.

"Do not mention your disgusting heretical books under my roof," Don Miguel warned. "Your mother says that if the Dominicans had not taught you to read Hebrew and exposed you to such filth, none of this would have happened. And in that she is right."

Ramón said nothing. God would have to forgive him for not defending the holy Talmud under the circumstances.

Miguel turned to his wife. "Go to your bed, woman. I wanted you to hear with your own ears that I did everything in my power to change his mind. Now that you have heard, leave us alone. And you can sleep well. It is going to be all right. I promise you."

Ana rose on still-shaking legs. It was hard to believe that even her powerful husband could draw good from such a thing as this. But she wanted to believe it; she would try her best to do so. Nodding to both of them because she did not trust herself to speak, she left the room.

"Now," Miguel said. "Here is what we are going to do. . . ."

They talked long into the night. It was sunrise before the plan had been discussed from every angle and the details made final. "One last thing," Miguel said as they rose to leave the room. "I am curious to know if this letter of credit that we propose to honor is genuine. You might as well begin immediately using your knowledge of Hebrew to the benefit of the house. Tomorrow go through the old records. Those from the time our ancestors wrote in that language are in the storeroom in the garden, under lock and key.

"Be careful you are not seen or we will have the Inquisition to deal with despite all our efforts. But tell me if you find any mention of this Benhaj." He waited a moment, then reached into a secret drawer in his writing table. "Take this too. I wish to know what it says." Miguel pressed the pendant into the palm of his son.

Forty-eight hours later Felix Ruez Zaban sat again in the study of Don Miguel. On the table between them was a leather chest, bound in brass, as long as his arm and four hands high. It was locked. Felix eyed it hungrily. "You have discovered that I told the truth. The document is genuine, no?"

"The document is genuine, yes. At least, there was a Benhaj

Mendoza who ruled the house nearly two hundred years ago. He accomplished very little, so I'd never heard of him."

Felix was not particularly interested in the history of the Mendozas. "Is my money in that chest?"

Don Miguel smiled. "You are young and impatient, my friend. In business that is not wise. Take some wine with me. It is special, and I think you will enjoy it."

There was a silver ewer on the table, and from it Don Miguel poured two goblets of drink. The wine was dark and golden brown. It had the scent of hazelnuts and a creamy richness that soothed the palate with the first sip. "Very nice, don't you think?"

Felix didn't answer immediately. He took another swallow and rolled it around on his tongue. Then he held the goblet away from him, peered into it, and sniffed again. "Most unusual," he murmured. Despite the avarice that was making his palms sweat, he was above all a vintner. He took another sip. "Unusual but delicious. What is this, Don Miguel? How did you come by it?"

"I came by it very simply. I went to the town of Jerez de la Frontera and bought it from a small bodega."

"But that is not very far, four days ride. I have been in Jerez de la Frontera. Never have I tasted such wine as this."

"No? Well, perhaps next time I go I will bring some back for you as well. Now, Felix, to business." Miguel Antonio released the clasp on the chest and lifted the domed lid. The interior was lined with red velvet, and it was filled with gold coins that winked in the dim light of the shuttered room. "Here is your thousand ducats." Actually there were only nine hundred and forty-seven, all he'd managed to come up with. Hopefully that wouldn't matter.

Felix bent forward. His eyes glittered with excitement. "I have never seen so much money before. Whatever my ancestor did for yours, may they both rest in blessedness."

"Amen," the older man said, making the sign of the cross. With ceremony he produced the letter of credit. "I may tear this up?" Felix nodded. Don Miguel ripped the document into small shreds and pushed them to a corner of the table. He stood up. "Now, wait a moment and I will call a servant to carry this to your home. And perhaps we should arm him."

"Yes," Felix said. "That is wise. Wait until my wife hears. She didn't believe you would pay attention to a paper so old."

"The nonsense of a woman. Any man in Spain knows that the house of Mendoza honors its debts." Don Miguel started for the door, presumably to call the armed guard he'd suggested. At the threshold he hesitated. "Felix, I wonder if—No, of course not. You are a poor man, you must take what profits are available to you. Only the rich can use their wealth to make more wealth."

The younger man narrowed his eyes and looked hard at the elder. "I am not so poor at this moment. I have a thousand ducats. What are you hinting at, Don Miguel?"

Miguel Antonio moved away from the door, but only a short distance; he did not return to his chair behind the writing table. "It crossed my mind that perhaps you are brighter than your ancestors have been. In fact, I'm sure you are. After all, you found the document. But still . . ."

"I am brighter than my father and grandfather, certainly. I have plans for my bodega and my vineyards. With this money, and if the weather is kind and we have a good crop this year, I intend to buy a bit more land."

"In the hills outside Córdoba? Ah, yes. But that will yield the same wine your family have produced for generations. Quite good, of course, but it won't do."

"Do for what? What are you talking about?"

Miguel made a great show of studying his visitor. "Perhaps . . . Why not? Why shouldn't a man who has always been poor have an opportunity to be rich? Sit down, Felix. Listen to me." Now he returned to his chair and casually, as he passed by, he dropped the lid on the chest of gold. It no longer winked at them.

"I am investing in a vineyard, Felix. A whole hillside of vineyards. In fact, I have already bought them. In Jerez. And the bodega I spoke of, the one that makes this extraordinary wine, I have bought that too. The wine is made by a special method devised by the family who formerly owned it. Each year after the grapes are pressed, the wine is blended with that of previous seasons. A little brandy is added. There is a very clever method of aging and drawing off, but you would understand the details better than I. I know only that with the Jerez method, there cannot be a bad year. No matter how poor the harvest, the wine of previous seasons tempers it."

"But that is remarkable. I have never heard of such a thing."

"You have tasted the wine. Here, have some more." Miguel refilled both their goblets.

"It is even better than I first thought," Felix said. "Don Miguel, could I learn this method? If you would permit me to see how it is done, it could change my life."

"My young friend, but of course. For the debt my ancestor owed yours. If that is what you want, you have it. However, I was thinking of something a little more, shall I say, challenging?"

"Yes? What? Tell me."

"I have been able to buy this bodega only because the family is dying out. Only one old man is left who makes this particular wine in this particular way. There are others doing something very similar in Jerez, but their wine is not as wonderful. Anyway, my problem is that I require a *vinatero*, someone to oversee the growing of the grapes and the making of the wine. The old man will teach him, but it is better if he is someone who already knows winemaking."

Felix leaned back. His fingers were drumming on the arm of his chair; other than that, he was making a great effort to remain calm. "I know winemaking, Don Miguel. I was practically born in a bodega. I can tell with only my nose what wine is good and what is bad."

"Yes. That's what I was thinking. But what good is it to you if all I do is offer employment, Felix? That is no way to repay a debt of honor." He thumped on the chest of gold. "Neither is a mere thousand ducats."

Don Miguel leaned forward and his voice dropped to a whisper. "I have not told you the best part. I have a contract to send abroad as much of this wine as can be made. Not to our colonies. The ... er, other direction. There is a certain island-people who are mad for it. They call it sack."

Felix's eyes bulged in his head. "England!"

"Shh, lower your voice!"

Felix complied. "We are at war with them," he spat out in a hoarse whisper. "How can you—"

Miguel raised his hand. "Ask me no questions about that. Suffice to say that it can be done. Trade goes on, whatever kings and queens do."

Felix shook his head. "Only the Mendozas could manage such a thing. No wonder you are so rich, Don Miguel."

"Yes," the older man agreed. "Money makes money. That is a rule of life. Never forget it. And that brings me to the heart of this discussion. I feel honor bound to offer you a chance to increase your thousand ducats. Felix, would you like to be a partner in this venture? If so, we will call this chest of gold and a year's labor in the bodega sufficient to buy you a one-tenth share."

It was on the tip of Felix's tongue to say yes immediately. He was so excited he could hardly sit still. To be a partner with the Mendozas was a guarantee of wealth and status. No Ruez until now had been so close to such glory. But he made himself hesitate. "Perhaps one tenth would not be quite enough, Don Miguel. I have a family—four children and another coming. Perhaps two tenths?" His voice dropped at the end. He was already regretting his audacity.

Miguel Antonio hesitated and simulated great thought. "Yes," he said finally. "Yes. I agree."

They clasped hands on the arrangement.

"Twenty percent," he told Ramón later. "I was quite prepared to give him fifty. Now, help me get these ducats back to the storeroom."

The story Don Miguel told Felix was true in all but one particular. He had bought the vineyard and the bodega some months before. But until yesterday he had not intended to try to ship the Jerez wine to England. It was possible, that was true, but given the state of affairs between Philip of Spain and Elizabeth of England, it was very difficult and expensive. Only the need to get Ramón out of the country had given him the idea and made him decide to chance it.

Managing also to avoid turning over all his ready gold to Felix Ruez was a bonus. So perhaps the fortunes of the house were on the upturn again. Pray God it was so, and that the good luck extended to Ramón. He would need it.

The would-be Jew left his father's house a week later. His first destination was Amsterdam in the Low Countries, not as dangerous as the second leg of the journey would be, but still not easy. The Low Countries were Spanish territory, but the Protestant heresy was spreading mightily there, and no matter how vigorously the Inquisition proceeded, it seemed impossible to stamp out. Traveling in his garb of a Dominican aspirant, Ramón met with courtesy from the authorities—and with hostility from the people. He was a Mendoza; he managed.

In the city on the Zuider Zee the difficult part truly began. He was to find a man his father knew. "He will deny it, as well he should," Miguel had explained. "But between you and me, he is a Jew despite his Christian baptism."

Because this Marrano was in debt to the family, Miguel Antonio had been sure of at least his initial cooperation. The rest depended on the son. So it proved to be. Ramón spent a month under the Netherlander's roof, and at the end of that time much was understood on both sides. The goal was achieved. Passage was arranged to England, but by a long and circuitous route, and certain names had been whispered as those of the proper persons to find in London.

The England that Ramón Mendoza was so eager to reach would have been a poor choice had others been available. Beautiful it certainly was, and prosperous, and alive with art and ideas and great plans for the future. Under Elizabeth Tudor the island kingdom was gifted with a measure of stability; still, conflict raged with Spain and France from without, and religious acrimony prevailed within.

Now, in the reign of Elizabeth I, daughter of Anne Boleyn and Henry VIII, the break with Rome was becoming final and the Mass was being suppressed, and the Book of Common Prayer adopted as the norm of worship throughout the land.

As for the Jews, officially there were none in any kingdom under the English crown. It had been an earlier king, the Plantagenet Edward I, who solved the Jewish problem in his part of the world. He expelled them from the realm in 1290.

Though England had always been more vigorous in her application of papal sanctions against the people of the old dispensation than any country in Europe, the ban was not enforced with vigor and so there were Jews in England in the last quarter of the sixteenth century. A community of Sephardim trickled into London after they were hounded from the Iberian peninsula. They practiced their religion in utmost secrecy and masqueraded as Protestants fleeing the Inquisitors. This fiction was recognized for what it was by the English, but the foreigners were tolerated because they were a channel of trade with Spain and Portugal. War, as Don Miguel had pointed out, could not be allowed to interfere with business.

By the year 1588, when Elizabeth told her troops at Tilbury, "I know I have the body of a weak and feeble woman, but I have the heart and stomach of a king . . ." and when England rejoiced at the defeat of the Spanish armada, all was accomplished as Don Miguel intended. Ramón, the once aspiring Dominican, was secretly Avraham the Jew—and openly Raymond Mendoza, the Protestant. He had a wife and three children, a thriving trade in the importation of sack from Jerez, and a house on Creechurch Lane in the East End of London within sight of the Tower.

Thanks to his efforts, and those of Don Miguel—and the vintnering skills of Felix Ruez—the house of Mendoza had ridden out its financial crisis on a wave of sherry wine.

"Fascinating, as you promised, Father." Robert put the leather-bound book on Benjamin's writing table.

"I think so," the older man said quietly. "I think it's a most remarkable document."

Robert studied his father. He was a fine man. Kindly, prudent in business, devoted to his wife and children, Benjamin was not the sort one expected to brew complex schemes. Still,

Robert suspected his father's motives at the moment. The thought had been nagging him for hours. The question burst from him now. "Why did you give me this?"

Benjamin bent over to return the history to the drawer. Robert couldn't see his face when he spoke. "For the same reason I sent you to Spain."

"I thought that was because you had invested such a huge sum in the Mesta affair."

"Oh, that was part of it. At least it was convenient that you could deal with the matter." He locked the drawer while he spoke. "But I'd have thought of some other excuse if there had been no attempt to break the Mesta."

"Excuse for what? Dammit, Father, why are you talking in riddles?"

"Calm yourself, lad. And don't be impudent." He checked the drawer holding the book once more, then, satisfied that it was securely locked, sat up. "Now, listen to me. Your brother Liam is my eldest son. When I die, he will take charge of the Mendoza interests."

"I know that. I've always known it."

"Don't interrupt. What Liam will inherit is what we hold and administer here in England. In the normal way of things you would work under him. Liam will be, how shall I put it . . . a crown prince. And a good one. He's competent and honest. But you, Robert, are a great deal more. You I wish to see as king."

Robert stared at his father, part of his mind understanding what the old man meant, the rest of it rejecting that under-standing. He shook his head.

Benjamin leaned forward to deflect that unspoken denial. "You know the story now. You must see that our claim is beyond question, the line unbroken. Ramón Mendoza was Miguel Antonio's son. Ramón was my nine times great-grandfather, you are his tenth great-grandson in a direct line of descent. But this is not a matter to be settled in a court of law. It's a moral question. And our moral claim is unimpeachable. We may not be religious men, but we have kept the faith. We remain somehow Jews, for all that we don't attend a synagogue. At least we circumcise our sons and we've made no other allegiance as they have in Cordóba."

There was a light tap on the door and a maid entered carrying a tray. "Ah, coffee," Benjamin said. "Thank you." He motioned the servant to leave and himself filled the cups from a silver pot. "Tea's fine in the afternoon, but in the morning a man needs coffee to get the blood flowing."

Robert took a long sip, using the time to marshal his thoughts. "The Inquisition still exists in Spain."

"True, but it has no teeth, as you yourself reported. And the times are changing, lad. It's in the very air we breathe. That foul London air your mother's always complaining about will spread to Madrid and then to Córdoba, Robert. It's written on the wall. There may be some difficult times, one needs to be most circumspect, but the opportunity will never be so perfect. Domingo is dying. All the reports I receive confirm your information. He won't last another year. And Pablo Luis is an embittered cripple with no interest whatever in anything except slaughtering innocent bulls."

"Does Domingo know what you have in mind? Does he agree?"

Benjamin smiled. "Of course not. Domingo has made himself believe that when the time comes, his malformed son will rise to the challenge, as Mendoza men have before. Besides, he doesn't want to admit that he'll soon be dead. He thinks he has time to arrange things, to get Pablo sorted out."

This was the man whom Domingo had accused of being cautious to a fault. And Robert had agreed with that judgment. "Father, I am understanding what you really mean, aren't I?"

"I'm sure you are, Robert. It's been in my mind since it became obvious that Domingo would never have a healthy son with his full wits about him. That's why I was at such pains for you to learn Spanish. You will be the next hidalgo. I intend that you shall go to Córdoba and rule the house of Mendoza."

❧ 7 ❧

"Sing, little Gypsy, and maybe these loudmouthed idiots will be quiet."

Sofía couldn't see the man calling to her. The café on the Calle de los Ciegos, the street of the blind, was thick with smoke, the smell of slopped wine so strong the fumes darkened the air. She pushed her way through the crowd, holding her ruffled skirts close to her body as she struggled past a table of *toreros*, distinguished by the long pigtails hanging down their backs. The bullfighters were engaged in a furious argument about last Sunday's bulls, but one of them stopped talking long enough to reach out and pinch her buttocks. *"Buenos noches, Gitanita."*

Sofía pulled away from him, but she smiled. Everyone called her *Gitanita*, little Gypsy, and all the men tried to fondle her. She was accustomed to it.

In the fourteen months since she left the Triana, she'd learned a great deal, most of it unpleasant. She was a woman without the protection of a father or a husband, and thus presumed to be the rightful prey of every male in Spain. Worse, she was a Gypsy and she was poor. No matter that she could sing anywhere people gathered and be welcomed back again and again;

no matter that those who listened to her showered her with coins, she could barely survive.

It had always been necessary to pay the landlords a percentage of what people gave her, but in sophisticated cities like Valencia and Toledo and Madrid they took almost all her earnings in return for permission to entertain their guests. If she sang in the open air, in the plazas and wide boulevards, she was accosted by the Re de los Mendigos, the king of the beggars, head of the beggars' guild, and made to give up an even larger share. Still, Sofía felt safe in the northern capitals far from Andalusia and the Gypsies who knew her, citadels of greed though they were.

She had been singing in this particular Madrid café for a week. There was no formal arrangement, but they'd come to expect her, even arranged a sort of stage. For the past two nights the landlord had made a great show of swinging her up to a corner of the bar he'd cleared for the purpose. He started to do so now, but paused with his hands around her waist. "The man I told you about is here, *Gitanita*."

"Where?" Sofía stretched her neck to see over the crowd.

"Over there on the left. The one without a hat."

"He's old. And why is he sitting with the three *majos*?"

"I expect for the same reason any man talks to *majos*, because they get women for him. But he paints them too."

"I don't know . . ." She shook her head in doubt.

"Don't be a fool. At least talk to him. But not now, later. Now you must sing." He lifted her onto the bar. Sofía adjusted her new ruffled skirt. The green one Fanta gave her had worn out beyond repair; this one was violet edged with black lace. She'd made it herself, eaten almost nothing for a week so she could afford the cotton cloth. She'd made a black blouse, too, and trimmed it with more of the lace. She wanted a black mantilla, but she hadn't enough money to buy one. Instead, she wore flowers in her hair. The flower sellers all knew her, and she got a special price. Pink roses tonight, pinned to the bun drawn tightly at the nape of her neck.

"Quiet, you fools!" the landlord shouted. "Quiet so the *Gi-*

tanita can sing." The hush began slowly with those closest to the bar; gradually it spread over the room.

Sofía still sang the songs of the South and the flamenco, but one thing was different—these days she sometimes used castanets. Among the Gypsies the curved wooden clappers held between the thumb and the palm belonged to the art of the dancer. Sofía adopted them because the crowds adored their sharp, clattering sound, and because a man in Valencia had given her a pair beautifully carved in chestnut. Now she raised her hands over her head and began clicking the castanets. Only when the quiet was complete except for that sound did she fill the café with her songs of love and revenge, and the joy and the pain of life.

"The painter can't hear you very well," the landlord told her later. "But he says he can feel the rhythm of your music. He says it enters his bones."

"He's deaf?"

"Yes. He got the fucking disease a few years ago. But he still fucks."

She had learned not to flinch when they spoke to her in the language of the streets. It was yet another price she paid for her lack of male protection.

"And doubtless that's what he wants with me. Which I don't want. So why should I bother to meet him?"

"The virgin *Gitanita*." The landlord pinched her cheek. "Everyone says you keep your legs tightly crossed, *mi niña,* and maybe you do. But the painter doesn't want you for that, he has plenty of women to warm his bed. He wants only to put you in a picture."

"And for that he'll pay?"

"Yes, so he says."

She hesitated a moment more, then nodded.

The landlord led her through the crush to the painter's table. The three *majos* were still with him, but they moved aside and made a place for Sofía. "Don Francisco," the landlord said, "here she is, as I promised." He turned to Sofía. "This is the greatest painter in Spain, *Gitanita,* Don Francisco de Goya y

Lucientes. My most distinguished customer. See you don't offend him."

"Little Gypsy," Goya said. "It's a name of sorts, do you have another one?"

"I'm called Sofía." She knew she had to speak up, but her throat was dry from all the singing and the smoke of the men's cigars. The painter leaned closer; he hadn't heard her. "Sofía," she shouted.

"Ah, I see. A good name. They tell me you're from Seville, Sofía. Are there many blue-eyed Gypsies in Seville?"

She shook her head.

"No, I thought not. But your eyes are a color such as I've never seen. I wish to try to put that color in a painting. Will you pose for me?"

Sofía hesitated. "I'm not sure, Don Francisco. I mean no disrespect, but I've never done anything like that. I wouldn't know how."

"There's nothing to know. You will simply sit and I will paint. Just the head and shoulders, I think. You can keep your clothes on. Three reales an hour."

"For how many hours?" It was tempting. Here perhaps was some money she could both earn and keep. The landlord had already told her he wouldn't ask for a portion of the model's fee.

"Four hours, maybe five," the painter said. "I won't know it's done until it's done."

Sofía hesitated, then agreed. Maybe if it took him long enough, she would be able to buy a black mantilla.

"Good," Goya said. "Good. I'm pleased. Come tomorrow." He told her the address of his studio. "Here, I've written it down. Just show this paper to someone if you get lost. A priest, someone educated like that."

"There is no need, Don Francisco. I can read." Sofía tucked the note between her breasts.

He hadn't heard her, he'd already turned away to speak to the man on his left. but the *majo* next to Sofía heard and he studied her with sudden interest. He was dressed in the flamboyant style of the men of his trade, an overlong cape and an outsize broad-brimmed sombrero trimmed with peacock feathers. Beneath the hat his hair was dark auburn. For a moment Sofía stared back at him, then she turned away. It was time for her to sing again.

"Señorita." The auburn-haired man stepped from the shadow of a plane tree and put himself in Sofía's path.

She'd been walking slowly, watching a water carrier and his donkey. The animal was laden with two brimming water butts. She had been told that there were seven hundred fountains bringing the water from the surrounding mountains to the city. A fantastic number, but perhaps it was true. One thing she knew was true—she'd seen it with her own eyes—in Madrid no woman filled and carried her own bucket. The rich didn't even send their servants to the fountains. The work was assigned to official employees of the government, and they alone could bring water to the houses of the city. There were others assigned to collect the city's garbage, and still others who gathered the manure from the streets.

She'd also heard that almost two hundred thousand people lived in Madrid. Before she came here she wouldn't have believed there were two hundred thousand people in the whole world. No wonder everything was organized, even the procurers and their women. Sofía looked at the auburn-haired *majo,* but she didn't greet him.

"Señorita," he said again. "I wish to speak with you."

She tried to walk past him. "I do not wish to speak with you, señor."

The *majo* moved to block her path. "Why not? You've just left the painter, haven't you? How was it? Did the master turn your face into a portrait all Spain will talk about?"

"All Spain talks about everything Goya does. As to my portrait, I don't know. It isn't finished yet."

"And you've been in his studio for four hours. I know, I watched you go in. That's twelve reales. Did he pay you yet?"

Sofía shook her head.

"You're lying," the man said with a grin. "I know for a fact he pays his models after each sitting."

Sofía put the hand clutching the coins behind her back. "No, no. He didn't pay me; I swear it."

"Don't worry. I'm not going to ask for part of it. I have a beautiful *maja*, she keeps me very well."

She believed him. He wasn't after her money. That gave her confidence. "Your *maja* is stupid. All these women who lay with men then give the money to *majos* are stupid. What does she get out of it?"

The man laughed. "I won't tell you what she gets out of it, but I'll show you if you like." Sofía tried again to push past him. He put out an arm to stop her. "Wait, that's not why I want to talk to you. I have a proposition, but it doesn't involve me, and it will cost you nothing to listen. Come, we'll have a glass of wine and discuss it."

She went because it was easier than arguing with him, and because it was a beautiful afternoon and she had nothing to do until after ten, when she would go to the café in the Calle de los Ciegos and sing, and because the thought of returning to the lonely hovel she slept in was depressing.

He took her arm and guided her past the new museum they were building on the meadows of the Paseo del Prado to a place where they served the strong, fruity red wine of the Rioja region, drawing it from huge oak barrels that lined one wall and carrying it in pewter pitchers to the benches where the customers sat. The room was filled with *majos*. It was easy to spot them because of the way they dressed, as if they were proud of what they did. There were other women too, pretty ones wearing the latest fashions, doubtless the *majas* who supported these parasites. "I don't like it here," Sofía told the man who'd said his name was Pedro. "Say what you want to say quickly."

"One drink together and I'll explain, then you can do what you want." Pedro summoned a boy wandering through the crowd. He brought his pitcher and filled their cups and marked a number on the wall above their heads. "*Saludos*," Pedro said, toasting her with his eyes as well as his drink. "You are beautiful, *Gitanita*. I hope the master does you justice in his painting."

She didn't answer. It was not to tell her she was beautiful that he'd brought her here, and by now he knew that she wasn't interested in being any man's *maja*. Better an ordinary *puta*, if it came to that. Better a whore who went by the name and at least kept what she earned for herself. Sofía was sick to death of always having to give part of her money to some man for a reason he devised. So far she had survived by selling her voice. If she ever had to sell her body, she would do it on her terms.

"I have a friend," Pedro said finally, "as important and influential in his way as Goya is in his."

"You seem to have a number of powerful friends. What do they see in you, I wonder?"

The *majo* flushed. "And you have a tongue like an old witch. I begin to think I've made a mistake."

"Yes, you probably have." She started to stand up. Pedro grabbed her arm and pulled her back to the bench.

"Sit down. And shut your mouth for a few minutes. I don't think I like you, *Gitanita,* and I know you don't like me. But I have a commission to fill and I think you're the *chica* I've been looking for. When you said last night that you could read, were you lying?"

"No, I wasn't lying."

"Where did you learn?"

She didn't know the answer to that. She'd learned to read and to count somewhere in that past of which she remembered nothing. "It's no business of yours."

Pedro shrugged. "Have you ever read a book?"

At last he'd piqued her interest. In fourteen months Sofía thought she'd heard every question a man could ask. They were all designed to get him something he wanted, but at least this one was different. "No," she said hesitantly. "Not a real book. Where would I see a book?"

"I don't know, but you said you could read."

"I can. Can you?" He nodded. "That sign over there, then," she said. "I'll tell you what it says." She read out the list of the various bodegas from which the wines came, and the prices charged for each of them.

"Amazing," Pedro said when she was through. "I've never met a woman who could read. At least, not one who wasn't rich and titled and the wife or the daughter of nobility."

"I suppose you go around mostly with the wives and daughters of nobility."

This time Pedro ignored the barb. "The man I told you about, my influential friend. He has asked me to find him a companion." Sofía started again to rise. "Damn you, will you sit down. It's not what you think. He wants someone he can talk to. He has a wife but she's fat and ugly and she bores him. He wants someone who is beautiful to look at and who will also be able to talk to him about books, and—" He paused for effect. "And about music. He said maybe someone who could play the mandolin or the guitar, but if he heard you . . ."

"That's all?" Sofía was sure he was lying. "He wants only to talk about books and music? And what will he give for this?"

"Everything," Pedro said simply.

"What do you mean?"

"Just what I said. He will give his companion a house to live in—actually he already owns it, a little place near the Toledo Gate, and he will buy her food and clothes. Everything, as I said."

"And what will she give you?"

"Nothing. My arrangement is with the gentleman. He will pay me. It will not concern you."

"Why me? Why not some highborn lady?"

"Highborn ladies do not usually take such posts."

"Some do," Sofía insisted.

"I know, but he wants someone who has nothing to do with his world, someone who is entirely different. Well, what do you say?"

"No."

"Why not?"

"I don't trust you. I think you're lying and I don't believe this business is as innocent as you make it sound. I'm a singer, not a whore."

Pedro shrugged. "Suit yourself. It's a pity, because he's waiting to speak to you. That man over there."

She couldn't help being curious. Sofía looked in the direction he'd indicated. Only one man in that corner wasn't dressed like a *majo*. He was a gentleman wearing a brown frockcoat over a cream-colored waistcoat and breeches. Not a young man, his hair was white. He was looking at her intently. "That's him?" she demanded, turning back to Pedro.

"Yes. Walk a ways with me. He will follow. We arranged it all earlier. You and he can talk, that's all. Then you can decide whether you want to go on with it. You have everything to gain, *Gitanita,* and nothing whatever to lose."

She never went back to Goya to finish sitting for her portrait. She simply forgot about it, because from the moment Pedro introduced her to Javier, everything changed.

Sofía moved into the house near the Puerta de Toledo the first week in May of the year 1801. Pedro and Javier had both called it a little house; Sofía thought it a mansion. There were five rooms built around a central patio. There was a tree in the patio, a mimosa heavy with feathery yellow blossoms on the day she arrived. The scent of the mimosa perfumed the rooms, and when she stepped out her front door she could see the royal palace. "It suits you?" Javier asked.

"It's magnificent." Sofía threw her arms around him. "You are magnificent, Javier." She still didn't understand why he wanted her, why he gave so much in return for so little, but Sofía had stopped worrying and begun blessing her good fortune. Maybe this was what Fanta had meant when she said the cards promised Sofía a wonderful future.

"I only hope you won't be bored because I can't be with you very often." Javier had already said this a dozen times.

"I won't be, I promise you. I shall feel like a princess."

"I hope so. You delight me, Sofía. I want you to be happy. Now, let us sit here and you can tell me what you thought of the book I gave you last week."

"I loved it. I loved Don Quixote best, but all the people in the story were wonderful."

"Characters," Javier corrected her gently. "That's what the people in a story are called. And did you think them all wonderful? Didn't you think it was cruel of some of them to mock Don Quixote?"

Sofía pursed her lips and thought for a moment. "It didn't occur to me, but yes, you're right . . ." They spent an hour discussing the novel, then she sang to him for a while. He liked best the soft sounds of the *soléas*. She never sang flamenco for Javier.

"Lovely," he murmured when the last notes died away. "Lovely."

There was a tap on the door. Sofía looked up, startled. "*Adelante*," Javier said, then, to Sofia, "Don't be frightened. It's just the maid."

A maid! It had never occurred to her that she would have a maid.

"My dear, this is Juana. She will look after you."

Sofía 'saw a woman as old as Fanta, with just as forbidding a face. Not exactly a maid, a guardian perhaps. Someone to spy on her and tell Javier what she did when he wasn't around. "I don't need a maid."

"Yes," he insisted. "I think you do. Besides, Juana has been with me for years. She is an excellent cook. You'll quite enjoy her food."

Sofía turned to the maid. "Can you stew hedgehog?"

The other woman paled. "I do not cook such filthy things."

"No, I thought not. Javier, this won't do. I'm a Gypsy and I have Gypsy ways. You knew that when you began with me."

"I love your ways, my blue-eyed Gypsy," he said, smiling. "But if you are to stay here, then so is Juana. Now, what do you choose?"

She looked around the room and thought of the shelter behind a stable that until now had provided her only protection from the wind and rain and cold and cost five reales a week. "I will teach you to stew hedgehog," she told Juana.

The maid never did learn to prepare the Gypsy delicacy, but she taught Sofía other things. "I have prepared your bath, señorita," she told the girl that first night after Javier had left.

"What are you talking about?"

"Your bath, señorita. It's ready in the kitchen by the fire."

Sofía followed Juana more out of curiosity than anything else. There was an oval copper tub sitting on the floor beside the coal stove. It was steaming. "What have you got in there?"

"Hot water, Doña Sofía. And herbs to make a sweet smell."

No one had ever called her Doña Sofía, not even Javier. She stepped closer to the tub. "It's not convenient to bend over so far," she objected as she reached into it preparing to splash her face. "And it's too hot."

"Not like that," Juana said quietly. "Take off your clothes, I will show you."

Sofía considered for a moment. "Do rich women do what you are telling me to do?"

"Yes, the young and beautiful ones particularly. Taking baths has become the fashionable thing to do."

Without another word Sofía began undressing. She had reminded Javier that she was a Gypsy because it had suited her purposes to do so. But she had decided to learn the ways of *busne* women. That's why she had made this arrangement with Javier. As a Gypsy, her life was in peril and she had to struggle or starve; as a *busne* she was safe and everything she needed appeared like some miraculous gift from heaven.

"What do I do now?" she demanded when she was naked.

"Step into the bath, Doña Sofía. I will wash you."

At first she thought all her skin must be burned away. "I'm scalded!"

"No, no, señorita. It feels hot for only a moment, then it's comfortable. Sit back, you will see."

Gingerly Sofía leaned back and allowed her whole body to be submerged. A sensation of relaxation and peace flooded over her. "Juana, I think this may be a very good idea. Have you ever had a bath?"

"Oh, yes, señorita. My previous lady insisted that I be very clean and smell sweet."

She started to ask who Juana's previous lady had been, but the maid was scooping the perfumed water out of the tub with a china pitcher and pouring it over her head. Then she began rubbing Sofía's hair with the leaves of a lemon tree. It smelled wonderful, it felt wonderful. All her questions disappeared in a new and remarkable peace.

"You are more beautiful than ever," Javier said when he came the next day. "And you smell delicious."

"I didn't smell so good before, did I?" Sofía asked.

"Let's just say not as nice as now. Now you smell like a lady."

"Good. That's what I want to be."

"You shall," Javier promised. "I will teach you and Juana will look after you. Will this make you happy, Sofía?"

"Very happy."

It did, and being happy was apparently all that was expected of her. When Javier came, he talked with her about what he'd said she must call literature, and she entertained him with sad, sweet songs. Then they would share a meal prepared by Juana. While they ate he discussed wine vintages and how best to cook and serve such delicacies as pheasant. He also offered patient instruction in the proper use of cutlery and table linen, and taught her to drink from a stemmed glass rather than a cup.

If she had to choose the one thing most remarkable about her new life, Sofía would pick the glassware. In the caves of the Triana she drank from a tin cup, in the posadas and cafés from cups made of dark brown earthenware, but in the house Javier provided there were cups of delicate china and glasses the colors of the rainbow. The first time she saw them, Sofía felt an intense stab of pleasure, as if the glass were part of some memory, some key to who she had been before she was a Gypsy. She could never hold on to that, never part the curtain that shrouded her past, but she continued to find joy in the emerald and indigo goblets that graced the table in the house near the Puerta de Toledo.

For his part, Javier seemed delighted to teach her all these things she had never expected to learn, never even considered. Apparently such delight was enough for him. He held her hand while they were together and kissed it when he left; apart from that there was nothing physical between them. Sometimes Sofía wondered if without knowing it she had died and gone to heaven.

"Domingo is dead." Benjamin Mendoza made the announcement without fanfare on a December day in 1801.

Robert thought about the man who had been his host two years earlier. "When did it happen? How?"

"He died three months past, in September. This damned blockade of Napoleon's slows down our news from Spain, not to mention our shipments of sack. As to how, peacefully apparently. In his own bed. His heart stopped and they buried him with full Catholic pomp. The official notice talks about his grieving widow. The letter from my unofficial source says she attacked his mistress at the funeral. Made a spectacle of herself."

"I expect Maria Ortega was a match for Doña Carmen."

"You said you never met her."

"The wife? No. I met the mistress, though, a remarkable-looking woman."

"Yes, you said that too. You'll have to deal with both of them, but it shouldn't be too difficult."

"You haven't changed your mind, then?" Robert asked.

"Of course not. Have you forgotten everything we talked about?"

"I haven't forgotten. But . . ."

"But what? Robert, if you've no stomach for this, tell me now."

He didn't answer immediately. He looked around the comfortable, familiar room with its lifetime of associations, ten lifetimes of associations, and thought about all he was heir to. "I have the stomach for it," he admitted finally. "I didn't realize how much I wanted it until you talked about it. Since then I've thought of little else. I think I'm possessed."

"Power," Benjamin said. "That's what men fight and die for."

"A short time ago I'd have said money, now I think you're right."

"We're both right." Benjamin went to the window and leaned on the sill. Little had been done to this house since the sixteenth century. It was two-storied and half timbered, and the windows were small and threaded with lead mullions. His view of the Tower of London was distorted by the wavy old glass in the window, but he could see that symbol of the life and death prerogatives of the crown. "In our times power *is* money. In previous ages it was other things, perhaps. I'm not sure. But I know that now wealth rules, whatever the crowned heads dream about when they sleep."

"Have you told Liam?" Robert asked.

"About Domingo's death? No, not yet."

"I was referring to your plans."

"No, I haven't told him about them either." Benjamin glanced at the clock on the mantel. Its brass pendulum swung steadily. "He should be here any minute. We'll tell him together."

Liam Samuel Mendoza had been named Leo by the rabbi who officiated at his circumcision. The Anglo-Irish name Liam had been an affectation of the boy's mother. Both names meant the same thing, lion. Liam looked the part. He had a great mane of sandy hair and a strong beaked nose, but he had little else in common with the fabled beast. He was a slow, plodding man, reliable and usually calm. Until recently Robert would have said that Liam took after their father. Now he wasn't sure whose nature his brother had inherited. "So Domingo is dead," Liam repeated after his father gave him the news. As if he had to struggle to memorize it.

"Yes. Two months ago. As I said." Today Benjamin had less patience than usual with his eldest son.

"So Pablo Luis is now head of the house."

"Pablo is the hidalgo," Benjamin agreed. "That title has passed to him by law. And I suppose he fancies himself head of the house of Mendoza, if he thinks about business at all. But he's not."

An expression of mild surprise passed over Liam's face. "If not Pablo Luis, then who?"

"Your brother Robert."

Liam looked from Robert to Benjamin then back again. "Did you arrange this with Domingo when you were in Spain?"

"I arranged nothing," Robert said. "It's all Father's idea."

Liam repeated the series of questioning looks, twisting his head from one man to the other. "I'm sorry, I don't understand."

"Godstruth, lad!" Benjamin exploded. "Can't you see the logic of it? In Córdoba there is no one of the family to take on the leadership. The only son Domingo left behind is a crippled maniac who chases around the country wallowing in bull's blood. You must take over here in England after me, so Robert is the obvious choice, the best choice. With you here and Robert in Spain, the house of Mendoza will prosper as never before."

Nicely done, you old fox, Robert thought. Liam's going to feel honored rather than slighted. He was right. In a few moments Liam was enthusiastically discussing plans for the future.

"We're going to do this without any drama," Benjamin said. "Robert is simply going to return to Córdoba with all possible speed and take up the slack ropes Pablo Luis will undoubtedly be trailing behind him. I think the hunchback will be more than glad to have someone relieve him of the burden."

"He loses by default," Robert said quietly. "If he cooperates, that will be the cleanest way."

"Clean or messy is unimportant," his father said. "Just do it. You're a match for that obsessed idiot, I trust. And you'll find help where you least expect it. I haven't just thought of this, and I've not been idle the past twenty-six years. Now, Liam, you'd best go. You're expected at the admiralty in an hour, I believe."

"More ships?" Robert asked when Liam had left.

"One more at least. Nice for us that as well as fathering a bastard daughter on Mrs. Hamilton and becoming a vice admiral, Nelson found time to attack Copenhagen."

"More of that quest for power you were speaking of earlier," Robert said.

"Of a sort, but war doesn't really enrich the men who conduct the battles. They're pawns of higher forces. By the way, I have it on reliable authority that our new prime minister is going to sue for peace, sign some kind of a treaty with Napoleon. I think Pitt meant for him to do so, that's why he resigned and maneuvered Addington into his place. It's easier if the man who's been shouting war isn't suddenly the one to shout peace."

"Thank God for whoever does it. If he's successful, we can start shipping sack again."

Benjamin nodded. "Yes, we will. But whether it's war or peace, our role is to control the purse strings of those who control the armies and navies. That's power, lad, and that's why you leave for the Continent tomorrow." He placed a small box on his writing table. "I have something for you. Take a look at this."

Robert opened the box. Lying on dusky blue velvet was a medallion about three inches long and two wide. He studied it a moment. "This inscription is in Hebrew, isn't it?"

"Yes. I know you can't read the words, but can you guess what this is?"

"No, can't say as I—" Robert looked up. His father was smiling. "By God, I do know," Robert murmured. "The pendant, the one the old record spoke of. The token Felix Ruez presented to Miguel Antonio in 1575 to prove the truth of his claim."

"The very same. At least I imagine it must be. What I know for sure is that Ramón Mendoza brought this with him to England. It has been passed from father to son ever since. I'm giving it to you now."

From father to eldest son, most probably. Robert understood why this presentation hadn't been made until after Liam left. He cradled the thing in his palm. "Can you tell me what it says?"

"It's a line from one of the psalms. 'Im eshkacheck Yeroslalayim tishkack yimini tidbak L'shoni,'" Benjamin quoted. "'If I forget thee, O Jerusalem, let my right hand forget her cunning.' There's a Mendoza legend that says the line was adopted as the family motto sometime in the seventh century, when they fled persecution in Córdoba and went to Tangier. The patriarch of the time is supposed to have had this carved over the gates of his house in Africa. To remind his children and theirs that Córdoba was their Jerusalem, their true home."

"The seventh century," Robert whispered. "Incredible."

"I suppose it is. The story also claims that a later Mendoza financed the first invasion of the Moors into Spain. To regain a foothold in Córdoba, naturally."

"Do you think all this can be true?"

Benjamin shrugged. "The history? I don't know. But whether or not it's true, it's appropriate. Don't you forget, Robert. Not what you read of Ramón's story, and not what you know of England. You'll need all your cunning, lad. It won't be as easy as I told Liam. But you'll prevail and the house of Mendoza will be richer and stronger than in all her history."

It was the same circuitous route as last time, and for the same reason, the French blockade. The night was misty and cold. Robert sat on the deck of a two-masted Dutch whaling ship, huddled against the chill and leaning on a pile of neatly coiled hawsers.

The whaler would take him to Rotterdam. From there it would be overland to Spain; by coach when he could arrange it, on horseback when he couldn't. He knew what to expect, the rest of the journey would be even less comfortable than this. The squared hull of the wooden whaler rode the choppy water like the flat hand of a child slapping waves at the seaside. She was empty now, but he could still smell the stink of the whale oil that normally filled the hold.

The captain was a Dutchman, as squat and unlovely as his craft, but just as reliable and suited to his task. Years before he'd served on Mendoza ships plying between Southampton and Cádiz. That's where he'd learned English, and become one more in the vast link of contacts that made the Mendoza empire work. When the Dutchman wanted to strike out on his own, Benjamin Mendoza had lent him the money to buy his first whaler. He'd paid interest on the loan, and a share of the profits on the cargoes of his first five years. But he still knew there were favors due. He approached his passenger. "Comfortable, Mr. Robert?"

"As comfortable as I need to be, Captain Graumann."

"Good. I brought you this." He offered a tin mug.

Robert took it, expecting tea, and tasted rum. "Thank you, it's welcome."

"I'll leave you to your thoughts, then. We'll make port by sunup."

Robert's thoughts were mostly of that last private conversation with his father. They'd had a valedictory ring to them, as if the old man thought they might not see each other again. The salt spray stung his cheeks. Like tears perhaps. He wasn't the sort of man to weep, hadn't done so since he was a child, but he could taste sadness on his tongue. It warred with the rising excitement that was making his blood sing.

The pendant was around his neck: he could feel it pressing against his flesh. He'd looked up the entire psalm before he set out. It was the hundred and thirty-seventh, the one that began "By the waters of Babylon we sat down, and how we wept when we remembered Sion." He wasn't weeping, but he remembered.

❦ 8 ❧

Robert's carriage entered the Patio del Recibo through broad double doors leading from the Calle Averroes. The coachman reined in his horses beneath the huge chestnut tree that dominated the entrance courtyard. The spreading canopy of silvery branches were shadowed with a hint of green, the February promise of Andalusia's early spring, and of shade when the heat of summer came.

Robert opened the carriage door and jumped to the cobblestones without waiting for a footman. Three servants in the maroon and gold Mendoza livery stood by the entrance to the interior of the palace. He recognized one he'd seen two years before, Juan, the majordomo. Juan was looking at him with a mixture of suspicion and confusion.

"Close those doors to the street," Robert ordered. "And see that my trunks are taken in immediately, and that the driver here is paid and gets something to eat before he leaves." He headed for the door the servants guarded.

"With all respect, señor. We were not told to expect a visitor. And the house is in mourning."

"Of course it is. So am I. I'm not a visitor, Juan, I'm a member of the family. Robert Mendoza, don't you remember me?"

"Of course he does, and so do I." Maria Ortega entered the

patio through a smaller door to the right. "Welcome, Don Robert. We did not expect you, but welcome."

She was just as remarkable looking as before. Almost as tall as he, and most unusual for a Spanish woman, a redhead with green eyes. And she was still here. That was the most interesting fact of all. "Good afternoon, Doña Maria. I'm delighted to see you again, and only sorry the circumstances are not happier."

"The sight of you lightens our grief." She spoke formal words, but Doña Maria's green eyes sent dancing messages of pleasure. She turned to the servants, issuing orders in rapid succession. Robert walked into the house without waiting for her to precede him.

Three hours later Maria Ortega sat with him in one of the smaller dining rooms. "I thought we would take our meal here. Not to do you less honor, only because it's more restful after your long journey."

"Indeed," Robert agreed. She'd placed herself at the head of the table, and she wore black lace, like a grieving widow. "I didn't see this room last time," he said. "It's charming." There were three proper walls, the fourth was a series of open arches fronting a patio where a fountain played between a double rank of cypresses shaped into ruched tiers by generations of gardeners skilled in topiary.

"Yes, I think so. Are you warm enough?"

"Delightfully warm." A charcoal brazier burned beneath the table. Robert had lifted the long table cover and draped it over his lap in the fashion he'd learned on his previous visit.

"I hope you enjoy your dinner, Don Robert," Maria said. "The cook has a special touch with *cerdo adobado*."

He took a forkful of the pickled pork without hesitation. "Delicious." It wouldn't be so easy as the brazen lady thought, Robert reflected. He'd eat pork or anything else when the stakes were so high. "How is Doña Carmen?"

Maria shrugged delicately. Her shoulders were creamy white, set off by the black gown. "The same, I imagine. One can hardly tell. Let us speak of more pleasant things. Tell me of your journey."

She wasn't beautiful in the conventional sense. Her face was too angular, her eyes too knowing, but she was utterly compelling. Her dark red hair was drawn back in a thick twist, held in the Andalusian fashion by a tall jet comb, and there were rings of jet in her ears. Moreover, her figure was magnificent.

She leaned forward, giving him a good look at the gentle curve of her full breasts. Robert felt his groin tighten. There wasn't time for dalliance. Not at this time and not with a wench already far too involved in the affairs of this house. He pulled his gaze away, but knew she'd noticed his reactions. Robert motioned to the footman standing in the shadows by the sideboard. "More pork, man. It's delicious, Doña Maria. I shall tell the cook so myself."

He pleaded tiredness and escaped to his room before midnight. It was the same room he'd had before, large and luxurious, with a balcony looking over yet another of the patios. An oil lamp burned on the ornately carved table that filled one corner. Its wick was turned low, casting a limited circle of light.

Something moved in the shadows. Instinctively Robert reached for the pistol he'd kept tucked in his waistband since he left London. It wasn't there. He'd decided that tonight for the first time in weeks he could dine unarmed. Damn! Now he'd pay for that bit of self-indulgence.

The creature who stepped into the light of the oil lamp recognized the motion. "You need not fear me, sir. I'm hardly a match for you. We didn't meet when you were here last. I keep out of sight mostly. But I'm a friend."

He was a dwarf who stood no higher than Robert's waist and whose head was so outsized it looked as if it must topple from his shoulders. "Who are you?" Robert demanded. "What are you doing here?"

"My name is Harry Hawkins. I knew your father."

"You're English? When did you know my father?"

"I was born in the same house you were. On Creechurch Lane. To a scullery maid who worked in your kitchen. Most men made as I am finish up living in a cage and being exhibited for money. Thanks to your sainted father, I avoided that fate.

He called me by a word in the old tongue of your people, a mitzvah. Do you know what that means?"

Robert shook his head, unable to take his eyes from the deformed man, yet feeling guilty because he was staring.

"A mitzvah is a divine commandment, also a good deed. Mr. Benjamin said I was his mitzvah and he would be mine. He had me educated, and it turned out I had a head for figures. I was working for him when you were born. I remember that day, how joyful everyone was because the house had another son."

"Why are you here?" Robert had relaxed now, and he dropped into a chair by the table with the lamp and motioned the dwarf to do the same. "When did you come to Spain?"

"Soon after you were born your father sent me to Córdoba."

"To spy for him," Robert said. "That was the reason, wasn't it?"

The big head shook. "No. That's an obvious kind of conclusion, but it's not accurate. I had become, by the grace of God, converted to the true religion, a Catholic." The dwarf crossed himself piously. "It's not safe in England for Catholics. Nor for Jews, for that matter. But unlike your family, I insisted on practicing my religion openly."

And that would have meant his employer and guardian must pay the huge annual fine demanded of all who didn't conform to the established church. Benjamin would never have tolerated that, however much he pitied this poor creature. "I understand," Robert said. "All the same, you have spied for him, haven't you? Father told me he had sources of information here."

"I don't call it spying," Harry Hawkins insisted. "Spying is not Christian. But how many men would have called me a divine commandment, do you think?"

"Not many."

"No. So when I realized what was happening here, and that it could hurt your father and his family, I wrote. That's not spying."

"What was happening here?"

The dwarf looked at the decanter and glasses sitting on the

table. Robert noticed and poured a tot of brandy for each of them. "What was it you felt you had to tell my father?"

Hawkins swallowed his brandy in one gulp. Robert wondered if carrying around that huge head was painful.

"I wrote him that Don Domingo was squandering the Mendoza resources, that there was almost nothing left."

"You're lying."

"I don't lie, sir." With such quiet dignity, he had to be believed. "Almost a year ago I wrote your father how things were. I never had a reply. It got much worse just before the hidalgo died. I was going to write again, but now you've come. I presume your father sent you because of my news."

"I know nothing of your information. I don't believe my father did either. He'd have told me. You're sure you wrote this letter?"

"Of course I'm sure. I don't—"

"You don't lie. So you've said. And I believe you, Harry Hawkins. But you can also believe me. This is the first I've heard of your news. Because of the war, no doubt. Our correspondence has been in a shambles since the blockade. Now, I think I'd best know more. How bad is it?"

"As bad as it can be," Hawkins said. "There's no bullion. Absolutely none. And practically no reales. In short, the cash position is a disaster. The house is living on credit rather than extending it."

"Sweet God in heaven!" Robert poured them each another brandy. It was the rough, strong stuff of Spain, not the refined cognac of the French. It went down his throat like a shaft of fire and hit his belly like a burning coal. Good, just what he needed from the sound of it. "What about the houses, the lands? The Mendozas own half of Andalusia."

"True," Hawkins agreed. "They do. More like two thirds, perhaps. And a lot of the rest of Spain as well. But nearly everything's been put up as collateral of one sort or another. The thing is, sir, Don Domingo was very secretive. I never knew who his creditors were. I still don't. One thing I can tell you, just before he died Don Domingo took another loan from a man in Madrid. He gave the *cortijo* as security."

The *cortijo* was a vast country property south of the city. It had been given to the family by the Castilian king who turned the Moors out of Córdoba in the thirteenth century. The many farms and olive groves of the Mendoza *cortijo* were valuable beyond belief. "What did he get for it?" Robert asked.

"Ten thousand reales."

"Ten thousand? That's a joke, the *cortijo* is worth ten times ten million reales."

"I know. And there's more, sir."

Robert groaned. "You'd best tell me, whatever it is."

"Don Domingo has promised the king thirty million reales. In some seventeen months, sir. Before July of 1803."

"Thirty million!"

"Yes. I don't think Don Domingo was right in his head at the end. I think..." His voice trailed off.

"Come on, man. What do you think? You're my only source of information at the moment, so if I'm going to make some sense out of all this, you have to tell me everything."

"I think Maria Ortega was putting things in his food. Things to make him mad." He whispered the words, and he didn't look at Robert when he spoke them.

"Good God, I knew she was a vixen, but . . . Why would she do it?"

"That I don't know, sir. I've tried to find out. I know she leaves the house and has meetings with strangers. But I'm not made for following people and being unobserved. Children stare at me. Adults, too, sometimes. They call out and jeer. I'm useless at that sort of thing."

"Don't apologize for what's not of your making," Robert said softly. It wasn't hard to imagine how grim life must be for this poor creature. "You've done remarkably well, Harry Hawkins. I think you're going to be my mitzvah too."

The dwarf left by a rope ladder dropped over the balcony, the same way he'd entered. Robert watched him climb down the thing with remarkable agility, then flung him the end with the curved iron grappling hook. Hawkins disappeared into the shadows of the moonless night. Robert turned back into the bedroom and saw a bit of folded paper that had been pushed beneath his door.

His first thought was that the note must be from Doña Maria. Inviting him to her bed no doubt, convinced that yet another Mendoza could be caught by his cock. He bent to retrieve it. "Come to the wine cellars tomorrow at four." There was no signature, but he was sure it wasn't from the Ortega woman. She still imagined herself queen of this palace. She'd not set up a meeting in such an unlikely place during the siesta. So someone else in this remarkable house had secret things to tell him.

Robert followed the hulking figure leading him deeper into the labyrinth of passages beneath the sprawling mansion. "Here," she said at last. "We can talk here and none of her spies will hear us."

Doña Carmen was as repulsive as the stories reported—a body so swollen out of shape it almost didn't seem human, eyes that were mere slits above bloated cheeks. She was draped in black cloth that hid everything but her face. Perhaps there was some sort of curse on this place; perhaps everyone who lived here became hideously ugly. No, the dwarf had been born on Creechurch Lane. It was simply that these malformed rejects had grudges to settle and were willing to make common cause with him. At least, that was his assumption. "What is it you want from me, Doña Carmen?"

"Justice."

"What that is rather depends on who's making the judgment," he said evenly.

"I want her dead." Her voice was a harsh whisper. "I want her shamed as she has shamed me."

"I take it you mean Doña Maria."

"Don't speak her name in my hearing! I want that *puta* to suffer as she has made me suffer."

"Have you spoken to your son about her?" Robert kept watching her face, trying to read the eyes he could barely see.

"Yes, right after the funeral. He said he would do something, but I haven't seen him since then. And she's still here. Lording it over my house, acting as if Domingo were not dead and everything was the same."

"Nothing ever stays the same, Doña Carmen."

"I wanted him to die too," she said as if she hadn't heard him. "And he did. Not as I planned it. I wanted the Inquisition to burn him, but I never found it—"

"Found what?" he interrupted.

"The evidence to give to the Inquisitors. That plaque he told you about. But he died anyway. Peacefully in his bed, that's what everyone was told. Hah! He was on top of her, rutting like an animal. I was watching them. I always watched them. She had to push the corpse off her and fix him so it looked as if he'd been sleeping alone."

Robert forced back a grin. Not a bad way for a man to die. Domingo had been lucky to the end. And the mess he'd made was left for someone else to clean up. "Why are you telling me all this?"

"You must get her out of my house. I'd kill her myself, but she has many friends and they would avenge her. I'm a helpless woman. I can't defend myself against her friends."

"What friends? What are you talking about?"

"She sees people. Powerful men meet with her secretly. Domingo never knew, but I watch her. I watched them both. I know everything that goes on in the palace."

Robert would wager the poor creature did. And he was glad to have corroboration of at least some of Harry Hawkins's suspicions. "For your sake, I'll get rid of her, Doña Carmen. But you must do something for me."

She looked at him suspiciously. "What? I'm a poor, defenseless woman. What could I possibly do for you?"

"I must speak with your son. I want you to send word to the new hidalgo. Tell Pablo Luis he must return to Córdoba. Do you know where to find him?"

"Perhaps." She shrugged, and even that ordinary movement was made grotesque by her affliction. "He will be with the bullfighters. Wherever the best corrida is taking place. Madrid probably."

"Send a message that he must return immediately, that you need him. Tell him his duty as a son will not allow him to refuse you. Tell him anything you like, just don't mention that I'm here and get him to Córdoba. Will you do that?"

"Will you punish the *puta* for how she has made me suffer?"

"Yes. Do we have a bargain, Doña Carmen?"

"*Sí*, Englishman, we have a bargain."

Robert took the first opportunity. The next morning he breakfasted in his room. When he went downstairs and asked for Doña Maria, the servants told him she'd gone into town. "To the dressmaker, señor."

Did young women go to dressmakers here in Córdoba? He had no sisters, so he couldn't be sure, but his mother's seamstresses all came to her. More confirmation of the dwarf's suspicions, perhaps. Pity he'd not been down in time to follow her. But he was in time for the more important task. Robert motioned a footman to follow him, then returned to the upper part of the palace and the private chambers.

"What is all this?" Maria Ortega returned through the Patio del Recibo as he'd hoped she would, and looked in astonishment at the pile of trunks and boxes he'd put there.

"Your things, Doña Maria. Your services are no longer required at the palace." Robert lounged by the door, leaning against it, arms folded. None of the servants were in evidence, but he spotted a dark shape behind the curtains of a window on the floor above.

"My services? Who are you to tell me what is or is not required here? I will speak with Don Pablo. He is the hidalgo."

"Yes. But Don Pablo is not here and I am. Now, señorita, I've ordered the coachman to take you wherever you wish to go." He raised his hand and a small carriage pulled forward. Another signal and three servants appeared and began loading the woman's belongings.

"This is outrageous," she sputtered. "I won't go."

"Yes, I think you will. My name is Mendoza, Doña Maria. Yours is not. And the wife of my late cousin has requested that you leave the palace. If you insist that I summon the guards, I will do so. Frankly I thought you'd prefer to avoid that."

She stared at him defiantly a moment longer, then turned away. A footman helped her up into the carriage. Robert stepped forward and handed her a leather purse. "Your wages for the next two months. Thirty reales. That's correct, isn't it?"

He knew her official salary had been fifteen reales a month. Hawkins had brought him the ledgers and he'd seen it recorded. He'd also established the fact that she spent a hundred times that each week by virtue of Domingo's indulgence. That's why he'd kept back the rope of pearls when her jewelry was packed. Not to effect some petty reclamation, just so she would understand that he was aware of her excesses. But she didn't know that yet. For a moment he thought she would refuse the purse, then her hand whipped out and she snatched it.

"You will regret this, Englishman," she whispered. "I promise you will regret it."

In the first weeks after his arrival, Robert easily forgot about Maria Ortega and her threat, as he was preoccupied with another woman. Córdoba ravished him. She was the most beautiful creature imaginable. He wondered how he had managed to resist her spell on his first visit. Perhaps because then he had not dreamed of possessing her. Now he did.

All during February and early March he walked the streets from dawn to dusk. He fell irrevocably in love with the twisting alleys that led to small perfectly composed tableaus that surprised the eye with exquisite harmonies of white walls against a door, a window, a pot of flowers. He was seduced by broad avenues lined with orange trees, by tinkling fountains, by splendidly adorned public buildings and secret patios. Córdoba sang to him, but he was afraid her melody was a dirge.

Benjamin had said it. Money is power. Their plans had been about Robert wresting control of a magnificent fortune from an obsessed cripple. They hadn't discussed how to rescue that fortune when it was in danger of being lost forever, or how he was to find thirty million reales before July of next year, or do battle with Pablo Luis when he still couldn't find him. The hidalgo hadn't responded to his mother's entreaties. Robert had yet to see him or discover where he was.

He'd done the obvious thing, written to London asking for bullion and advice. So far there was no reply but it was still too soon to expect. Or his father might not have understood the message, phrased in guarded words lest it fall into the wrong hands. One good thing he'd discovered, the precarious financial position of the house wasn't yet common knowledge. Domingo had been mad in many ways. The amount he'd lost fighting the Mesta was beyond belief, but he'd remained secretive and circumspect to the end. The vultures weren't yet alerted by the smell of blood.

Cold comfort, he thought. He was standing on a palisaded bridge that ended in a tower at the far shore of the Guadalquivir. The Romans had erected this defense of the city, probably with the help of the Mendozas. He was prepared to believe the old myths after reading Ramón's story. Perhaps there had been Mendozas here as early as the first century, and if so, they'd doubtless lent money to the Roman Procurator who governed Córdoba. Then to the Goths and the Visigoths who came after them. And according to his father, the family had financed the invasion of the Moors in 711. Five hundred years later the Arab rulers no longer suited them, so Mendoza gold flowed to the Christian kings who pushed the Moors back into Africa.

"And all for nothing," he whispered to the chill March wind that abraded his face. "All so I could come along in 1802 and preside over the pillaging and the rape." Robert turned from the fortified bridge and walked back to the palace.

Hawkins was waiting for him in the entrance hall. The dwarf sprang out of the shadows beside the blue marble pillars that stood on either side of the broad stairs. "Godstruth, you startled me, Harry. Must you always sneak around corners?"

"Forgive me, sir. It's my habit to hide. People don't like to look at me. They—"

"Yes, yes, I understand. Well, what is it?" No reason to be

so brusque with the little man, just that his mood didn't allow for kindness and soft words.

"News, sir. It came while you were out and I thought you'd want to know right away."

"What news? From my father?"

"Not from Mr. Benjamin, sir. Not personal news. It's a treaty. Between Napoleon and Addington. The British and the French have made peace at Amiens. You don't look pleased, sir. It means the end of the blockade. We can ship more sack."

"Yes, I realize that. And it's a good thing. You've done well, Hawkins. Send word to Cádiz that a cargo should leave immediately."

"I've already done that, sir."

"Good." Robert turned away. Miguel Antonio and his son Ramón had saved the family fortune with sack, but times were different.

"Mr. Robert," the dwarf said softly. "Could I trouble you a moment more?"

Robert paused with one foot on the stairs. "Yes, of course. What is it?"

"I think I've discovered the name of the man in Madrid."

He turned back to the dwarf. "Have you, indeed? How?"

"The code, sir. The one Don Domingo used to write down the names of the people he borrowed from. I've sorted it out. I understand it now."

Robert had seen the little black book with Domingo's scrawls. He'd puzzled over it for days, then given up. "God almighty! That's wonderful, Hawkins. Now we can begin to make some progress. Come to my room and bring the damned book. If we know who, then we'll soon know how to get them off our backs."

He bounded up the stairs like a man reprieved from hanging. He'd go see that bloody gouger in Madrid. He'd raise ten thousand reales—a sum like that wasn't out of reach—and pay off the bastard. Then the *cortijo* and its wealth and income would be clear, and his to use for his own ends. It was a start, by God, it was certainly a start.

* * *

Sofía was carried along by the crowd surging toward the Plaza Mayor. She could smell the bulls penned at one end of the vast rectangle ringed by a solid phalanx of buildings.

The crowd of aficionados called out wagers to one another and arranged meetings for after the fights. They were Madrileños of every class and circumstance, just risen from the siesta, ready to enjoy themselves, and to bask in the April sun that warmed the afternoon.

Sofía allowed herself to be pushed forward, swallowed by the tide of people. She wore somber gray unrelieved by jewelry or flowers. Her dress did not identify her as a Gypsy, or even an Andalusian. It was similar to what other fashionable women wore, a fitted bodice covered by the ends of the shawl over her hair, and a skirt that belled out from her waist and stopped above her ankles. Sofía didn't want to attract attention.

Inside the high walls of the plaza she found a space to stand with her back to the banner-bedecked podium with its high-backed chair occupied by the official president of the event, the alcalde. The mayor of Madrid was elected by the members of the city's guilds, and the Madrileños had more affection and respect for him than for their king. The alcalde's wife sat beside him. People clustered around the pair like bees seeking honey; others waved or called out greetings.

In ten minutes the vast space was filled except for the sand-covered circle in the middle that was reserved for the fight. She spotted some children high up on the roofs of the surrounding buildings. Gypsy boys probably. She sometimes saw Gypsies in Madrid, though she recognized none of them and she made certain they didn't see her. Sofía pulled her shawl forward so it shaded more of her face, and waited. Soon the great spectacle would begin; even now the three toreros who would fight were praying to their special patron, El Cristo de la Salud, in the chapel behind the plaza.

Out of the corner of her eye she caught a flash of motion. The alcalde had waved his square of white linen. It was time. Trumpets and drums struck the opening notes of the paso doble. Slowly the procession made its way into the plaza. At its head were the three toreros who would fight. Behind them

in separate files marched the retinue of each—their banderilleros, their picadors, their ring servants. Lastly came two teams
of three mules which would be used to drag away the dead
bulls.

How splendid they all were, how richly dressed, how brightly
tasseled and caped and hatted and belled. The procession paced
slowly across the sand to the alcalde and bowed. The crowd
roared its approval when he threw the bullpen key to a servant,
who caught it deftly in his hat. They roared even louder when
a moment before the recessional began, the alcalde's wife leaned
forward and tossed her silk scarf to the tallest of the three
toreros.

Sofía was not moved by the colorful drama. She wasn't particularly interested in the corrida. She was there to observe the
alcalde and his señora. She could dare to look more closely at
them now that the ceremonies had begun and the couple were
fully occupied. It was a sight she found extraordinary because
the mayor of Madrid was Javier, her protector, and his wife
was not the fat and ugly woman Sofía had been told about.
She was young and pretty and very gay, and Javier obviously
adored her.

"What's wrong, Sofía?"

"Nothing is wrong."

"Yes, something is. I know you, my dear. It's been almost a
year. I know you very well."

"Javier, why do you keep me?"

He did not look surprised by her question. He lay down his
fork and considered it. "Let me answer with another question,
why do you stay?"

She fingered the brooch pinned to her bodice. It was a
sapphire. Javier had given it to her because he said the jewel
matched her eyes. "You know what my life was like before I
met you. You've been very good to me, Javier."

"But now?" he asked. "You've learned everything I had to
teach you, Sofía. Yet you stay."

"Where would I go? Besides—" She paused, wondering if
he could possibly understand. "There's one thing you've given

me that I don't think you're aware of, but it's the most important thing. You've given me time to hate."

"You're right. I'm not aware of that. I don't associate hatred with you, my dear."

Sofía's voice trembled. "You mistake me, Javier. I am not a saint and I know how to hate." She stood up, too agitated to remain at the table. "I told you about my child, what happened to her. I told you how she died."

"Yes. Then it's your Gypsy husband you've learned to hate?"

"Not learned. I said you gave me time to hate him. What I feel about Paco was born before I met you, before I left the Triana. But that first year, while I struggled so to stay alive, I almost forgot. It almost pushed Paco from my mind."

"And now?"

"Now I have many hours in which to make a plan."

"A plan of revenge," Javier said. "There have been many such over the centuries, Sofía. They almost never work the way they're meant to. Revenge and hatred are strong emotions, my little Gypsy. They cloud the mind. If you want to achieve something, you have to be very deliberate. Then perhaps you will succeed. Tell me, what have you decided to do about this Gypsy murderer?"

"I haven't decided anything yet. Nothing seems exactly right. But I'll think of something. Now I have time and I'll think of something."

"And that's why you stay?"

She shook her head. "Only part of the reason. Perhaps a small part, I'm not sure. But you've never answered my question, why do you keep me? What do you gain? You've asked me for very little, Javier."

"I imagine you expected it to be different. Whatever I promised in the beginning, you must have thought that sooner or later I'd want to share your bed."

"I did think that once." Sofía let her eyes roam over Javier's familiar face. He was patient with her scrutiny. "I thought it," she said softly, "until I learned you were the alcalde, and until I saw your wife."

The silence lasted for some minutes. Finally Javier spoke.

"The corrida, that must be how you found out. You must have come to a bullfight."

"Yes," she admitted. "Quite by accident the first time. Just because I was near the Plaza Mayor and I had nothing better to do. I've gone many times since then."

He laughed softly. "Funny, that never occurred to me. I knew you weren't an aficionado, but I didn't allow for a woman's whim. Victoria would be amused and tell me how stupid I am."

"That's your wife, isn't it? Victoria must be her name."

"Yes."

"She's very pretty."

"And much younger than I. But I love her dearly, and I believe she loves me."

"Then why?" Sofía leaned over the table, banging her small fist on the dark mahogany. "Why, why, why?"

"Sit down, my dear. I have a story to tell you."

They talked for another hour. When the conversation was ended, Sofía walked with him to the front door of the little house. The night was spring warm and the moon was full. They stood together for a moment, Sofía leaning against the door, toying with the ends of her lace scarf. "Very well," she said at last. "I'm not promising anything, but you can bring him here whenever it suits you."

"Thank you." Javier leaned forward and kissed her cheek. It was the most intimate caress they had ever shared.

❧ 9 ❧

"We have met before," Pablo said.

"Yes," Sofía agreed. "But that was a long time ago. I didn't expect you to remember."

"I've never forgotten your eyes or your voice. I recognized you the moment I walked in the door."

"Javier didn't tell you I was here?"

"Nothing except that I must come to this house and meet someone. I thought it must be a torero."

Sofía smiled. "And are you disappointed? I'm told you're a devout follower of the bulls, hidalgo."

"I am. But I love the flamenco as well. No, señorita, I'm not disappointed. At least I won't be if you'll sing for me."

She didn't use the castanets. Javier had told her Pablo Luis was a purist, someone who understood the art. The hidalgo would say the castanets were meant to accompany a dancer. Sofía raised her arms over her head and began clapping. The friction made her palms sting. She was out of practice. Javier preferred other music to the flamenco. No matter, he wasn't here this evening. Just Pablo Luis Mendoza, whom he'd sent. Like a *majo* after all, she thought. And I'm a *maja*. No, not really. No money was involved in this transaction. "He's bitterly lonely," Javier had said. "There are those who think the bulls are enough for him, but I know him well and he's a cultured and sensitive man, one with a great interest in Gypsies, by the way. I never thought I'd be fortunate enough to find a Gypsy when I began searching for a companion for Pablo Luis."

"A companion, not a bedmate?" she'd asked.

"Perhaps. That's up to you, Sofía. My only concern is that he love you and be comforted by you."

"And you want me to believe that this is some act of Christian charity on your part? That you've taken all this trouble and gone to all this expense only to prepare me to comfort Pablo Luis Mendoza? And only because he's your friend?"

"Believe what you want," Javier had said with a shrug. "My reasons are my affair. I'm simply asking if you'll do it."

"What if I said no? How could you have been sure I'd agree to such an arrangement?"

"In the beginning I didn't care whether or not you agreed. I was taking a woman out of the gutter and making her into my own creation. I expected simply to force her to do what I wanted."

"But now?"

"Now I've grown fond of you. I won't bend you against your will, Sofía. All I ask is that you meet him and see whether you can do as I wish."

So tonight she was in the pretty little parlor of the house she'd lived in for over a year, giving a private flamenco performance for the hunchbacked ruler of the greatest fortune in Spain.

She sang two songs, one about a woman who waited for her lover, one about a young girl's dreams of romance. Pablo listened attentively to both, and smiled his appreciation when she was finished. "There's another one I remember," he said. "You used to sing it for my mother. It's about revenge."

There was something in his eyes. Desperation, she decided. "Do you think often about revenge, Don Pablo?"

His laugh was bitter. "Against whom? God? The fates? If I knew where to revenge myself, I would do so. As it is . . . Sing the song, please."

Still, she hesitated. "How is Doña Carmen?"

Pablo shrugged. "The same. I haven't seen her since my father died. She wants me to come to Córdoba. Some cousin from England is visiting, but I haven't time. There's a young torero I'm grooming for his *alternativa* in July. He fights as El Sevillano, but he's a Gypsy, like you."

Sofía had not admitted to Javier that she'd met the hidalgo before, and that, plus the fact that Don Pablo had known her so long ago, made her nervous. It gave this man a power over her greater than any Javier possessed. She did not want to talk about Gypsies. "I'll sing the song about revenge for you, shall I?"

"I'd like that a great deal, señorita."

She took a deep breath, lifted her hands, and began. *Ay, madre mía. Ay, mi amor. Soy la victima de destino muy duro....*

Pablo began to clap too. Yes, she remembered now, he knew the Gypsy rhythms. In Córdoba he had stayed out of sight and clapped, but he'd never joined her song as he did now. *"Soy la victima de destino muy duro...."* The victim of a hard fate. He was that, for all his wealth. Her nervousness melted away. Sofía felt a wave of tenderness for him, a strange echo of what she'd felt for tiny Sara. In an odd way Pablo Luis seemed to her as helpless as her child had been.

A jasmine twined round the window of the bedroom in her little house. It shed its scent in the June night. Sofía breathed in the sweet smell and stroked the bare skin of the man who lay beside her. There was no moon; the room was in total darkness despite the open window. With the most delicate and tentative of movements she touched his withered arm.

"Don't," Pablo whispered harshly.

"Please, you mustn't be ashamed. No part of you offends me."

"Why not? Every other woman I've been with was repulsed by me."

"Whores, that's all they were. I'm not a whore, Pablo. I care for you."

He made a sound deep in his throat—half pain, half

triumph—and rolled on top of her. He was turgid with the need he'd restrained these many weeks, until tonight, when she'd encouraged him, finally led him to her bedroom and to her bed. But he was no practiced lover. He couldn't woo her with playful caresses or take her with passion mixed with gentleness. Pablo found the opening he sought and drove himself into her and let his desire drown his shame. In seconds it was over. "I'm sorry," he murmured.

"Don't be. I'm not sorry."

He didn't answer for a few seconds. "In truth neither am I. I love you, Sofía. You can laugh at that, tell everyone how Pablo Luis, the hunchback, has made a fool of himself over you, but it's true. I love you."

"I know," she whispered. "That's why we're here."

That was the real reason. Not because of Javier and whatever devious scheme had led him to make Sofía into a woman Pablo could love, then bring them together. Not because she had no choice. She could have refused; Javier said she could and she believed him. Certainly not because she loved Pablo. Whatever she felt for him, it wasn't the love described in the songs she sang. It was tenderness and pity and warmth. And the realization that of all the men she'd known, only this one truly needed her.

"I'm not laughing at you," she whispered. "I'll never laugh at you, Pablo. I swear it."

The Alley of the Dead Dog was a twisted passageway bent between two narrow lanes in the poorest part of Madrid. A gutter ran down its center, stagnant water thick with swill and the urine of men and animals. The cobbles on either side were barely wide enough to allow a man to walk without putting his feet in the stinking mess in the middle. Two beggars approached each other from opposite ends of the alley.

"*Por aquí,*" one whispered when they met by a low door in a crumbling wall. He pushed it open and waited. The second beggar was stooped, apparently with age, but he had to bend yet farther to enter the room. The first man followed a little more easily.

The cellar was fetid and dark, the roof just high enough so the first beggar could unfold himself to his considerable height. Not an old man after all, a young one. "A strange place to do business," Robert said.

"It has been a strange business. And I'm well known. This is one of the few places I'm not likely to be recognized."

"You mean that here in the underbelly of your fine city they don't care about the alcalde who serves the rich."

The first man lit a candle and set it on a keg that would serve as a table. In its sudden light his smile looked like a death's-head grin. "Is it different with the lord mayor of London?" Javier asked.

"No, I expect not. Politics matters little in a place like this. And there are places like this in every city in the world."

"Agreed." Javier reached into the rags he wore and produced a folded paper. He lay it on the splintered wood of the barrel. "My part of the bargain."

"And here's mine." Robert placed a leather pouch beside it. "Do you wish to count it?"

The alcalde shook his head. "I do not believe that after all this you would engage in such an obvious kind of risk, señor."

"No," Robert agreed. "I would not."

It had been almost impossible to arrange this meeting, even after he knew the name of the man in Madrid from whom Domingo borrowed ten thousand reales. He had to raise the money by selling some things from the palace—Maria Ortega's pearls for a start, a few gold ornaments, and part of the table silver. Simple enough for most men, but for a Mendoza to be seen doing so would have been an announcement to the world of the family's plight. He'd needed agents and then agents of the agents, a series of veils between himself and the buyers. It had been done, but with great difficulty and too much time.

After that it took yet more time to inform the alcalde of Madrid that he was known as the secret creditor of the late Domingo Mendoza, and that the debt was to be paid and the security returned. Robert picked up the document and read it quickly.

"You're satisfied?" Javier asked.

"Entirely." Robert stretched out his hand and held the paper to the candle. A corner of it caught fire, and he held it until his fingers were almost singed, then dropped it to the dirt floor of the cellar and watched it burn to nothing. "Done," he said when only a smudge of ash remained.

"Done," Javier agreed, stuffing the money pouch into the front of what passed for a shirt.

Robert looked at the other man, trying to see behind both the disguise and the guarded eyes. "Now that it's over, can I ask what your aim was?"

"That shouldn't be hard to understand. The Mendoza *cortijo* is enormously valuable."

"But to think that for a debt of ten thousand reales it would ever be allowed to pass to you . . ."

Javier smiled again. "One hears rumors, señor. Nothing definite, but a bit of talk here or there. A hint that the mighty Mendozas may not be so mighty after all, that an old man's foolishness was leading him to squander what generations of wiser men had created. In such a situation, it can be worth taking a small risk."

"So we meet at last, Cousin. I regret that I could not be your host in Córdoba, but other affairs have kept me occupied."

"Yes," Robert agreed. "So you've said. How fortunate that we find ourselves in Madrid at the same time."

Pablo gestured with his good arm. "Fortunate, I agree. And this house is certainly large enough for two of us."

It was a twenty-room mansion isolated at the outermost edge of Madrid. Besides being much smaller, this house had none of the exquisite beauty of the palace in Córdoba. It was grand without being elegant, a four-square hulk built a century earlier by a Mendoza who died before he had the chance to occupy it. Robert knew there was a lien on the property. He wondered if his cousin did.

"Sorry this place isn't more comfortable," Pablo said. "It's been used very little. I think I'm the first Mendoza in generations to come frequently to Madrid."

"It's quite comfortable," Robert protested politely. "I'm grateful for your hospitality, Pablo. Your mother was kind enough to suggest that I use it while my business keeps me in the city. We didn't know you were here."

"Of course. Stay as long as you like. I'm not sure of my plans beyond Sunday, but the servants are competent. You'll have no difficulties."

And how long will we keep up this polite chatter, Robert wondered, this little dance of discovery while we take each other's measure. "As long as I'm not inconveniencing you."

"Not at all," Pablo assured him. He cocked his head and studied the Englishman. "We seem to have something in common, the color of our clothes. Few men dress in black in Spain these days. Perhaps they do in England?"

"Not really. Colored frockcoats and breeches are very popular. I've just never cared for them."

"My reasons are different," Pablo said wryly. "But you will have assumed that. Do you know when the black cape and sombrero went out of fashion in Madrid?"

Robert shook his head, and Pablo continued. "With Charles III in 1776. Your Parliament was worrying about the Declaration of Independence by the American colonies, and in Madrid they were making a law that no one could wear the *manteleta* or the broad-brimmed hat. Some idiot convinced the king that it was too easy to conceal weapons and identities in such clothes."

"Your cape is illegal?" Robert couldn't suppress a smile. "The jails of Spain must be very full if even clothes are regulated by law."

"It's not illegal now. There was a riot on Palm Sunday of that year. The masses were as determined to wear the things as the king was that they wouldn't. Fortunately there was a clever man among the fools of the court. The Count of Aranda decreed that anyone could wear what he wanted, but he also made the black *manteleta* and sombrero the official dress of the hangman. Since no one wanted to look like a hangman . . ." Pablo waved his one good arm.

"An interesting story."

"There are many interesting stories in my country," Pablo

said softly. "If you know them, they may help to explain our character. Unless you understand that, you can't know us, even though you speak our language. Do you follow the bulls, Cousin Roberto?"

"I prefer Robert, if you don't mind. And I've never seen a bullfight."

"Ah, I thought not somehow. Perhaps you will be my guest at the corrida this Sunday afternoon? It's the *alternativa* of a young man I've been interested in for some time."

"With pleasure," Robert said. "I do want to understand Spain, Cousin Pablo. Very much."

The noise was deafening. Robert would not have believed so many people could cram themselves into the Plaza Mayor. They stood six deep behind the barriers erected to mark out the ring where the fights were to take place.

Only the alcalde and his wife were seated, raised above the throng in ceremonial chairs on a decorated dais. Robert looked at Javier. Quite a different man from the beggar he'd met with a few days earlier. Today he was resplendent in his robes of office, and smiling at everyone. His wife was a pretty little thing, but her charms paled when compared with those of the young woman who had accompanied Pablo Luis.

Robert tried to look at her without being obvious. She seemed somehow familiar, but if he'd met her before, he couldn't remember where or in what circumstances. When Pablo introduced them, she had given no sign of recognition. Now she turned her remarkable blue eyes in his direction, and Robert was caught staring. He groped for a remark to cover his embarrassment. "Are you an aficionado, Doña Sofía?"

"Not really. I've come here about a dozen times, that's all. Don Pablo promises we'll see something spectacular today."

She looked to Pablo Luis for confirmation, but the hidalgo hadn't heard her. He was studying the bulls penned in the corner and watching the gate through which the toreros would soon enter.

Sofía turned back to the Englishman. He hadn't stopped

looking at her since they were introduced. Except for his brown-gold eyes, he sported no color. His hair was as black as his clothes. He was an eagle, she decided, a powerful bird of prey, ever on the alert and ready to pounce. There was a sense of strength about him; he seemed wrapped in the aura of his powerful family. How easily he could be taken for the hidalgo.

Sofía adjusted her fan so she could see Javier. He had just signaled with his white linen square. "Look," she said. "They're about to begin."

Pablo raised his good arm and pointed to the fighters entering the ring. "¡Mira! There he is, leading the procession." He turned to Robert. "The torero who is to take his *alternativa* always fights the first bull of the afternoon."

Robert started to speak, but his cousin wasn't paying attention. He'd turned to Doña Sofía. "Now, my dear, what do you think of my Sevillano? Wait, don't tell me. Not until after you see him fight."

Sofía was grateful he gazed again at the arena and didn't look at her. She clutched the barrier with both hands and leaned forward, trying to comprehend that the godlike creature displaying such confidence in the face of death, was Carlos. God in heaven, it couldn't be. But it was. The torero to whom Pablo was so devoted was the same Carlos whom Zocali and the others called a coward, the man who had deserted her when she needed him most.

Robert was aware that the woman beside him was agitated, but perhaps it was simply the excitement of the event. The preliminaries were over now, and they were unlocking the pen, summoning the first bull of the corrida. A few seconds passed and nothing happened. Then a black monster surged onto the sand. "Sweet God," Robert murmured. "I'd never have imagined the creature was so huge."

"Over a thousand of your English pounds." Pablo spoke without looking at the other man, his eyes focused on Carlos standing alone, utterly relaxed, the fighting cape—dark pink on one side, yellow on the other—dangling loose from his right hand. "Now is when the bull decides to fight," Pablo said. "He's looking for the herd and peace, he sees only the man, and commits himself to a fight to the death."

Robert saw a flash of motion. Black hide, rose cape, and the gold and silver and blue of the bullfighter's elaborate costume twisted together in a spiral of graceful movement. For a moment it seemed that man and bull were one entity, then the animal charged across the ring and the first mighty olé of the afternoon surged from the collective throat of the onlookers. "What's happening?" he demanded. "I thought the lad must be dead."

All Pablo's attention was on the ring now. He didn't hear the question. It was Sofía who answered. "It was a wonderful pass. A full veronica, remarkably fine, very close to his chest."

She leaned closer to the Englishman, talking as much for her sake as his, because talking stilled the clamor of thoughts and fears buzzing in her head. "They call this the *tercio de varas*. It's the first act of the fight. It includes the torero with the cape and then the picadors."

The crowd screamed once more, drowning out her words. "Watch," she shouted in Robert's ear. "Watch how he lures the bull forward with the cape, then uses it to lead the animal past his body."

Carlos stood absolutely still, his position classically correct. His blond hair had been plaited into the traditional pigtail of the bullfighter. The braid hung halfway down his back in exactly the prescribed manner. He was perfect. They could hear him calling to the bull, making soft sounds and fluttering the cape. The animal charged and Carlos controlled him with complete confidence, leading the animal backward and forward with the cape in another series of stunning veronicas; each time the horns came closer and closer to his thighs, a hair breadth from slashing the flesh.

"Olé! Olé! Olé!" The palms of the crowd seemed to smoke with the ferocity of their clapping.

"Look!" Unconsciously Sofía grabbed Robert's arm. "Look at that!"

Carlos had led the bull into what appeared to be another veronica, but at the last moment he swung the cape up over his head as if he were going to put it on. The pink and yellow folds expanded like a flower in the brilliant sunshine, hung there a moment, then fluttered closed. The bull surged past on the strength of his own momentum. "A farol," Sofía whispered. "I've seen it before, but never like that."

Robert was conscious of her hand gripping his arm. Her fingers dug into his flesh with surprising strength. "*Mi madre,*" she breathed. "He's on his knees!"

The bullfighter had indeed gone to his knees in the face of the bull. But it wasn't an accident, as Robert first thought. It was yet another of those remarkable movements of the cape. The bullfighter had no chance to jump out of the way if there was a mishap. He controlled his enormous opponent on the strength of his art alone. He completed another heart-stopping pass, and when he rose to his feet and extended his hand to the crowd, they exploded in a frenzy of appreciation.

The bullfighter stepped behind the barrier. "What's happening now?" Robert demanded. "Is it over?"

"No, now it's time for the picadors."

Two men on horseback entered the arena. They carried long lances and their horses had one eye blindfolded. "So they will move only counterclockwise around the fence," Sofía explained. "And nothing must be on the bull's right. That's his natural line of exit."

With El Sevillano out of the ring for a brief time, Pablo relaxed his concentration slightly. "This is the part few understand," he told his cousin. "But the bull is given the pic not to torture him, just to wear him down a little, and to lower his head for the charge at the end."

Robert made no comment. It looked like wanton cruelty to him, no matter what Pablo said. A few minutes later it was over and the horses left by the same gate they'd entered. "The *tercio de* banderilleros now," Sofía murmured. "The second act. The torero will place them himself because this is his *alternativa.*"

El Sevillano returned to the arena. He carried two pointed sticks. Robert estimated each to be about two feet in length. They were decorated with ribbons and streamers, and almost before he realized what had happened the torero had run past the bull and planted them on either side of the creature's withers. The crowd cheered again. It seemed he'd done it in a fashion that pleased them. It had been fast enough, God knew.

"Six banderillas," Sofía explained. "Three pairs. Also to lower the bull's head for the final charge. But to excite him too. They say that a good bull grows stronger and braver under punishment."

All six were in place almost before she finished speaking.

A hush fell. The atmosphere changed. A moment before the olés of the crowd had merged into a continuous cheer of approval; now the aficionados were silent. The trumpets sounded a few bars of the paso*doble*. Another man appeared in the ring. "That's Pepe Talosa," Sofía whispered. "He's very famous and a full matador. He actually confers the *alternativa* on Carlos."

Robert looked at her. "Who's Carlos."

"El Sevillano. That's his real name."

She looked flustered. Robert wondered why. Then his attention was drawn back to the circle of sand. The second bullfighter had given a sword and another cape to the first. The crowd was still waiting in silence, but they cheered again when El Sevillano saluted the alcalde. "He's dedicating his bull to the mayor," Sofía explained.

The man, Sofía had called Pepe Talosa left the ring. It was all up to the young one now. Robert did not need to be told that this was the final act of the drama. He could read that in the faces of those around him, in the way Pablo Luis leaned forward as if he were connected by some invisible cord to the young man with the sword, as if they were one person.

"*Buena fortuna*," Sofía whispered.

Robert heard her. There was something going on here he didn't quite understand. Something too intense and personal to be merely part of this arcane sport or art, or whatever it was. He had no time to puzzle about it now. The torero had draped the cape over the sword and, manipulating both with one hand, he was leading the bull into another series of intricate movements.

The danger in which he placed himself was obvious, even to someone who understood few of the fine points. And apparently he did it well. The olés came thick and fast, the colorful blend of man and beast spun like a child's top on the sand. Robert was caught up in the heat and the blazing sun and the virtuoso display, until he was shouting along with everyone else.

Sofía held her breath. It was impossible to imagine that Carlos could equal the capework he had already shown them. He didn't. For five minutes more, shielding the sword with the muleta and holding both in one hand, he was even more graceful, more elegant, more totally controlled and fearless.

A single trumpet sounded. The crowd stilled.

Carlos paused. He held out his arm and turned full circle, including every onlooker in the gesture. He would kill for them; the bull was theirs.

His glance traveled the plaza until it rested on the face of Pablo Luis. He started to turn away, then looked again. His eyes locked with Sofía's. They spoke silent words across the bloodied sand, but beyond that second's hesitation, there was no outward sign that anything had happened.

Carlos drew himself to his full height, stood staring at the bull, who stared back at him, then rushed forward. His body arced upward in a leap of startling height, and while he was still in the air he buried the sword to its hilt in the single vulnerable spot between the bull's shoulder blades.

El Sevillano had killed as incredibly as he fought. He had dispatched the animal with one thrust delivered *a volapié,* with flying feet. The massive black body shook, the beast staggered for the time it took to draw a breath, then sank to the ground. Sofía felt Pablo Luis shudder, as if he, too, had performed this perfect finish to a perfect bullfight.

The people did not respond immediately, awed by the pure poetry of motion they's just seen. Then flowers rained onto the sand, tossed by every woman present. The cheers shook the ancient walls of the Plaza Mayor.

Those shouts would echo the length and breadth of Spain. There was not a town or a village in the land where what had been done this day would not be talked about. Pablo leaned past Sofía to Robert. "Remember what you have seen here, my English cousin. We have bared our soul for you, and you have been present at the birth of a legend."

Sofía knew he would come. She sent Juana to bed and waited for him by the open door of the little house near the Puerta de Toledo.

She heard his pounding footsteps before she saw him. Then he rounded a corner and ran toward her, stopping a few yards before he reached her side.

Carlos stared at her. It was very late, after midnight, and the full moon shone on Sofía's dark hair, lit her astonishing eyes. "It really is you," he whispered.

"Yes, it's me." Her heart was pounding. Looking at him like this, after so long, she was made dizzy by a storm of feeling. Anger, surprise, even the echo of love; Sofía could not distinguish one emotion from another. She seemed to experience everything at once.

"Today, at the corrida," Carlos murmured, "I was sure it was you. Then I told myself I must have been mistaken. Tonight, in the taverna where we were celebrating, I asked Pablo about the woman who had been with him—"

"And he told you my name?"

"No." He took a step closer to her, touched her shoulder as if to prove to himself that she was real. "No, he said very little and I didn't want to seem . . . too interested."

Sofía nodded, acknowledging the truth he had recognized, perhaps without realizing he recognized it. "Where is the hidalgo now? And how did you find me?"

"He is still celebrating. I am afraid he is very drunk. The others, all the people who are suddenly my great friends, they, too, are very drunk. People say more than they should when their bellies are full of wine. Someone mentioned a woman who lives near the Puerta de Toledo who—" He broke off as if he didn't want to say more.

Sofía looked at him a moment longer, then stepped aside. "Come in. We cannot talk in the street."

* * *

"Nothing has changed," Carlos said.

"Everything has changed," Sofía insisted.

"Because you thought I deserted you four years ago?"

"You did desert me."

"No. Why can't you understand?" Carlos sat stiffly on a small couch covered in pale pink brocade. He had grown accustomed to luxury these past years, accustomed to the ways of the *busne* gentry, but he still could not associate those ways with Sofía. It was difficult to believe that he was sitting with her in this fine house and that she was mistress of it. The *busne* had reclaimed her; it was as if her years with the Gypsies had never happened. "I left to get enough money to buy you from Paco," he repeated. "I didn't desert you. I was obeying the law of the Rom."

"So you said. But it came to the same thing, Carlos. You were gone and I was married to that pig, and in the end he murdered my child. How do you expect me to feel?"

"I understand how you feel about Paco. Just not that you blame me. What was I to do, Sofía?"

"You could have taken me with you. Instead, you ran away and left me behind, and everything happened as I told you."

"I thought they would wait two years." Carlos ran his fingers through his hair in a gesture of frustration. He didn't have it in the pigtail tonight, it was swept back and caught in a simple clip. "Until Joselito told me you were married, it didn't occur to me that Zocali would ignore the law and shorten the betrothal time."

"Zocali was eager for his money. You all wanted something from me. The only one who turned out to be different was Fanta." Sofía rose from the couch and paced the room. "Only Fanta really cared for me. Now I can't go back and find her because they will stone me if they see me. The tribe believes that I killed Sara. What do you think of that, my fine matador? Imagine. They raised me and are the only family I know, yet they think I murdered my daughter."

"Fanta is dead," he said softly.

Sofía stopped pacing. "When?"

"A year ago. I see Joselito sometimes. He told me."

She sat down hard on a small green stool upholstered in moiré silk and buried her head in her hands. "A year ago. Fanta was the nearest thing to a mother I ever had and she died a year ago and I didn't know. That's what my life has become, Carlos. I am cut adrift like a log floating in a stream."

"No, you're not alone." He crossed to her, took both her hands in his. They were limp and icy cold. "You're mine, Sofía. You've always been mine. Marry me now. I'm the greatest matador in Spain. You'll have jewels and the finest gowns. We will . . ."

She pulled her hands away and allowed herself a small laugh. "Carlos, don't you wonder how I come to be living in such a house as this? Don't you wonder what I was doing at the bullfight with Pablo Luis Mendoza? He may be your *apoderado*. Surely you know he's not an ordinary manager of *toreros*. He's the richest man in Spain."

"I know that, but . . ." He looked around as if seeing the house for the first time, then looked back at her. Sofía wore a dress of pale blue silk trimmed with black lace. Her hair was swept back into a bun twisted with a rope of shimmering pearls. More pearls glowed in the brooch at her breast.

He leaned forward and grabbed her shoulders, shaking her. "Tonight, the things people hinted at. I didn't believe them. But it's true, isn't it? He's your lover. That obsessed hunchback has bought you? It's because of him that you're here in this house?"

"Not exactly as you think." She pushed his hands away and stood up. "But it comes to the same thing. How else could I survive, Carlos? What do you think a woman on her own with no money and no family and no protection can do? She can be a *puta* or a *maja*, or she can have one wealthy, discreet protector. I am fortunate to be in the third category."

"A *puta*," he said through clenched teeth. "You can make any fancy *busne* explanation you want. You're still a whore."

Sofía's hand shot out, catching him across the cheek. She wore a diamond ring and it slashed his skin and drew blood. "How dare you! You have fewer brains than the bulls you fight.

And a lot less courage. You can kill as many *toros* as you like. You're still Carlos the coward."

He lunged for her, his hands gripping her arms, his strength bending her backward. "*Puta!* Little whore! You're a cheat and a liar. A *busne* vixen. I wish to God I'd left you for the bandits. I wish I'd let El Hambrero eat you alive."

For a moment it was as if a curtain were torn and behind it Sofía saw such horror as her mind could not contain. She gasped and stopped struggling. "Oh, my God . . . Holy Virgin . . . It was El Hambrero that night in the mountains . . ." Her body shuddered with sobs. "I remember. God in heaven, I remember. There was a woman and he cut off her breast and ate it. Then a baby . . ."

"Don't! For the love of Jesus, Sofía, don't remember."

He crushed her to him, all thoughts of vengeance disappearing as her memories triggered his. "It was the worst night of my life. I never wanted to tell you about it. I was glad you'd forgotten. Forgive me for reminding you now. Forgive me, Sofía. Oh, God, I love you so much. I've always loved you. It doesn't matter what you've done. You're still mine. I saved you and you belong to me . . ."

His words went on and on. She didn't hear them. She was aware only of the strength of his arms around her, and the memory of those same arms carrying her to safety so many years before. It was as if the two occasions were one. She clung to Carlos as the only safety in a world of terror beyond imagining. She could hear the screams, smell the burning flesh, see the huge man on the white horse with blood streaming down his beard while he chewed human flesh. "Hold me, Carlos," she begged. "Keep holding me. Don't let him get me. . . ."

"Shh. There's no one who can hurt you. I'm here and we're together and no one can touch you."

For the first time he kissed her lips, tasted her mouth. Even the salt of her tears was sweet to him. Carlos felt her soft flesh melting against his hardness, felt the silk of her gown slide above her waist and the curves of her hips and her buttocks tremble beneath his hands. "You're mine," he whispered again. "You're mine."

They sank to the carpet still locked together, and he finally possessed her. Carlos took her the same way he had rescued her that night in the hills behind the flaming pueblo of Mujer-gorda—in haste, acting purely on instinct, and with no thought for the future.

"What else do you remember?" he asked later, lying beside her in the dark, his face buried in her long black hair, intoxicated with the scent of lemons that clung to her.

"Nothing else. I always thought if I remembered that night I'd remember everything. Who I am, where I came from. But I don't. I remember only El Hambrero."

She shuddered again and he gentled her with soft kisses and stroking hands. "It's all right, *mi amor*. Nothing can hurt you now."

Sofía wanted to believe him, but she knew it wasn't true. "Listen to me, about Pablo . . ."

"Don't mention his name. I want to forget he was born. I want to forget he ever touched you. We'll go away somewhere, Sofía. He'll never find us."

"No."

"I don't understand. What else can we do?" He propped himself on one elbow, studying her face in the milky light of the moon that shone through the window.

"It's too late to run away together, Carlos. We had that chance years ago and we didn't take it. I can't leave Pablo. He needs me."

"You'd let him— I don't believe it! I won't believe it. Don't you understand anything? You belong to me. By right. I brought you out of that inferno and you're mine."

"No, you listen to me for once." She sat up. Her breasts were magnificent, soft and full, tipped with dusky rose. She was heedless of them, once more the Gypsy she was raised to be.

"I told you as soon as you came here tonight. Everything is changed. I am who I am now, not the child I was then. And you've changed. You're not a half-Gypsy freak barely tolerated by Zocali and the rest. You are El Sevillano and all Spain is at your feet. You owe that to Pablo Luis Mendoza. We both owe him everything. I will not see him destroyed. Either by you or by me."

"I cannot live knowing he is touching you here." He put his hand on one breast. "Or here." The fingers of his other hand moved between her legs. "Does he do this to you? This?"

He caressed her intimately, exciting her flesh with kisses such as she'd never experienced, with touches unlike any she'd ever felt. "Does he make you sigh as you're sighing now, *mi amor*? Can he make you tremble like this? Gasp for breath like this? Tell me!"

In reply she spoke his name. One long word that lasted the length of a final shuddering sigh of release. "Carlos, ahhh . . ."

"Well?" He fell back on the carpet, breathing as hard as she was, his skin sheened with the sweat of her passion as if it were his own.

"I cannot leave Pablo," she whispered. "You choose, Carlos. I won't, because I can't."

He flung himself on top of her and gave his answer by pounding her body with his.

The messenger rode through the Puerta del Sol, bent almost parallel with the mane of the bay stallion, one hand clinging to the short reins, the other flailing the animal's powerful left haunch. Ahead of him looming in the moonlight was the forbidding stone hulk of the Palacio Real. He swerved to avoid it and any questions from the guards. An alley on his right was the better choice. The walls of the buildings on either side almost touched the horse's flanks, the pounding hooves splashed stinking sewerage onto the rider's boots. It did not slow him.

There was no time to ride to the stables in the rear of the isolated house on the Calle del Campo—he was still at a full gallop when he reined in by the front door. The bay reared back on its hind legs and neighed loudly in protest. The rider was out of the saddle before the horse's front hooves regained the cobblestones. "A message for the hidalgo," he shouted while he banged his gloved fist on the foot thick oaken door. *"¡Urgente!"*

For nearly two minutes he kept up his ceaseless pounding on the wood. Finally the door swung open on massive black iron hinges. "Are you crazy?" the old majordomo demanded. "Who are you and what are you doing here disturbing us in the middle of the night?"

"I have a message for the hidalgo," the man repeated. "He must leave at once for Córdoba. Doña Carmen is very ill. They think she may be dying."

❦ 10 ❧

The room was airless, the windows tightly closed against the evil vapors that everyone knew carried disease. The bed was on a raised dias against one wall, hung with black curtains. Dark wool carpets were strewn across the marble floor, and, like the bed, the chairs and chests that filled nearly all available space were draped in black. It was not mourning in advance. Doña Carmen had chosen the decor long before she succumbed to this fever.

The smell of blood and urine and dung was very strong. "We've applied leeches every day for a month," the doctor explained to Pablo Luis. "And given her a calomel purge each of these last six days. I regret, hidalgo, there's little more we can do."

Pablo waved a dismissive hand and approached the bed. She seemed thinner. Perhaps the treatment would not cure the fever, but something had relieved the swelling that plagued her these last years. He bent over her, close enough to hear the stertorous breathing and smell the sour breath. "*Mamina*," he murmured, using the affectionate name of his childhood. "It's me. I'm here."

The black eyes opened, focused on him. Carmen tried to lift one hand to touch his cheek and failed. She parted her lips, made a sound. Pablo bent closer. She opened her mouth wider, struggling to force out words that would not come. There was only that whispering noise from her throat. But she must speak. She must tell him that the Englishman was a Jew, and that he lusted to control the house, that the dwarf was his spy. They wanted to deprive Pablo of what was rightfully his. "Jew," she managed to croak.

"I know, *Mamina*," Pablo whispered. "I know. It doesn't matter."

She had to tell him how much it mattered. She must make him understand that his only weapon was the Inquisition. He could find the plaque and denounce the interloper to the Inquisition, then his inheritance would be safe. She managed to form the first part of the word. "Pl—" she whispered. Then she died.

The priest circled the open coffin, sprinkling the corpse with holy water shaken from a palm frond set in a jeweled gold handle. The aspergillum sparkled in the glow of dozens of tall candles, and a shaft of topaz-colored light entered through a stained glass window set behind the altar. Despite all this illumination, most of the cathedral of Córdoba was in shadow. The sanctuary was obscured by its surroundings. The triumphant Christian kings had taken as spoils the vast mosque built four hundred years earlier by the Muslim caliphs, and created within it a Christian church, but the massive sweep of the architecture of Islam defeated the victors.

A forest of marble pillars stretched as far as Robert could see in every direction. The pillars supported arches of different colored stone carved in Moorish filigree so intricate it looked like woven thread. He had no difficulty imagining barefoot Arab men prostrate in prayer, their white robes luminous in the dim light, their scimitars still by their sides. The accoutrements of Catholic worship seemed to Robert a mere and temporary intrusion.

He stood beside Pablo Luis near Doña Carmen's bier, in the place reserved for family. The service droned on, but Robert ignored the buzz of Latin. He glanced at the corpse. Looking at her now, he could almost believe that once she'd been a great beauty. Death had vanquished the bloat that deformed her for the last years of her life. A black mantilla was draped around her hair, and she was dressed in a black satin gown. She looked pretty and peaceful, not like the lunatic who had conspired with him in the wine cellar beneath the palace.

The funeral mass ended and Robert and Pablo turned to follow the coffin on its final journey. The procession left the half light of the church the local people still called *la mezquita,* the mosque, and entered the wide patio that surrounded it. The sunshine of the August afternoon blinded Robert. He closed his eyes and opened them again. Maria Ortega was standing a few feet away, watching the coffin. He saw the hatred and the triumph in her face. The woman knew too much. She was what his father would call a tag end, something remaining to be dealt with. But other things first. The burial. Then Pablo Luis.

It was after dark before the two men were alone in one of the many parlors of the palace. "We've business to discuss, I suppose," Pablo said.

"I won't burden you with that tonight," Robert said. "There are important things to talk about, but tomorrow is time enough."

"I shan't be here tomorrow. Carlos is fighting in Valencia on Sunday. Doña Sofía is meeting me there. I leave at dawn."

"Doña Sofía will be patient. As for the bullfighter, surely he can manage one corrida without you."

Pablo took a sip of sherry. "No doubt he can fight brilliantly without me. It's my need that takes me to Valencia," he added quietly, "not his."

"I see."

"Do you?"

"I think so. But what are you going to do about all this?"

Robert waved his arm in a gesture that encompassed everything the great mansion was and represented. "Neither the palace nor the affairs of the house of Mendoza will run themselves, Pablo."

The other man shook his head. "I haven't the interest or the skill for business. But you know that. It's why you're here, isn't it?"

"I'm not sure I understand—"

"Yes, Robert, I think you do. It's odd, you know, having a hump on your back and a crippled arm. It makes people think there must be something misshapen in your brain as well. There is nothing wrong with my brain, Cousin. Don't underestimate me."

"You think I have?"

"I'm not sure, but if you imagine that I don't know you hunger to control the house in Córdoba, then yes, you do."

Robert waited a few moments before answering. "Someone must control it," he said finally. "It won't run itself," he repeated. "You must realize that."

Pablo stood up. "Do what you like. I'm going to bed. Oh, Robert, there's one other thing. The dwarf, Hawkins. You know he's your half brother, don't you?"

Robert's astonishment showed on his face.

"No, I see you didn't know." Pablo chuckled. "My father told me years ago. Why else do you imagine Benjamin was so solicitous of the poor creature's welfare? Good night, Robert. And adios, I suppose. I shan't see you in the morning. I've ordered the carriage for first light, as I said. God knows when I'll be in Córdoba again. I hate this cursed palace. Stay as long as you like. Look after things here. That's what you want, and it makes no difference to me."

Robert looked from the ledger he was studying to the dwarf sitting on a high stool at the table across the room. "Hawkins, tell me something, who was your father?"

"Don't know, sir. I never knew him, and my mother never said. Hawkins was her name, Sally Hawkins."

"Oh, I see." He didn't see at all. He'd been studying Harry Hawkins every chance he got since Pablo Luis left a fortnight earlier. He still could find nothing of Benjamin in the little man's face or his truncated form.

The notion of sharing blood with the poor sod didn't bother

Robert. Harry Hawkins was made as he was through no fault of his own. What stuck in Robert's throat, the lump of disbelief he couldn't swallow, was the idea of his father having a scullery maid as his mistress. And in his own house. He remembered the way Benjamin had looked when he'd told him about Don Domingo and Maria Ortega. "A wife's a wife," he'd said. "A mistress is something else. A man shouldn't keep them under the same roof. . . ."

God knows, Robert understood that sometimes a man couldn't control his appetites. His own were giving him rather a lot of discomfort lately. His occasional forays to the whore houses of Córdoba were neither satisfying nor safe. He didn't trust those silk sheaths. He'd seen what that kind of disease could do to a man. The risk was too great. He'd have to find a woman of his own. No more whores.

He sighed. He'd told himself that at least six times in the fourteen months he'd been there. This resolution probably wouldn't outlast the others. He'd get the ache in his groin, the hunger like no other hunger, and—

There was a knock at the door. "Shall I see who it is, sir?"

"Yes, Hawkins. And if it's not urgent, put whoever it is on half pay for three months. The servants know they're not to disturb us here." That had been Domingo's rule; he thought it a good one and kept it in force.

The dwarf opened the door and stepped into the passage between the counting room and the palace, closing it behind him. In seconds he was back. "It is urgent, sir. A messenger from Cádiz. He's brought a letter from London."

Robert took it and glanced at the red wax seal. "It's from my father, Hawkins. The first in six months. I was beginning to think he'd forgotten me." He opened it eagerly and scanned it, taking in the elegant handwriting that he recognized at once as Benjamin's. When he looked up he was smiling. "No wonder it took so long, it can't have been a simple thing to arrange. Order a carriage, Hawkins. And an armed guard. There's a very important shipment waiting for us in Cádiz."

"Bullion, sir?" the dwarf asked softly.

"Bullion, Hawkins. Enough to keep our promise to King Charles and a bit over. A little capital at last, so we can begin buying our way out of this unholy mess."

The sleek three-masted merchantman was anchored almost a mile offshore. Six men rowed the hired longboat, but it took an hour to reach her. Robert sat in the prow, listening to the slap of the oars in the water. They drew closer, and he studied the graceful eighty-foot sweep of the *Queen Judith*'s wooden hull.

Like her sister ship, the *Queen Esther,* she was pierced for sixteen cannon, eight to port and eight to starboard. He counted five black muzzles aimed at the longboat. *Queen Judith* was fully armed and clearly had a much larger crew than the nineteen that usually manned a merchant ship.

The ship rode low in the water, her square sails furled. They were close enough now for him to see the red ensign of British shipping that flew from her mizzenmast, and below that the maroon and gold flag of the house of Mendoza. The longboat pulled alongside. Robert stood up. "Ahoy, *Queen Judith!* Permission to come aboard?"

A seaman leaned over and swung a lantern so that it lit the longboat. Confirmation of what his spyglass had doubtless already told him, as was his question. "Who asks?"

"Robert Mendoza. Where's your captain?"

"Right here, Mr. Robert." Rudi Graumann came to the ship's railing. "Permission granted. Bos'n, put a rope ladder over for our visitor."

The sturdy hemp ladder was dropped and Robert scaled it and swung himself onto the deck. "My father wrote that you were in command, Captain Graumann. Are you working for the house of Mendoza again? What happened to the whaling fleet?"

"Nothing's happened to it. At least I hope nothing has. Mr. Benjamin asked me to take this one voyage, because I would know you by sight, Mr. Robert. He seemed to think that was important."

The way the Dutchman smiled told Robert that Graumann

knew the nature of his cargo. "Did he now?" Robert said, chuckling. "Well, my father was always a cautious man."

"Come below, sir. We can talk more comfortably there."

Robert nodded, but he turned to the longboat before following Graumann. "Back to shore with you. You'll be paid as soon as you arrive in the harbor."

"By the freak, señor?" the lead oarsman whined. "Do we have to get our money from the freak?"

"If you want any reales at all, you'll take them from Señor Hawkins. And be polite about it. He's not going to infect you, you superstitious fool." Robert turned to Rudi Graumann. "My clerk is a dwarf, heaven help him. Doesn't make him any less intelligent or trustworthy, but these Spanish idiots think he's been marked by the devil, or some such ridiculous nonsense."

"I imagine it's more trouble to him than it is to you, sir."

"Yes, Captain, you're right, it is. Now, let's go below and I'll have some of that wonderful rum you always have aboard."

They spoke in the owner's cabin. It had been prepared for Robert since the *Queen Judith* left her home port of Blackwall-on-Thames. "It's been a peaceful journey, sir. We're carrying a crew of thirty, just in case. Every man handpicked twice over. First by your father for trustworthiness, then by me because he knew his job."

"Thirty, eh? That explains the ten cannon. But they look too pristine to have been fired. I take it you had no trouble?"

"None, thank God. We loaded the cargo at midnight and set sail at dawn. No pirates or privateers were meant to know what we were carrying, and apparently none did."

"Good, and no French Navy to worry you either. Will I offend your Dutch soul if I point out that Britain once more rules the seas in peace, Captain Graumann?"

"Not my soul, Mr. Robert. But maybe my head."

"Oh, why's that?"

"I don't know what you think of things—as for me, I don't believe this peace between Napoleon and England will last."

Robert took a long drink of rum and picked up the cold meat pie the ship's cook had provided. "Do you know something, or is that just a guess, Captain?"

"A guess—I imagine that's what you would call it, sir. But it's a guess based on what a lot of folk are saying in London and Rotterdam."

The pastry tasted marvelous. He hadn't realized how much he missed good English food. "Frankly I can neither agree nor disagree. Córdoba's the end of the world in some ways. It doesn't buzz with news and gossip the way London does."

"I've always heard that Spain is different. Cut off, you might say, sort of keeps to itself."

"Yes, at least the people do. It's all tied up with their religious fanaticism. But it's a beautiful country all the same, fascinating." Robert swallowed the last mouthful of pie and brushed the crumbs from his shirtfront. "Now, are you prepared to bring your ship into harbor and unlade her, Captain?"

"Whenever you say, sir. And I admit I won't mind being rid of the cargo. At least the hundred tea chests marked Assam."

Robert smiled. "So that's what we're carrying back to Córdoba. Assam tea. Not much profit in that here. Spaniards are addicted to coffee. Never mind, Captain. Some cargoes are better than others. You'll return with sack. Five hundred kegs of sherry wine from Jerez. And one special keg that's for my father's personal use. An amontillado that's twenty years old. Lovely stuff. See that he gets it, will you?"

"I'll do that, sir. When do we hoist anchor?"

Robert glanced out the porthole and then at his fob watch. "As soon as the tide allows. Right about now if I timed it correctly."

The Dutchman nodded. "The tide's just turned, Mr. Robert, and the wind freshened with it. You timed it perfectly. We'll make a seaman of you yet."

"I doubt that." He was starting to feel bilious, the rocking of the merchantman making the meat pie and the rum fight in his belly. "But there are men waiting in Cádiz, and the sooner we get this rather special tea offloaded and on its way to Córdoba, the happier I'm going to be."

"Mr. Robert, may I ask you something?"

"Anything you like, Hawkins. I've been wondering when you

were going to tell me what was on your mind. Somehow I don't think it's that." Robert jerked his head in the direction of the hundred tea chests that rode in a wagon behind them. Each wooden crate held one hundred sixteen-ounce bricks of gold bullion, which made each worth roughly six thousand pounds sterling, or five hundred thousand reales. Together they totaled fifty million reales. Enough for King Charles, damn his avaricious soul, and then some. Precious as the gold was, Robert wasn't seriously worried about getting it safely to Córdoba.

Outlaws were a fact of life in Spain as anywhere else, but a dozen men on horseback flanked the carriage on either side. Each wore maroon and gold Mendoza livery; each was armed with musket and sword. Robert himself had a pair of pistols tucked in the waistband of his breeches. It had been a choice between being obvious and looking invincible, or being subtle and looking innocent. Robert had chosen the first alternative, and so far they were unmolested. He was confident they'd remain so.

"It is and it isn't the bullion," Hawkins said. "I'd like you to break the journey, sir."

"Break it where? Why?" He eyed the dwarf, wondering if perhaps he'd been mistaken to trust him. Maybe the many protestations of loyalty had been a trick and he'd swallowed the bait. But he didn't think so. All Robert's instincts told him that Harry Hawkins was as devoted to the house of Mendoza as he claimed to be. "You'll have to give me a damned good reason to stop before we reach Córdoba."

"There's someone I want you to meet." The dwarf was looking at him intently, trying to convince him by sheer force of will. "It's vital, sir. And we go right by. There may never be a better chance."

"A chance for what?"

"For you to reverse everything Don Domingo did," Hawkins said. "To put the Mendozas on the side of the angels and earn God's blessing."

"The side of the angels," Robert repeated softly. "That would probably be a first for the Mendozas."

Hawkins saw no humor in the remark. "I know. That's why

it's so vital. Just an hour, sir. That's all it will take. And we'll be perfectly safe. I swear it."

He was persuasive. And Robert was curious, and bothered by what Graumann had said, and by the feeling of being cut off from news. Besides, the guard was as formidable at rest as they were on the march. "Very well, an hour. No more, and not if we have to go out of our way."

Hawkins's face was a study in joy; his small body fairly trembled with delight. "I knew it was time. I've been praying to the Virgin to show me the proper moment, and he has. It's not out of our way at all, Mr. Robert. Look up there on the left."

"You mean that stone fortress on the hill? What lion's den are you suggesting I put my head in, Hawkins?"

"None, sir. It's a holy place, the Monastery of the Precious Blood of the Savior. We'll be safe and welcome, I promise you."

Robert walked beside the monk who'd introduced himself as Brother Elijah. They were in a far corner of the monastery orchard, surrounded by trees heavy with apricots and peaches. Apples and pears and pomegranates ripened nearby. He waited for the other man to speak, studying him all the while. The monk was as tall as Robert himself, and just as thin, but he had the holy fire of fanaticism burning behind his eyes. Robert was mystified. What might Hawkins imagine he and this brown-robed monk had to discuss?

"You are not a Catholic, señor?" the monk asked.

"No, I'm not. Did Hawkins suggest you could convert me?"

"Not to the holy faith, though I will pray for you, Don Robert. Perhaps in His mercy God will show you the errors of the Protestant heresy."

Brother Elijah paused. Robert had the clear impression that the monk was waiting for him to deny that he was a Protestant. Well, he could wait until hell froze over. Robert had no intention of handing the Inquisitors another Jew to burn. He was conscious of the pendant with the Hebrew lettering that he still wore beneath his shirt. Mind, they wouldn't need that. All they had to do was pull down his breeches and they'd know. Still, wearing the pendant was stupid. He'd hide it somewhere safe as soon as he returned to Córdoba.

The silence lengthened. Finally the monk made up his mind. "I will trust you. On Harry's word. Let us sit down, Don Robert. No one will overhear us, I promise you."

"I'm not much bothered if they do or they don't," Robert said easily. "I've no secrets to tell you, Brother Elijah."

"I know. But I have some to tell you. Not secrets perhaps. Truths. The sort that no one in Spain is supposed to speak aloud. Harry tells me you have Spanish blood, for all you're an Englishman."

"That's true."

"Of course it is, you're a Mendoza. Descended from the mighty house that has shaped so much history and done so much damage . . . And yet, do you know, I have been thinking a great deal about the Mendozas lately. On balance you have been less bad for Spain and Andalusia than those higher in the aristocracy. And you're a good deal richer than all of them."

Robert thought of the bullion surrounded by guards in the forecourt of the monastery. "Frankly, yes, we are. Do you want some sort of contribution for your good works, Brother? Is that what this meeting is about?"

"Not exactly." The monk pushed back his brown hood and turned his face to his guest. Robert realized that the man was younger than he'd first thought. A livid scar stretched from his right ear to the corner of his narrow mouth. Now, how would a man of God get a scar like that? "Let me begin by admitting that I am not what I seem," the monk said.

"No, I was just deciding the same thing." Robert put his hand on the butt of the pistol still at his waist. He'd not been searched or asked to disarm, and he hadn't offered to do so. "What are you, then?"

"Nothing that threatens you," the monk said quietly, noticing the movement of Robert's hand. "What I mean is that I'm not a simple man at peace with his God. That's what we're supposed to be, but I'm not."

"Peace isn't always easy to come by, at least not the sort you mean."

"No, but that's what I came here to find—peace, time for prayer. I haven't been successful."

"Am I permitted to ask why?"

The monk clenched his fists in his lap. "Because the suffering of my fellow Spaniards gives me no rest. How well do you know us, Don Robert? Are you aware that we are a nation still in the Middle Ages? That the aristocracy despises the Bourbon monarchy, that our politics are rotten and ruled by personal animosity and reciprocal fear, that the upper class has absolutely no patriotism and is moved only by greed, that their disdain for those beneath them has made us a country of a few rich and a great many poor who have no hope of being anything else?"

"I've heard all those accusations," Robert said. "I don't know that they're entirely accurate."

"Every word is true." Brother Elijah gestured at the orchard. "Look at this. Paradise, isn't it? But do you know why there is lush farmland in Andalusia? I'll tell you. Because the Moors dug canals for irrigation. No Christian ruler before or after them bothered. In the far north they have enough natural water. Here we have the canals of the Arabs. In the rest of the country there's nothing but arid wasteland."

The monk rose, began pacing, his hands tucked into the sleeves of his robe, the knotted cord at his waist swinging as he moved. "Spain lives by bringing in silver and gold from her colonies. You, sir, live by lending money that almost inevitably is to be repaid by the next treasure ship from America and the Indies. How long do you imagine those distant lands will allow themselves to be raped for the benefit of the so-called mother country? We've seen revolution in North America and in France. Soon we'll see it in Spanish America as well."

Robert leaned back, trying to take the measure of the man who spoke so passionately. He was not, as he'd admitted, what he seemed. "Let us say that I agree with your assessment, for the sake of our discussion at least. What remedy do you propose, Brother Elijah?"

"Napoleon."

Robert caught his breath. "That's a strong cure for any disease. It could well kill the patient."

"The patient, as you call her, is Spain. And she's already dying. The very same conditions I described existed in France before the revolution. That's what made it happen."

"And brought in the rule of the guillotine," Robert reminded him.

"Yes. That's my point. Napoleon is a much better choice than civil war. He has put an end to the atrocities in France."

"Perhaps. But as you pointed out, I'm not a Spaniard. I don't involve myself in your politics."

The monk sat down again, leaning toward his visitor, his speech fast and sure, the result, as he'd said, of long hours of thought. "You're a Mendoza. And I'm told that at the moment you control the house here in Spain, de facto if not de jure. That kind of power can never be neutral. You must be with us or against us, Don Robert. There's no other way."

"With or against whom?" Robert asked quietly.

The other man's body relaxed slightly, the passion under control once more. "A small group seeking to make this a country where there is justice and freedom."

"Your Church hasn't much of a record in that regard."

"Not my Church, only the venal men who sometimes act in her name. This time they must not prevent her from taking the side of the angels."

It was the same phrase Hawkins had used. The Mendozas can be on the side of the angels, he'd said. Perhaps. Be that as it may, Robert had no intention of missing this opportunity to discover exactly what these angels planned to do. "I can make no commitments," he said slowly. "But I will hear what you have to say. And I won't put the house of Mendoza in open opposition to you without telling you first."

"Do you swear to that, Don Robert?"

"I give you my word, Brother Elijah. My word as a Mendoza. It comes to the same thing."

"Yes, I believe it does." The monk reached into the deep pocket of his brown habit and withdrew a folded bit of paper. "Here is the name of the person who can tell you more."

Robert took the note but didn't look at it. "One question—what's Harry Hawkins's role in all this?"

"Harry is one of us in spirit," the monk said. "Though there's little he can do, poor creature. But he prays for us. He's a saint, you know."

Robert waited until they were once more on the road to Córdoba to look at the name written on the slip of paper the monk had given him. His eyes widened in surprise and he read it a second time, then he turned to Harry Hawkins. "You're an Englishman still, aren't you, Harry?"

"Depends what you mean, sir."

"What I say. A son of English soil, devoted subject of his gracious British majesty, King George III."

"No, not exactly, sir."

Robert drew back in exaggerated horror. "What? Treason, I say!"

"Don't mock me, Mr. Robert. I was born in England, yes. My blood's English blood. But, as I told you, I've been here twenty-seven years, as many years as you've been on this earth. I speak the language of Spain, follow their customs, eat their food. And Spain, thank God, is a Catholic country."

"So your loyalties are here," Robert said softly. "Yes, I understand. But how much do you know of this gaggle of revolutionaries you're involved with?"

"I'm not involved with any revolutionaries," the dwarf protested. "I simply believe in justice, Don Robert. My confessor introduced me to Brother Elijah. He thought I could help him because of my position with the house of Mendoza." He shook his outsized head. "I never could until today. It's the answer to prayer that you came, Mr. Robert. And that I was able to take you to the monastery."

Robert didn't reply. The monk had said the dwarf was a saint. Perhaps he was. More important was how much Hawkins knew of the people involved in this secret group and their aims. Most important of all, who had a higher claim on his loyalty, the house of Mendoza or Brother Elijah?

*   *   *

Robert kept a tight rein on his horse and slowed him to a canter, deliberately holding back and making the other rider come to him. These foothills of the mountains north of Córdoba were mostly scrubland, fit only for grazing goats. This place was called a ranch, but he saw no cattle, and no horses other than the two that were now only a few feet apart.

"Good afternoon, Don Robert," Maria Ortega said.

He took his time before answering, studying her. She looked very fine. She sat sidesaddle with practiced ease, her polished boots gleaming beneath her long black skirt and short black bolero jacket. Her hat was black too. The dark outfit was relieved only by the gleam of her red hair and the cluster of yellow marigolds tucked beside her ear beneath the hat's broad brim. "Thank you for coming to meet me, Doña Maria."

"Brother Elijah told me to expect word from you. So I wasn't surprised when it came."

"Ah, yes, the passionate monk," Robert said softly. "Am I to believe that he's the explanation for your . . . shall I say, your alliance with Don Domingo?"

"I was Domingo's mistress for the cause, yes," she said frankly. "You needn't mince words with me, Don Robert."

"And how was that cause served? That's what I can't figure."

"We cannot succeed without the house of Mendoza. Certainly not here in Andalusia, quite probably not in all of Spain. There was no hope of getting Domingo to cooperate willingly. He was not a man of vision. I had to use other methods."

"They won't work with me, señorita."

"I know. So I thank God that Brother Elijah has convinced you."

Robert shook his head. "I only said I would listen and talk further. I'm committed to nothing."

"It's a beginning."

"If you want more, you'll have to tell me who else is involved."

A rabbit scurried through the brush and Maria's horse backed. She tugged expertly on the reins and brought him once more to Robert's side. "I can't do that. I don't know most of them anyway. That is how we protect each other. The Inquisition still uses torture, and none of us can be sure we will be glorious martyrs if we're put to the test."

"Except Harry Hawkins, perhaps. Your Brother Elijah tells me he's a saint."

"He may well be," she agreed. "Because of what he has to bear. But he knows nothing that could incriminate anyone else. Nothing about me, for instance."

"Or about the true motives of Javier, the alcalde of Madrid?"

He could tell by her eyes that he'd struck home. It had been a guess, a blind shot, and it had found its mark. "Javier is absolutely committed to our cause," she admitted.

"So you arranged for him to lend Domingo ten thousand reales and get the *cortijo* as security. You helped him get a foot in the door, a bit of control over the house of Mendoza. That is what happened, isn't it?"

"It's what I tried to make happen. We need the Mendoza influence. I already admitted that."

"If you want my help, you'll have to convince me you're worthy of it. And that it is in the best interests of the house of Mendoza for you to have it. Otherwise I'll be your enemy and I won't lose. Make no mistake about that, Doña Maria."

"No, never fear, I won't." She turned her horse's head in the direction from which she'd come. "I have to go now."

"But we'll speak again?"

"Whenever you wish. Adios, Don Robert."

"*Hasta luego,* Doña Maria."

She started to ride off, then swung her mount around and rejoined him. "One question, if I may." He nodded. "What did you do with my pearls?"

"Sold them. Thanks to you, there was a shortage of cash for a time. That isn't true any longer."

"I see. I'm glad you've solved your problems, Don Robert, but it's a pity about the pearls. They were a particularly fine strand. I was quite fond of them."

It was October before Robert saw Doña Maria again. This time he went to the house. It was little more than a simple farm cottage, a single-story structure made of adobe and nestled into the side of the mountain. It was chilly up there at night. A fire of pine logs burned in the grate and warmed the thick white walls and the red tile floor. "Do you live here alone?" Robert asked.

"With only three servants. A friend kindly lent me this place when you turned me out."

"Don't expect me to apologize for that. You deserved it."

Maria leaned over and poked the fire, raising a brief flurry of aromatic sparks. "Perhaps. At least from your vantage point."

"From anyone's. You suborned Domingo, shamed his wife."

"For the cause," she said. "I told you that."

"And did you murder my cousin for your cause?"

She raised startled green eyes to his face. "Murder! No! Who told you that? Domingo died of a heart attack."

"So I've heard. I also heard that in the final days you were giving him something to make him mad. Perhaps it also killed him."

She shook her head. Tonight the flowers in her hair were white, and they cast pale shadows on her cheek. "I gave him opium—to deaden the pain. He was in constant agony. I'd been giving him opium for years. It probably lengthened his life, not shortened it."

"I see."

Without waiting to be invited, Robert poured himself a tot of brandy from the decanter sitting on her table. She raised one arched eyebrow but said nothing. "I imagine opium also deadened Domingo's senses," Robert said. "Made him more manageable. It must have been fairly easy to get his signature on various documents when he was drugged."

"Yes," she admitted. "But my original intentions were good."

"I believe there's an old saying about that, señorita. Something about the road to hell."

She stood up, leaning against the mantel of the fireplace. "You may call me señora. I've been married. Tell me, do Jews believe in hell?"

"I'm not here to discuss theology."

"No, neither am I. What have you decided?"

"Nothing. I still don't know enough of your plans."

"Simply to wait until the right moment to rid ourselves of this incompetent king, and to invite Napoleon to help us do so, if that seems possible."

"Spain will become part of France in that event."

"No," she insisted. "It never will. Napoleon is far too wise to imagine that Spaniards will forfeit their independence. We will be an ally of France. And following her example, there will be a change in our laws. The Inquisition will be banished. Ordinary people will have an opportunity for a better life."

"And pigs will fly," Robert said softly. "Doña Maria, you are mouthing the nonsense of liberals and reformers everywhere. The world seldom accommodates idealists."

"It will happen. You'll see that it will. Especially if you'll help us, commit the wealth and the influence of the house of Mendoza to our side." She spoke with passionate conviction. Her cheeks glowed with color. Her lips grew moist and parted. Beneath a green velvet gown her breasts rose and fell with each breath she drew.

"You're a remarkable woman," Robert said. "I can't help but admire your devotion to your cause, whether or not I give it much chance of success."

Maria looked at him for a long moment. "I'm a free woman," she said finally. "Regardless of the way society views my freedom. I do what I want, take what I want, just like a man."

"And what you want is for Spain to be something other than what she is, and your wanting is to make it happen."

"That's not what I meant."

"What then?" he asked.

"I want you. Don't look like that. I'm not speaking of anything permanent. I mean now. Here. Don't you find me at all desirable, Robert?"

"Yes, I do. But I'm used to choosing my women, not being chosen by them."

"Then you don't know what you've been missing. Compliance isn't passion, Englishman. You have a lot to learn." She unlaced her bodice while she spoke and dropped it from her shoulders. Her breasts sprang free. They were as magnificent as he'd first judged them to be. "Come here," she said, and he went, unable to resist.

Maria moved into his arms like the practiced courtesan he knew her to be. And she was right—her unbridled appetites, her responses to his caresses, were unlike anything he'd ever known. She demanded pleasure and showed him how to supply it, and he found himself more excited by the giving than he'd ever been simply by pleasing himself with an acquiescent whore. When her strong legs gripped his hips and she moved beneath him in a frenzy of desire, he found himself climbing a pyramid of delight, spurred ever higher at her urging.

"More," she whispered. "More. Not yet, not yet. More." And finally. "Now, now I want all of you."

He reached the pinnacle and gave himself up to ecstasy.

It was dawn before he was dressed and ready to leave. "I still haven't promised anything," he reminded her.

She was stretched naked on the couch beside the dying fire, languid, sated, her dark red hair streaming loose, her flesh creamy soft with loving. "I know. I never thought to win you over with lovemaking. This was for me, not Spain."

"And for me?"

"I hope so, yes."

"Yes," he agreed.

"You'll return to me, then?"

"I want to," he admitted.

"Then do so. I'll always be happy to see you. Whatever happens about the rest."

He nodded and started to leave, then stopped. "I nearly forgot. I brought you something."

He gave her a small packet and she opened it, then looked up at him with a wide smile. "My pearls."

"It took a while to buy them back, or you'd have had them sooner."

"I'm happy to have them now. Thank you, Robert." She slipped them around her neck and they lay lustrous and lovely against her naked breasts.

❧ 11 ❧

Dawn was a hint of gray in a wet, black world. The line of carriages battled thick yellow mud that clogged the spokes of the wheels and splattered the flanks of the horses, then clung to them like a chalk shroud. On the horizon Seville was obscured by sheets of rain, a misty goal at the end of an impossible journey. "A poor beginning," Pablo said. Neither of his two companions answered.

Sofía pulled her cloak closer. She was chilled deep inside herself. Sitting between Carlos and Pablo, she was frozen by an iciness that touched her soul. She could feel no body heat reflected from either man, no hint of the fires she shared with both her lovers.

This is the cold of death. The thought came with the suddenness of revelation, and once born, it would not leave. Someone would die this week in Seville. Perhaps she? Sofía didn't know. But there would be death.

Pablo leaned forward, moving the velvet folds that curtained the window of the carriage. "Look."

Carlos and Sofía looked in the direction of Pablo's pointing finger. There was a line of robed and hooded men on the crest of a hill to their left. They held short, stout weapons, a multitude of snakelike leather thongs attached to ebony handles. The only sound was the whistling of the whips as the men walked slowly, beating their own backs and shoulders.

"*Los flagelantes,*" Carlos whispered.

The trio in the carriage watched the men descend the hill and move out of sight. "The excesses of Holy Week in Seville." Pablo sighed. "I'll never understand them. But I suppose you two are accustomed to all this."

Sofía didn't answer. Carlos grunted something barely intelligible.

Did he wonder? she thought. Did it puzzle Pablo that when the three of them were together, Carlos and she were virtually mute? Oh, God, why had she come? Because Pablo wanted it. "It will be wonderful, Sofía," he had insisted. "Stop worrying about the Gypsies. They can't touch you when you're with me. It's the most exciting corrida of the season. Semana Santa in Seville, how can you miss it?"

He was like a child in his newfound zest for living, his delight in being with her, his need. She couldn't deny him. So she was there, sitting between the two men who each had an irrefutable claim on her body and her soul.

There was a house waiting for them in Seville. For the Mendozas there was always a house waiting. This one was borrowed, Pablo explained. From a grandee who owed the family so much money, he never wanted to be in the same town at the same time as the hidalgo. Like the others Sofía shared with her protector for weeks or days at a time, this house was big and beautiful and fully staffed. "I'd much rather have his house than repayment of his debt," Pablo said, chuckling. "The poor fool doesn't understand that. Maybe he doesn't know it's Robert who worries about the Mendoza coffers, not I."

Sofía allowed a maid to remove her cloak. How easily she accepted such services now. In the ten months since Pablo took her to bed and assumed control of her life, she'd become practiced in the mannerisms and prerogatives of a lady accustomed to wealth.

They were expected and everything was prepared. Sofía moved closer to the fire crackling in the gate. A footman brought wine, and she drank it eagerly.

"Will you come with us to the *ganaderia*, my dear?"

"No, Pablo, I think not, if you don't mind."

"Of course not." He took her hand, pressed it to his lips. She could feel Carlos's eyes watching them. Pablo seemed oblivious to that malevolent stare. He never noticed. She was screaming inside and he never noticed that either. "What is it like when you and he are alone?" she'd asked Carlos.

"Different," he'd said. "When I'm with him we talk about the bulls, the fights. We are the same as we've always been."

Sometimes she created an imaginary conversation for them. "I make love to her quickly," Carlos would say. "I don't sleep beside her the way you do. I take her wherever and whenever we have the opportunity. And you should see her, Pablo. You should see how she writhes and moans, how she craves what only I can give. With you she's sweet and gentle, with me she's a bitch in heat. . . ."

There would be no such tale told this afternoon. The matador and his *apoderado* would go to the ranch providing the bulls for this most prestigious of all corridas. They would inspect the animals that Carlos would fight in three days time, when Holy Week was ended and the fiesta of Easter began. They would discuss courage, tactics, bravery, a new movement of the cape that Carlos was perfecting. They would not talk about Sofía.

"I'll stay here," she said. "Take care, Pablo. Wrap up well. It's cold."

He smiled at her and touched her cheek. "Don't worry, little one. Rest. Will you meet us at church later?"

"Yes, of course."

Like the cathedral in Córdoba, the one in Seville had been a mosque for some five centuries. Its single tower had been built by the Moors, and it still gave the church the name every Sevillano used, La Giralda. It stood on the edge of the neighborhood once occupied by the Jews of the town, now known as the barrio de Santa Cruz.

She had been in La Giralda only a few times. All her previous Holy Weeks in this city had been spent in the Triana, kneeling with Zocali and Fanta and the rest in the Church of Santa Ana. Today the great arched spaces of the cathedral were dark and draped in black and mourning purple. She glanced at the massive litters bearing the heroic-size statues that would later be carried through the streets. Standing at the back of the church waiting for the penitents who would shoulder them, the tableaus were static and unimposing.

"Over there," Carlos said, finding her in the crowd of worshippers and taking her arm. "He's waiting for you."

His fingers burned her flesh. "Did he say anything?"

"He said a lot. It was all about the bulls. I've told you and told you, he doesn't suspect a thing."

"Carlos, we can't—"

"Shh. Not here. Come, he's waiting."

She joined him where he stood to the left of the high altar. Pablo Mendoza was above gossip, insulated from it by his enormous wealth and his total lack of interest in society. Like almost everyone else, the Church was in the debt of the Mendozas. Not even a bishop would dare to criticize what Pablo did. If anyone in Seville was scandalized by the hunchbacked hidalgo appearing in public with his mistress, they would say so only when no one could hear.

The procession entered from the rear; priests and bishops vested in purple were led by a white-robed acolyte carrying a black-draped crucifix, others with candles, and yet others swinging censers that wafted clouds of fragrant incense. They approached the altar in double file, each pair genuflected, then they divided and moved to either side of the long choir. Mass of Wednesday of Holy Week had begun.

When it was over, the various societies who had vowed themselves to this public profession of sorrow for sin formed up around the statues and hoisted the pallets draped in velvet and silk and woven gold. Barefoot, carrying their enormously heavy burdens and wailing their sorrow, the penitents brought the images into the streets.

Seville was alive with people, an ant heap of flesh. Throngs surged forward to touch the holy figures paraded past them, but they fell back and cleared a path when the hidalgo was recognized. Pablo and Carlos and Sofía reached the Plaza of Santa Maria la Blanca just as a clock somewhere chimed five times. They stood and watched the procession approaching on the Granada road. A dozen matadors dressed in their *trajes de luz* carried the image of El Cristo de la Salud, the patron of the bullfighters, into the city from its home in the hamlet of San Bernardo. Carlos knelt in the street as they passed.

The flagellants appeared again, beating themselves until they drew blood that stained their white robes. The rain finally stopped and there was an apricot sunset that kissed the city with flames.

It went on all night. At dawn, lying beside a sleeping Pablo in the curtained four-poster of the absent grandee, Sofía could still hear their cries of remorse.

She, too, was a penitent. Why wasn't she out there in the night, weeping and wailing and screaming her grief to the heavens? She was a betrayer of trust. Not just Pablo's, Sara's too. Another year had passed and she had not tried to avenge her daughter's murder. She had not looked for Paco. First ease had deadened her hate, now fresh guilt served the same purpose. Somewhere outside a man begin to sing the classic *saeta*, a spontaneous outpouring of his devotion. The song floated in through the open window, and Sofía listened until his voice faded and her cheeks were wet with tears.

For forty-eight hours the processions continued. Each followed a prescribed route, each had a particular priority established years before, and was jealously guarded by the guilds and confraternities that sponsored them.

The Virgin de la Esperanza appeared from the parish church of La Macarena, and that of Jesus del Gran Poder from the Church of San Lorenzo. In the Calle del Sol they acclaimed the Virgen de las Angustias, and the procession of the Virgen de la Soledad was borne along the Calle de Trajano. Late in the afternoon of Good Friday the last statue was carried across the Triana bridge. The river reflected the wounds of the martyred body of the savior, El Cristo de la Expiración, and the Sevillanos gave themselves up to a final agony of grief.

"It's over at last," Pablo said. "Sweet Jesus, what a strange city this is. A strange city in a strange country. Do you know why El Colón chose Seville as his center of operations and not Cádiz?" Sofía shook her head. "Because," Pablo continued, "in 1492 Cádiz harbor was full of ships crammed with the Jews their gracious Catholic majesties had just expelled. We're given to excess, my dear. It seems to be part of our character. In Seville most of all. They say three of the flagelantes died. Beat themselves to death. Some years it's more, isn't it?"

Sofía nodded. She watched the procession disappear in the direction of the cathedral, then looked toward the Triana hills. "Some people have a lot to be sorry for."

He saw the direction of her glance. "Not you," he said gently. "Forget it, little one. It's over. They have no claim on you any longer. Besides, it's Easter now, or it will be the day after tomorrow. Enough of penance, it's time to celebrate." He took her hand. "Since I found you I have learned how to enjoy a fiesta."

Having purged itself of anguish, Seville was ready to celebrate with him. The brilliant late April sun shone on the Plaza de Toros on Easter Sunday, and the aficionados screamed their joy at the closeness of the passes of the matador who was their own, El Sevillano. "Olé! Olé!" they shouted, and their cheers echoed and reechoed in the plaza. As an unknown Gypsy boy they had despised him; when he took the name of their city because it was also his, Carlos became their idol. "Olé!" they shouted again as he executed another series of veronicas and finished with the cape behind his back in a stunning *gaonera*.

"He gets better and better," Pablo murmured. "More fearless with every bull he fights."

Less caring of his life each time he made love to her, Sofía thought.

She searched the faces of the crowd for any that were familiar. Once she thought she saw Zocali, another time Paco. A second glance proved it was neither man. They wouldn't recognize her now anyway—not as the woman of the hidalgo in a satin gown and a *madrileño* lace shawl—and if by chance they did, they would do nothing. The aura of wealth and privilege that surrounded her put her beyond their reach. Sofía knew it, but she kept looking, reaching for another fragment of her past that had disappeared almost as completely as those early years she could never remember.

On the bloodied sand of the arena Carlos killed his bull, and amid the wild cheering of the crowd the president of the corrida awarded him both ears as a mark of his stunning bravery and skill.

"You'll have to decide now," Maria said. "You can't keep sitting on the fence."

"Why not?" Robert stroked her hair lightly and listened to crickets chirping a May song beyond the window. She pleased him, this woman. She did not share the single-minded obsession of Brother Elijah; he had come to believe that the devotion of Maria Ortega to the cause of the liberals was a fascination with power, not a thirst for justice and equality. Robert was at ease with a woman who was not a dangerous fanatic, but simply lusted to be near the throne, so Maria's charms had not paled these seven months. He did not love her, but he understood her. Sometimes he enjoyed talking to her as much as bedding her. "You think because they've broken the Peace of Amiens anything is different?"

"Of course it's different. England refused to leave Malta, and she has declared war on France. Napoleon has rightly decided that England will be his enemy until he invades her."

"Thank you for interpreting the situation for me," he said gravely. "I never understood politics until I had you to explain them."

"Stop teasing me. You're a Mendoza. You understand very well."

"And who are you? That's something you've never told me, Maria. Who are the Ortegas that they leave you free to do whatever you want?"

"No one makes me free. I take my liberty, Robert. I thought you understood."

"Maybe." He cracked an almond and chewed it thoughtfully. "Doesn't answer the question though. Who spawned you? Even you must have parents."

"Of course I have. Had, rather. They're both dead. My family is from Barcelona, in the North. I haven't seen them in years."

He wanted to ask how many years, but he thought better of it. If he did, she'd probably scratch his eyes out. He guessed she was over thirty. Perhaps thirty-five. Seven years his senior. And though she admitted having been married, she would never say if her husband still lived or, indeed, tell anything about him. She'd told him a more important fact, however. "There's something you should know. I'm barren."

So the husband, whoever he'd been, probably wasn't sorry to let her disappear into the life she chose. And Robert needn't worry that she'd present him with a bastard child. It was a perfect arrangement—except that she kept nagging him about this choice she thought he had to make.

Robert, did not intend to make a choice. As far as he was concerned, there wasn't one to make. He would wait and watch. Napoleon was expanding his power in Switzerland and Italy and creating vast camps and harbors and arsenals at Boulogne, Calais, Dunkirk, Ostend. His intention was obvious—he meant to invade England, as Maria said. But to do that he had to move his troops and supplies across the Channel, and Addington had commissioned Nelson to prepare a fleet to destroy every French vessel. It was a time to wait.

Maria was still chattering. He gave up his reverie and turned to her. "For heaven's sake, woman, stop talking. I don't ride all the way out to this miserable ranch in the dead of night to listen to your nagging." He laughed when he said it, and she took no offense. Instead, she twined her arms around his neck and lifted her mouth to be kissed. He took her slowly, luxuriating in the pleasure she provided. Thank God he didn't have to bother about those infernal silk sheaths.

A week later Doña Maria sent a messenger with a note that said merely "Come." That was unusual. She never summoned him. He went to the ranch of his own accord whenever it suited him, and she was always waiting. He decided to obey her command. It might be important. If it was merely cheek, he would deal with it quickly. As soon as he handed the reins of his horse to a servant, he knew she wasn't alone. He could see an unfamiliar carriage near the stables to the right of the house.

"Robert, these men must speak with you. Javier you already know, the other gentleman is—"

"Permit me to introduce myself merely as Manolo, Don Robert." The man who had interrupted Maria clicked his heels and bowed. He wore a dun-colored frockcoat and brown satin breeches, but the clothes did not sit comfortably on his short, muscular form.

Handsome sod, Robert thought, but he'd wager the man usually wore a uniform of some kind. Maria busied herself pouring glasses of sherry. Robert took one and sipped and continued to wait. He sensed that Javier was studying his face, and he turned to him expectantly.

"So you've outfoxed me," the mayor of Madrid said.

Robert smiled. "I'm not exactly aware how, but delighted to hear of it nonetheless."

Javier smiled too. "You, Don Robert, have taken charge of what I thought by various methods to control. You've turned out to be the Trojan horse."

"An army of Greeks, all by myself? Remarkable, and I never realized."

"Robert!" Maria said sharply. He turned to her quickly, his brown eyes flashing a warning and she looked away, visibly chastened by his sudden anger.

"Perhaps we'd best get to the point," Robert said. "I take your meaning, Don Javier, but I'm not sure where it's getting us. You wanted to see me, gentlemen, about what?"

"About thirty million reales," Manolo said quietly.

"Indeed? That's a lot of money."

"It's the amount the house of Mendoza has promised to lend the king in less than two months," Javier said. "And despite all Maria's efforts to see that it couldn't happen, and all my maneuverings to see that it wouldn't happen, you brought the money from England to Cadiz. Now it's waiting at the Palacio Mendoza until you decide to hand it over."

"I would say that your spies were efficient," Robert said. "But I wasn't particularly secretive about my movements."

"No," Manolo agreed. "That was an interesting course of action."

"The Mendozas seldom hide their light under a bushel, señor."

Javier refilled his sherry glass. "I believe you have an expression in English, 'rattling one's saber,' something like that."

"Yes, I've heard the remark." Robert tipped some of the pale fino into his own glass and waited again.

Manolo cleared his throat. "Permit me to clarify. Javier and Maria, acting from the most patriotic of motives, made enormous efforts to deflect the aid of the Mendozas from Charles—"

"Who is the rightful king of Spain," Robert interrupted.

"The rightful king, yes. As Maria Luisa is the rightful queen. Please, Don Robert, let us recognize that all Spaniards are united in wanting the best for the nation. The argument is only about what is best and how to achieve it."

"Very well, I can accept that. And though I'm not a Spaniard, I, too, want the best for your country. I bear Spain no enmity, Don Manolo. So why should I renege on a promise made by my house to Spain's legitimate ruler? I presume that's what you're suggesting."

"Not exactly," Javier said. "We ask you only to stall a bit. Possibly to send the thirty million reales through a mediator rather than directly."

"What mediator did you have in mind, the First Consul for Life of France?"

"Napoleon will be king of France soon," Maria said quietly. "I have that on good authority."

"Fine." Robert lifted his glass. "Gentlemen, I've decided to make myself king of Córdoba, or all Andalusia perhaps. Since it seems that anyone who likes can declare himself a royal, why not me? Would you care to join my court?"

"You mock us, Don Robert," Manolo said softly. "But we speak of serious matters that we feel deeply. Charles IV is a blathering idiot, the Infante Ferdinand is little better. The Queen, may God bless her, is the only one of the family fit to rule. And she requires a consort worthy of her."

Ah, yes, he had it at last. Manolo was a Spanish diminutive of the name Manuel. So this was Manuel de Godoy, the royal guardsman said to be Maria Luisa's lover. And it appeared he lusted for higher honors. Robert did not allow his face to betray his insight. "Let us speak seriously, then. What would you have me do?"

"Delay the payment to Charles," Javier said again. "And consider the possibility that your thirty million reales might be invested more wisely. For the greater benefit of your house, perhaps."

"What benefit?"

Manolo cleared his throat. "The right of the house of Mendoza to establish a Spanish national bank."

Good sweet God! The plum Domingo had nearly choked trying to swallow, the right to control every shipload of gold and silver from the colonies, to issue banknotes as legal tender. "It's an interesting notion," he said softly. "But who is going to grant such a franchise?"

"The ruler of Spain," Manolo said. "He will sign a decree and it will be done. By fiat. I think, Don Robert, you and I both know that's the way things are accomplished."

"Perhaps," Robert said after some moments.

"Perhaps what?" Javier demanded.

"Perhaps everything will happen as you describe." Robert set his empty glass on the table. "There are forty days before the thirty million reales are due in Madrid. Shall we wait and see what happens in that time? Now, Doña Maria, gentlemen, good night to you. Thank you for a most interesting conversation."

When they were in Madrid Sofía still spent much time in the little house behind the Puerta de Toledo. Pablo had bought it from Javier and given her the deed. On this June Sunday she sat at her dressing table, preparing herself to be beautiful at the corrida that would take place in a few hours. The rose silk gown she would wear hung on the door of the wardrobe; at the moment she was dressed in only five petticoats. Her breasts were exquisite, particularly when she lifted her arms to fuss with her hair. Pablo was stretched on her bed, watching her, his adoration plain in his eyes. "I love the fact that you are without shame," he said softly.

She didn't understand at first. "Oh, you mean these." She cupped her hands beneath her breasts and laughed. "Gypsy women are taught no modesty above the waist."

"Then I'm glad you were a Gypsy for a time. Because now you are my *Gitanita*." He paused for a moment. "Sofía, there's something I want to ask you."

Her heart beat faster. Every day she expected the accusation she wouldn't be able to deny, the charge of her infidelity. But Pablo didn't seem angry. Rather, he was embarrassed. "What is it?" she asked, leaning across the space between them to touch his cheek tenderly. "You can ask me anything."

"Am I incapable of fathering a child?"

She pulled back, stunned. "No! I mean I don't know . . . What makes you—"

"It can't be you. You've already borne a daughter. I thought that because I can make love I can sire, but maybe not, maybe because of . . ." He lifted his shriveled arm, then dropped it and whispered, "It must be me. You aren't pregnant and we have been together a year."

Sofía turned away and toyed with the silver-backed brushes on her dressing table. "Do you want a child, Pablo? A bastard child?"

"Not a bastard, no."

"But that's what it would be."

"Not if we married."

She did not answer for a few seconds. "I'm already married, you know that," she said finally. "I'm the wife of Paco. We were married in the crypt of Santa Ana. A marriage blessed by the Church," she added bitterly.

"These things can be arranged. The Gypsy Paco isn't the point, my dear. I'm the point."

Sofía shook her head. "No, it isn't you. It never occurred to me that you would think that. I have made certain not to conceive. I assumed you wouldn't want me to."

It was his turn to be startled. "How could you do something like that?"

"It's not difficult. The women of the tribes know what herbs to use."

"But that's murder. I thought that was the very thing they blamed you for—about your daughter, I mean."

"To interfere with the child in the womb or after birth is murder. That is against the law of the Rom, though *busne* women were always asking for herbs to expel the baby once it started. What they got was never more than a bit of parsley chopped up and made to seem something else. But there are other plants that make a woman barren for however long she chooses. The law of the Rom doesn't forbid those."

"The law of the Church does," he said stiffly.

"I thought I was doing what you wanted, Pablo. If I've displeased you, I'm sorry." She wasn't sorry. How could she have a baby and not know if it was Pablo's child or if Carlos was the father? What if she gave birth to an infant with blond hair and gray eyes. What would Pablo think then? No, it was impossible.

"I don't think you're sorry." He stood up and moved behind her, looking at her face reflected in the mirror. "Look at you and look at me. Why would you want a child that might be marked like its father." He turned away. "It was stupid of me. Sometimes I convince myself you really care for me, and I forget."

Sofía jumped to her feet. "Pablo, don't say things like that! It's not true. I do care. I really do. I know the man and I don't see the afflictions. You must believe me. Don't go . . . Please . . ."

He had shut the door behind him before she finished speaking.

Twenty minutes later, when the maid Juana knocked and entered, she was still sitting at the dressing table half dressed. "*Doña Sofía, el matador está aquí.*"

She shivered. Think of the devil, Fanta used to say, and you will see the tip of his tail. "Tell him to wait in the patio. I'll come soon."

She wiped the tears from her eyes and patted fresh powder on her face. She looked at the rose-colored gown, but she wasn't yet laced into her corsets and she didn't wish to take the time now. Sofía slipped a yellow satin dressing gown over her shoulders, then tied it tightly at the waist and picked up a black lacquer fan. Her hands weren't trembling, she noticed. She was very calm, and sure of her decisions.

Carlos waited by the pink-blossomed oleanders in the central courtyard. He wasn't yet wearing his *traje de luz*. "What are you doing here now?" she asked. "Why aren't you dressed for the fight?"

"I'm looking for Pablo. There is some problem with the bulls. The ones we saw at the ranch the other day haven't come. They've sent others in their place."

"He's not here. Juana must have told you."

"Yes, she did."

"Then why didn't you go to look for him somewhere else?"

He took a step forward and touched her shoulder, his fingers inching down toward her breast. "I wanted to see you anyway. No, don't push me away. What's wrong?"

"I had an argument with Pablo, I'm upset. Go away, Carlos."

His eyes narrowed. "What did you argue about?"

"Not what you think. Pablo wants to marry me."

"You can't," he snarled. "I won't permit it. Besides, you're already married."

"I know. He says that can be arranged."

"Arranged how?"

"I don't know. The Mendoza wealth, probably. They can buy anything, why not an annulment?"

He tried to pull her into his arms, but Sofía pushed him from her. "Don't. It's broad daylight, you fool. Juana could be watching."

"Damn Juana. Does she spy for Pablo, do you think? Maybe he knows everything. Maybe he's toying with us like a cat with a pair of mice. Run away with me, Sofía. Let's leave all this lying and pretending. How can we go on in such a miserable existence?"

"Pablo doesn't spy on me. He trusts me. That's what makes it so terrible, and that's why I can't leave." She fanned herself.

The summer heat was oppressive even in the shade of the oleander trees and the twining vines. "He wants a child."

"*Dios mío,* why do you torment me like this? You can't have his child. And if you did, could you be sure it was his?"

"No. That's why I won't do it." She sounded so calm, so sure of herself. How could she say these things and pretend they weren't tearing her apart? Because she had to, just as she had to say the rest of it. "I've decided something. I didn't plan to tell you until after the corrida, but since you're here—"

"Tell me what?"

"That I've decided to end it."

"I don't understand."

She snapped the fan close. "Yes, you do. You and I, it's over. I won't go on deceiving Pablo like this. Leave, Carlos. Don't come back. At least don't come back without Pablo."

"Just like that," he said softly. "The hunchback offers you marriage and you turn me out."

"It's nothing to do with marrying Pablo. I don't know if I'll do that. I know only that I can't keep living with the fear and the pain you bring me."

"What about my pain?"

"I can't be responsible for that, Carlos."

"You are responsible. Ever since I pulled you out of the hell of Mujergorda you have been my reason for living. You are in my debt, Sofía. You owe me your life."

"No!" She spat out the word. "Don't say that ever again. I'm tired of hearing it, Carlos. I'm tired of being beaten with that stick. Go away. For the love of God, just go away. Every woman in Spain adores you. They throw flowers at you, swoon at your feet. Go take the spoils of the matador and find someone who won't hate you and herself each time you touch her."

He lunged for her, grabbing the fan from her hand and flinging it across the patio.

"Leave me alone. Are you mad? I'll scream . . ."

His arm whipped out and struck her across the face—once, twice, three times. The blows were much harder than the single one she'd dealt him that first night so many months before.

Sofía sank to the ground, collapsing at his feet in anguished sobs. The yellow robe opened, exposing her breasts.

"Gypsy men all beat their women, I'm told," a soft voice said. "It's their custom, isn't it?"

Sofía raised her tear-stained face. Pablo stood beside the jasmine vine, his black hat and cape backed by the shining green leaves and fragile white blossoms. Everything he knew showed in his eyes; they were liquid with grief. "No," Sofía whispered. "It's not what you think. Carlos and I knew each other as children. We never admitted that to you, but—"

"Stop," he said. His voice was still normal. Only the eyes screamed at her. "No more lies, Sofía. They aren't necessary any longer. Odd, that a beating can be as intimate as sex." He turned to the matador. "Carlos, you have to dress—you're expected at the corrida in less than an hour. If you don't hurry, there won't be time for your prayers." He looked at Sofía again. "I apologize for disturbing you. I came back only to say I was sorry about our quarrel earlier, and to ask you to come with me to the plaza and watch Carlos in yet another triumph. Too bad, isn't it? How very sad the whole thing is, and how stupid I've been."

The hidalgo could not stay away. He stood in his usual place by the barrier in the Plaza Mayor. Around him the crowd screamed its excitement as the bullpen was unlocked and the first bull of the afternoon came through the gates. It was not the animal Pablo expected; this one was red with wide horns at an uneven angle. The small dart planted in his withers displayed the colors of the proper ranch, but this was not the proper bull. There was something not quite right in that first charge—a slight swerve perhaps.

The crowd sensed something wrong. He could feel an undertone of concern beneath their shouts of ecstatic expectation. Pablo took a deep breath and felt a surge of joy war with the despair in his heart. Suddenly he knew exactly what would happen, and he was glad.

Carlos stood behind the burladero, the screened gap in the

barrier reserved for the fighter. His most trusted assistant, a man Pablo had found for him when his training began four years earlier, entered the ring and played the bull with the cape a time or two. To fix it, as they said, to give the torero an opportunity to assess his opponent.

Come out, matador, Pablo thought. Come out and see what's waiting for you.

Usually he trembled when Carlos began his first passes. It was as if his withered arm held the cape, as if he, Pablo, were the reason for the wild cheering, as if he drank deep of the intoxicating danger and the lust for blood and victory. Today his whole body shuddered at the charge of the animal. Today he was not the matador but the bull.

I'm going to kill you because you have killed all there was of life in me. I have so little and you have so much, and even that little you profaned and stole from me. See my horns. Look at them. Look at them before they gore you to death.

The toss came in the second *tercia*, in the act of the placing of the banderillas.

See my contempt for you, matador? I do not even choose to kill you when you are making one of your famous passes. I deny you the honor of death in a moment of glory. I do it as you go by me now. You have dismissed the banderilleros and chosen to place the sticks yourself. Because you are crazy with joy today. Today you think you have finally banished the humpbacked fool and the woman is yours. But you will not live to enjoy her, matador. Know that as you charge past me and I turn my head and drop it and lift you. Both my horns are in your belly now, matador. When I fling you off, they will rip upwards, and cut out your heart.

Twenty minutes later someone remembered the hidalgo who had been the matador's *apoderado* and closest friend and went to look for him. He was still standing by the bullring, weeping as if his own life had ended.

It was Pablo's manservant who found him the next morning. The hidalgo had hanged himself from the chandelier of his bedroom in the Mendoza mansion on the Calle del Campo. He wore a bullfighter's *traje de luz* of maroon and gold. No one had ever seen him dressed thus before. He must have had the suit made secretly, probably years earlier. It was specially tailored to accommodate the hump on his back and his crippled arm.

❧ 12 ❧

The two years since Pablo's suicide had been fraught with crises, and decisions that Robert alone could make. He, an Englishman, was the hidalgo. Sometimes he wondered what people thought about that. Nothing, if their reactions to him this chilly October morning were anything to go by.

Wherever he walked in Cádiz, Robert saw hectic preparations for the Fiesta of San Rafael to be held in a few days on the twenty-fourth. No one paid him any attention, certainly they seemed totally unaware of the drama waiting to be enacted a few miles away.

Robert was not unaware of it. He had wagered everything on one calculated gamble. He was going to win because he had to—anything else was unthinkable. He would celebrate with Cádiz. Music, song, dancing in the streets—a party as only Spain could make a party.

There were posters everywhere, crude but colorful drawings announcing a week long corrida and the visit of some singer called La Gitanita. A flamenco artist from the look of her. The posters bore little more than sketching, but they indicated a woman wearing a ruffled Andalusian gown with her arms raised over her head and castanets in her hands. Robert paid scant attention to the posters. Time for that later. Now he was waiting for two men, his brother Liam and Harry Hawkins.

Liam came first. He arrived the night of the eighteenth, in a carriage surrounded by an armed guard. He kept glancing over his shoulder as if the hounds of hell were chasing him.

"Stop looking so damned frightened," Robert told him. "It's Villeneuve and his armada Nelson's after, not you."

"It's hardly his lordship that worries me," Liam said stiffly. "Spain and England are at war. I'm an enemy alien."

"So am I. Don't forget I'm an Englishman too."

"The way you look, I might have forgotten. Have you adopted all their ways, Robert?"

"Not all, just the ones that suit me. In any event, no one in Spain is bothered by one civilian more or less, no matter his nationality. Come upstairs, we can talk in comfort."

He led Liam to a suite of rooms over the sprawling Mendoza warehouse. In the sheds at ground level, consignments of sherry awaited shipment. Above them was an apartment of six large rooms lavishly furnished with typical Spanish formality.

"Very grand," Liam said, surveying the spacious salon. Stiff gilt chairs with red velvet seats lined the walls; behind them hung tapestries depicting hunting scenes. The polished oak floor was covered by a Turkey carpet woven in dark maroon and dull gold. The center of the room was occupied by a carved ebony table on which stood half a dozen many-branched silver candelabra.

"Not my taste, Domingo's," Robert explained. "Or perhaps some hidalgo before him. I haven't bothered to find out, since I'm seldom here. I just came now to meet you and—" He broke off. "Never mind, come into my study. You'll find that homier."

He'd furnished the study to suit himself—two large, comfortable chairs upholstered in soft green leather, a number of small tables supporting brass oil lamps, a big desk carved from African teak, and shelves of beautifully bound books in Spanish and English. "Better?" he asked.

"It's very nice. But I still think we should have met in Gibraltar."

"Feel safer there, would you? British soil and all that. But I need to be here, Liam. And I need to talk to you."

"That's what your letters have been saying for the past six months. Frankly, if Father hadn't insisted, I still wouldn't have made this journey."

Robert poured wine for both of them. "Father sent me here to take over Córdoba. I've done it."

"So you have. I'm not denying your accomplishments, Robert. Business has never been better from the Spanish end, and thank God it has. At home we're in a real mess."

"The taxes?"

"Yes. That damned government."

"But it's all to defeat Napoleon. You despise this self-styled emperor, don't you, Liam?"

"Of course I do. But the battle's to be won or lost at sea. They'll never defeat Napoleon on land."

"Perhaps," Robert said. "It's all up to Nelson, then? In your opinion?"

"Yes, but much good he does us when his ships chase off to the West Indies on some game of hide-and-seek with that ass Villeneuve. A pox on both of them."

Robert looked out the window toward the harbor. It was cluttered with masts. "They're not in the West Indies now," he said quietly. "Nelson's a few miles out to sea, and the Spanish and French armadas are right here in Cádiz."

"I know that. I'm not blind, man." Liam rose and went to stand beside his brother. "What are they waiting for, do you think?" Despite his hostility to the whole business of military maneuvering, his voice was tinged with awe. "God, they look invincible."

"As to what they're waiting for, I'm not sure. But they are bloody good ships. I built and paid for fifteen of them."

"Fifteen! Fifteen warships to attack England. You *have* turned Spanish, haven't you? I was joking before—apparently I spoke the truth."

"Stop looking at me like that. Sit down and listen. This is why I sent for you. I couldn't put it in a letter. I had to make a choice, Liam, and I chose."

"Spain rather than England."

Robert slammed his fist on the table. "The house of Mendoza rather than any single nation on God's green earth. That's what we're about, Liam. That's what you and I were born to, whether we like it or not. Because Spain is allied with France, she was obliged to contribute ships to that fleet down there. And if Napoleon wins, we win."

"Depends on who the 'we' is, doesn't it?" Liam demanded. "I could say that if England wins, we win. The English Mendozas win."

Robert knew there was truth in the remark, but he wouldn't admit it. He'd fought that battle with himself for months before he made his move. Then, after Pablo hanged himself, after Napoleon declared himself not king, as Maria had predicted, but emperor, after half a dozen more meetings with Manuel de Godoy and Javier and Elijah, he had decided. Because the prize they offered was beyond his power to refuse. "The Mendozas are one house," he told his brother. "One entity. And——" He paused, took a deep breath, then said it. "If we prevail here, we are to be empowered to create a national bank of Spain."

Liam stared at him. The enormity of the announcement stunned him. "You're sure?" he croaked at last.

"I'm sure. I have it in writing from the man who will be king of Spain, and a confirmation of sorts from the new emperor himself."

"But fifteen ships," Liam repeated. "You paid for the building of all of them?"

"Yes. Fifteen ships of the line. Four of them three-deckers mounting better than a hundred guns."

"Great God! What did it cost?"

"Nearly two hundred million reales. Better than three million pounds sterling. Father provided the seed money, by the way. I was persuaded that Charles IV was not a worthy recipient of the bullion Rudi Graumann brought."

"But the rest—you must have pledged everything." Liam was reeling with the scope of the gamble, and with the fact that the whole incredible sum was wagered against the country that had sired him, and Robert.

"Near enough as makes no difference. Practically all our loans are secured by gold and silver due from the Spanish colonies. I pledged those."

Liam turned ashen. "All of them?" he asked in a harsh whisper. "Every farthing the house will earn for—"

"For the foreseeable future," Robert interrupted. "I spread the risk among bankers here and in Switzerland and Prussia and Italy. There's no single heir to Córdoba's power if I lose. For God's sake, Liam, have a drink. Get hold of yourself. I had to do it. There was no other way to raise the money. I couldn't very well ask you or Father. Especially since I'd heard about the taxes. But think of it, Liam, we will become the bank of Spain. We'll have a stranglehold on every precious cargo that docks on these shores, complete control over the purse strings of the nation."

"And if you lose?"

"Why do you keep saying *you*? If *we* lose is more like it."

Liam shook his head. The mane of light hair had some gray in it now. He looked older than his thirty-six years. "No, you're wrong. You made this decision of your own accord, Robert. You didn't consult me or Father and—"

"I couldn't. Dammit, Liam, why can't you see that? Letters take weeks, sometimes months. I had to decide."

"You didn't consult us," Liam continued as if he hadn't been interrupted. "But you're not the house by yourself, Robert. You're not some . . ." He searched for a word. "Some Medici prince or Oriental potentate. You don't rule by divine command, by your own fiat."

Robert waved a dismissive hand.

Liam stood up, visibly drawing his dignity around him. "Very well, you've made your decision. There's nothing I can do to stop it now. They're out there, your warships and Napoleon's. And Nelson's. We'll just have to see what happens, won't we?" He turned to go.

"You're staying, surely," Robert said. "I've had a room prepared for you here. I presumed—"

"Thank you, but I think I prefer a public house. Just for a few days, until I can make arrangements for another overland journey." He nodded toward the harbor crammed with warships. "There's not much hope of getting home that way."

"Liam, listen, I have a source of information. Whatever happens, we'll be the first to know. We can use that to advantage. There's this dwarf, Harry Hawkins is his name. Absolutely trustworthy. I put him on a fishing brig a few miles offshore. He can see what happens and he'll send word."

"I don't think I care for that sort of advantage," Liam said stiffly. "But I remember Hawkins. Father sent him away the year you were born. I was just a nipper of six, but he's not the sort one's likely to forget. Poor sod, I hope you haven't put him in mortal danger too."

Four days later, at first light, a messenger raced down the port street toward the Mendoza warehouse. He was a boy of ten and he'd been brought ashore in a swift cutter. Others were behind him; the brigantine he'd been on was not the only fishing boat near the Cape of Trafalgar on the twenty-first of October. The dwarf had told him he would earn a beating if he didn't get this letter into Don Robert's hands before anyone else brought the news to Cádiz.

The child was breathless and sweating when he dashed through the big doors of the warehouse. Despite the hour, a few men were trundling kegs of wine from one place to another. "Where is the hidalgo? This is for him, *urgente*."

"Right here." Robert stepped from the shadows in the rear of the cavernous space. He'd not slept more than a few hours since his meeting with Liam. He had spent this night inspecting a shipment from one of the bodegas in Jerez, for lack of some other outlet for his nervous energy. "Give me the packet, *niño*." He studied the boy's face. The lad was trying to look grown-up and implacable, but something of what he'd seen showed in his eyes. "Bad, was it?" Robert asked softly.

The boy nodded. "Terrible, Don Robert. Everywhere blood. Everywhere. The sea was red."

It was on the tip of his tongue to ask who had emerged victor from the carnage, but he wouldn't do it. For one thing, the lad could be mistaken. They had heard the boom of the cannons all yesterday; the echo had been carried to shore on the easterly breeze. In a battle such as this must have been, no inexperienced child could be sure which ships were sunk and which still afloat. Besides, he wanted to be alone when he learned his fate. "Well done, *niño*," he said instead. "You'll be rewarded." He motioned to a man nearby. "See he's given drink and food. I'll be above and I'm not to be disturbed."

"*Sí*, Don Robert."

He climbed the stairs to his apartment and stopped to wash the dust of the warehouse from his face and hands before going to his study and opening the packet. It was wrapped in oilskin. Inside were four closely written sheets in Harry Hawkins's neat hand.

We could see both sides quite clear, Nelson's twenty-seven vessels, and the combined force of thirty-three under Ville-neuve and Admiral Gravina. Nelson himself was aboard the *Victory*. I could see him plain as you like with the spyglass. Wearing all his medals he was, sir. Looking very grand. I admit I felt some pride. Every ship had added more topsail, so we knew it wouldn't be long. Then, about half eleven it was, the man with me who can read the signal flags told me the *Victory* was sending a message down the British line. "England expects that every man will do his duty"—that's what it said, sir. I couldn't hear them, but with the spyglass I could make out the seaman cheering. It was hard not to be impressed with them, sir. Nothing like that happened on our side. We had the advantage of them in ships and firepower, but the men didn't look to have that same hunger for battle. I hope you'll forgive me for saying so, Mr. Robert, but I think that's why it came out as it did.

Robert stopped reading and stared out at the harbor. The weather had changed, and during the night a strong wind had blown the gun smoke from the horizon. The Atlantic glittered in the rising sun. How peaceful it looked now.

He'd been so sure, so convinced the risk was nowhere near as great as it seemed. Despite everything he'd said to Liam, the thought that he might gamble and lose had never really crossed his mind. With one brilliant stroke he'd intended to make the house of Mendoza in Córdoba a seat of such power it would be first for generations to come, not just in Spain but in all Europe. He'd even entertained the idea of expanding into North America. And it was gone, all the power and all the glory.

He didn't need to read the rest of Hawkins's letter, but he felt compelled to drink every bitter dreg.

I'm fairly sure Nelson is dead, but what's certain is that they won. Nineteen of our ships surrendered, sir. The rest were sunk. God save us, Mr. Robert. God bless the house of Mendoza. You did the right thing, sir. I'm sure of it. And even though it looks bad now, I know God will remember that you acted rightly and you'll be blessed.

Ever your humble servant under Jesus Christ,
Harry Hawkins

Robert folded the sheets carefully and rewrapped them in the oilskin. Then he pulled on his cloak and left the warehouse and went to the public inn where Liam was staying. He found his brother breakfasting in the taproom at a table in the rear. He was alone and no others sat nearby. Giving the Englishman a wide berth, no doubt.

"Here, you can read it and cheer." He threw the letter on the table. "The news will be all over soon enough. I saw some small boats heading for shore on my way over here. But this is the first word."

"Nelson won?" Liam whispered the question.

"Yes. And so have you, at least according to the way you put things the other day. No bank here, but Napoleon will never dare to invade England after this. What's more, Britannia rules the waves for good and certain now. Probably forever."

"Robert, listen, I'm sorry. I mean it. I've been thinking. I know you did what you believed was best. What happens now? What about Córdoba?"

"Córdoba's dead. It will take a while for the last rattle. Most of the loans aren't due for some time. The blood will trickle away slowly, and the corpse will have a fitting tomb. The palace and nearly all the Andalusian holdings are still free and clear, but Córdoba's dead."

"Will you be coming home, then? Father will want to know."

"I don't think he will. I doubt Father will be eager to see me after this."

"You're wrong, Robert. You're his favorite. One error in judgment won't change that."

Robert shook his head. "Yes, it will. Anyway, I've no interest in going home. I'll just stay here and sit by the deathbed. That's an old Spanish custom, Liam, sitting beside a corpse until it gets cold and starts to stink. Let's say it's one of the ones I've chosen to adopt."

Robert was drunk for the next three days. Eventually, when he could pour no more wine or brandy down his throat, he staggered back to the apartment above the warehouse and passed out.

He woke naked in stifling darkness. The curtains around the bed and at the window were drawn, and while he had no memory of it, apparently his manservant had undressed him. Robert pushed aside the tapestry hangings and stumbled to his feet. Sweet God, how his head ached! He made his way to the window, tugged the cord of the curtains, and threw open the casement. Judging by the sun, it was late afternoon, and warmer than it had been. He breathed deeply and felt the fresh air enter his lungs and revive him a bit.

"Indalencio!" Crossing the room to pull the bell rope seemed too difficult. He preferred to shout. "Indalencio, get in here. I need you!"

"Sí, señor. I am here."

"A bath, man. Sweet God, I stink. And a drink."

"The bath is prepared, Don Robert. I have been keeping it hot." The valet was half Robert's size, but he took the hidalgo's arm in an offer of support.

Robert shook it off. "I can walk, Indalencio."

He staggered to the dressing room, where a copper tub full of steaming water waited. A huge kettle hung over a brazier filled with burning charcoal, its spout issuing yet more steam. The warm, moist air of the small room comforted him even before he lowered himself into the bath.

"Ah, that's better. Now, Indalencio, a drink. I'd ask for the hair of the dog, but you wouldn't know what I was talking about, would you?"

"No, señor. But I have prepared a drink for you." The little man held out a silver goblet.

Robert took it and sniffed suspiciously. "Smells like sherry. Oloroso. But it's warm."

"*Sí*, Don Robert. *Vino oloroso caliente* with a raw egg. *Está muy bueno ahora.*"

"Hair of the dog," Robert muttered. "Just like I said." He emptied the goblet in one long swallow.

Half an hour later he was washed and dressed in clean clothes. Physically he felt a great deal better. As for the rest, no bath could ease his mind. A walk perhaps. Clear the cobwebs from his brain.

It was dusk, but the streets were empty. The Spaniards usually paraded at this hour, greeting and examining one another, the young men ogling the young women and the señoritas returning the scrutiny from behind their fans, trying to elude the watchful eyes of their chaperones. Robert noticed a string of lanterns suspended around the plaza where the bullfights took place. Ah, yes, the Fiesta de San Rafael. No one was likely to allow the defeat of an armada to prevent a fiesta. But they wouldn't stage a corrida after dark. Curious, he walked to the plaza.

A man sat on an overturned crate at the end of the narrow street that debouched onto the open square. He barred the way. "*Qué pasa?*" Robert demanded.

"A concert, hidalgo. To enter, everyone must pay one real. Even the nobility," the man added, enjoying his moment of power.

He was too curious to take offense and fished in his pocket for a solitary coin to give to the man. They had erected a wooden stage at the end of the plaza where the president of the bullfight usually sat. Two men sat there now. One had a guitar, the other a tambourine, but neither was playing. Robert heard the sound of castanets from someplace to their right. Of course—the flamenco singer the posters had advertised.

The sound of the castanets went on for a moment before she came into sight. It caught the attention of the crowd, stopped their chattering. They were leaning forward expectantly by the time the tambourine joined the rhythm of the castanets. A few seconds later the man with the guitar ran his fingers over the six strings, and the most erotic melody in the world rippled into the night.

She walked on slowly, still making music only with her fingers. She was dressed in a black and red Andalusian gown, tight to her hips, flaring out in a sea of ruffles below. There was a tall comb in her hair and red roses tucked behind her ear. He knew her, he was sure of it. He couldn't see her clearly enough to be certain, but . . .

Then she opened her mouth and that incredible, haunting voice of such stunning purity made him remember everything.

"I didn't connect Doña Sofía with the Gypsy girl in the posada near Seville until tonight," he told her later when they walked together on the street behind the wharves.

Sofía didn't smile. "In a way neither did I, until a year or so ago. She was part of one world, the hidalgo's woman part of another."

"But you put them together."

"When I had to, yes."

"I'm sorry."

She was startled. "Why should you be sorry?"

"It never occurred to me that you would be in need. I simply assumed that Pablo had made some kind of arrangement."

How could she explain what her *true* need had been? Could the hidalgo have given her absolution for her sins? Washed the blood of Carlos and Pablo from her hands? No, nor could she explain that nothing else would satisfy her.

"It wasn't your responsibility," she said. "And I wasn't really in need. I had my house in Madrid, a lot of jewels. I was in no danger of hunger, Don Robert. Don't feel guilty on my account."

"Please, in a way we've been through a great deal together. Can we be just Robert and Sofía? And if there was no need, then why . . ." He let the question trail off. What she did was none of his business.

"Why do I sing in public and remove myself from polite society?" she supplied. "No, don't be embarrassed, it's an understandable question. But a mistress, even the mistress of a Mendoza, is never really in polite society." He thought of Maria Ortega, but she was still speaking and the notion melted away. "Besides, there was a need, though not the sort you meant."

"What, then?"

"The need to be independent, the need not to rely on anyone but myself for securing my future."

"So you went back to singing in posadas." He was unconvinced of that wisdom, and his voice betrayed it.

"No," Sofía insisted. "Not the way I did when you saw me years ago. I travel with two musicians, the men you saw tonight, but they are employed by me, not the other way around. And I sing only by prior arrangement, and only at the most important fairs and fiestas in Spain. I do not beg for coins after a performance, Robert. I'm paid because people pay to see me."

"Like a matador," he said, then regretted the analogy. "Sorry, that was thoughtless of me."

She shrugged. "It's been a long time. You are entitled to forget."

"But not you?"

Sofía turned to him, studying his face in the milky moonlight, wondering how much he knew or had guessed. She read no accusation in his brown eyes. "A long time, but a lot of blood," she said softly. "No, I haven't found it easy to forget."

"Matadors risk their lives every time they enter the arena. And Pablo Luis was a haunted man from the moment he was born. None of it was your fault."

"Perhaps."

He noticed her pull her shawl closer around her shoulders.

"You're cold. I shouldn't keep you talking out here at this hour. You're staying at the inn, I imagine."

Sofía nodded, and they turned and began walking back toward the town. "When will I see you next?" he asked before he left her.

"I sing here for the last time tomorrow night. Then I must leave. I'm to sing again next week. In Córdoba, as it happens."

"Will you dine with me after tomorrow night's performance?"

"If you like."

"Yes, I do like. You're a breath of fresh air, Sofía. I find that very welcome at the moment."

"Something's bothering you, isn't it?" she asked. Then, with a degree of perception that surprised him: "The defeat of Admiral Gravina and the armada was a business reverse for you, wasn't it?"

"You might say so," Robert admitted. "But we have more pleasant things to discuss. Until tomorrow evening, *Gitanita*."

She held out her hand and he kissed it, then bowed and turned and walked away.

He was amazed at himself, chasing after a woman when his life was in shambles, his dreams blown to bits off the white cliffs of Cape Trafalgar. Yet he wanted her. He wanted to stifle the agony of defeat with the fire of . . . what? Sex? Not exactly, victory of a sort.

"Sofía, ride with me to Córdoba, send your troupe on ahead. We're both going to the same place, so why not?"

"You're not staying in Cádiz?"

He smiled and poured her more wine from the decanter on the table in the dining room of the apartment above the warehouse. "There's no need to stay now."

She looked at him speculatively. He disturbed her, he'd disturbed her ever since that day she stood beside him in the Plaza Mayor in Madrid and Carlos took his *alternativa*, and she explained the bullfight to Pablo's English cousin. "You lost a great deal to Lord Nelson, didn't you?"

"Yes."

"Particularly cruel, since he's a fellow Englishman."

"Was. It's been confirmed. Nelson was killed in the battle."

"Do you take some consolation in that?"

"No, why should I?" He toyed with a forkful of venison roasted with pears and juniper berries. "I had no personal animosity toward him. It was a matter of business."

"But you're English, so was he," she said.

"I'm a Mendoza."

Sofía stared at her plate. "Family?" she asked quietly. "Are you saying that's the highest loyalty?" To whom should she be loyal? Who had spawned her? Where?

"It is for me," Robert said. "Or at least it was."

"Pablo didn't feel that way."

"I know, that was his problem. My cousin couldn't accept the destiny he was born to. He wanted to change his heritage for something else. That never succeeds."

Sofía shook her head. "You're wrong. About Pablo's problem. About heritage—" She hesitated. "I'm not sure."

"Forget Pablo, you knew him better than I. But what about heritage? Why aren't you sure about that? Haven't you returned to your own?"

She laughed, but it was a bitter sound. "I knew that's what you were thinking. But you're wrong. I'm no more a Gypsy than you are."

He protested, reminding her that he'd seen her years earlier, before she went to Madrid and became a different woman. She told him her story. "But the world of the Gypsies is the only one you remember," he said finally. "So it's the one that claims you and that makes it your true heritage."

Sofía put her hand over her heart. "Here, it does not feel so." Then, before he could say anything else, she stood up, gathering her lace shawl and her fan. "It's late, I must go."

"What about my suggestion. Shall we ride together to Córdoba?"

"We'll ride together," Sofía agreed.

A day's journey brought them into the glazed golden light of inland Andalusia. Sofía felt its warmth, but it was not the sun making her blood hot. She was drowning in him. He sat across from her in the splendid carriage blazoned with the maroon and gold arms of the house of Mendoza and looked at her with those warm brown eyes, and she felt as if she could not breathe.

The first night they stopped at a nondescript posada. Robert looked at her questioningly. She almost nodded. She wanted to give in to him. Not because it had been two years since she had known that particular pleasure. No, this had nothing to do with that. And that's why it was so dangerous. "They must have two rooms free in this place," she said lightly. "It doesn't appear there are any other guests."

The next afternoon they came in sight of Seville. "There's still some daylight," Robert said. "Shall we go on for another hour? I know a small inn near Carmona. It's very nice."

"Yes," Sofía said. "I'd prefer that."

The inn was simple and unpretentious, but nestled by the side of a stream. "It's charming, Robert."

"Have you ever sung here?"

"With Paco, you mean? No, I don't think so."

Robert was busy giving instructions about the servants and the horses. She approached the landlord. "Two rooms, one for the gentleman, one for me."

She saw the contempt in the man's eyes. A lady did not travel with a man who was neither husband nor brother. Sofía stared at him, daring him to make some remark. "Sí, señorita," was all he said.

Her room was high under the eaves of the pitched tile roof. It had a balcony looking out to the stream and beyond, to Carmona's steep hills and neat whitewashed houses. Sofía stood there long after midnight. She looked at the darkened houses and thought that in many of them men and women, husbands and wives, must be making love. She turned her eyes back to the inn. Robert's room was across from hers. A light still shone behind the curtains.

She imagined him sitting in his bed, propped up against the feather pillows, reading perhaps. Did he wear a silk nightshirt or one of linen? Perhaps he slept naked. How easy it would be to find out. She could sneak through the corridor and knock on his door and he'd welcome her. She knew he would. What are you doing to me, Englishman? What am I allowing you to do to me? An owl hooted the only reply.

She did not join him for breakfast in the taproom the next morning, preferring to take her coffee and fried bread in her chamber. After she ate she ordered a bath. The maid fussed that it was too much trouble. No guest ever asked for a bath. Sofía insisted and she got her way. When it was time to dress she chose from her trunk a blue gown with a matching blue cape. She knew what the color did for her eyes. The carriage was waiting in the forecourt when she descended the stairs.

"Good morning, Sofía. Did you sleep well?"

"Very well, Robert. I hope you did too." His eyes were mocking her, as if he knew of the long vigil she'd kept on the balcony.

"I was restless," he said. "I stayed awake a long time."

"What did you think about?" she asked.

"You."

She had expected the answer. Sofía touched the scarf draped over her hair and felt his glance follow her hands as she adjusted its fall over her breasts.

"You look very beautiful this morning. I can't decide which suits you better, Andalusian or *madrileño* dress."

"They both have their place."

"Yes," he agreed. "Everything has a place, a time in life."

"Your sleepless night has made you into a philosopher."

He laughed and helped her into the carriage, and the touch of his hand singed her skin.

Robert climbed into the carriage and sat across from her. "I know a woman who thinks she's a free spirit," he said. "Most people would think so. But you make her look hidebound by convention."

"Convention never served me very well. I've learned to do without it," she told him.

They were quiet for the first hour. We've exhausted all the idle chatter, Sofía thought. Now we must speak the truth or be silent. I choose silence because I don't know what the truth is.

No, that's not so. I do know, but it terrifies me. So long, two years of teaching myself to feel nothing. Now this.

She couldn't look at him, afraid her control would snap if she did. She watched the road and the lush fields on either side instead. Then, when the noon sun was high overhead, he said, "I have a surprise for you. We're lunching in a special place today."

"Another of your charming inns?"

"No. We're on Mendoza land now, Sofía. We have been for some time. This is the family *cortijo*. It was given to us by Fernando III, they say, because a Mendoza helped him to finally defeat the Moors and claim Córdoba for the *reconquista*."

"The Mendozas have been part of most Spanish history, haven't they?"

"All of it, if the stories are to be believed. I'm forced to admit we've changed sides with remarkable ease."

Something flickered in his eyes when he said that. Had he backed the French and the Spanish against Lord Nelson and the English? If so, he'd lost, and perhaps that lost wager was tormenting him now. "We all have to make choices," she said softly. "At times they prove wrong—that's destiny, luck if you will. But your ancestor won quite a prize. This is beautiful land, Robert. Wonderful."

"Mostly it's farms and orchards and little shacks the laborers live in, but there's one house a bit more comfortable, if not very grand. I'm told that some Mendoza built it in the fourteenth century. I don't know if that's true. It's a fairly primitive place. Delightful all the same though. I think you'll like it."

He'd sent word ahead and two servants, a man and his wife, had opened the house and were waiting for them. The woman had made a stew of wild rabbit and bitter oranges, and she served it to them in front of a blazing log fire in the large room which, with the kitchen and two small bedrooms, was all there was to the house.

"The family have always resisted the notion of a large country hacienda," he explained. "I don't think any Mendoza has ever actually lived here."

She toyed with her meat, her throat too tight to swallow. Still, she maintained the pretense of casual chatter. "Have they always lived in Córdoba?"

"Yes, whatever 'always' means. I don't know exactly when the first Mendoza came to the city. But one thing is certain— they were there long before the present palace was built. The original one burned down in thirteen something. So this one could almost be called new. Less than five hundred years old, an upstart."

He grinned at her, and her heart leapt and her hands trembled, and she was sure he must see what she was feeling. He gave no sign.

"All the same, the palace is extraordinary. You must see it."

She didn't meet his eyes. "Is the Patio of the Orange Trees still there? Is there still a reflecting pool and pink roses?"

"Ah, I see. I didn't realize Pablo had taken you to the palace."

"He never did." She told him about singing for Doña Carmen when she was a very young girl.

"So your life has been entangled with the Mendozas a long time," Robert said. He reached across the table and with one finger lightly traced a line on the back of her hand. "What would the old Gypsy fortune-teller who raised you have said about that?"

"She'd have called it destiny."

"Then she'd have been right. I've known you were part of my destiny since the first moment I saw you."

No more pretense. It was time to choose. She turned her face to his, looking at him intently. "The first moment you saw who, Robert, the wandering Gypsy singer or Doña Sofía?"

"Both. Both women intrigued me, even before I knew they were one and the same."

Sofía withdrew her hand from his touch and lifted her wineglass and drank. She didn't so much make up her mind as give in to a force she couldn't resist. "Robert," she said quietly as she set down the glass. "Do you want to make love to me?"

He gasped in shock, then threw back his head and roared with laughter. "You are a wonderment, *Gitanita*. I doubt there's ever been your equal."

"That doesn't answer my question."

Would he be perverse enough to refuse her, to tell her he picked his own bedmates and managed his own seductions? She saw the notion flit across his face, but the fire smoldering in her eyes kindled answering sparks in his. "Yes, damn you. I do. I'm not sure I trust you, Doña Sofía. But I want you, yes."

"Very well. Can that door be bolted?" She nodded toward the door that led to the rest of the small house. "Those two bedrooms aren't very inviting. Besides, they're cold. And the kitchen won't do."

He walked to the door and drew the heavy bar across it. When he turned back she was naked, standing by the fire, letting its leaping flames make rosy shadows on her creamy flesh.

They loved violently at first, an explosive union that was the culmination that had been awaiting them for years, then once more with tenderness and seeking. When it was over, a sea rose within her, a great tide of peace. So many journeys, so much wandering; at last she had come home.

The room was dark now, lit only by the dying fire. "Why?" Robert asked softly. "Why me, and why here and now?"

"Because that's why you brought me here." Joyful to be able to speak the words, aware that she had given herself entirely and there was no turning back. "Because you need me. Because for the first time in my life I know the meaning of love."

She felt him retreat from her though he didn't move.

Her words burned his ears, seared themselves onto his heart. He'd been amusing himself, trying to escape—even if only for a few days—the anguish he knew was waiting. But fate had tricked him again. Sofía had offered him a gift beyond price at the very moment when he had no choice but to refuse it. "Sofía, listen to me. I can't . . . I mean that right now things are—" He stopped speaking, realizing that words were less than useless, a cruel joke.

She lay very still. The tide of passion receded and left her alone on a barren shore. I've lost him, she realized with sudden clarity that did not cushion the pain. I never had him, but I've lost him. Then she understood. She had escaped punishment so far. Two men had died because of her. Her daughter's murder remained unavenged. A river of blood—how could she help but drown in it? For a moment she wished she could, but that would be too easy. Hell had begun. Losing Robert was her payment for sin, the wages of the blood she'd spilled.

He did not attend either of her two performances in Córdoba. The whole town came to hear La Gitanita and cheered her wildly, but not the hidalgo of the house of Mendoza. On her third morning in the city she forfeited any residue of pride. She knew, but she could not accept what she knew without a struggle.

All the shutters on the palace windows were closed, the gates were shut, too, and no one answered when she rang the great brass bell hanging beside them. Had he gone, perhaps? But even if he had, there would be servants. Sofía walked around the walls, remembering the times she'd gone there before. In the Calle Judíos she stopped in the exact spot where she'd first seen Pablo Luis. It seemed she could see him now. His ghost went ahead of her. She shook her head and banished it and walked on.

The door she remembered was exactly as it had been. Doubtless it still led to the Patio de los Naranjos. She tried it, but it was bolted shut. Farther on in the little alley that still had no name she put up her hand and played her fingers over the marks Fanta had made long before. There were others as well. Some Gypsies who came after them had carved three parallel lines beneath the circle with the dot inside. Fanta's sign had meant that Gypsies were welcome. The additional lines changed the meaning to Gypsies were regarded as thieves. So Doña Carmen had come to hate them at the end because none of Fanta's prophecies came true. Not for me either, Sofía thought. You promised me a great destiny, Fanta. Instead, I'm a whore and a murderess and the only man I love doesn't want me.

She had come all the way around now, back to the gates leading to the Patio del Recibo. She hesitated, trying to decide whether to ring the bell again. There was a small door for foot traffic cut into one of the tall gates. It opened and a child came out. No, not a child, a man, but a dwarf. He held a linen handkerchief to his face and carried a black satchel. *"Señor, disculpa me, pero está por dentro el hidalgo?"*

He looked at her a moment before replying. She saw that he was weeping. "No, Señorita," he said. "The hidalgo is dead."

Sofía gasped. "He can't be dead. I saw him just three days ago."

"He still walks," the dwarf said quietly. "He breathes. But he's dead. I don't know what your business with him may be, señorita. But go away. There's nothing for you here." He turned and looked back at the gates. "There's nothing for anyone alive. This is a tomb."

She watched him walk away, then ran back to the little door that led to the Patio de los Naranjos and pounded on it until her hands were bloody, and screamed Robert's name until her throat was hoarse. Once she was absolutely certain he was standing and listening to her, separated from her only by the thick wood of the door, but he said nothing and gave no sign. After an hour Sofía admitted defeat and left.

For a while Robert sat beside the reflecting pool beneath the orange trees and listened to her voice calling him, heard her small fists beating against the thick wood of the door. When he could stand it no longer, he went inside.

I love you. It was such a simple phrase, had been spoken by men and women so many times since the world began. *I love you.* When she whispered those words, he had known his fate in one painfully lucid moment. His future was to be nothing, to have nothing—because he had nothing to give. She loved him, that beautiful, exciting woman, and he could easily love her. But if he allowed himself to do so, it was the ultimate betrayal, the final rejection of everything he'd been born to and already destroyed. To accept Sofía's love, to return it, was to avoid his just punishment, to escape the agony he had brought upon himself and must endure. And as the greatest shame, to make her share in the degradation that was rightly his alone.

All that night he paced the many splendid rooms of the Palacio Mendoza. Her voice seemed to follow him. Long after Sofía had given up and left, he heard the echo of her cries.

Robert knew they would haunt him always; they were one more refrain in the ghostly chorus of reproaches that had come to dwell within these ancient walls.

A pair of enormous chandeliers hung from the ornately plastered ceiling of the state dining room. Robert stood beneath them and thought of Pablo Luis. He went to the windows and tested the heft of one of the thick silken cords that looped back the embroidered curtains. Then he turned away. To seek oblivion was an act of cowardice little different from accepting Sofía's love.

He ran from the dining room, his pounding feet echoing in the empty corridors. There was a long gallery on the second floor of the east wing. Portraits of Mendozas long dead hung on the walls. Robert stood and stared at them. He was drenched in sweat and his heart was pounding, but he threw back his head and summoned the energy for a mighty shout, a screaming cry of anguish that was also a vow. "I will endure. The fault was mine and I will endure the punishment."

The priest hesitated. He held the quill in his stiff old fingers, but he did not sign his name. The woman waited and watched him. "Señorita, there are other ways—"

"No, not this time."

Her blue eyes were unwavering. They were dark shadowed now, a result of her recent ordeal, but yet beautiful. Still, he did not sign. "What you ask me to do is a sin," he murmured. "To swear to what I know is not true."

"A very small sin, Don Lorenzo. It has to be you; no one else in this pueblo can read or write. And you will be believed."

"But I will have perjured myself."

"Only you and I know that." Sofía leaned forward. "Two thousand reales, Don Lorenzo. Enough to build a new church, and to dig a well so your people need not walk a mile to the river in order to get water. Where else will you get two thousand reales?"

"Nowhere," he admitted. "Very well, I will do it." He'd already said that twice, a week earlier when she proposed her bargain, and this morning when she brought the document for his signature. Still, he hesitated. He read the words one more time.

I, Lorenzo Gonzales Rudin, parish priest of the village of Encinasola in the province of Andalusia, do hereby attest to the fact that the woman known as Sofía, La Gitanita, gave birth to a son in this village on the twenty-ninth of February in the year of Our Lord One Thousand Eight Hundred and Four. This boy was baptized by me when he was four days old and given the name Rafael Pablo Mendoza Sofía according to the laws of God and Holy Church.

"It is all true except for the date," she reminded him.

"Except for the date," he agreed. The son had been born a week before, on the twenty-ninth of July 1806, but she insisted on making him swear the child was born two years and some months earlier. "The name," he said hesitantly. "Perhaps if you did not use the name of quite so powerful a family—"

Sofía stood up. "Sign it or not, Don Lorenzo. But decide now. I have a carriage waiting. If you refuse, I will find some other priest who needs two thousand reales."

Don Lorenzo signed his name in small, cramped letters, as if he hoped the angels wouldn't notice.

Sofía took the document and put it in the leather satchel she carried, then she passed him the chamois bag containing the money. "Thank you. I hope you enjoy your new church, Don Lorenzo."

"Señorita, whatever your reasons for this deception, and I agree they are not my affair, you must make your peace with God. You cannot live with this sin on your soul."

"Yes," she said, "I can live with it. The problem will not arise until I must die with it. Adios, Don Lorenzo."

The carriage stood outside the priest's house. The coachman helped Sofía climb into it, and waited for his next order. "To Caceres," she told him. "But drive carefully." She leaned over and moved the lacy white blanket that half shielded the infant's face. The woman holding the baby smiled at her. "He has been sleeping all the while, Rosa?"

The wet nurse nodded. She could make no reply other than a movement of the head because a few years before, bandits had come to Encinasola and killed her family and raped her and afterward cut out her tongue.

She had borne a child as a result of that terrible night, but it had lived only a few days, for which she was grateful. Then, while her breasts were still full of milk, a neighbor had died in childbirth. Rosa had given that child suck and nursed it for two years, and the child's father gave her food and a roof over her head in return for the service. Afterward there had been another, whose mother had sour milk, and now the lady with the blue eyes like jewels who had come here and birthed a son who must be a bastard, or why else all the secrecy? Rosa did not care, the lady was taking her to Caceres, a city three days journey from this village, where everyone knew Rosa's shame. She smiled again and nodded at Doña Sofía.

The carriage left the pueblo and took to the open road, its movement steadier now. Sofía reached out and took the child in her arms. Just a month old and already he was beautiful. I love you, little Rafael, with your fuzz of dark hair and your eyes that are blue now but may someday be brown. I'm glad I hadn't the foresight to prevent your birth. You're my treasure, and I will protect you. You will grow up believing that your father is dead, that he died before you were born. You will never know the pain of rejection from the man who is your father but doesn't wish to be. It doesn't matter, my angel. I can give you enough love for both a mother and a father. I must leave you with a nurse for much of the time so that I can earn our daily bread, but I will take care of you, my Rafael, until someday you claim your heritage. When that day comes, my son, you will be ready.

The carriage lurched over a pothole and Sofía almost lost her grip on the infant, but she hung on.

Book Two

espite Nelson's great victory at Trafalgar, by the autumn of 1810 Napoleon's decree that no country in Europe might trade with the nation he called "perfidious Albion." It had so injured British industry and commerce that thousands were unemployed, and millions were on the edge of destitution. That year English exports to continental Europe sank to less than eight million pounds sterling; in 1811 the figure was under a million and a half. Revolution was in the air. The Luddite weavers went about smashing the machines they hated, and decrying the industrial revolution that had looked to make Britain the greatest power on the globe.

Violence at home was compounded by impending violence abroad. While fighting with Napoleon, Britain was heading for another war with America, and exports to the former colonies were now less than one sixth of what they had been. The government saw the only cure for their problems as higher taxes, and the burdens became so great that the entire economy of the country was near collapse. Eventually one bankrupt businessman took a pistol to the lobby of the House of Commons and killed the prime minister, but that, of course, solved nothing.

Manuel de Godoy's ambitions went far beyond sharing the bed of the Queen of Spain or introducing the reforms that radicals like Brother Elijah and Maria Ortega envisioned. De Godoy wanted a kingdom. When it looked as if he might fail in Castile, he dreamed of conquering Portugal. Napoleon had already told the Portuguese that they must stop all trade with England, and when they refused had sent an army of twenty thousand men into Spain, poised to march into Lisbon. Now de Godoy raised an army of his own, and unable to resist this combined threat, the Portuguese royal family took ship for Brazil. The French swallowed Portugal and Napoleon sent three more armies into Spain. To assist his Spanish allies, naturally.

But who governed Spain? The heir apparent, the Infante Ferdinand, mounted a plot against de Godoy. Godoyistas fought Ferdinandistas in the streets until disgusted with their carryings-on, and with the constant presence of the French troops, the populace of Madrid rose in revolt and captured de Godoy and threw him in a dungeon. King Charles, utterly bewildered, abdicated in favor of his son. But the Emperor of France had not given his approval to this move, and French troops marched on Madrid and liberated de Godoy. Napoleon refused to recognize Ferdinand as king, and summoned all parties to a conference across the border in Bayonne.

The Spaniards knew that the upstart emperor intended to end the Bourbon dynasty and give them a Bonaparte as king. On the second of May 1808 they gathered in their thousands in front of the Palacio Real and stoned the French troops and tore some of them apart with their bare hands. The French fired into the crowd, volley after volley ripped flesh and pulverized bone. Perhaps the only Spaniard to win that day was Goya; he stood on a hill and surveyed the scene and later painted a masterpiece called *El Dos de Mayo*.

Now Ferdinand lost all heart for the terror he'd unleashed and he abdicated, restoring the crown to his father. Charles IV did not have the stomach to return to his furiously angry subjects and his adulterous wife and her scheming lover. He offered the kingship of Spain to Napoleon, and he in turn bestowed it on his brother Joseph after two earlier choices declined to become ruler of so passionate and violent a people. The Bourbons and de Godoy would be supported in royal splendor at Marseilles, but what was money compared to the throne of Spain? Satisfied with his bargain, Napoleon rode leisurely back to Paris, acclaimed at every step as the invincible master of Europe.

The new king took over a Spanish nation in revolt. The peasants armed themselves with knives against the French carbines and the Church raised the cross against this Joseph Bonaparte, who, though he had agreed that Catholicism would be the only legal religion in Spain, they condemned as a Lutheran and a Freemason and worse, a man who spoke not a word of Spanish.

This was an Iberian conflict, marked by those fires that burned with such particular ferocity on this peninsula. There was an orgy of amputations, castrations, crucifixions, beheadings, hangings, and impalings, spurred on by the Church, who called their flock to insurrection in the name of God, His Immaculate Mother, and St. Joseph. Goya made a series of drawings he called Los Desastres de la Guerra, that later the world might know.

❧ 13 ❧

The Palacio Mendoza had been many things; now it was a prison. Robert had dismissed all the servants except Indalencio. Harry Hawkins begged to be allowed to stay. He pleaded that he had nowhere else to go and that service to the Mendozas was his only reason for being alive, but the hidalgo would not relent. In the end the dwarf left sobbing, and Robert barred the gates and locked the windows and drew the curtains of thick crewel and luxurious damask that once he'd described to his mother in such terms of glowing praise.

In the fourteen patios the roses and jasmine and bougain-villaea first rampaged over the walls, then burned up and died because there were no gardeners to prune them, or give them water during the long months when Andalusia was hot and dry. Many of the trees survived, their roots sunk deep into the hidden streams of the earth, but the oranges and grapefruits and lemons and pomegranates rotted on the branch, except for those few Indalencio picked for his master's infrequent meals.

Robert ate seldom and at odd hours. Most of the time he didn't know if it was night or day. The only light in the palace was candlelight. For weeks at a time he avoided the sunlit patios, especially the Patio de los Naranjos, where he'd stood and listened to Sofía pound on the door and call his name.

Each time her small fist struck the wood his body had jerked —she was beating his flesh, stabbing him, putting the final nails in his coffin.

He would never forget. Not Sofía and not his vow to endure, to suffer the punishment that was justly his—but that promise screamed at the accusing faces of his ancestors had been his final expression of emotion. Since then he was a walking corpse. The fires inside him had gone out and the cold of death had come. He was a ghost, of no use to any man or woman alive, least of all himself.

Córdoba is dead, he'd told Liam. But not just Córdoba. His life force had been centered on one thing and by his own hand he had destroyed it, had flung his inheritance to ravening dogs and lost it. It was the sin for which no Mendoza could be forgiven.

Benjamin might have been able to forgive, but Benjamin died and Bess soon followed him. There remained Liam, but he had concerns of his own and when Robert didn't answer his letters he stopped writing. After all, there was no longer any profit to come from Córdoba. The leadership of the house of Mendoza had passed to England, but like his country, Liam was struggling to survive, and he was ill equipped to seize the opportunity. Certainly he didn't have time to worry about the brother who had turned traitor in Spain. He was preoccupied by an apparently fruitless quest to salvage something of what Benjamin had put into his hands in England.

In Córdoba, too, the death throes were not quick. The agony was prolonged as one by one the loans came due and the profit that should have flowed from the treasure ships into the Córdobés coffers went to the creditors of the house of Mendoza. Men spoke of the decline of the once mighty fortune, but not as much as they might have done in less hysterical times. A French army occupied Andalusia, and here as everywhere they were harried by the bands of *guerrilleros* who attacked them by night and were gone as swiftly as they had come, asking no quarter and giving none.

Robert knew what was happening. The news seeped in even through his high walls and battened gates, but he heard it as a man apart from other men, a creature no longer involved in the affairs of the living. He had narrowed his world to the forty-six rooms of the Palacio Mendoza, and he paced them hour after hour, staring at the walls now shrouded with cobwebs and leaving footprints in the thick dust that coated the marble floors.

One night in 1809 Maria Ortega came, letting herself in through a door that led from the Calle Judios to the Patio del Fuente with a key Robert didn't know she possessed. Indalencio found her sitting beside the cracked remains of a lapis lazuli fountain that had once dripped water into a basin carved from a single piece of rose quartz.

"Doña Maria, I did not know . . ."

"Where is the hidalgo?"

"I'm not sure, señorita. Here somewhere, but . . ." He shrugged helplessly.

"Find him, bring him to me. I must speak with him."

In a few minutes the servant returned. "I am sorry, Doña Maria. He will not see you. You must leave."

"Tell him I will not leave until I speak with him. Tell him that if necessary I will sit here until I rot. You can't throw me out bodily, Indalencio. You're not big enough."

Half an hour later Robert entered the patio by one of the secret paths and appeared at her side in the moonlight. Maria gasped, then clasped her hand over her lips. In the four years since she'd seen him his hair had gone totally white. His eyes were the staring eyes of a madman, and his face was ravaged with deep lines of despair and self-hatred. He wore a tattered black frockcoat now much too big for him, and black breeches stained with grease and dirt. But he was her last hope. In a moment she recovered herself. "Good evening, Robert."

"Go away."

"Not until I speak with you."

"I have nothing to say to you, we have nothing to say to each other. Go away."

"Robert, for God's sake, listen to me. Things are happening beyond these walls. Terrible, incredible things. You can help stop them. You *must* help stop them."

He laughed a strange, brittle laugh. "Look at me, Maria. Dead men achieve nothing. Ghosts can't save Spain."

She stood up, drawing herself to her full height so their eyes were level. "Yes, Mendoza ghosts can. There is no leadership, Robert. No voice of authority to speak against the violence the priests and bishops are inciting. You could be that voice. Your name will make people listen. Everything we fought for, everything we believed, is being soaked in blood. It has to end."

"What I fought for was the house of Mendoza. You knew that. I never pretended otherwise. I lost and I ruined the house and now there's nothing left. I'm the last of my line in Córdoba, and I'm dead."

She tried another tack. "Napoleon has issued a new constitution for Spain. Have you heard? Do you know what it says?" He didn't answer, didn't look at her. "It's marvelous, Robert. It could bring new glory to the house of Mendoza. He's abolished all feudal monopolies. That means the end of the Mesta. I've been told privately that he's still willing to grant the Mendozas the right to create a national bank of Spain."

"What Mendozas? Didn't you hear me? I'm all there is, Maria, and all there ever will be, and I'm a corpse. There's no money for this bank and no one to be the banker. So for pity's sake, if you feel any pity, go away."

She went on as if she hadn't heard him. "The constitution says something more. The Inquisition is also abolished. There will be freedom of religion here. You can be a Jew again. All the Mendozas can be Jews. That's what you wanted. You never told me, but I knew."

"You let yourself in, go the same way you came." He started to leave.

"Robert, wait, listen to me. Just a moment more, I beg you. Harry Hawkins sent you a message."

The name triggered something in him, some spark of life. "Poor Harry. How is he?"

"Not well, but very happy. When you sent him away he went to Brother Elijah. He's a lay brother at the monastery now, but he has a fever. It comes and goes, but it weakens him more each time."

"That doesn't surprise me," Robert said softly. "The Mendozas are finished, as I said."

She didn't understand his logic, but she dismissed it as unimportant. "Harry has sent a letter with me." She held out an envelope, but Robert made no move to take it. "Go on," she said, as if tempting a child. "Take it, it's for you. Harry says you can save yourself and your house and all Spain."

He laughed that mirthless laugh again. "That's not a letter, Maria. That's the philosopher's stone, the one that turns dross into gold. Somehow I don't think Harry Hawkins is empowered with such a gift."

He left her, and this time she couldn't stop him. She sat by the silent fountain until it was nearly sunrise, studying the rich blue stone and tracing the cracks in its once-beautiful form. At last, knowing herself to be defeated, she got up and went out into the street. But because she was not a woman to give up hope easily, she left the letter behind.

For a week Robert did not return to the Patio del Fuente. When his aimless pacing finally did take him there, he didn't see the envelope. The drifting leaves of autumn had covered it in a dry brown shroud.

He sat where Maria had sat and tried to recall what she looked like, what her body had been like so long ago. He could not. The only face he could summon from memory was Sofía's. The only touch he ever imagined, hers. Sometimes he caught himself wondering if she ever thought of him. But he banished such speculation as he banished all else—remembering was not a fit activity for a corpse.

A cold wind blew and Robert shivered, then looked down and saw that the breeze had disturbed the leaves and uncovered the letter. He hesitated, almost touched it, then snatched his hand away.

How beautiful this fountain had been once. It was very old, probably the work of *mudejares,* the Arabs who remained behind after the Moors left and were artisans to the Christian rulers. The old manuscript Benjamin gave him to read years before in England spoke of a Mendoza who brought in *mudejares* to decorate the palace.

So many had gone before him; who would come after? What would happen when at last his body accepted what his mind knew to be a fact, and he stopped breathing and his flesh rotted? The French had left him alone so far. Because he was the one man in Spain who didn't plague them? But when he died, perhaps French troops would be quartered in the palace. Or Spanish patriots would defend themselves from this place. Had there ever been a time when no Mendoza claimed this land? No matter, such a time was coming soon. Then someone would see all this faded magnificence, and remember that once men of strength and courage ruled here—until one man betrayed them all.

But maybe . . . Hesitantly he took the envelope in his hands and opened it. Some minutes more passed before he could bring himself to read what the dwarf had written.

> You must not give up, Mr. Robert. You're the only one who can help Spain now. That's why I'm going to tell you what I've never told you before. It has always been my prayer that you'd come to the true faith. It still is. But if the old ways can save the house of Mendoza, then I'll not set myself against them. Look in the little room in the west wing off the Patio de las Mujeres. Beneath the mark on the wall there's a stone in the floor that will come up if you use a lever of any sort. God bless you, sir.
>
> Ever yours in the love of Jesus. . . .

The Patio de las Mujeres had four stone filigree screens across each corner. It was said that during the brief time the Mendozas lived as Muslims, the women of the house were kept in purdah there. True or not, this was the oldest part of the palace, perhaps a section that had not been destroyed by fire five centuries earlier. The room Harry had directed him to was small but exquisitely proportioned, with a faded mosaic frieze of russet and green acanthus leaves running below the ceiling.

The mark on the wall was a space about two feet square. There was a hole at each corner, where something had once been fastened. Harry Hawkins's revelations had nothing to do with this ancient scar. Everyone knew about it. When Robert first came to Córdoba in 1799, Domingo had showed him this mark. "They say the plaque hung here," the old hidalgo had explained.

"But you don't know what it said or what happened to it?"

"No." Domingo had shrugged. "Neither of those things, as I told you."

"Still, you haven't repainted this wall or filled in the marks of the nails?"

Domingo crossed himself. "God forbid. No one's ever done that. It's a kind of family legend This mark stays on the wall, though no one knows why anymore."

Robert no longer cared why. He turned his eyes to the floor. It was formed of large stones fitted together without mortar, not unusual considering the period in which the room had been built. He'd brought a short crowbar with him, and he inserted it in the stone immediately below the mark on the wall. It was easier than he'd expected, the merest amount of leverage lifted it free.

He propped the stone against the wall and carried a candle closer. Where the stone had been, there was only the dirt on which the floor had been laid. He scratched at the earth with his nails. Solid, compacted by centuries. There was nothing. He was on a fool's errand.

He had started to lower the stone back into place when he saw the words carved into its underside. A single line of crude print, but in Hebrew characters he couldn't read. He cursed in frustration, then moved the candle so another part of the stone was illuminated. Another line of words, these in Spanish. Some later hidalgo had translated the Hebrew. *Hay un tesoro en la cueva.* There is a treasure in the cave. It looked like Domingo's hand.

So the old man had known Hebrew after all, or perhaps he had Hawkins search out a translation for him. Yes, that made more sense. It would explain how the dwarf knew about this message. But it was nonsense. There wasn't any cave, and if there was a treasure, Domingo would long since have plundered it.

Robert let the stone fall back into place. More old stories, legends of the glorious Mendoza past. They couldn't help him now. Nothing could help him because he was a dead man. He lay on the floor and fell asleep beneath the mark on the wall, the last remaining sign of some ancient pact made by his ancestors with God or the devil. Or perhaps both.

The faces of the campesinos were ruddy in the firelight. They were brown, seamed faces more accustomed to the sun in their fields than this smoky cave between La Rambla and Puente Genil, and they did not smile when they looked at Sofía. Their expressions were grave, serious—and adoring. For two hours she'd been singing the songs of Andalusia that gave them hope; mostly fandangos, some flamenco, lastly a poignant Sevillano *saeta*.

· "Enough, *Gitanita*," Juan Sanchez said. "You must be tired. Rest now." He was a small, stooped man with arms that seemed too long for his body. His followers called him El Mono, the monkey; the French called him a plague out of hell. To ordinary Andalusians he was a hero.

"I can go on if you like." Sofía was tireless when she was with them like this, in their hidden enclaves, seeing the loneliness and the determination on their peasant faces. "If it pleases you, I'll sing more." Behind her Enrique strummed a chord on the guitar. In the days when she lived in Madrid and had servants, he'd been her coachman; then, in a sense, he had led her into war.

"Everything you do pleases us," Sanchez said. "But we've promised to bring you safely to Jaen tomorrow. They won't thank us if you arrive with a sore throat." He stood up and extended his hand. "Come, we've made a place for you to sleep."

They had put clean straw in the rearmost part of the cave and made a rough curtain from some burlap sacks. "It's not what you're used to," Sanchez said. His smile showed the gaps where his teeth should be. "But it's the best we have."

"It's what I've been used to for two years." Sofía smiled back at him. "There's no place I'd rather be."

The words came easily, the struggle was behind her.

When the fighting began, Sofía was convinced it had nothing to do with her. She had her own battles to fight, her own griefs. And she had Rafael. She had become famous, she was on her way to becoming rich—such victories insured her son's future—and she chose to ignore the French troops in the streets.

"Doña Sofía," her coachman had said one spring day in 1809, "I cannot drive for you any longer."

They were in Madrid, in Sofía's house by the Toledo Gate. That night she planned to have Enrique take her to Cáceres for another of her secret visits with Rosa and Rafael. The thought of losing the servant she trusted did not please Sofía. "What do you mean? Why not? I thought you were happy with me, Enrique, I thought you liked—"

"I have been happy," the man interrupted. "Now there is no time for happiness."

"Because of the war, that's what you mean, isn't it?"

"Sí, señorita, because of the war."

"Listen to me. What you're saying is foolish. One *guerrillero* more or less, what difference can it make?"

Enrique had shrugged. "Very little perhaps. Still . . ."

So be it. There were other coachmen for hire. Sofía had made up her mind to let him go, but she asked him to remain in her employ one more week, just until she could find someone else. "It must be a trustworthy man, Enrique. You understand."

"Of course, *Gitanita*. Someone for Cáceres. Yes, I understand."

Cáceres, where what was left of her heart remained. God! The pieces of it that had been hacked away. The family she had never known and couldn't remember, the daughter Paco had murdered, the permanent shame he'd seared into her flesh because she had never avenged the child, Pablo Luis and Carlos . . . And Robert. Robert Mendoza had made her drink rejection to its final bitter dregs. But in spite of himself, he had given her the greatest blessing of her life. Rafael.

They had set out for Cáceres that night. It was to be the final time Enrique made the journey with her. Once, as he helped her into the carriage, Sofía had felt his eyes on her. They seemed a reproach. "Listen," she started to say. "Listen, I cannot expect you to understand, but—" She had stopped speaking. She could not explain to a simple creature like Enrique that she had no emotion left to spend on a war she barely understood, a war which she could do nothing to stop.

The road southeast from Madrid was well traveled, but not usually by night. These journeys were dangerous and would have been even without the dragoons and the *guerrilleros,* but Sofía dared not visit her son by daylight. If the world knew she had an illegitimate child, she would never again be invited to sing in public.

Enrique was a skilled driver and they made good time, then, when they had been on the road about four hours, he suddenly reined in the horses.

Sofía leaned out the window, gazing up at the driver's high seat. "What is it, Enrique? What's wrong?"

"Look, señorita." He gestured with his whip.

She turned to see what he was pointing at. A series of huge wooden crosses had been erected on either side of the road. On each hung a crucified man.

"*Madre de Dios,*" Sofía whispered. "No, I don't believe it. No, no, no!"

Enrique climbed down from his perch, more intent on the victims than on his mistress. Sofía watched him walk toward the first cross. She wanted to look away, but she couldn't. She retched and reached into her bag for a square of linen to press against her mouth. Enrique was standing a little ways away, staring up at the first in the long line of impaled corpses. Sofía could not help herself. She had to leave the carriage and look too.

She went and stood beside Enrique, but he ignored her. For long seconds she stared at the frozen grimace of agony on the face of the crucified man, then she looked at her driver. Tears were rolling down his cheeks.

He began to walk along the row of crucifixes—slowly, pausing for a few seconds before each one. Sofía followed him. She was shaking and gagging, but she could not leave. Not until they had paid their silent homage to each victim and Enrique took her arm and began leading her back to the carriage.

They heard a moan.

Sofía froze. Enrique's grip on her arm tightened, then he let her go and turned and ran back to the scene of the slaughter, searching for the man who was still alive.

She watched him. When he stopped she knew he'd found what he sought. Enrique was standing in front of the final cross on the right side of the road. Sofía was not aware that she had moved until she stood beside him. "Is he . . ."

"*Sí*, I think so. I think he is alive. I saw his mouth open and close."

Sofía dropped her handkerchief and stretched out her hands. She wanted to tear the man down off the cross, but even as she made the gesture she knew it was futile. His feet were crossed and an enormous iron spike had been driven through the flesh and bone of his ankles into the wood of the upright. Both his wrists had been mutilated in the same way. There was not as much blood as she would have expected, and what there was had dried earlier in the sun. Rivulets of brown stained the man's arms and his feet.

"He has drawn himself up so that he can breathe," Enrique whispered tonelessly. "That is how crucifixion kills. The weight of the body sagging on the spikes makes it impossible to breathe."

"Oh, my God. Oh, my God." It was all she could find to say. Then: "But now? Now surely he is dead?"

"I do not know. Perhaps."

"Ten pietas . . ." The lips barely moved, but the whisper could be heard. "Ten pietas."

Have pity. How could she? In the name of God, what could she do? Sofía felt the tears running down her cheeks, and she saw Enrique's. But if they wept an ocean for this creature, that would not in any way ease his agony. Let him die, she prayed. Dear God, let him die. The man moaned again.

Sofía drew one deep breath, then, with absolutely no fore-thought, she opened her mouth and sang.

The notes of the *saeta* were pure and true, her voice did not betray her. No matter what, it could be counted upon. She did not take her eyes from the face of the crucified man—once she thought he smiled at her—and she sang and sang and sang.

"It is enough, Doña Sofía." Enrique touched her arm. "Enough now. He is dead. We must go."

She let the notes die away, float into the void of the night. "He is dead? You are sure, Enrique?"

"I am sure. It took a long time, but—"

"No! It can't have been long."

"It has been, I promise you, señorita. Near an hour, I would guess. Your songs eased him."

Sofía knew they had. She knew, too, that she must go to war.

In the cave of the *guerrilleros* Juan Sanchez was still looking at her, studying her face as if he could not believe she was there. "I saw you once a few years ago, Doña Sofía, before the war. You were singing in the gardens of the Alhambra in Granada. I could not afford to buy a ticket, but I climbed over the wall when no one was looking. I never dreamed then that you would sing just for me and a dozen others like me."

"None of us dreamed this would happen. Are you from Granada?" she asked.

"I was, now . . ." He shrugged. "I am from hell, or so the French say."

"But when it's over, when we've driven them out, you'll go back to Granada."

"Perhaps, but I don't think so."

"Why not?" She was surprised, the attachment of the campesinos to their home ground was legendary.

"There's nothing there for me now but blood. The dragoons murdered my wife and four of my children. The fifth they blinded and she died a few weeks later. I was in the olive groves some way from the house. I heard everything but there was nothing I could do. The dragoons said we were harboring *guerrilleros*. Until then we'd never even seen a *guerrillero*. So I became one."

Sofía had heard hundreds of similar stories. There was nothing she could say to offer comfort to people who had suffered as these had. She could only sing. She touched his cheek with her palm. "Good night, Juan Sanchez. I hope you sleep well."

El Mono kept his hand pressed to the cheek she'd touched as he walked back to the fire. One of the men was drawing with charcoal on a bit of hide. Sanchez went and looked over his shoulder. "The eyes aren't right. She has bigger eyes." The man made a few more marks with the charcoal. "Better," Sanchez said.

It had become a kind of competition. Every group of partisans La Gitanita joined for a few days had one of their members make a sketch of her. When the men met, they compared them. The drawings circulated. Some had even fallen into the hands of the French, and it was rumored that there was a price on the woman's head. Other people denied that even the French would put a price on the head of a woman, but it made little difference. They would have to catch her first and the *guerrilleros* passed her from hand to hand like the treasure she was.

There was the sound of a scuffle outside. Sanchez dropped the picture and pulled his knife in the same motion. His other hand reached for a blunderbuss leaning against the wall. In less than five seconds every man in the cave was armed and ready. Another man came in, pushing a Frenchman in a blood-soaked blue uniform ahead of him. The dragoon had only one hand; the other was severed at the wrist. The Spaniard who'd captured him held up a leather dispatch box. The hand that had carried it was still chained to the handle. "It was easier to cut through the flesh than the chain," he said. "*Muy buenas noches a todos.*"

"Why have you brought the pig here?" Sanchez asked.

"He speaks a little Castilian. I think there are things he could tell us, but why should I have all the fun myself, eh?"

El Mono nodded. "Good, but take him outside. She is sleeping." He jerked his head toward the back of the cave. "We don't want his screams to disturb her."

In the morning Sofía and Enrique left with three of the others. When they descended the hill from the cave she saw the body of a man in a clump of trees by a stream. He was naked and his arms and legs had been spiked to the ground with chestnut palings. She could never get used to the atrocities. She turned her head as they went by.

"Don't worry about him, *Gitanita*," one of the partisans said. "A Frenchman who ate something that didn't agree with him and choked to death." She could not stop herself from looking at the man one more time. They had cut off his manhood and shoved it into his mouth.

❧ 14 ❧

The yellow stone walls that enclosed Caceres rose atop a steep hill. Built by the Romans, reinforced by the Moors, and retained by the Christians, the walls were crenelated battlements studded with towers; they made the city a fortress. Sofía's carriage, a small, half-open phaeton, had been stolen for her. It raced toward the city. Sitting behind the driver, she strained forward, as if the impetus of her body and the force of her will could make the two horses run faster.

Enrique was the coachman. He cracked his whip constantly, urged on by the knowledge of her desperation. "Almost there, Doña Sofía," he called over his shoulder, but his voice was snatched by the wind.

The phaeton was the only thing that stirred the sultry June air, the dust-covered black leather body of the small carriage cut a swath through the still, hot afternoon. Ahead, a pall of greasy black smoke hung over the city, growing larger and more noxious as they neared their goal. Be alive, Sofía prayed silently. Be alive and safe, my angel. Mama is coming, Rafael. Be alive.

"I think the gate is closed!" Enrique yelled.

"No, it can't be." Sofía could see that it was, even as she

denied the possibility. The immense doors of the Puerta de San Antonio were shut tight, sealing Caceres off from the world.

Two armed guards stood outside the gates. They wore the livery of the Golfines, virtual rulers of Caceres since the fifteenth century, stronger than ever now in 1811 because, having rejected the usurping king in Madrid, the only authority most Spaniards recognized was local. "*No pueden entrar!*" one of them shouted as Sofía's driver reined in beside them. "You can't get in. The duke's orders."

"We have urgent business here." Enrique flipped a coin at the guards. "Open the gates."

The coin fell at the men's feet, but neither of them bent to take it. "*No pueden entrar,*" the first guard repeated. "The city is poxed."

Sofía had huddled in the shadow of the half roof of the phaeton; now she leaned forward. "Please, I must get in. I'll pay you anything."

"*Lo siento.* I'm sorry, señorita. No one goes in and no one goes out. Those are my orders." He took a step closer to the carriage. The face of the doña was hidden by the hood of her dark cape. He'd heard stories of a mysterious woman who came and went, whom no one ever saw clearly. She undoubtedly did so with the permission of his master; there had never been orders to bar her. Today, however, everyone was barred. It had been so for two weeks, ever since smallpox had broken in the town. "*Lo siento,*" he repeated.

Sofía pushed back the hood, revealing her face. She saw the startled recognition in the guard's eyes. He was young, just a boy really. Not old enough or hardened enough to hide his feelings. "Will you not do it for me, *mi niño*?" she asked.

"*Gitanita,* I didn't know—"

"No one in Caceres knows when I come. But now you do, because I'm desperate."

The second guard had stood impassively during the exchange; recognizing that something remarkable had happened, he came closer. "It's La Gitanita," the first whispered. "She says she has to get in, she says she's desperate." The second guard was older and more experienced. He wasn't going to be fooled by a pretty face masquerading as a heroine. What would La Gitanita be doing in Caceres today? He peered into the carriage. Sofía let him get a good look at her before she pulled her hood forward.

"*Mi madre*, it is you. But no, *Gitanita*," he said anxiously. "For the love of God and His Holy Mother, what will Spain do if you get the pox?"

Sofía spoke slowly, all her intense need in her words, looking first at one guard, then the other. "*Mis niños*, the treasure of my life is behind those walls. If I can't save it, I'll never sing again. And whatever my poor songs have meant to Spain . . . Well, there will be an end to them."

The impasse held them all in silence. The only sound was the labored breathing of the pair of chestnut geldings who stood heads down, steam rising from their flanks. The guards looked at each other, at the coachman, at the woman whose face was known from Andalusia to Galicia, whose music had become a rallying point for the resistance to the French invaders. Finally the young one motioned the driver closer. "Go to the right," he whispered. "To the gate off the Plaza Socorro. They open it every day around this time. Only for a few minutes, to bring in fresh food and medicine." He shuddered. "And to take out the corpses." The driver nodded and cracked his whip and the horses pulled the carriage forward.

The phaeton halted a short way from the cobblestone plaza outside the walls. "I'll come with you, Doña Sofía," Enrique said. "We can leave the carriage here."

"No, you stay with the horses. Wait for me. There's no reason for you to expose yourself, Enrique."

He protested but she wouldn't give in, and she crossed the plaza alone, head bent, cloak pulled tight around her as if it were winter, not the warm and humid early summer.

No one paid her any attention. The men outside the open narrow door were obviously terrified and eager to be done quickly. The figures passing them the burlap sacks full of corpses were nuns in black habits. Their coifs jutted out from either side of their heads, cutting off any side vision, and their faces were covered by heavy black veils. Sofía slipped past them and in the silent, desperate melee no one chose to notice.

The streets were empty, the terrified citizens of Caceres all hid in their houses, windows shuttered and curtained against the evil vapors that all knew carried the dreaded pox. She raced up the Calle de Gloria and into the warren of narrow alleys behind the palace of the Golfines. *I'm coming, my angel*, she promised in urgent silence. *I'm coming, Rafael.*

The door of the house where a few years earlier she'd hidden her son and Rosa was locked. Sofía fumbled with the large key, almost dropping it in her haste. Finally she was inside. She didn't stop to lock the door again, but almost automatically, her eyes raking the patio for any sign of Rafael, she shot the iron bolt.

Outside, a figure moved closer. A short, stocky body made a grotesquely broad shadow in the afternoon sun, and a powerful arm reached out to try the door. Bolted. Curse the whore to hell. Another opportunity lost. The figure receded into the shade of the walls and resumed a vigil of many days.

"Rafael! Rosa! Where are you?" Sofía sped from room to room. They all opened off the central patio, and each time she found no one she returned to the sunlit space studded with small palm trees and tried another. "I'm here. I came as soon as I heard. I'll take you away. Rafael, answer me, darling. It's Mama . . ."

The only reply was the sighing of the fronds of the squat *palmeras* as she brushed by them. But there was something else, a faint whimpering coming from somewhere inside. A cat, perhaps. No, a child. Rafael!

She called again, then paused and listened. For a moment all she heard was the terrified beating of her own heart, then the whimper once more. It came from the direction of the kitchen, but she'd already been there and it was empty.

Sofía returned to the kitchen. There was no fire in the grate. She put her hand over it. The embers were long cold. She smelled stale smoke, but she couldn't tell if it came from in there, or if it seeped in through the small tightly closed and barred window, evidence of the pyre of corpses they were burning beyond the walls of the city. "Rafael," she called again. Softly this time, so he wouldn't be frightened. "It's Mama, darling. Where are you?" The answering whimper was a little stronger.

She looked around her wildly, trying to judge the direction of that single heartrending sound. There was a small door beside the fireplace, almost hidden by a chair. She flung the chair out of the way and pulled at the door. It was bolted from the inside. There was a keyhole and Sofía knelt down and put her eye to it. She could see nothing but blackness. The stairs were steep, she remembered that. She'd gone down them only once, when she first brought Rosa and Rafael there. The stairs led to a small wine cellar and food store. It was damp and dark. In God's name, why was Rafael locked in the wine cellar? Where was Rosa?

"Rafi," she called softly through the keyhole, using the pet name she'd given him long before. "It's me, darling. I can't get in, the door is bolted on your side. You'll have to come up the stairs and open it. Can you hear me, Rafi?"

"*Sí, Mamacita.*"

The simple words filled her with joy. He was there. He was alive. "Come up the stairs, darling. Open the door. You're a big, strong boy, you can do it."

She heard the padding footsteps, tentative at first, then racing toward her. She could even hear his breathing as he struggled to throw back the heavy bolt. It seemed an eternity before he succeeded, but he did, and the door opened and she grabbed her child and held him in her arms. "Rafi, Rafi, thank God. I came as soon as I could, darling. Oh, God, let me look at you."

Sofía pushed the shock of dark hair off his forehead, studying his face, terrified that she would see the telltale yellow pustules. His face was unmarked. She grabbed his hands, looking at first one, then the other in the dim light of the shuttered kitchen. They were clean. She pushed up his shirt, only half registering that it was filthy and hadn't been changed for days, and examined his back and his chest. The smooth baby skin betrayed no sign of the pox. She hugged him fiercely, in an ecstasy of relief so strong it made her dizzy.

"We were hiding," he said, small arms tight around her neck. "You smell so good, *Mamacita*. It smells funny in the cellar. That's where Rosa and me were hiding so the bad sickness wouldn't get us. But she went to sleep and she won't wake up. I keep shaking her and calling and calling and she won't wake up. I'm hungry, *Mamacita*. I didn't have any breakfast."

Sofía sat him on the pine table, ignoring the layer of dust that covered it. She found a piece of cheese in the larder cupboard beneath the window. It was old and hard, but it had no mold. "Here, darling. Eat this now. We'll get something more in a moment." She watched him gnaw on it. His front tooth had come out the month before, but the new one was in now. It was a perfect white tooth, just as everything about him was perfect. The small, sturdy body, the dark curly hair that was like hers, and the tawny Mendoza eyes—they were all perfect. And he did not have smallpox.

"Listen, my angel, you must stay here and not move. I'll be back in a moment."

"Where are you going?"

"Downstairs into the cellar. I have to see Rosa, darling. Then we'll go."

There was a candle in a rough clay holder on the table, and Sofía carried it to the tinderbox beside the fireplace. The oily smell of the partly burned cotton in the box assailed her as she searched for the flint and the steel. She didn't know where anything was because she never did such homely tasks in this house, not anywhere, for that matter, not for years.

She found what she was looking for and willed her hands to stop shaking. After a few tries she struck a spark. The tinder caught and she poked a brimstone-tipped match at it. The smell of sulphur rose acrid in the air as the match burst into flame. Sofía lit the candle, blew out the match and closed the lid of the tinderbox to smother its flame. "Remember, Rafi, don't move. I'll be right back."

She had to bend to descend the stairs, and even at the bottom she couldn't stand upright because there wasn't full headroom in the tiny cellar. She moved the candle around, casting flickering shadows on the damp stone walls. The corpse was huddled in the farthest corner.

She knew it was a corpse before she approached it. Death was apparent in the stiff, unnatural position of Rosa's arms and legs, in her absolute stillness. But Sofía had to be sure; she owed that much to the woman who had served her so devotedly and loved Rafael as intensely as she did.

The funny smell Rafi had mentioned came from the body. It was the smell of sickness, not decay. The corpse had not yet begun to rot. Perhaps she hadn't been dead very long, or the moist cool of the cellar had preserved her. Sofía bent closer, moving the light of the candle over Rosa's body. Her black dress betrayed nothing; it covered her from neck to ankles. Rosa was as modest in death as she'd been in life. Her face was turned to the wall.

Gingerly Sofía reached out and tried to turn the head. It was already stiff and wouldn't move. She'd have to roll Rosa over to see her. Sofía hung back, repelled by the thought. But she must do it. She couldn't just leave without some final act of thanks. She prodded the body with her foot, and it flipped over and landed with a soft thump. Sofía moved the candle, then choked back a scream of horror. Rosa's face was swollen beyond recognition. The pustules had all scabbed over, and a red-brown crust covered her like excrement.

"*Mamacita.*" Rafael was at the top of the stairs. "Please, *Mamacita,* come up here. I don't want to stay alone . . ." He put his foot on the first stair.

"No, don't come down. I'm coming up now." Sofía ran up the steps, pushing her son out of the cellar ahead of her and slamming the door behind them.

"Did Rosa wake up?" the boy asked.

"No, darling, she can't. Rosa has gone to be with God."

He started to ask more questions. "Shh, not now, Rafi. We'll talk about it later. I'm taking you away from here now." She lifted him into her arms and ran out of the kitchen into the patio. She had to put him down to open the iron bolt on the door to the alley, but she picked him up again as soon as it swung open. Sofía took no care to close it again. All that she wanted of Caceres was in her arms; the devil could take whatever she left behind.

She had given no thought to how she was going to get herself and Rafael out of the city. The door to the Plaza de Socorro would doubtless be closed by now. But there would be a guard and she would bribe him the way she'd bribed the two at the San Antonio Gate—with her face and her fame, and the symbol she'd become of the country's determination to be rid of the Bonapartes and all their works.

She felt the body hurtling toward her before she saw it. A shape lunged for her. She saw the flash of a totally bald head in the sunlight, the glitter of a single gold earring in the shape of a snake, the lethal gleam of an unsheathed knife. She screamed and hung on to her son as Paco's powerful arms tried to pull him away from her. Her traveling boots were strong leather and she kicked fiercely, aiming for the groin but missing.

After her one scream of terror and surprise they struggled in silence. Sofía kept waiting for the knife to descend, and even as she kicked and twisted she was trying to protect Rafael's back from its thrust. But it didn't come. Instead, Paco tossed the knife away and used both hands to tear at her grip. He was trying to grab the child from her, to kick her away and take Rafael. She hung on with the ferocity of a wild beast.

It had all happened in seconds and only now did the little boy know fear. "Mama! Mama!" His arms clung more tightly around her neck. Sofía had no breath with which to answer or reassure him. She aimed another kick at Paco's groin and missed again. He had hold of Rafael's waist and had almost pulled him away. Then the child's cotton breeches tore and the Gypsy was left holding air. He cursed and lunged again.

"Señora, *qué pasa?*" A man ran toward them, a priest in the brown habit of a Franciscan friar. "*Qué hace, Gitano!* Leave them alone!"

Paco paused for a moment. He stared at Sofía and at Rafael, then at the priest. The Franciscan was almost upon them. Paco turned and ran.

Sofía sagged against the wall, heaving for breath, still clinging to Rafael, who was sobbing with terror. The priest had reached them now.

"Are you all right? Who was he, what did he want?"

Sofía made no attempt to answer his questions. "Thank you, Padre. You saved us."

He looked at her. Her hood had fallen off and her hair come free of its bun in the struggle. Still, he recognized her. "La Gitanita, it is you, isn't it?"

Sofía nodded.

"What are you doing in Caceres of all places?" He didn't wait for a reply. "No matter, you can tell me later. Here, give me the child."

She continued to cling to Rafael, unable to make herself give him up even to this benign stranger. "It's all right," he said gently. "I'm Father Alfonso. I mean you no harm, I promise you. Give me the child and come. You need care and shelter, both of you. I know a safe place." Reluctantly, but knowing that she had no choice, Sofía passed over her son.

She did not know Caceres. She had gone there as often as she could, but always she arrived by night, spent a day or two with Rafael and Rosa during which she never went out of the house, then left, again by night. She had no idea where Father Alfonso was taking them as, carrying Rafael, he sped through adjoining alleys and across a broad plaza fronting a church. He passed the church and turned right, darting down another alley, then stopped and opened a door set in a high stone wall. "In here, Gitanita. It's all right, I promise you." He stepped aside for Sofía to precede him.

She was in a study of sorts, a small square room with a large crucifix on one wall, a table and two chairs, and rows of books. She reached out her arms and the priest returned her son to them, then she collapsed into one of the chairs, clutching Rafael, who had stopped sobbing but who clung to her as if he would never let go.

Father Alfonso looked at mother and child a moment, then without a word he let himself out of the room through a door

different from the one they'd entered. In a few minutes he was
back. A black-robed and veiled nun followed him, carrying a
tray with two glasses and a plate of cakes.

Sofía gasped when she saw the nun. "Where are we?" she
demanded.

"In the Casa de los Infermos," the priest said. "But don't be
frightened. I told you it was safe, and it is."

"How can it be safe? No one leaves the Casa de los Infermos
alive. Besides, she's one of the corpse tenders."

"Yes, at least that's what everyone calls them. They refer to
themselves as the Sisters of Hope. She can't speak to you, by
the way, they take a vow of silence. Eat something, señorita.
Give something to the child. Sweet things are good at a time
like this. The sugar gives you energy."

He took a glass from the tray the nun held and offered it to
Sofía. She hesitated. "Please," he said again gently. "There's
nothing to fear. I'm a doctor as well as a priest."

Sofía took the glass and sipped from it. She tasted the sweet
hot chocolate drink that all Spain had become addicted to since
cocoa beans were discovered in Spanish America. "Here, Rafi.
It's good." She held the glass to the little boy's lips and he took
a sip, then pushed it away. "No more? But you said you were
hungry. Look, there are cakes too."

"I'm not hungry anymore. My throat hurts."

"It hurts because you were crying. Drink a bit more, you'll
feel better."

The child shook his head. "I hurt all over, *Mamacita,* not
just my throat."

Father Alfonso took a step closer. "Let me look at him,
señorita."

Sofía pressed Rafael closer to her. "No, I know what you're
thinking, but he's not poxed. I checked everywhere. There's
not a mark on him."

"The marks don't come until later," the priest said gently.
"Please, *Gitanita,* I can help. Allow me to do so."

Once more she gave up her son into his arms and watched
as he examined each part of the small body. The silent nun
watched, too, and it was to her that Father Alfonso spoke. "The

first stage. He has a fever, climbing steadily. Here, take him. You know what to do."

Rafael screamed as the black-robed woman lifted him. Sofía jumped from her chair. "No! They handle the corpses. They're diseased."

The Franciscan put himself between the mother and the nun who held the boy. "Señorita, listen to me. The sisters are not carrying the disease. They cannot carry it. But the child has already come into contact with it. He has smallpox. You have to accept that. There are things we can do, but the only thing you can do is pray that he has a mild case."

Sobbing Sofía collapsed into the chair. She saw the nun carry Rafael from the room. She heard him screaming for her. She was powerless to help him, and that was the worst agony of all.

Alfonso went to a table and returned carrying a small glass. "It's brandy. Drink it, you'll feel better."

She drank the fiery liquid and gave him back the empty glass. "He was with his *niñera*," she said dully. "She died of the pox before I came. I don't know exactly when. Maybe last night, maybe this morning."

"How old is the child?" the priest asked.

"Eight years." She lied without hesitation. Here she was on solid ground, following the plan she'd made when Rafael was born, the one from which she'd never deviated.

"Small for his age," the priest said. "I'd have guessed a bit younger." She didn't reply. "I did not know La Gitanita had a son," he added.

"No one knows. Rafael has always lived here in Caceres with Rosa, the *niñera*. She looked after him for me. I came every few weeks, but in disguise." She buried her face in her hands. "This time I came too late. I was with the *guerrilleros* in the hills near Zafra. Everything's so confused. The English Army has given up trying to starve out Badajoz. They're pulling back into Portugal again. I didn't know there was pox in Caceres until a few days ago. Then I had to wait until they found a carriage for me." She began crying again. "I came as soon as I could, but it wasn't soon enough."

"Please, señorita, calm yourself. Perhaps it was. In the early stages—" He broke off. Talking about the disease would only make it worse for her. "Don't give up hope, señorita. Tell me about Badajoz. They say the French never came out to fight."

"In the hills we heard that Don Arturo attacked the town twice, but the English ladders were too short to reach the top of the walls, and they wouldn't fall to battering."

"We Spaniards have built too well for our own good, it seems now." The priest smiled wryly. "And this Don Arturo, the generalissimo the English call Wellington? He's a good general?"

"The *guerrilleros* say he is a lion. I trust them."

"So do I," Alfonso said. "This whole thing is remarkable, you know. Napoleon made one miscalculation, he didn't realize that he could capture the Spanish throne but never the Spanish people. And every peasant who kills a Frenchman shouts at the moment of victory, 'For the Virgin and La Gitanita.' They've canonized you, señorita."

"They're not that foolish," Sofía said. "They know I'm not a saint. But the songs I sing are their songs. I represent their country and remind them what they're fighting for, that's all."

"It's a very great deal. The Church and Spain are in your debt, *Gitanita*." Then, because talking about all this had calmed her somewhat: "Do you want to tell me about the Gypsy who attacked you?" She didn't reply. "Is he the boy's father?" Alfonso asked gently.

Sofía's head shot up. "*Madre de Dios!* How could you imagine that animal to be Rafael's father? Of course he isn't."

"Who is?"

"That's none of your affair, Padre."

"I see." So the boy was a bastard, as he'd suspected. There were those who said that La Gitanita had many lovers. Others insisted it was only calumny spread by the French, because the peasants who adored her would never accept such immorality. Bad enough that the queen had taken a lover and thrown them all into this nightmare, now the symbol of resistance too? "I see," he repeated.

"I doubt that you do." Sofía stood up. "When can I see Rafael?"

"I'll take you to him now."

He led her through a series of dark passages. A few times they passed the silent, black-robed figures who never greeted them or acknowledged their presence. They came to a small winding stair, and the priest stepped aside and motioned for Sofía to ascend.

When she did she was in a small room at the top of a tower. Rafael was in a bed covered by a clean white sheet. One of the nuns sat beside him. There were windows on all four sides of the room and each of them was open. "The evil vapors..." Sofía dashed to one of the windows and tried to pull it closed. "God in heaven, what are you doing? Are you all mad?"

Alfonso grabbed her arms and dragged her away from the window. "Listen to me—I told you I was a doctor. The disease doesn't come from the air. A man in England has proved that. Edward Jenner has shown us it comes only from contact with another victim. And if the patient survives that infection, he's protected for life. We deliberately give the disease now. It's called vaccination and—" He broke off. She wasn't listening to him or absorbing his words. Her entire body strained toward the small figure in the bed. He released her and she ran to kneel beside her son.

"The important thing now is to keep the fever from mounting too high," Alfonso said. "That's why the windows are open. If we do that, the case may be less virulent. If it is, he'll live. We'll know in two days, señorita. When the first pox come."

"Look." The priest pulled back the sheet. "A few here on his chest and his belly. Turn over, *mi niño*, let your mama see the rest of you." He rolled Rafael over gently. The boy was compliant and peaceful, and he looked much better to Sofía than he had the day before. "It's been a week and there are no more than a dozen pustules here on his buttocks and his back. God is good, señorita. It's the mildest possible case. Your son will be fine."

She knelt beside the bed and reached out, but the priest stopped her. "Don't touch him," he whispered. "He's highly contagious now."

Sofía allowed herself to be moved a bit back from the bed. "Did you hear the padre, my angel? You're going to be all better soon and we'll go away."

"I itch, *Mamacita*."

"I know, my love, but you mustn't scratch. It will make scars."

The nun approached and swabbed the sores with a bit of linen she'd dipped into an evil-looking concoction. "The herbs help the itching a bit," the priest said. "They can't stop it entirely."

Sofía thought of Fanta and her potions. She longed to take the linen from the nun and dab Rafael's body herself, but she knew they wouldn't let her. "Promise me you'll try not to scratch," she told him. "Then you will still be my handsome boy when we go on our trip."

"Where will we go, *Mamacita*?"

"It's a surprise," Sofía said. A surprise to her, too; she had no idea where to take him. But she'd think of something. "I'll tell you when you're all better," she promised Rafael.

Later she sat again with Father Alfonso in his study and asked the question she hadn't dared to ask before, because her terror for Rafael had been enough to bear. "Will I get the pox now?"

"Well, it's wise to be cautious, but I think not. It's been a week and you show no signs. I believe you may be one of those naturally immune to the disease, señorita. It's not uncommon. I myself am. And that means you can't infect anyone else either. Infection comes only from contact with a pustule."

The Franciscan gripped the crucifix that hung from the rope tied around his waist. "The ways of God are strange, *Gitanita*. In those books there"—he gestured toward the shelf—"are reports from the Jesuits working in China. Those heathen knew a thousand years ago what good Christians are only just learning. The Chinese doctors pulverize the scabs from a pox victim and blow a bit of it up the noses of people who have never had the disease. If they're fortunate, they get a mild case. Then, as I said, they're immune."

"All these nuns, you told me they couldn't give the disease. Are they all naturally immune as well?"

Alfonso shook his head. "No, they haven't been blessed in that way. Their order was founded for women who have been poxed and recovered. Women who have no place afterwards except in a convent." He lowered his voice and did not meet her eyes. "That's why they veil their faces. In some cases the ravages of the disease can be quite terrible, señorita. But they're immune now, as Rafael will be. Where will you take him when he's well?"

"I'm not sure. I have a house in Madrid. At least, I had. But they say the French keep watch on it, that they would like to capture me."

"No doubt," Alfonso agreed. He hesitated, then determined to go on. "Señorita, forgive me, but I must speak frankly. Have you thought of taking your child into Portugal? Away from Spain."

"Why would I think of such a thing?"

"Because if you simply disappeared, you would remain a wonderful legend and continue to give those who defend Spain and the Church hope and something to fight for. But—"

"But if I appear with a bastard child, I destroy the legend," she said quietly. "I hadn't thought of it. I've been too worried about Rafi, but you're right, of course."

"Then you'll go to Portugal? We have many houses there. I could send you to one of our convents with a letter of introduction. I can arrange everything."

"No. Thank you, but no, I won't go to Portugal."

"But you agreed—"

"I agreed that you were correct in your assessment of my situation," she said. "Not in the solution."

Alfonso was silent for a moment. "You're a strange woman, *Gitanita*. I'm not sure I understand you at all."

More important, Sofía thought, the priest didn't understand Rafael. Didn't know he was a Mendoza and that if she did what he said, the heritage Rafael would lose was an empire, not a nation and a nationality. And the priest didn't know about

Paco, who had somehow found out about Rafael, and who was
bent on kidnapping him for ransom. Otherwise he would have
killed one or the other of them in the street. "I would be grateful
for help all the same," she told the priest.

"Whatever I can do, I will do, *Gitanita*. I owe you that as a
Spaniard and a son of the Church."

"You saved my son's life. You owe me nothing. Rafael and
I are in your debt, Padre. We'll repay it someday. In the meantime, we need something more. Have you found Enrique and
my phaeton?" She'd sent them to look for her driver and carriage
the first day.

"We found the driver, yes. I didn't say anything before because I didn't want to add to your worries. Your Enrique was
a bit the worse for wear, and there is no phaeton. He was
attacked by thieves while he waited for you."

She was visibly upset. "You should have told me, Padre. Was
Enrique badly hurt?"

"No, as it turned out. I saw him this morning and he's almost
recovered. Just a blow on the head."

"Thank God." Sofía thought for a moment, then looked up.
"Listen, what I need now is a closed carriage and four strong
horses. We'll leave as soon as Rafael and Enrique are well
enough to travel."

"A carriage can be arranged. Where will you go?"

"To Córdoba," she said quietly. "Rafael and I will go to
Córdoba."

❧ 15 ❧

The carriage that stopped at the Posada del Potro at sundown carried no luggage strapped to its roof and the driver wore no recognizable livery. The only occupants were a black-veiled nun and a small boy. The innkeeper was puzzled, but these were strange times. "*Sí, señores,* how can I help you?"

"We need a room," the driver said. "Something decent for the sister and the child."

The innkeeper hesitated, then shrugged and motioned them inside. "Up there." He gestured to a balcony above the open courtyard. "Six reales for the night. In advance."

The driver paid. "I'll want a bed as well," he said. "And stabling for the horses."

The child stared at the landlord but didn't say a word. The nun kept her black-veiled face modestly cast down and was also silent. The arrangements were made, more money changed hands. The boy and the woman mounted the stairs and disappeared into the room the landlord had indicated.

"Did I do it right, *Mamacita?*" Rafael asked, his eyes twinkling with excitement. "Did we fool him?"

Sofía threw back her veil and hugged him. "You did it perfectly, darling. You were wonderfully scary. I bet he has something to tell his wife tonight!"

"What happens now, *Mamacita*? What's the next part of our—" He paused. "I forget the word."

"Adventure, darling. Our adventure. And the next part is very hard. Do you think you can do it?"

Rafael drew himself up very straight. "Yes, I can."

"Yes, I'm sure you can. You must stay here alone, my love. But it won't be for long, and Enrique will be sitting right downstairs watching the door, so you'll be perfectly safe as long as you don't go out or open the window." She was checking the locks on the window even as she spoke. They were secure. And there were shutters she could close. "It will be very hard, Rafi," she said, turning to him. "I know it will be. But you must do exactly what I say. Promise me you will."

"I promise, *Mamacita*."

"They don't give alms in there, *hermana*. You're wasting your time." The man walking past the gates of the Mendoza palace made his comment to the nun, then continued on his way. Sofía waited until he was out of sight and looked to make sure no one else was in the road. It was long past dark, and the Calle Averroes was empty.

She rang the bell. Nothing happened. She rang it again. Once before, six years ago now, she had stood here and tried to get in and finally gone away defeated. Tonight she would not go away. She rang the bell a third time. The brass was tarnished black and the rope pull so rotten that it came loose into her hand. Sofía threw it down in disgust and banged on the door with her fist.

A peephole of about a hand's width and breadth had been cut into the gate at eye level. It opened. She could see a part of a face: grizzled, slack-jawed, the eyes dull and uninterested. "Yes, what is it? We have no business with nuns here."

"I must see the hidalgo."

"The hidalgo sees no one. Go away."

The man started to close the tiny door, but Sofía pressed her face close to the opening. "Wait. Listen to me," she whispered urgently through the black veil, her voice tinged with menace. "If you don't let me in, I will put a curse on you. Your hair will all fall out, then your teeth, next your arms and your legs will fall off, and finally your private parts." She could see the terror on the servant's face even before she finished describing the terrible things that would befall him.

"*Madre de Dios*, you're not a nun, you're a devil."

"A witch. And I will curse you. I'm starting the curse now." She muttered some gibberish.

"*¡Ay, qué malsuerte!* No, wait ... I'm opening the gate now. See, I'm doing it. ..."

Not for nothing had she spent so much time with the simple peasants of Spain these three last years. They were more superstitious than Fanta and Zocali and the rest of the tribes combined. She slipped into the Patio del Recibo before he pulled the gate all the way open. "Quick, shut it. Good, now tell me, where is the hidalgo?"

"I don't know. I swear, I don't know. The palace is very big. He goes from one room to the next. Sometimes I don't see him for days."

"Very well, I will find him. Stop bobbing up and down like a fish in a barrel. Listen to me, are there any other servants?"

"No, *hermana,* no. Only me, I swear it."

"Good. I want you to leave here for a while."

"Leave? Why should I leave? This is my home, I live here. I have no place to go."

"Yes, I understand, that's why you stay. A roof over your head and nothing to do." She looked at the debris that was knee-deep on the cobblestones of the patio. The litter of years had blown over the walls and been left to rot; bits of paper and fallen leaves and broken branches were a tangled mess everywhere except along a rough path that had been swept, or more likely kicked, from one of the doors to the front gates. Weeds had planted themselves in the refuse and flourished on either side of the makeshift track. "Go away," Sofía repeated. "After midnight you can return."

The servant still hesitated. "But—"

"Go, or I'll start the curse again!" She pulled the door open and pushed him out of it and, ignoring his murmured, terrified protests, shut it behind him. There was a large, rusted key in the lock, and she turned it and put the key in her pocket. Then she took a deep breath. Where to begin? At the beginning. There was no other choice. Sofía walked toward the first door she saw.

The filth was incredible. The once-glorious curtains hung in tatters from broken windows, but at least that allowed moonlight to enter the enormous rooms. What she saw in the milky reflection chilled her soul. The walls of reality had crumbled and she was looking through the breach at a lunatic world spun free of its axis.

Cobwebs hung from chandeliers in which the last candle had guttered away years before. Most of the furniture was scattered and broken, gilt arms and legs hacked off for firewood. The seat covers of the sofas and chairs were in shreds, and creatures had gnawed loose the horsehair stuffing. She heard the soft slithering noise of rats scurrying ahead of her as she walked, and realized it was they who had stripped the remains of the Mendoza citadel to line what must be a kingdom of nests.

In one enormous salon the stench of a dead rodent was overpowering. Sofía gagged and fought the urge to turn and run. There was no place to run to, she reminded herself, not for her and not for Rafael. She choked back her nausea, willed her legs to stop trembling, and went on.

For some twenty minutes more she wandered through this vista of horrors, then at last she found him.

Robert was in a small room that had a frieze of mosaic leaves running around the top of the walls. He sat on the floor, staring straight ahead. Apparently he neither saw nor heard her. Of all the terrible things she'd seen tonight, this was the worst. Sofía was shattered. All her strength and determination leaked away through the mortal wound made by the sight of him. If this was Robert, her dreams were nightmares and her hopes a mockery.

In less than seven years the young, virile Englishman who had captured her body and her soul had become an old man. His hair and his beard were both white, and long and straggling; his body was thin and stooped, his clothes filthy. His mind must be gone. The Robert she'd known and loved could not be contained in that broken shell.

She closed her eyes, then opened them again. He was still there, still staring at the wall, still a cruel caricature of what he'd been. She started to turn away. There was no hope for her here. No future for her child could be built on this ruin. *You have a great destiny.* She heard Fanta speaking the words she had spoken so long ago. A great destiny. If not here, where? If not now, when?

"Robert," Sofía said softly. "Robert, look at me." He did not move for some seconds. She repeated his name. "Robert, can you hear me?"

At last he turned his face to her. She bit her lip to keep from crying out. His eyes were black holes; two deep lines ran from his nose to his chin. The unkempt beard covered the lower half of his face. But the voice—*Madre de Dios*—the voice was the same. "Of course I can hear you. Who are you? How did you get in here?"

Ordinary questions asked in an ordinary tone, and in that deeply resonant voice she'd never forgotten. Somewhere deep inside Sofía a spark of hope fluttered to life and her determination was reborn. Whatever else he might be, Robert wasn't mad. She didn't answer him immediately. She crossed the floor and stood in front of him, and lifted her veil and tossed it back over the black coif that covered her head. "It's Sofía, Robert. I must speak with you."

He looked up at her, squinting in the gloom. Did something flicker in his eyes, some hint of caring dredged from the past? She couldn't be sure; it happened too fast. "Sofía?" There was no emotion in his tired voice. "Yes, it is you, isn't it? Have you become a nun? How extraordinary. I'm afraid I have nothing to say to you in any case. Go away, Sister Sofía."

"No, I won't go away. We have a very great deal to say to each other, Robert."

He didn't answer; instead, he turned his head and shouted, "Indalencio!"

She almost laughed aloud with the joy and hope of it. He shouted. He was annoyed, imperious, demanding.

"Indalencio, get your useless old carcass in here! I want you to show this nun the way out."

"You're wasting your breath," Sofía said. "If this Indalencio is your servant, he won't answer. I sent him away so we could speak privately."

"Did you? Too bad. You shouldn't have. The old thief is quite adequate as a corpse tender." He leaned against the wall and closed his eyes, the glimmer of life gone once more. "I'm tired. Leave me alone."

She knelt beside him and grabbed his shoulders, astonished anew at how thin and frail he'd become. But that didn't matter now because she knew the truth, and she knew what she had to do. She shook him as fiercely as she dared. God in heaven, he might break in her hands. Well, if he did, so be it, he was no use to himself or anyone else as he was. "Listen to me, damn you! I know you've been hiding here for years, all Spain knows. But it's over. You're Robert Mendoza and you can't run away from that anymore. I won't let you. You owe something to the Mendozas who will come after you."

He made a sound between a laugh and a groan. "There are no Mendozas to come after me. I'm the last of my line, Sofía. The last gasp of the mighty Mendozas of Córdoba. Pitiful, isn't it? All that glory, then me."

She slapped him across the face. Once, then again. Hard slaps that stung her palm and left a red stain on his hollow cheek. Except for the way his body jerked, he made no response. "You're disgusting. Your self-pity is sickening. But I'm going to save you in spite of yourself, Robert Mendoza. Now, get up." She got to her feet, dragging him after her. "Where's your bedroom, your dressing room?"

Robert didn't answer, but he followed her, as docile as a child. It was as if there were two people warring inside him, the man he'd been and the ghost he'd become. For the moment the ghost held sway. She led him out of the room to the square patio with the stone filigree screens and looked around, trying to decide which direction to take. A movement in one corner caught her eye. "Indalencio, is that you? Well, that's your name, isn't it? Get out from behind there. Make yourself useful, you foolish old man."

"I came back, *hermana*. But only to help you. Don't curse me, please. . . ."

"Stop whining. And stop calling me sister. I'm not a nun. Where is the bedroom of the hidalgo?"

"He doesn't have a bedroom. I mean not anymore. He just walks around and sleeps wherever—"

"Yes, yes, I know. Take us to his former bedroom."

She kept hold of Robert's hand as Indalencio led them up a narrow flight of servants' stairs and along a series of corridors. The only light was the moon and the candle he carried, but she could see well enough to identify dirt and desolation everywhere. Still, it was much better than what she'd seen so far. These private quarters of the Palacio Mendoza had weathered the years of neglect more successfully than the public rooms below. Probably because the two men lived entirely downstairs and the upper floors were left to molder in peace.

"Here," Indalencio said, stopping in front of an intricately carved oaken door. "This was once the room of the hidalgo."

She pulled Robert into the room. He stumbled after her, seemingly unaware of what was happening. Sofía saw another door that must lead to the dressing room. "Is there a bathing tub in there?"

"*Sí, hermana*, I mean señorita."

"Get water. Hot water, lots of it. And soap."

"*Sí, sí, inmediatamente*." He stopped speaking. "But I can't. There is no way to heat water, the stove isn't lit."

"Then light it, damn you! *Ahora, tu entiendes?*" He nodded. "*Bueno, ¡sales tu!*"

Indalencio scuttled away and she turned to Robert. "Now, let's get these filthy clothes off."

It was almost four in the morning when Sofía returned to the Posada del Potro. The gate to the street was closed and barred, but when she pressed her face to the iron grating she saw Enrique sitting in the courtyard holding Rafael in his arms.

He'd wrapped him in a blanket and the child was sleeping. "Psst . . ." She made a soft hissing sound. "Enrique, let me in."

"*Gracias a Dios*." He lay the boy down gently, then rushed to the gate and began unbolting it. "I was terrified for you, Doña Sofía. You were gone so long. And the little boy became frightened. He never came out of the room, but I could hear him crying. So after the landlord locked up, I went upstairs and got him and brought him down here."

"Thank you. I don't know what I would have done without you these last weeks, Enrique. But there's no time to talk now. We're leaving immediately. Forget about the carriage and the horses, you can come for them in the morning. It's not far, we can walk."

They went back into the street together, Enrique carrying Rafael, Sofía leading the way. She had taken the key to the door that led to the Patio de los Naranjos before she left, and now she let them back into the palace that way. Indalencio was nowhere to be seen. She wondered if he'd run away in terror. No matter, tomorrow, she would think about the problem of servants. "Come this way, Enrique. The place is a pigsty, but we'll deal with that later. Up these stairs. Be careful, they're so filthy you might slip."

"I won't slip, señorita," Enrique said softly. She was magnificent, his *Gitanita*. He thanked God and all His saints that the robbers in Caceres hadn't killed him, that he'd lived to continue to serve her.

There were stubs of candles everywhere among the debris. They were useless because Sofía had no idea where a tinderbox or a flint might be. The moon was gone now, but they had starlight to guide them along the corridor. In its hard blue glow she noticed that the walls were decorated with murals; beneath the covering of dirt was a hint of jewellike colors depicting another world.

They came to the carved door to Robert's room, and Sofía paused. "Wait here a moment." She took another key from the deep pocket of the black habit, opened the door slightly, and peered inside.

Indalencio had brought a lamp when they bathed Robert,

but he'd assured her that the tiny quantity of oil it contained was the last fuel in the palace. She'd left it burning with the wick turned down as far as she dared. It still flickered weakly and gave just enough light for her to make out Robert's form in the big bed. He was restless, turning and muttering in his sleep. But he was there. Sofía closed the door and didn't bother to lock it.

They walked a few paces more down the wide corridor. "Rafael and I will sleep in here." She opened the door to another large chamber she'd spied out before returning to the posada. A shaft of light entered from the corridor, a ghostly pathway leading her on. The room was draped almost entirely in black, but there was a big four-poster on a dais, and the bedclothes, though crumbling and yellow with age, were reasonably clean.

Enrique moved aside the hangings and lay the sleeping child on the bed. "*Mamacita*," Rafael murmured. Sofía leaned down and kissed his cheek.

"I'm right here, my angel. Sleep now." She straightened up and turned to Enrique. "There's a small room at that far end of this passage. You can sleep there."

He nodded but didn't say anything. When he let himself out of the chamber Doña Sofía had chosen for herself and her son, Enrique took off his cloak and made a pillow of it and stretched out in front of the door.

When she woke, it was still the black of night. But it couldn't be. Sofía got up, careful not to disturb Rafael, who was curled into a little ball beside her. She could see a faint line of light to her left, and she went toward it, arms stretched forward to guide her through the unfamiliar room. She tugged at the curtains blocking the suspicion of light, and they parted amid a cloud of dust. Golden sunlight burst into the chamber. Sofía drew a deep breath of wonder. Despite the filth it was magnificent.

She was looking out a pair of windowed doors to a balcony above a patio, and beyond that was spread the many angles and walls and cornices and gables of the Palacio Mendoza. Red roof tiles glowed in the sun. Here and there patches of verdant green moss and tiny succulent plants had lodged in their cracks and made intriguing patterns. She opened the doors and stepped outside. The flowers and trees of the patio below had long since withered and died, but through their skeletal remains she caught a glimpse of a fountain in some rare rich blue stone. Beneath her, nudging the railing of the balcony, a remarkably persistent bougainvillaea made a patch of vivid purple and green.

"*Mamacita?*"

She turned back to the bed. Rafael was sitting up and rubbing his eyes. "Good morning, darling."

"Where are we, Mama?"

"In a palace. In your palace, Rafi. Come see."

He clambered down off the high bed and went to join her. Sofía picked him up. "Look, isn't it splendid?"

"It's very big," he said somewhat uncertainly. "Is it really a palace?"

"Yes, it is. And it's really yours."

"Am I a duke, then?"

"No, my love. You're not a duke, you're a prince." She swung him around and set him down. "Let's explore a bit, shall we? We can start right here with this room."

Sofía moved around it. She quickly discovered that the black hangings all came down if she tugged at them. Behind them were mosaics and tapestries. The coverings had protected sharp reds and mellow blues and soft yellows. "They must be the only things in this place that aren't covered by six years of dust. Look, Rafi, I wonder what's behind those doors."

There were a line of them covering one wall, and the keys were in the tiny locks. Sofía opened the doors and saw row after row of gowns and squealed with pleasure. "They're old styles, but they're magnificent. Don't you think so, Rafi?"

"I like them better than that black dress you're wearing, *Mamacita.*"

"So do I. I shall change at once."

Sofía selected a pale pink gown trimmed in heavy white lace. It was the simplest one she could find, and thus the least out of fashion. She spotted tortoise-shell brushes and combs on a dressing table in one corner and began fixing her hair. The alabaster jar that had once held beeswax was empty, so she couldn't sleek it back. A number of soft curls escaped the bun at her neck and curled around her face. Never mind, it was the best she could do and it wasn't unflattering. "Well, Rafi, what do you think?" She turned for her son's approval, but he was gone. "Rafi, where are you?"

"Right here. Look, I picked some flowers for your hair." He came in off the balcony clutching a spray of the purple bougainvillaea.

"Rafi, how could you reach that?"

"I hung over the edge. Don't worry, I'm a very good climber."

He spoke with such grave solemnity she had to laugh. She dropped a deep curtsy and took the flowers from his hand. "Thank you, Prince Rafael. I shall wear them with pride."

She'd just pinned the purple blossoms behind her ear when there was a light tap on the door. It brought Sofía immediately face-to-face with the reality that awaited her in this desolate place. "*Adelante*." She took a deep breath and prepared for whatever might come.

"Doña Sofía, I found some water and some coffee and some milk. I thought you and the child—" Enrique was holding a tray with two cups. He stopped speaking when he saw her. "Forgive me for being so bold, señorita. But you look very beautiful."

"Thank you, and thank you for the coffee. Have you seen anyone else?"

"No one. And the señor who is sleeping down there"—he jerked his head toward Robert's room—"hasn't appeared. I listened and I could hear him breathing, but I didn't go in."

"Very good, Enrique. We're going to stay here for some time. Perhaps a long time. And neither Rafael nor I can live in this filth. I want you to go into the town and get some women. Bring them back here to clean. You'd better stop and order some food as well, and make sure that at least one of the women is a decent cook. We'll worry about a majordomo and footmen later. Right now what we need are sensible señoras who know how to scrub."

The coachman cleared his throat. "Doña Sofía, forgive me, but . . ."

"Yes?"

"But what about money? They will expect to be paid, probably in advance. If I had any, it would be yours, Doña Sofía, but I don't. Those miserable thieves in Caceres took my last real, and we've spent everything the priest gave us for the journey."

"At the moment I have no money," Sofía admitted. "If I'd been better prepared before we went to Caceres, it would be different. As it is . . ." She shrugged. "But you won't need money, Enrique. Tell the señoras that they are coming to work in the Palacio Mendoza. Tell them the hidalgo is well again and he's summoned them. Tell them there will be plenty of money. The Mendozas make reales out of air, everyone knows that."

Enrique looked doubtful but determined. "I will try, Doña Sofía." He turned to go. There was a man standing in the doorway, watching them. He was as tall and thin as a scarecrow, and his white hair and white beard made him resemble some ancient prophet. He was staring at Doña Sofía and the child. Enrique stepped protectively in front of them looking as though he wished he had a weapon.

"It's all right, Enrique," Sofía said. "This is Don Robert, the hidalgo. We are old friends. Go and do as I've told you."

She waited until the coachman's footsteps had died away, then she said, "Good morning, Robert. Do you feel better after your bath?"

"Where is the black habit? I thought you were a nun."

"I told you I wasn't. That was a disguise. I don't know whose gown this is, but I hope its owner won't mind my borrowing it."

He laughed, but it was not a pleasant sound. "It was Doña Carmen's. This was her room, but, as you know, she's long dead, like all the Mendozas. Who is the boy?"

Rafael had been hovering behind Sofía, peeping out from around her full skirt at the terrifying-looking stranger. Sofía drew him forward. "My son, Rafael Pablo Mendoza. Rafi, this is your cousin Robert."

Robert shook his head. "You're lying. Pablo had no son."

"Yes, he did. Here he is."

"I don't believe you. Pablo would have mentioned him."

"It makes little difference whether you believe me. Rafael was born some months after Pablo died. I have the papers to prove it. Signed by a priest."

Robert looked at the boy a moment longer, then shrugged. "It doesn't matter now."

"Yes, it does." Sofía took a step toward him. "All this is Rafael's heritage. You have no right to destroy it."

"All what? A crumbling palace, a name that's been dishonored? Sofía, you must be the most stupid woman in Spain. Why don't you change your son's name? At least protect the poor little bastard from the infamy of being a Mendoza."

Sofía stiffened. Then she kissed Rafael. "Wait here, darling. Cousin Robert and I have to speak privately for a moment."

She stepped forward and pushed Robert out of the room. He was a figure cut from paper, a shadow of a human being. There was no resistance. She pulled the door shut behind them and only then did her rage show.

"You miserable, lying, cowardly wretch! Don't you ever dare to call my son a bastard. He's a Mendoza, do you hear me? A Mendoza. He needs no other pedigree, no other stamp of approval from man or God. Certainly not from you." She slapped him again, twice, the way she had the night before, but this time in fury, not cold calculation.

And this time Robert resisted.

He grabbed her wrist and held her arm away from him. "Enough. Strike me again, Sofía, and I'll strike you back. I swear it. As for what I said about the child, I apologize. Not because it was untrue, but because I said it in the boy's hearing. His parents' sins are no fault of his."

She was conscious of how weak his grip was. She could break away from him easily. His gesture was a memory, a response he'd once learned that was now mere mimicry. But it was the first sign that he still remembered that once he'd been a man and it made her heart sing. "Very well, Robert," she said quietly. "I apologize for striking you. Shall we talk about the future?"

"I have no future."

"But I have, and my son has. And we're here and we can't leave. There's no place for us to go. My home is in Madrid and right now I can't return there. After the English liberate us, well, we'll see."

He cocked his head and studied her, something in her words triggering old memories, old concerns. "So Spain expects to be liberated by the English, do they? How strange life is," he added dully, dropping her hand and starting to turn away.

"England will liberate Spain," she insisted, eager to draw him into any discussion that strengthened his hold on the here and now and banished old ghosts. "Wellington will drive out the French. And the *guerrilleros* will help him."

Robert shrugged. "Perhaps. I suspect Spain will find the English as avaricious as the French, or any other conquerors. By the way, where is Indalencio?"

"I haven't seen him. I think perhaps he's run away, taking God knows what with him. I suspect he's been robbing you for years, Robert. I checked the stable last night and it seems he's sold off all but two of the horses."

"It doesn't matter. I'm not going anywhere." Robert started for his bedroom.

"Robert, one more moment, please. You agree that Rafael and I can stay?"

"If you like. That doesn't matter either."

"It matters a great deal. You'll see that in time. We're agreed, then, Robert? I'm to be mistress here, since there's no one else?"

He walked away without replying.

Enrique returned within the hour. A small army of women followed him into the palace. There had to be at least thirty of them. "*Madre de Dios,* why so many, Enrique?"

"They insisted."

Sofía looked over the recruits standing beneath the chestnut tree in the Patio del Recibo. Each of them carried something. Flowers mostly, but one had a bucket full of still-squirming fish, and another held a squealing baby pig in her arms. "I don't think I understand," she murmured.

"It's for you, señorita. No one would come when I said the hidalgo wanted them. They insisted someone gave him the evil eye and now he's a madman. They said it was bad luck to enter the Palacio Mendoza. So I told them La Gitanita was there, then they all insisted on coming. And bringing you things." He waved toward the troop of women. "Most of their men are *guerrilleros*. They all want to meet you, Doña Sofía."

She had to greet each one personally, kiss each one on both cheeks, murmur a word about how brave their husbands and fathers and brothers and sons were. It was over an hour before the ritual ended. While it went on, one woman attracted Sofía's attention. She approached her now. "What is your name, señora?"

The woman curtsied. She was a great giant of a creature, as tall as any man, and her shoulders were as broad as Robert's had been in the old days. But it wasn't her size that appealed to Sofía; there was a clear intelligence behind those dark eyes, and the mark of leadership in the woman's strong jaw. "I am called Angelina, señorita."

"Very well, Angelina. I would like you to take charge here. There is an enormous amount to be done. It will take a long time, I realize that. But at least it will be easier if there is someone to direct things."

"Sí, señorita," Angelina said gravely. She tugged at the skirt of her long black dress and gave a tightening pull to the sash at her waist. *"Bueno, mujeres, ahora comenzamos a trabajar."*

Angelina gave rapid directions, the women fanned out into the ground floor rooms of the palace and began an onslaught of cleaning and polishing and airing. Thanks to Angelina, it was as organized as a campaign planned by Wellington or Napoleon. Sofía walked behind them, delighted to note that among the rubble they were finding some furniture worth saving. It was carefully separated from the great pile that could serve only as firewood.

Rafael ran from room to room, enchanted by the wonders

of the palace. He discovered the delight of straddling the ebony banister of the great staircase in the foyer and sliding down it until the marble pillar at the base stopped his descent.

A young woman was sweeping the marble stairs. She watched the child with indulgent affection. Were any children anywhere loved as Spanish women loved them? Sofía wondered. The girl felt Sofía's eyes on her and asked shyly, "Is he a son of the house, señorita? I did not know there were any children in the palace."

She'd planned to pass him off as some distant Mendoza relation. Now, looking at the earnest face of the girl, seeing the respect for the legend of La Gitanita in her eyes, Sofía couldn't do it. "His name is Rafael. He's my son."

"*Sí,* I thought so," the girl said. Rafael ended another journey down the banister, and she caught his hand and helped him climb off and stroked his curly hair. "He looks like you, señorita. Please God, he will grow up to be as brave, and bring you as much honor as you have brought to Andalusia."

So much for Father Alfonso's worries about her fall from grace. Perhaps the men of the country might blame her, never the women. And they would see to it that their menfolk behaved.

Angelina appeared. "Señorita, I have arranged that we will clean only downstairs today and perhaps tomorrow. There is so much to do, the rest will have to wait."

"A good plan, I agree."

"But where is your room, señorita? We must clean it immediately."

Sofía led Angelina up the stairs to the chamber where she and Rafael had slept the night before. "*Bueno,*" the woman said. "I will send someone up here right away." She looked around at the many doors leading off the corridor. "Señorita, the hidalgo . . ."

"He is resting," Sofía said in answer to the unasked question. "And Angelina, he's not mad. That's a wicked rumor. You must see that it is stopped. The hidalgo doesn't have the evil eye. You know that I was a Gypsy and I know such things. He has been ill, that's all. He is going to get well now."

"Praise the Virgin and all the saints," Angelina said. She crossed herself dutifully, but Sofía could see that her heart wasn't in it. It would take a great deal of time and effort for Robert to earn back the respect of the people of Córdoba.

"Perhaps he will join us for lunch," Sofía said. "Then you can see for yourself that he isn't mad. We will have lunch, won't we?" As soon as she said the word, she realized she was starving.

"¡Ay, mi madre! What do you take me for, señorita? Of course there will be lunch. Right now the best cook of Córdoba is preparing it. Her name is Puri and in the kitchen she's an angel. Out of it, well, that's something else. But don't worry, I will see that Puri behaves."

"I'm sure you will. Very well, I shall tell the hidalgo that we dine at three. Is that possible?"

"Whatever you wish is possible, *Gitanita*," Angelina said. She moved off, majestic in her bulk, to give instructions about cleaning the señorita's room and serving her lunch.

Sofía went to Robert's door and opened it. The room was empty. She sped down the stairs, her eyes darting into every room as she raced through them looking for him. He was nowhere in the main wing. She remembered where she'd found him the night before, but lost her way once or twice as she tried to retrace her steps. Finally she came to the patio of the stone screens and the small room with the mosaic frieze of acanthus leaves. Robert was there. So was a cowering old woman.

"Sofía, since you seem to be in charge here, kindly tell this crone she can clean anything she likes, but she's not to touch that wall."

"What wall?"

"That one, with the mark."

She followed the direction of his pointing finger. "It's a very old stain, Robert. It needs a good scrubbing and some fresh paint."

He took a step toward her. "Listen to me, you can do what you like, I told you it doesn't matter. But that mark is not a stain, at least not the sort you mean. It stays." He fixed her with those eyes that had grown so dull and dark in the past years. Was she fooling herself to think there was a suggestion of the old tawny glow in them now? "Swear to me that you won't let anyone touch that mark," he repeated.

No, she wasn't fooling herself. He really cared deeply about this peculiar request. That he could care deeply about anything was a blessing.

"Of course it will be as you say, Robert." She turned to the woman still standing in the corner holding her bucket and her rags. "Señora, you heard the hidalgo. That wall is not to be washed. You may merely brush away the dust. And be very careful, do you hear? Those are the orders of the hidalgo."

"*Sí,* señorita." The woman returned to her task.

"Robert," Sofía said, turning to him. "We are lunching at three. Will you join us?"

He shook his head and walked away without another word.

She didn't know where the kitchen was, but she followed her nose. The smell of roasting meat wafted through the halls. It led her to the very rear of the east wing. She opened a pair of high double doors and she was in an enormous room with a red tile floor. A steaming kettle sat on the cast iron coal stove that stood in one corner. There were four huge fireplaces, each large enough to roast an ox, but only one of them was lit. On a spit in front of it a small pig was twisting slowly, dripping savory fat into a pan below and turning mahogany brown.

A woman with iron-gray hair but the body of a young girl stood at a raw pine table, wielding an enormous knife over a mound of cabbage. "You must be Puri," Sofía said.

The cook turned to her and immediately dropped the knife and curtsied. "*Sí, Gitanita, a mi me llaman Puri.*"

"Your food smells wonderful."

She had to choose between the impression created by the hair and what the woman's figure conveyed. Sofía decided on the hair. Puri could not be a young woman.

She wondered what Angelina had meant when she said this one was a devil outside the kitchen. Perhaps she'd find out, but fortunately she'd made it Angelina's responsibility. "Puri, I want you to prepare a tray for the hidalgo. He is getting better very quickly, but he will not yet join us for meals. Make him a tray and have someone carry it up to his room. Angelina knows where it is. Do it every mealtime until I tell you differently. If he's not there, have the tray left outside his door."

Sofía walked slowly out of the kitchen looking at everything. She had been in many great houses with Pablo, but never behind the public face in the domestic areas. Here were whole rooms filled with china and glass, and others whose many cupboards were crammed with linens for the tables and the beds. She opened one door, expecting to discover another such storeroom and found instead a deep closet with shallow shelves that held all manner of bottles and jugs and vials. This was the *farmacia* of the palace. Its stores were covered in dust and cobwebs, but the pictures that identified the contents of each container were intact.

She lifted one glass bottle, blew off the dust, and saw a crude drawing of a woman giving birth. Sofía pulled the cork and sniffed the viscous green liquid that still remained on the bottom of the bottle. It was familiar. Years before she had watched Fanta mix the herbs she gave to women in labor, and this smelled as that had. A large jug with a picture of a quill pen contained powdered charcoal for making ink, another was identified by a picture of a winged insect and held the powdered gray leaves of a plant whose name she didn't know but whose smell told her at once it was a moth repellent.

Sofía smiled, closed the cupboard door, and walked on. It calmed her, seeing all this, the inner workings, as it were, of the once-magnificent Palacio Mendoza. There was nothing here she could not master, nothing whose purpose she could not identify. She could oversee this great mansion and bring it back to life because she could understand it. Knowing that gave her a sense of peace.

She turned a corner and came across a door different from all the others. Most of the entrances and exits in the palace were arched; this door was lower than the rest, and rose to a marked point. It was framed in wood pockmarked with age, and like its shape, its lock was different from the other doors. For a moment she was tempted to see where it led. Not now, she decided. One of these days she would investigate. There was time. She had made a beginning last night and today—with Robert, God help him, and with the palace. Somehow she would restore and secure Rafael's inheritance. Meanwhile they were safe. For now that was enough.

❧ 16 ❧

The child was a mystery. All during the long hot months of July and August Robert watched him. He spied on Rafael around secret corners and from behind hidden doors. Sometimes he tried to figure out how old the boy must be if he were Pablo's son, born after Pablo died. He couldn't come to grips with the problem; his mind was clouded, unused, unaccustomed to grappling with numbers or the progression of time. Ten? No, seven, or maybe eight. How long since Pablo hanged himself? Robert couldn't remember. But the child looked younger than seven, and surely it had been at least that long since Pablo died. Sofía must be lying.

Once the lad spotted him. He stared for a moment, his eyes growing big with terror. Then he murmured, "Good morning, Cousin Robert," and ran away.

Robert watched the retreat of the small, sturdy form. He put a hand to his face, felt the wild full beard, and moved his fingers through the long, snarled hair. He had become a creature that frightened children. So be it. The boy was nothing to him, let him be frightened.

But Rafael's eyes haunted him. Those brown eyes with the flecks of gold were Mendoza eyes. Sofía was telling the truth, this was Pablo's son. Or perhaps . . . No, that was ridiculous. She wouldn't lie about that.

So much thinking after so little made his head ache. He escaped back to his room, but the next day he watched Rafael again.

Years before, when such things mattered, Robert had chosen his bedroom carefully. Of all those in the palace, only this one had a small spiral staircase connected to its balcony. The staircase descended into the Patio del Incienso.

In the old days he often went down to the Patio of the Incense late at night, and walked among the scented plants and breathed deep the heady perfume. Once a sandalwood tree had grown in the center and musk roses had lined the walls. After that there had been debris and filth and dead things, and he'd stopped sleeping in his bedroom or walking in his special patio. Then Sofía came. And the child. Now the Patio del Incienso was bare of everything except raw brown earth and a few brown twigs with pale tips that betrayed recent pruning. The army of women had recruited a slightly smaller army of men, and the fourteen patios of the palace were under attack.

One hot September afternoon Robert put a tentative foot on the first step of his balcony stairs, then stopped and studied the man digging in the earth below.

He was an old man, a peasant whom decades of Andalusian sun had made a dark, dried prune, but he had wonderful hands. Robert had watched him working on the roses and the tree. The man cut them with love, with a kind of communion between his shears and the plants, and somehow he'd coaxed them into life. Tiny buds were already swelling. When the winter rains came there would be new leaves; someday perhaps there would be flowers again.

The gardener's back was to Robert. He was kneeling by a patch of bare earth beneath a niche in the wall. "*Buenas tardes, hidalgo,*" he said without turning round. "*A mi me llaman Tito. Son bonitas las flores, no?*"

Robert didn't see any flowers, pretty or otherwise. He didn't answer.

The gardener moved aside slightly. He had just put a bright red geranium in the earth. "*Por la santa,*" he said, indicating the weathered stone statue of Teresa of Avila that lodged in the niche.

From the dim mists of memory Robert recalled the other reason he'd chosen this particular room. Teresa of Avila had been descended from a family of so-called "new Christians." Her blood was Jewish blood. It had amused him to contemplate what the Inquisitors made of that. "*Sí, por la santa,*" he said now. "*Sus manos son buenas,*" he added.

Tito looked at his hands, trying to see what was good about them, then glanced up at the hidalgo. "*Ellos me sirven,*" he said.

"Will they serve me?" Robert asked.

The old man looked puzzled. "I will do whatever you wish, hidalgo. If you will tell me what it is." Perhaps Angelina and La Gitanita were right. They said the master wasn't mad. This didn't sound like a madman, though he looked like one.

"Have you ever shaved a man?" Robert asked.

Tito was startled. "Me, señor? No, only myself. I work on a small farm. On your land to the south, hidalgo."

Robert wasn't interested in the *cortijo.* He'd all but forgotten it existed. He was interested in Rafael, and in looking presentable enough so that perhaps the child would talk to him. "I want you to shave me," he said. "Come up here."

There was a charcoal brazier in his dressing room. Robert had found some charcoal and lit it. The coals were white hot, the copper kettle over them steaming. Next to the brazier was a sliver of brown soap he had salvaged from the back of a drawer, and he'd stropped a series of razors and laid them out on a small table. "There's everything you need, Tito. Just pretend I'm a tree or a rosebush." Robert sat down on a stool and waited.

An hour later he was clean-shaven and his hair was short and neat. Tito had worked with trepidation at first, then with enthusiasm. It was as the hidalgo had said; he need only pretend the man was a plant and it was easy. "You are transformed, Don Robert," he said. "Look." He caught up a mirror in a silver frame and held it so that the master could see his face.

The glass was cracked, but Robert could see himself well enough. He looked in silence for a few seconds. "Very good, Tito," he said finally. "I'm well pleased."

"Have you told your mother about our talks?" Robert asked.

Rafael shook his head. "No, sir. Because you said I shouldn't, but..."

Robert put a hand on the boy's dark curly hair. "But it bothers you to keep things from her, eh?"

"Yes, sir."

"Don't worry about it anymore," Robert said. "I will tell her myself. Tonight."

It remained very warm this first week in October. Sofía had decreed that meals be served in the small dining room open to the Patio of the Cedars. Robert joined Sofía and Rafael there. Her eyes betrayed surprise, but not her voice.

"How nice you look, Robert. I'll have them lay an extra place." She rang a small handbell. Angelina appeared. "The hidalgo is dining with us. Please bring china and cutlery." Sofía turned to her son. "Say good evening to Cousin Robert, Rafi."

"Good evening," Rafael said, then he giggled and looked down at his plate.

Robert smiled at the child. "So, Rafael, shall we tell our secret?"

Sofía frowned in puzzlement and looked from one to the other.

"We're old friends," Robert said. "We've been meeting in the Patio de los Gatos. No one has yet arrived to take it apart and put it back together, Sofía. Your hordes seem to have missed it. Rafi and I have long talks there, and the cats join us sometimes."

"There are a million cats, *Mamacita*. A million million maybe. Cousin Robert says they've always been there. In the old days the servants fed them. Afterward, all those years when there weren't any servants, they lived on the rats," he added matter-of-factly. "Sometimes I bring them milk and bread."

Sofía smiled at her son, but her most dazzling smile was directed toward Robert.

Two weeks later he found her in the counting room. "I've been looking everywhere for you. How did you find your way in here? What are you doing?" He gestured to the ledgers she'd spread out on the writing table.

"I found my way in through that old door beside the kitchen. I wanted to see where it led. As to what I'm doing, I'm looking over the accounts."

"You can read?"

"Yes." She dismissed his startled expression with a wave of her hand. "Robert, I think there will be some rents from the *cortijo* this year."

"How can there be?" He sat down on the stool that Harry Hawkins once used. "No one has collected Mendoza rents for years. Why should anyone start paying again now? And that's what I wanted to see you about. How are you paying the wages of all these servants?"

"I'm not paying their wages. I keep a careful record of everything, and I've promised them I'll pay when I can. They are content with that for the moment."

"That's what Tito told me," he said. "It seems you're a heroine. I never knew."

"You never knew much of what was going on. You still don't." Sofía closed the ledger with a snap. "There are no French troops in all Andalusia now. Did you know that?"

He shook his head.

"Wellington drew Soult and his dragoons north to Badajoz in June and they haven't come back. The *guerrilleros* were able to return to the land. I'm told the olive crop is excellent. That's why I think there will be some rents. I'll arrange to collect them, shall I?"

"Why ask me? You seem to do exactly as you please here."

"I tell everyone I'm acting on behalf of the hidalgo. As I thought we'd agreed." She looked at him. "White hair suits you. Especially since you've filled out. You're looking quite handsome again, Robert."

He acknowledged the compliment with a curt nod of his head, then paid one of his own. "And you are more beautiful than ever, Sofía. But where does that leave us? You've done wonders here with soap and water"—he waved his arm to include the entire palace—"but you can't make bullion out of soap and water."

"Does that bother you?" she asked softly. "I thought you had given up worrying about the Mendoza fortune."

"I had," he admitted. "Until . . ."

"Yes?"

"Until you told me Pablo had a son and I met Rafael. He's a fine lad, Sofía. It seems a shame."

"That he'll have no inheritance? Yes, doesn't it? That's why I intend to see that he does."

"You can't," he repeated. "There's no capital. We have no claim on the gold or silver that comes in from the colonies. I signed it all away. Without that the house is bankrupt."

"Not quite. There are still the lands, Robert. And the vineyards in Jerez. Everywhere in Andalusia they're tending the vines again and making wine."

He narrowed his eyes and studied her. "You read your way through all this, didn't you?" He gestured to the rows of document cases and ledgers that lined the walls.

"Not all, but a good part of it. There was a time when the sherry trade made up nearly half the annual income of the house of Mendoza," she reminded him.

"That was a long while ago, when a much smaller annual income represented a much greater fortune. That's not how it is in modern times, Sofía. You can't build a new house of Mendoza with sack. Even if England were wealthy enough to import the quantities they used to, and if your beloved Wellington broke Napoleon's hold on Europe and trade between her and England could begin again, it wouldn't be enough."

She was torn between her delight at how he looked and sounded, almost like the old Robert reborn, and her distress at what he was saying. She frowned, then forced a smile. "But it's a beginning, isn't it, Robert? We can at least make a beginning. For Rafi's sake," she added.

He hesitated, then nodded gravely. "Yes, for Rafi's sake, I suppose we can."

At the end of October Robert set out for Jerez.

Sweet God, why was he so nervous? Because this was a trial. He had wanted Sofía to go. "I can't," she'd told him. "It can't be a woman, it has to be you. If they're to believe in Jerez that things have changed, it has to be you."

He knew she was right. So now he was on the road in an old carriage she'd found in the stables and had repaired. The coachman was Sofía's servant, Enrique. She'd dressed him in Mendoza livery she produced from air, as she produced so much else, and Robert had taken Tito as manservant. But despite the aura of normalcy, it was a trial, an attempt to see if he really was alive again, or merely a ghost going through the motions.

At first he was terrified of looking at the world beyond the walls of the palace. He kept the curtains of the carriage drawn and sat very still with his eyes closed. When at last he found the courage to open them, Tito had partially unveiled one window and Robert could see that Andalusia was green and lush and beautiful, and ripe with lingering autumn. "It looks as it always did," he murmured. "I thought the soldiers..."

"There were few battles here, Don Robert. The wounds of the land were from neglect, because the campesinos went off to become *guerrilleros*. Such wounds were not difficult to heal."

Robert nodded, pushed back all the curtains, and drank in the sights. He knew that another part of his resurrection was under way.

In four days they reached Jerez and the Mendoza bodegas in the high chalky lands surrounding the city. "Drive into the forecourt of that building over there," Robert told Enrique.

The main house looked as it always had, a yellow stone fortress on a slope above the town, looking down on the spires and domes of many grand churches. The horses were reined in on the cobblestones in front of the entrance doors. Tito got out and Robert followed him, ignoring the helping hand the old man offered. It was three in the afternoon, siesta time. The place was absolutely silent except for the song of a linnet in the branches of a towering oak.

Robert hesitated. He was sweating and starting to tremble once more. What did he do now? Think. What would he have done before he died and came to life again? Stride up to the front door? Ring the bell? No, neither of those things. Not himself. He would send a servant to wake the household and tell them the master had arrived. Except that he wouldn't have to, they'd have been alerted to his coming and everything would be ready. But that was then and this was now, and he had to do something besides stand there gawking like an addle-witted fool.

He had turned to Tito to order him to go forward and summon the steward when the front doors were flung open. A young man burst through them, pulling on a dark blue frockcoat as he ran down the three broad steps that led to the forecourt. "*Madre de Dios,* it is you, hidalgo, isn't it? My wife said it was, but I didn't believe . . ." He reached Robert and grabbed his hands and kissed them. "Welcome, Don Robert. I didn't know you were coming. I wasn't prepared, but praise the Virgin and the saints . . ."

Robert was overcome by the welcome, tears stung his eyes. Sweet God, he couldn't let this lad see him cry like a woman. He hid his emotion behind gruffness. "Who the devil are you? Where's Ruez?"

"You don't recognize me, hidalgo? I'm Federico Ruez. My father was the steward until he died the year before last. I met you six years ago, in Cádiz. I was working at the warehouse then. Don't you remember?"

Robert didn't, but he nodded. "Yes, yes, of course, Cádiz in '05." The year of Nelson and Trafalgar, the year of his entombment. "Your father's dead, you say?"

"Yes, hidalgo. Two years now. I came home then. I'd been in the mountains with Juan Sanchez and the *guerrilleros,* but when my father died I came back. There was no one else to look after things here." He finished buttoning his frockcoat and he stood straighter and composed himself. "But we mustn't stand out here in the sun, Don Robert. Please, *mi casa es su casa*." He extended his arm and ushered them up the steps into the house.

The young wife who'd spotted the arms blazoned on the carriage from her bedroom window was waiting for them. She kissed both Robert's hands and sent Tito and Enrique off to the kitchen in the company of a servant, then opened the door to the main salon and allowed the men to precede her. Another servant, this one still flushed with siesta, arrived with plates of figs and dates and sugared almonds.

Federico poured glasses of pale yellow amontillado and brought them on a silver tray. He raised his. "To your good health, Don Robert. And to our good fortune in seeing you here today."

Robert drank the wine and nibbled the foods they pressed on him. The wife whose name was Marisol remained with them a few moments, then excused herself. It was time to talk of business.

"Have you continued to make wine all the years I was ... ill?" Robert asked.

"All the years," Federico said. "But very little, because most of the workers were away fighting the dragoons. The year my father died, we made a total of less than two thousand butts. Last year the same. This year it is five thousand, only ..."

"Yes, go on lad. Only what?"

"Only there is nothing to do with them, Don Robert. We keep them in the *soleras* here. The warehouse in Cádiz is full. There have been no shipments for four years, hidalgo. But now you are here, so I presume ..." He looked eagerly at Robert and waited.

At last he understood the reason for the extravagant welcome, their joy in seeing him. He was their conduit, the means of trade. The family Ruez could make sherry with or without the Mendozas, but they couldn't ship it unless the English connection was alive and healthy. "You've heard nothing from my brother?" Robert asked. "Nothing from Don Liam?"

"Not a word, hidalgo, not for three years or more. They

say things are very bad in London. And until now, though the English ships could get to Cádiz, they couldn't come into the harbor. The English still rule the seas, I'm told. But what good is that since the dragoons would not allow us to trade?"

"Not much good at all, lad." Robert spoke slowly, giving himself time to think. "Come, show me the bodegas. We'll talk of trade after I've seen them."

Federico Ruez was a steward in the tradition of his long line. The wine caves were spotless, the butts stacked three high in the precise formation that allowed for the triple decanting of the *solera* system. There were careful records kept in a small office in each of the bodegas. Robert looked at them and listened to the young man's explanations and comments, and nodded sagely and said little.

He was thinking of Liam. Liam was the key, and he had not been in touch with his brother since the day six years earlier when they parted in Cádiz. He'd assumed that things had continued as always between London and Jerez, that he was coming here to face a steward who had been cheating the house and would now be made to restore the profits that belonged to Córdoba. The situation he found was entirely different. "Very good," he said when they had surveyed the last bodega, the one they called La Reina. "You've done well, Federico. Now we must go back to the house and talk."

"*Sí*, hidalgo, but if you can spare one moment more?" Robert nodded. "I want you to taste something in this small keg here."

He went to a miniature oak barrel with a spigot that stood on a shelf in the office and drew some dark amber liquid into a pewter tankard. Robert took it and sipped. It was sweet, but that was not its distinguishing characteristic. This was the smoothest sack he'd ever tasted. It was like velvet on his tongue, and it slid down the back of his throat in a silken wave of pure pleasure.

"It's remarkable. You made this?"

"*Sí*, Don Robert. I have been experimenting with a new grape my father planted when I was born. It's called Pedro Ximénez. A white, of course, but we can grow it on the less favored land, the *barros* rather than the *albarizas,* and get a higher yield than most."

"And it's this new grape, Pedro whatever-you-called-it, that makes this wine?"

"Not exactly, Don Robert. It's the must. If you fortify earlier than usual, add the brandy before the fermentation is complete, you get this . . . I don't know what to call it, hidalgo."

"Milk," Robert said instantly. "It's mother's milk, lad. How much of this stuff do you have?"

"Two hundred butts only. I began years ago, but with the war . . ."

"Yes, of course." Robert finished his "milk" and set down the tankard and led the way back to the house.

They had to brush the chalk from their shoes and their clothes before they entered. There were great brushes hanging beside the door for just that purpose. Federico even had the stuff in his hair. It was impossible to walk through the vineyards of Jerez without being covered by a dusting of white. "It doesn't show in your hair now, Don Robert," the young man said. Then he blushed. "I mean . . ."

"I know what you mean."

Robert smiled. He liked this lad, even if he was a touch more familiar than he should be. Apparently a new breed of Spaniard had been created in the last few years. Perhaps men who had fought as the *guerrilleros* had fought considered themselves the equal of their betters. Well, so be it. It might not be a bad thing.

Once again Marisol was waiting for them. There were more refreshments for the hidalgo, there was a room prepared for the hidalgo, there was anything the hidalgo might wish that it was in her power to supply. Robert said he would retire until it was time for the evening meal. He left Federico without another word about trade, and he could feel the young man's eyes boring into his back as he mounted the stairs.

They did not speak of business again until the following morning. "I can't offer you a simple solution," Robert said. "I'll write to Liam and see if he can dispatch ships, but at best it will take some months. In the meantime, can you continue to function?"

"*Sí*, hidalgo. But with difficulty. There's very little money and the men must be paid. Thank God we've finished with this year's vintage so we can operate with fewer people. But the coopers can't be let go. Unless we use the winter months to make oak barrels, next year we'll have to pour our wine on the ground. And I need some help in the *soleras,* though I'll keep as few as I dare."

"Try to survive," Robert said. "That's all I can offer you, Federico, the hope that if you survive, things will get better." He hesitated. "No, perhaps I can give you something more."

On a table in the room in which they spoke was one of the heavy glass bottles in which the wine was brought from the bodega to the house. "I have an idea. This new wine of yours, your 'milk,' let's plan to ship it in bottles rather than kegs. And let's put a mark on the bottle, a sign of some sort."

"What sign, hidalgo?" The younger man was eager to understand. "What will we gain by this plan?"

"A name. What if in all England people didn't just drink fino or oloroso or amontillado or just plain sack, as most of them call it? What if we could make people want only the sack from our vineyards, from our bodegas. Get me a bit of paper, lad, and a quill and some ink."

Federico produced the things he was asked for and Robert sat down at a table beneath the window. He dipped the quill into the ink and sketched a rough outline of the branch of an oak tree, and on it the form of a bird. "I mean this to be one of those linnets that is so common here, but you'll need an artist to render it true. Never mind, you get the idea. Now, below the picture—this." He wrote the word *Mendoza* in large letters, paused a moment, then made a dash and added the word *Ruez*. Beneath that combined name he wrote *sherry milk*. "These last two words are in English," he explained. "They mean *leche de Jerez*. What do you think of that, lad?"

Federico stared in wonderment. "*Mendoza-Ruez*. My name as well as yours."

"Do you know the story of how our two families became united in this venture?" Robert asked. Federico shook his head. "No? Well, I'll tell you someday. But what do you think of calling your new wine sherry milk?"

Federico broke into a broad grin. "I like it very much, hidalgo."

"So do I. Now I only have to figure out how to get it from Cádiz to the Tilbury docks, and we're away."

The carriage trundled steadily over the road northeast from Jerez. Robert ignored the scenery and remained deep in thought. When at last he came out of his revery he turned to Tito. "Where are we?"

"Returning to Córdoba from Jerez, hidalgo. You remember, we went to see your bodegas and vineyards."

"I know that, man. I'm not addled, Tito, not anymore. When will you be convinced?"

"I know the hidalgo is a man with a perfect mind, señor. I only meant—"

"Yes, yes. Stop fussing, Tito. Just tell me where we are."

The servant looked troubled. "I don't know this area, Don Robert. I've never been here before."

Robert gave up in disgust and stared out the carriage windows. The landscape told him nothing. Rolling green hills bathed in the westering sun, olive trees bent by the prevailing winds, a few late-blooming daisies struggling by the roadside, they could be anywhere in Andalusia. "Listen," he asked Tito, "have you seen a big monastery high on a hill?"

"A monastery? I do not know, Don Robert."

"No, you haven't! Because there it is." Robert stuck his head out the window and called up to the driver. "Enrique, take that road on your left. I want to call at the fortress up there on the hill."

Enrique clucked to the horses, drew on the reins, and the carriage obediently swung left. Robert settled back, drumming his fingers on his knees, his brow furrowed with concentration.

* * *

"I'm sorry," the monk at the entrance lodge said. "Brother Elijah is no longer with us."

So Elijah was dead. Pity, he'd have enjoyed asking the man what he thought of Napoleon now, after all the blood his schemes had helped to spill in Spain. But it wasn't actually Elijah he'd come to see. "Tell me," he asked the porter. "Is there a lay brother here named Harry Hawkins? A dwarf?"

The young monk smiled. "Oh, yes, I understand, señor. Many people come to see our saint. He's called Brother Francisco here. But I don't know if he can see you today. He's not well, señor. And it is late. Perhaps you can come back another time?"

"No, I can't. Tell him I'm here. Tell him Robert Mendoza wants to see him. I think he'll thank you for bringing that message."

Perhaps because of the Mendoza name the porter went to do as he was bid. He returned in a few moments. "Brother Francisco will see you, señor. He's in the garden."

Robert followed the monk out to the same garden where he'd walked with Elijah some nine years earlier. Harry was sitting in the sun near the orchard, in a strange contraption that looked like a chair on wheels. The two men clasped hands; both remained too English to kiss as Spaniards would have. The porter busied himself adjusting the cushions behind the dwarf's outsized head until Harry waved him away. "It's all right, I'm fine. Thank you, but leave us, Brother. I wish to speak with the hidalgo."

"So, Harry," Robert said when they were alone.

"So, Mr. Robert."

Silence. Until Harry said, "It's good to see you, sir. I've prayed for you every day." His eyes searched Robert's face and Robert had an uncanny sense that Harry Hawkins could read his mind, that he knew all the suffering of the past six years, and what it was that had at last brought him out of his self-made hell. "The ways of God are passing strange, Mr. Robert," the dwarf said. "But they always lead to our highest good."

Robert started to make some sharp rejoinder about pious sentiments. The words died on his tongue. There was something remarkable about this peculiar little man who had been Harry Hawkins and was now Brother Francisco, something not of this world, or any world Robert knew. "If you say so, Harry," he said softly. "Is it all right to call you that? I can't get used to thinking of you with another name."

"Of course it's all right. Sit down, Mr. Robert, on that bench over there. I can push myself near you, like this." He did something with the big wheels of his chair and it moved easily over the path. "Clever contraption this, isn't it? One of the carpenter brothers made it for me when the fever took my legs."

"I heard years ago that you were ill. Doña Maria told me—" He broke off, not yet ready to speak of Maria's visit to the palace while he was still a walking corpse, nor of the letter from Harry she'd brought.

"She came and spoke to me after she saw you. I just prayed all the harder, sir. That's about when my legs packed up, as it happens."

"What sickness do you have, Harry?"

"A fever that comes and goes, and a bad cough, though it's not too troublesome today. Something to do with my lungs, according to the brother infirmarian. It's no great worry, sir. God will call me when my time comes, so be it."

"I thought my time had come years ago," Robert said. "But it seems it hadn't."

"No, I knew you hadn't done all that needed doing. It is why I've prayed so hard for you to have another chance."

"A chance at what, Harry?"

The dwarf frowned. "It is not as clear as I wish it were, Mr. Robert. I know there's something you're to do, and I know it's important. It's something to do with the house of Mendoza. But I can't say more."

"Are you a soothsayer, Harry? Some kind of clairvoyant?"

"Perish the thought, Mr. Robert. Fortune-telling's a sin. It's just that if I listen very hard, sometimes the Lord Jesus or His mother, they tell me things."

"I see. Or, rather, I don't. Out of my line, Harry. You know me too well to believe otherwise."

"Yes, I do. Mr. Robert, what brought you here today?"

"I was passing," Robert said quickly. "And I thought—" He broke off. It wasn't true. "I had a compulsion to see you, Harry. Something I couldn't deny. I was on my way back to Córdoba from Jerez and it came on me when we were about half an hour from your monastery. I thought I'd left it too late and we'd gone by, but we went on a bit and there this place was up on its hill. So I came."

Harry smiled. "Passing strange, sir, as I said." A breeze came up, heralding evening, and he adjusted the light blanket over his knees. "Did you find the stone, Mr. Robert? The one in the room with the mark on the wall."

"Yes. Was it you who translated the Hebrew?"

"In a manner of speaking. Don Domingo found the message. He said it was an accident, but I think he'd discovered a reference in the old family records. Always reading them, he was. And what else would he have been doing prying up the floor? Anyway, he got me and made me look at the thing and asked if I could translate it. Because I'd been born on Creechurch Lane, sir, he thought Mr. Benjamin might have had me educated in Hebrew."

"As far as I know, my father was the last Mendoza to read Hebrew," Robert said. "I don't and neither does Liam." He waited to see if Harry might pick up that oblique hint about his parentage, but he didn't.

"No, I know. I told Don Domingo I couldn't do it, but I knew someone who maybe could. Someone who could be trusted not to report the business to the Inquisition. I copied the letters and brought them here to Brother Elijah and he translated them. Not many men in Spain can read Hebrew, but Brother Elijah was a scholar. Made little difference, as it turned out. We couldn't find any treasure. But then, we weren't supposed to. So Don Domingo and I just carved the translation into the rock below the original words and left things as they were. Then, after everything that happened, it seemed to me you might well be the one meant to discover the treasure, so I sent the letter."

"What did you mean about the old ways helping the house?" Robert asked.

"I can't say for sure, sir. But the words were in Hebrew after all. And Mr. Benjamin and yourself . . ." His voice trailed off.

"You don't hate Jews, do you?" Robert asked softly. "You may be the only Catholic in Spain who doesn't."

"I don't know about any others, sir. But I couldn't hate what Mr. Benjamin and yourself and Mr. Liam believe in, even if I think you're wrong."

"Believe in . . . Maybe that's my trouble, Harry. I don't know if I believe in much of anything."

"You will, Mr. Robert. I'm sure you will."

Robert smiled. "You think your prayers are going to make me a Catholic sooner or later?"

Harry didn't echo his light tone. "I can't say what they'll make you, sir. Only that it's my task to pray and yours to do something else."

"But you're not sure what."

"No, I'm not."

"Harry, listen. There's a boy, a fine lad. The son of Pablo Luis, born after the poor sod killed himself."

The little man smiled broadly. "So there's an heir to the house."

"Yes. If there's something for him to be heir to. At the moment it looks doubtful."

"You have to find the treasure, sir. Then everything will be fine. I'm sure of it."

"There isn't any treasure, Harry. There's not even a cave."

The dwarf frowned. "Ah, yes, I thought about it quite a bit. It occurred to me, Mr. Robert, that the old strongroom might be the place to search."

"In the passage to the counting room?"

"No, the one in the Patio de la Reja. Part of the palace was added quite late, sir. Less than a century past. The whole southeast wing was garden until then. After they built on, most of the garden disappeared. The bit that was left they called the Patio de la Reja. Got the name from the iron door covering the little hole in the rock that once was a strong-room."

"I don't know," Robert said doubtfully, thinking of the patio Harry meant. "The little hole's not big enough to be called a cave. And there certainly isn't any treasure in it." He stopped speaking because the dwarf was shaken with a sudden parox-ysm of coughing. "Harry, are you all right?" Robert pounded his back, but the hacking went on for some minutes before easing.

"Sorry, Mr. Robert," the little man said when at last he could speak. "There's not much I can do to control it."

He was weak and obviously exhausted by the effort to breathe. "Hadn't I better take you inside?" Robert asked.

"No need, sir. Here comes the brother infirmarian. It's time for vespers. He always wheels me into the church about now."

Robert watched the approaching monk. He was tall and thin, as Elijah had been. "I was sorry to hear that Brother Elijah had died," he murmured to Harry.

"Died? Who told you that?"

"The porter said he wasn't with you anymore. I just assumed—"

The big head shook emphatically. "He's not dead, sir. He left."

"Left? I didn't think a monk could leave. What about his vows?"

"Elijah was a special case, sir. He—" The infirmarian reached them and Harry broke off. "Will you come to vespers, Mr. Robert? There's a place for lay folk in our chapel."

"No, Harry, I don't think I will. But you take care of yourself. I'll try and call again next time I'm in these parts."

It was later, just after eight, when Harry knew. The monks were finishing compline, the last office of their day, and the Salve Regina echoed its praise to the Virgin in the vaulted choir of the monastery church. The saintly lay brother in the wheeled chair at the back stiffened, and the Latin words of the hymn died on his lips. Something desperately bad had happened at the Palacio Mendoza. Sweet Virgin Mary, Harry prayed, protect my brother and our house.

❧ 17 ❧

Angelina met Robert at the front door. He knew instantly that something was wrong. Her black hair was untidy and tears streaked her cheeks. "What's happened?" he asked.

"They're gone, hidalgo. La Gitanita and the child, they're both gone."

"How can they be gone? What are you talking about?" Robert struggled to control a sense of terror, a wave of nausea. His hold on reality was still so tenuous; the pit still yawned so deep at his feet. If Sofía had deserted him he would tumble into it and never come out. Forget that, don't think about it, listen to what Angelina is saying.

"Three days ago in the evening, the boy disappeared." Angelina held a black bandanna that served as a handkerchief, and she twisted it constantly in her raw-knuckled hands, her big body swaying back and forth in anguish. "We saw him in the Patio de los Gatos, then he wasn't there."

Robert ran his fingers through his hair, shook his head. "Angelina, are you telling me that Rafael ran away?"

"¡Ay, mi madre! No, hidalgo. He was taken."

"Taken by whom? Godstruth, woman, you're not making sense. Where is Doña Sofía?"

"I told you," she wailed. "La Gitanita is also gone. She was a crazy woman, screaming and running around the palace. Then, ay, hidalgo! She grew so calm she might have been dead. She went upstairs and when she came down she was a Gypsy. A real Gypsy, hidalgo, not like when she sings. Dressed like them, her hair like them. I didn't know her. You would not know her. Her own mother—"

Robert took a deep breath. "I understand, Angelina. What I don't understand is where she is."

Angelina wailed aloud again. "I don't know. Holy Virgin protect us, I don't know where she is or where the child is." She was sobbing and wiping her eyes with the bandanna.

Robert glanced at the carriage still in the Patio del Recibo. As far as he knew, there were no others in the stables, and no more horses. They'd all disappeared years before. "Did Doña Sofía leave on foot?"

"No, Don Robert," she murmured between sniffles. "She took the donkey of one of the gardeners. ¡Ay! a donkey like a common woman of the streets. All Córdoba thought the curse on this place was lifted. Now they will know that it isn't. The Palacio Mendoza is cursed, and we who work here are cursed, and it's all my fault because I told them—"

"*Callate!* Enough weeping, Angelina. Get hold of yourself. We're not cursed, by damn. We've been robbed, and the robbers will live to regret it."

He knew, sweet God, he knew what had happened and where Sofía had gone. She hadn't deserted him. The Gypsies had stolen Rafael for some arcane reason, and she'd gone to the Triana to get him back. But Sofía alone among hordes of *Gitanos*—it was insane. She'd never succeed without help. The blood coursed in his veins; rage filled him with strength. "Tell me again exactly when she left," he demanded.

Angelina stopped crying and looked at him. The white hair was the same, the dark brown eyes were the same, but the face was different. This was the face of a man—the fiery, strong hidalgo she had never seen but had been told once existed. "An hour after we knew the boy was gone, Don Robert. It can't have been more. It was Saturday in the evening. I think it was eight, maybe nine."

Three days ago, a few hours after he left Harry Hawkins at the monastery. Think, dammit, think. It would take her four days to get to Seville with a donkey. She couldn't be there yet. On a good horse he could do it in twenty hours, maybe less. A good horse. The pair who had pulled the carriage were gone from the patio now, Enrique had taken them around to the stables; but they were useless anyway, exhausted after their long journey. Besides, they weren't riding mounts.

"Angelina, send Enrique to the livery stables in town. Tell him to say I need their best stallion." He started up the stairs, calling out more orders as he mounted them two at a time. "And get out to the tack room and find my saddle. You'll know it's mine. It has my initials on the pommel."

She stared at him a moment, then she moved off like a mighty ship-of-the-line, all sails set and cannons blazing. "*Sí, hidalgo, inmediatemente*. Everything will be done exactly as you say."

Robert raced up the stairs. He hadn't touched them in years, but he was sure his pistols were still in his room.

A scattering of children played in the flat open plaza between the hills where sometimes the Gypsies made fiesta. They glanced at Sofía as she passed, then ignored her. Dressed in a blouse and a long skirt of homespun, with a shawl around her shoulders and braided hair and golden earrings, she looked as if she belonged. Sofía studied the children a moment. Rafael wasn't among them. No matter, she'd known it wouldn't be as easy as that. She ducked her head and entered the cave of the Zocali tribe.

She had forgotten how low and narrow this passage was, and how over the years the smell of thousands of cooking fires had permeated its walls. Sofía walked until she came to the place where the passage widened into a room, then she paused.

A woman sat with her back to the entrance. She was laying out cards on a rickety three-legged table. It could so easily have been Fanta, but of course it wasn't. It was Zocali's wife, Teresita. Sofía recognized the set of her thin shoulders. Another woman sat in a corner with a child at her breast. She glanced up and saw Sofía, and her face registered amazement, but only for a moment. Then she dropped her gaze and said nothing. Her name was Inmaculada. They had grown up together, been friends once.

Sofía's glance darted around the room, seeking Zocali. He wasn't there. She spotted Joselito. So far neither he nor the half dozen or so others in the cave had seen her, only Inmaculada, who continued to nurse her infant.

"A blessing on the fire," Sofía said. All eyes turned to her. "I have come seeking my father according to the law of the Rom. Where is Zocali?"

Teresita had half turned and was staring over her shoulder, her fingers frozen in the act of laying down a card. "My husband is dead. He died three years ago. A true daughter would have come to bury him." She spat on the floor.

"I did not know." Sofía turned toward Joselito. She weighed the possible consequences of a wrong guess, and decided to gamble. She took a step toward him and fell to her knees. "I claim the right to seek justice from the leader of my tribe, according to the law of the Rom."

"You have no tribe. You deserted our fire."

She could tell from the way he spoke that she had made the correct assumption. Joselito had taken Zocali's place; he was the elected leader of the tribe. "I am a daughter of this fire," Sofía said. "I have the right to be heard."

"You had such a right once. You forfeited it when you left." Joselito reached for a jug of wine, but he did not lift it to his mouth and his eyes didn't leave Sofía's face.

"I did not murder my child." Sofía knew she must take the initiative. "I swear it by Sara-la-Kali."

Teresita made a sound of disgust. She gathered up the cards and shuffled them, her fingers moving automatically while her attention remained on the intruder. "The time to say that was long ago. Instead, you ran like the *busne* whore you are."

Sofía did not bother to answer. Teresita had always hated her; she'd get no sympathy from Zocali's widow. Neither could she hope that her role among the *guerrilleros* would gain her status here. The Gypsies saw the war against the French dragoons as the business of the *busne*. They had taken no part. She kept looking at Joselito; he was her only hope. "Would I come here like this if I did not have a just cause? I did not kill Sara."

"We have reason to believe that is true," Joselito admitted.

"Did Paco confess—"

Joselito raised his hand and silenced her. "We do not speak of him."

"She has no place here," a man's voice murmured from the shadows. "That's the law of the Rom."

"I will decide what falls within our law," Joselito said. "She has come here of her own choice. She must have a reason." He raised the jug and took a long drink of the wine, then wiped his mouth with the back of his hand. "Death follows you," he said. "Carlos is dead, your child is dead."

The blood rushed from her head, she thought she would faint; then she realized he meant little Sara, not Rafael. And he knew about her and Carlos. She could read it in his eyes. "Carlos had his own destiny and he followed it," Sofía said. "We must all follow our destiny."

Joselito waited, studying her. Finally he nodded. "That is true. You may sit, I will hear what you have to say."

Sofía sat back on her heels and leaned against the wall of the cave. She had been in this position so many times; it was so natural. The dancing firelight, the long shadows and the close, fetid atmosphere—everything was as it had always been. The familiarity gave her confidence. When she spoke her voice did not betray the screaming anguish inside her. "My brothers and sisters, I have come to you because a great wrong has been done to me."

"Wait," Joselito interrupted. "You cannot claim whatever you have come here to claim until the old charge is settled. You deserted the tribe."

She had expected this, she was prepared. "Paco said I killed Sara, and everyone believed him. But I didn't kill her, Paco did. He flung her across the room and crushed her skull." Despite the passage of so many years, the words were a torment. Saying them made her heart ache for Sara as it was aching for Rafael. And they fueled anew her hatred for the man who was still her husband.

Joselito nodded. "I told you we know that now. But we have passed judgment on your husband. What about you?"

"She's a *busne* coward as well as a whore," Teresita murmured.

"*¡Silencio!*" Joselito roared. "Hold your tongue." He turned back to Sofía. "Have you been faithful to the law of the Rom?"

"As faithful as I could be," she said. "As my destiny allowed. I have not betrayed the fire. I swear that I've told no *busne* what I know of Gypsy things."

"You have not betrayed the signs?"

"Never," she affirmed.

"You have not spoken of the great trick or profaned the potions or accused any Rom before the *busne*?"

"Never—I swear it."

The voice from the shadows spoke again. "She has profaned the music. She sings our songs for money."

Sofía had placed the voice now. It was Tomás, Zocali's brother. He'd never liked her. But then, none of them had, except Fanta and Carlos and perhaps Zocali, and all three were dead. "It was Paco who first made me sing for money," she said. "In the end, because of him, I could only sing or whore. I chose to sing."

Joselito returned to the main question. "You did not murder the child?"

"No, I swear it by Sara-la-Kali," she repeated.

He stared at her a moment, then nodded. "Very well, but you deserted the fire years ago—why have you come here now?"

She took a deep breath. This was the hardest part, and everything depended on Joselito. If he was truly a guardian of the law of the Rom, she would succeed. "I have another child," she whispered. "A boy of seven years. Paco has stolen him."

"Is he your husband's son?"

"No. Rafael is not his son. The child is a *busne,* not a Rom."

"Then you are a whore," Joselito said calmly. "Just as Teresita has said."

"Perhaps. But my sins are not my son's. The law of the Rom says that children are a blessing, that they are not to be harmed."

"True, so why do you think . . ." he hesitated. "Why do you think the man who was called Paco will harm him?"

"Because he is evil. He is a wicked man, he does not honor the law. You all know that. He has stolen Rafael because he hates me. And because he wants a ransom. I have no money. When he learns that, what will happen to Rafael?" Her voice broke on the question. Asking aloud what she had asked herself for the four long days of the journey nearly destroyed the dignity she knew she must maintain. Sofía forced herself to swallow the tears that were so close to the surface.

No one spoke. Joselito continued to study her. He lifted the jug and drank some more wine. "Even if everything you say is true," he said at last. "What do you want us to do? Why have you come here?"

"I want to go to Paco's cave and accuse him and get Rafael back. I cannot do that without your help."

The atmosphere in the room changed. Sofía could feel the difference. A few feet shuffled. Teresita returned to laying out the cards, and Inmaculada shifted the position of the child in her arms. "What is it?" Sofía demanded. "Tell me!" She could no longer pretend a stoicism she did not feel. Her voice rose and tears streamed down her face. "Rafael is already dead, is that it? He's dead and you know it and—"

"Calm yourself," Joselito interrupted. "We know nothing. I swear by the fire."

"Then will you help me?"

"We can't."

"In God's name, why not?" Sofía stood up, drawing her shawl closer. She looked from one face to the next and saw nothing but blankness and disinterest. "Very well, if you are all unwilling to go with me, I'll go alone." She turned and began to walk away.

"Sofía, wait." It was the first time Joselito had used her name.

The first time he'd acknowledged by his tone that she was a human being as he was, that they had known each other for years, slept by the same fire, eaten the same food, were linked by common bonds. "If I could help you, I would," he said. "I can't. The law of the Rom won't permit it. This Paco is not here. Only his body is here. He has been banished."

Sofía understood instantly. To be banished was a punishment just short of stoning. It meant total spiritual exclusion. A Gypsy who had been banished ceased to exist as far as the tribe was concerned. No one spoke to him, no one acknowledged his presence or absence in the cave. If Paco was banished, she could find no help here. They would not speak to him or question him—that was the law—and thus they could learn nothing of Rafael's whereabouts. "When was he banished? Why?" Her anguish made her voice hoarse.

"Six months ago," Joselito said. "His own tribe pronounced the sentence. He did unnatural things with the daughter of his father."

Sofía sagged against the limestone wall of the cave. "*Madre de Dios,* then no one can help me. Rafael, oh, my God, Rafael . . ."

Someone pressed a cup of wine into her hand. It was Inmaculada. "If, as you say, he wants a ransom," she said softly, "he will not hurt the boy."

Sofía shook her head. "I don't know. I can't be sure. He hates me. He could do anything."

"How do you know it is your husband Paco who stole your child?" Joselito asked.

"Because he tried it before, about four months ago in Caceres. I saw him. He tried to pull Rafael away from me, but I fought him and then someone came and Paco ran away. And the night Rafael disappeared, people say they saw a bald Gypsy in the town. In Córdoba, where we are living. It has to have been Paco."

"The time is right," Joselito murmured. "While he was still one of us he would not dare to violate the law of the Rom in such a way. Someone might have found out. Now . . ." He shrugged.

Once more Sofía turned to go. "I must leave. I have to speak to him."

"I do not think you will ever speak to him," Joselito said to her retreating back.

Sofía froze. Slowly she swung around to face him. Joselito looked deeply thoughtful. "Why not?" she asked, her voice a hoarse whisper.

"Because he will hide from you. He expects you to come after the boy. That must be the whole point, Sofía. It's revenge he wants, not money. After you left, Fanta told everyone your husband lied, that it was he not you who had killed the child. She couldn't prove it and you weren't here to speak on your own behalf, but many believed Fanta. Life was not so—" Joselito hesitated. "So pleasant for him after that. And he couldn't take another wife, not even if one of the tribes would give him one, which they probably wouldn't. Maybe that's why he did such . . . such unspeakable things with his own sister. And so he was banished, and now he blames you and he wants revenge."

Sofía couldn't control her trembling. "Then Rafael is in worse danger than I imagined."

No one answered her. Joselito stood up and came to her side. "Come, I will walk with you to the outside." They went down the narrow passage in silence. When they reached the exit from the cave he took her hand. "Sofía, I'm sorry. I meant it when I said that I would help you if I could. But the law is the law. You know how it must be. If I hear anything about the boy Rafael, I will come and tell you."

"Thank you," she whispered. "I will be here. I have to find some way to speak with Paco."

"It is better if you return to the Palacio Mendoza," Joselito said.

"How did you know of—"

"I know everything about you," Joselito interrupted. "Even that you are called La Gitanita and what you did when the *busne* were at war. It is my duty to know. I am leader of the tribe now, and you are a daughter of the fire—whatever else you may be."

Joselito bent his head and stepped out of the cave first. It was night now, the children had left. But the plaza was not empty. "Stop right there," a voice said. Joselito looked down the barrels of two pistols pointed at his chest. "I'm looking for the woman known as Sofía, La Gitanita. Tell me where she is or I'll blow you apart."

"There is no need to do that, señor," Joselito said softly. "The woman is right behind me."

"Robert? Is that you?" Sofía pushed by Joselito.

"Sofía, thank God you're all right. Have you found Rafael?"

"No. And you can put your pistols away. This is the leader of my tribe."

Robert heard the words and he looked at her. She had become again the Gypsy he first saw singing in the posada. He wondered if Doña Sofía would ever return. He tucked the pair of pistols into his belt. "Are you saying the Gypsies didn't kidnap Rafael?"

"Not all the Gypsies. Just one. His name is Paco."

"You're sure?"

She nodded.

"Then where in hell is this bloody Paco? Why are we standing here talking? Let's go get him."

Sofía hesitated. She weighed the possibility that a confrontation would succeed. There were many Gypsies and only two of them, but Robert had his pistols. She had never seen a pistol in Paco's cave.

Joselito was silent, watching the two of them. Robert turned to him. "What's your name?"

"I am called Joselito. As Sofía has told you, I'm the leader of her tribe."

"Listen," Robert said. "This Paco, he's a big Gypsy with a bald head, right?" He turned to Sofía. "He's the one I saw you with that first night in the posada, isn't he?"

"Yes. He's my husband."

"Where is he?" Robert asked again. "Is he here?"

"He is, but not as you mean."

Sofía explained. Robert listened without interruption. "Very well," he said when she finished. "So no Gypsy can talk to him and he'll be on the lookout for you. But I'm not a Gypsy, he won't be expecting me. Take me to this cave of his and I'll deal with him."

Joselito drew a quick, sharp breath. To violate the sanctity of a Gypsy cave, to actually bring a *busne* there, was unthinkable. If such a thing happened, there would be war between his tribe and Paco's for generations. "She cannot do that," he said. "It is against the law of the Rom."

"What kind of law do you honor?" Robert demanded. "Doesn't it count for anything in your law that this Paco has stolen my son?"

Sofía gasped. Joselito looked at her. "This is the boy's father?"

"No, he's not," she insisted.

"Yes." Robert looked at her, not Joselito. "Yes, I am Rafael's father." He spoke quietly, without emotion. "That's the truth, isn't it, Sofía?"

She had fought too long, and she had lived with the agony of Rafael's loss for four endless days and nights. Sofía did not meet Robert's eyes. Her voice was so low, the two men had to strain to hear her. "Yes, but that changes nothing."

"It changes everything," Robert said softly.

Sofía opened her mouth, but it was Joselito who spoke. "*Sí,* it changes some things. A man's right to protect his son is the highest law of the Rom. You are not a Rom, señor, but perhaps . . . I cannot decide this alone, there must be a council of the tribe. Wait here." He turned and was gone.

"How did you know?" Sofía asked dully.

"Because I had all the time I was riding here to think of nothing but Rafael. And because of the way I feel about him. I love him, Sofía. As soon as I let myself listen to my instincts, they told me he was mine. Why did you lie to me?"

She shook her head. "I can't explain that here, now."

He nodded and didn't press. The minutes passed. "Where in bloody hell has this Joselito gone? What's taking so long?"

"He is speaking to the men of our tribe. You and I can do nothing but wait."

"You must know the way to this murderous bastard's cave. You were married to him."

Sofía shook her head. She was too weary to explain an entire way of life to Robert now. "Wait," she said. "It won't be much longer. And we will have a far better chance if—" Her words were interrupted by the arrival of Joselito and two other Gypsies.

Joselito motioned to Robert. "Come." Sofía started to follow them. "No," he told her. "You cannot be with us. This is something for men. The boy's father has the claim, not you." She stepped back and let them enter the caves without her.

There was no sign of Paco in the cave. A man stepped forward, Chichi, who had been elected leader of the tribe after Paco was banished. "Welcome, Joselito." His eyes did not convey the same meaning. They were not friends—besides, Joselito and the three men with him looked grave and angry. Chichi studied their faces. He paused when he came to the fourth. "You have brought a *busne* to my cave. It is against the law of the Rom. Why?"

"Because there is one here who has broken a higher law. One of you stole this man's son."

Chichi looked around at the men of his tribe. He saw no guilt in any of their eyes. "None of them would do such a thing. Of course, if a child should happen to fall into the hands of one of us, and if we happened to know that there was a ransom to be paid . . ." He studied his tribesmen again. Still there was no response. Chichi turned back to Joselito. "You are wrong and you have profaned my cave."

"I'm not wrong. And the criminal isn't one of these."

"Who, then? We are all here and—" The Gypsy stopped speaking. "Ah," he said. "I see." He jerked his head toward the darkest corner.

Everyone turned in the direction Chichi had indicated, but it was too dark to see. One of Joselito's men took a candle from the table and shone it into the dark corner. Paco was crouched there like an animal. He had become very thin since his banishment. He was filthy and his clothes were rags. His glance darted from place to place seeking an escape. There was none, Joselito and his men blocked the single door.

Joselito turned to Chichi. "This dog turd does not exist for any Gypsy. Let us go and leave him with the *busne*. The quarrel is between them."

It was a solution of sorts, but Chichi hesitated. The idea of leaving his cave to a *busne* disgusted him. Still, it was already profaned and they would need to purify it with many spells and rituals. Finally he nodded and led his men and Joselito's out.

Robert looked at Paco. "We have things to talk about, Gypsy."

"Nothing. I have nothing to say to you, *busne*. Put your gun away. It doesn't frighten me. If you kill me, you'll never find the boy. But you won't anyway." He laughed softly. "I'll never tell you where he is. He's in a safe place and every day he grows a little weaker and a little more thirsty. I go and see him and watch. I figure a week maybe. Then he'll be dead."

Robert stared for a moment at the face of total evil. Then he put away his pistol and drew a knife from the pocket of his frockcoat. "I think you will tell me what I want to know, Gypsy. It's only a matter of time."

All of Chichi's tribe and all of Joselito's were waiting in the plaza when Robert appeared. He had been alone with Paco for forty minutes. They had heard screams, but no shot. Now they noted that the *busne*'s pistols were tucked in his belt. He seemed very calm, but his white shirtfront and his black coat were soaked with blood.

A few of the women crossed themselves. "Is he still alive?" someone asked. Robert shook his head. Chichi darted back inside, no one else moved.

Robert searched the crowd for Sofía. She was standing by herself some distance from the others. Her eyes were closed, she seemed to be praying. "Sofía," he said softly. "I know where Rafael is. We can go get him."

She uttered one strangled cry of relief and ran to him. She saw the blood, but her only thought was for Rafael. "Is he all right? Where is he?"

"The bastard swore Rafi was still alive. He's in some old building. Number three Calle Santa Ana, do you know where it is?"

"Yes, yes I do." She started to run down the hill that led to the *busne* section of the barrio Triana. Robert ran after her.

"Sofía, wait!" Chichi raced toward them. Sofía paused for the few seconds he took to reach her. "This is for you." He pushed something wrapped in an old bandanna into her hands. "Your husband is dead." He looked at Robert and Sofía saw awe in Chichi's eyes. Or terror perhaps. "Paco did not die easily," Chichi murmured. "But he did not deserve to. We will not mourn him."

Sofía didn't answer. She shoved the thing he'd given her into the pocket of her skirt and turned and ran on. Robert hesitated a moment, exchanged one more look with the Gypsy, then bolted after her.

The Calle Santa Ana was a narrow alley a stone's throw from the river. They could see the masts of three ships at the nearby docks, and hear the sounds of movement aboard, but the alley itself was deserted. Robert looked around. There were many buildings and none of them had numbers. "He said it was a warehouse, but abandoned now."

Sofía didn't ask what he'd done to make Paco tell him so much. She didn't care. The stench in the alley was horrific, but she ignored it. She wanted to cry out for Rafael, to shout his name and listen for a response, but she didn't dare. This was a place of beggars and outlaws, of thieves who would kill for a single real. They spoke in whispers, and Robert had drawn one of his pistols. "Number three could be the third up from the river," she murmured.

"Yes." Robert moved closer to the mouth of the alley and counted the buildings. It was hard to tell where one left off and another began because the crumbling old walls seemed to run together. He identified the third door on the left and tried it. It was locked and bolted. "I could shoot the lock off," he said hesitantly. "But the sound is sure to bring trouble."

"Wait." Sofía turned and studied the third door on the opposite side of the narrow space. It was a pair of doors, really, and they were splintered and broken and sagged on their hinges. "That looks more likely, doesn't it?"

"I think so." Robert felt a surge of hope.

The battered doors were held shut by a large stone. He shoved it aside, and one of the wooden barriers swung free with a grating noise. They plunged forward and found themselves in a courtyard of sorts. The cobbles were slick with slime, river mud oozing in from an unseen source. Half a dozen cats yowled their displeasure at being disturbed, and scattered.

"Through there." Robert pointed to another set of doors. These were fastened with a bar of wood. He shoved it aside and pushed the doors open. They were in a cavernous space as dark as night. The stink was worse here—river sewerage mixed with cat urine. Robert cursed himself for not thinking to bring a torch, or at least a candle from the Gypsy caves.

"Rafi," Sofía called softly. "Rafi darling, are you here? It's Mama, pet. I've come to take you home."

They listened, but there was no reply.

"We've got to feel our way along the walls," Robert said. "There's no other way. You take one side, I'll take the other. Call if you find a door or any kind of opening."

It was a scene from the worst of nightmares. Once Sofía slipped and fell, and the unspeakable ooze that covered the floor soaked her skirt and coated her hands. She struggled to her feet and went back to clawing her way along the stone walls. She'd just come to a corner when she heard Robert calling her. "Sofía, over here. Follow my voice, there's some kind of staircase."

She joined him and they descended a narrow set of twisting steps that seemed to go down forever. Robert was in the lead. She held on to his shoulder so he could have one hand free to steady himself, the other to hold his pistol. They reached the bottom. "There's water down here. Hang on a minute. No, it's all right, it's just ankle deep. Rafi," he called. "Rafi, can you hear me? Are you there?"

Sofía thought she heard a muffled sound. "Rafi, it's Mama, darling. Where are you?" She paused and listened. "I heard something," she whispered to Robert. "From over there on the left."

They moved off in the direction of the sound Sofía thought— and prayed—she had heard. There were huge poles in the cellar, stanchions that supported the floor above. Robert found the first one when he bumped into it, the others he skirted carefully. They found Rafael tied to the fourth.

He was sitting in the water, gagged, and with his hands and feet tied around the timber pillar. Sofía knelt beside him, cradling him in her arms as best she could despite the position. "It's all right, darling, it's all right. We're here. We're going to take you home. It's all over, my love."

"Hang on, lad," Robert murmured. "We'll have you free before you can say 'jackrabbit.'" He put away his pistol and reached for the knife in his pocket. It was too dark to see, but he was suddenly conscious of the blood on the knife and how it had come to be there. He wiped it on his breeches before he cut the gag from Rafael's mouth.

"*Mamacita* and Cousin Robert," the child whispered. There was a tremor in his piping little voice, but his words were strong and sure. "I knew you would come."

"Good boy." Robert hacked at the ropes that bound Rafi's hands and feet. "A good brave Mendoza boy, just as I knew you'd be."

"I'm so thirsty," Rafi said. "I haven't had a drink for days and days. The Gypsy said he'd give me one, but he never did."

"Just a moment more," Sofía said. "Just a moment more, my darling, and we'll get you out of here and you can have all the drink you want."

"There, he's free." Robert tossed away the last cord and picked up the boy. They moved as quickly as they dared across the cellar to the stairs.

It seemed to take forever, but finally they were out of the warehouse at street level, then through the courtyard and into the alley. Robert paused and let his eyes adjust to the moonlight. He was looking around, trying to decide where to lead them next, when he saw a figure coming toward them.

"Here, take him." He shoved Rafael into Sofía's arms, drew his pistol and cocked it. The figure looked vaguely familiar, but it was backlit and hard to identify.

"Don Robert, Doña Sofía, it is you?"

"Enrique!" Sofía called out. "It's us. We have Rafael."

Enrique ran toward them. "Praise God and the Virgin and all the saints. I followed with the carriage, sir. It seemed like you'd need some way to get Doña Sofía and the child back to the palace once you'd found them. I went to the caves of the Triana and someone calling himself Joselito told me where you'd gone."

"Good man," Robert said. "You wouldn't happen to have a drink handy. The lad's got a terrible thirst."

Enrique smiled broadly. His teeth gleamed white in the moonlight. "In the carriage, hidalgo. It's waiting just behind, and I've a big jug of water from the fountain at the other end of town."

After his first brave words Rafael had said nothing. He merely clung to his mother, arms wrapped tightly around her neck. When at last they were able to give him the water he craved, he drank greedily, then he collapsed sobbing against Sofía's breast.

Robert looked at the child who was his son. He looked at Sofía hugging him to her, eyes shut in an ecstasy of relief. He did not feel in the least remorseful about the things he had done to the Gypsy in the cave. "Take us to the Palacio," he told Enrique. "Take us home."

The first rains of winter came three days after they returned to Córdoba. Robert stood at the small, barred window of the counting room, staring out at the mud churning in the road of the Calle Averroes. It occurred to him that if the rains had come before they found Rafael, the river would have risen, and with it the water in the cellar of the deserted warehouse. The boy would have drowned. If not, the Gypsy would have starved him to death. Either way, he would never have seen Rafael after realizing the boy was his son.

Sofía came in, went to the writing table, and busied herself with some papers.

They had not been alone since they left Seville. From the moment they entered the palace, Sofía had stayed at the boy's side. "Rafi is sleeping now," she said. "I believe it's his first real sleep. I've been watching him and he's completely peaceful. No nightmares. I thought I'd best see to these household accounts. While you were in Jerez I sold a few things so I could begin paying at least half wages to the servants. Don't worry, I was very discreet."

He ignored her domestic chatter. "Why did you lie to me?"

She hesitated, staring at the ledger. "I didn't dare to tell you the truth," she said finally. "I couldn't let you reject my child the way you rejected me."

"I didn't reject you. Not the way you mean. I was out of my mind, insane. I'd gambled everything on one roll of the dice and I lost."

"And Mendozas don't lose. I know. But you rejected me all the same."

"That afternoon in the house at the *cortijo,* you mean?" They stared at each other, the memory alive between them of those hours when their bodies had given and received so much pleasure. "The time when you said you loved me," Robert added softly.

"When Rafael was conceived," Sofía agreed. She felt a current between them—a mighty stream of power that chained her to this man and both of them to their son. Did he feel it too? She tried to read his eyes. They were studying her face, but she could not tell what thoughts were behind them. Did he know her feelings, did he realize that she still loved him? No, it was too soon. Too much had happened. "You rejected me from the moment Rafael began to exist," she repeated. "And again a few days later. I came here to the palace. I tried to see you. I pounded on every gate. I knew you were inside, that you could hear me, but you wouldn't let me in."

He nodded, his brown eyes still on her face. "I did hear you. I was in the Patio de los Naranjos."

"Then don't ask me why I told you nothing about Rafael. I would not let him face such rejection."

"I understand why you said nothing then, but not now, not since you brought him here. You must have seen how I felt about him. But if Rafael hadn't been kidnapped, I still wouldn't know he's my son. You wouldn't have told me, would you?" He took a step toward her. For a moment she thought he might take her in his arms. But he didn't, he demanded still more explanations and confessions. "That's the truth, isn't it?"

"Yes."

"Why? Damn you, Sofía! You had no right. He's my son. Mine as much as yours."

"No, not as much as mine. Not while you were half a man locked up in a prison you'd made for yourself. You had to come out into the sunlight, Robert. Then you would be worthy of Rafael."

"But you brought him here," he said. "Why do that if you were going to deny me the right to be his father?"

"I always intended to bring him here. I had no wish to cheat Rafi of his inheritance. The war made me act sooner than I planned."

Robert's shoulders sagged, and he looked away. Sofía felt the tension between them ease, then snap. She had been right; it was still too soon. Robert was almost healed, but not quite. He wasn't ready for her love.

He looked again at the muddy street and the sheeting rain. "It doesn't matter now, I suppose. What do I have to give him? A palace and some lands and vineyards, and no money to support them or build a future. I've been meaning to tell you, there's no hope of any return from Jerez. Not for some time to come."

He leaned against the wall, crossed his arms, and told her how it was at the bodega. "So most of the news is bad," he finished. "I wrote a long letter to Liam yesterday, but I don't hold out much hope for it. Even if I manage to get it to him, and if by chance he still wants to acknowledge me as his brother, and to unite London and Córdoba again. From what I hear of the conditions in England, Liam won't have the money to import sack, and the great British public has none to buy it with. Young Federico can concoct ambrosia, but if the gods don't come down from Olympus, there's no one to drink it."

She watched him with rising excitement. When he spoke, it was the old hidalgo speaking, with sureness and logic and a grasp of all the elements. When he'd came to the part about the new sherry Federico Ruez made, she'd wanted to laugh aloud. For a moment his eyes danced with the old fire, and his description of the wine almost made her taste it.

"*Leche de Jerez*. I like that, Robert, I really do. And the idea of shipping it in bottles with a mark on them is brilliant."

"Maybe. But much good it will do us with things as they are."

"They'll change," she said confidently. "If we just hang on, Wellington will change them."

He laughed softly. "Still counting on your great English god Wellington? Well, maybe you're right, and he'll work a miracle." He walked to the shelves and took down some ledgers. "Meanwhile I'm going to see what kind of rents we can look for from the *cortijo* and other sources. We may as well hang on, as you put it. There's not much point in giving up yet."

"No, there isn't."

Sofía walked to the door of the counting room, then paused and looked back at him. She wouldn't give up on him either, she thought. She would work and wait, and someday everything would be as it was meant to be. Someday he would love her as much as she loved him.

Later, in her room, she remembered the package Chichi had given her. She had not thought of it until then.

Sofía still had the skirt she had been wearing that night. Sodden and filthy though it was, the skirt was a symbol of the peace she'd made with the tribe, of her final release from the constant torment of hating Paco and praying for revenge, of the salvation of her son. She would never throw it away.

She shook it out and reached into the pocket. The package was still there, still wrapped in the filthy old bandanna. It was exactly as Chichi had given it to her. She undid the knot and opened it, and studied the thing she held in her palm. It was the earring shaped like a snake with a ruby on its tongue. The earring was still attached to Paco's ear.

❧ 18 ❧

On the fifth night after Rafael's rescue the rain ended, the moon waned, the wind dropped, and the stars shone like blue-white diamonds. The child slept peacefully. Sofía was restless, plagued with dreams and desires and hopes. Robert slept little. He thought of his son, and of his son's mother, and of his family in an England that seemed suddenly as far away as some distant planet in the heavens.

He heard the clock in the passage beyond his bedroom strike four. Sleep still wouldn't come. He flung back his covers and went to the doors of the balcony and opened them and stepped outside.

The cold hit him first—a piercing, biting cold he hadn't experienced since he'd left London eleven years past; then he saw the ice. It glittered in the starshine and rimed the railing of the balcony and the stubs of trees and shrubs in the patio. Frost in Andalusia in November; it was a thing unheard of, amazing. "The times are out of joint," Robert murmured softly, and wondered what sea-change all this heralded. He shivered and retreated to his bed.

In the morning the household woke to chilled stone walls and icy marble floors. Sofía ordered dozens of charcoal braziers to be lit and placed throughout the palace. The servants were sluggish and slow to respond, paralyzed by the remarkable weather. Angelina went about muttering prayers and incantations and making the sign of the cross. *"Este tiempo no es bueno, señorita. Hace mal."*

"It will be less bad if you'll do what I say," Sofía said tartly. "Have you told Puri to light the charcoal?"

"¡Ay! Of course I told her, but Puri does what she wants. She doesn't feel the cold because she burns inside."

"Angelina, what are you talking about? Tell Puri I want the coals made ready now. If she doesn't do it, she won't be working here tonight."

"Señorita, you cannot send Puri away unless you send Enrique away too."

"What do you mean? Enrique has been with me for years, he—" She broke off and studied the housekeeper. "Are you telling me that Puri and Enrique are having a romance?"

"Sí, señorita."

"But Puri's at least ten years older than Enrique, maybe more."

Angelina grinned wickedly. She put her hands to her throat. "From here up, maybe. From here down she's a young girl."

Sofía couldn't choke back her laughter. "Very well, if you say so. Go tell Puri that if she gets the charcoal ready, and if the braziers are lit within the hour, the hidalgo will make her the biggest wedding she's ever seen. I'll personally arrange everything."

"You'll help her get Enrique to marry her?"

"Why not? I'd help her do anything if it would warm this place up."

Angelina sailed off smiling. Sofía started for the stairs. She needed a second woolen shawl from her room. But the bell was ringing at the gates of the Patio del Recibo; she heard one of the gardeners hurrying to open them. She looked around. Angelina was already out of sight and none of the maids was nearby. Probably they were all huddled around the fires in Puri's kitchen. Sofía went herself to the door of the foyer.

A small black carriage had been driven into the patio. It was pulled by two undistinguished horses and it was unmarked. The driver wore no livery and the curtains at the carriage windows were drawn. As she watched, the door facing her opened, and a heavily veiled woman dressed in black started to descend. Just before her booted foot touched the cobblestones, the woman turned and said something. So there was someone else in the carriage. But whoever it was did not plan to come inside. The woman closed the carriage door and came toward Sofía.

"I have come to see the hidalgo." Her voice was that of one accustomed to giving orders and being obeyed.

"He is very busy," Sofía said curtly. "I handle all the affairs of the palace."

"Not this one. Please tell Don Robert he has a visitor."

The woman lifted the veil that covered her face. Sofía hated her on sight. She was neither young nor beautiful, but she emanated a vivid sensuality, and the way she spoke Robert's name made it obvious they were not strangers.

"Tell the hidalgo that Maria Ortega wishes to speak with him." She went past Sofía into the foyer and began to remove her gloves. Sofía didn't move. "Please, *Gitanita*," Maria Ortega said softly. "It is very important. I think Don Robert will be glad to see me."

Maria Ortega knew too much, not only intimate things about Robert, but about her. She knew who Sofía was; but all Spain knew who she was. And by now all Andalusia knew that she was living in the Palacio Mendoza. "Wait here," Sofía said.

She did not send a servant to fetch Robert. She went herself to his bedroom and knocked. "Robert, there's someone to see you."

Tito opened the door. Robert was just finishing dressing, looking into a mirror and tying the white stock around his neck. He didn't turn to face her. "What visitor? Can't you deal with it?"

"No. She wants to see you."

"She?" He paused in the act of reaching for his frockcoat. "Yes, an old friend apparently. Very attractive, rather like a queen. She says her name is Maria Ortega." She watched for his reaction. He didn't seem to have one. "Have you known her a long time?"

Robert grunted a noncommittal reply and finished buttoning his coat. Tito picked up a brush and attacked his shoulders. Robert shrugged away. "Not now, Tito. I'm brushed and polished enough for today."

He went past Sofía and started down the corridor without another word. She hesitated a moment, considered going about her business and leaving him to deal with his visitor. No, a pox on both of them. She wasn't a puppy to be summoned or dismissed at will. Sofía followed him.

Robert was already at the bottom of the stairs. Sofía watched his meeting with the woman. Maria Ortega had removed her cloak and her hat; her gown, too, was black. It set off her white skin and the red hair that gleamed in the dim light of the foyer. She held out both hands and Robert took them, then leaned forward and kissed her cheek. "It's good to see you, Maria. You look beautiful."

Sofía felt a stab of grief. It was over. She had lost him before she ever won him. The way this Maria Ortega threw back her head and studied Robert told a great deal. So did her words. "You are looking beautiful too. I heard the stories, Robert, and I wanted so much for them to be true, so I came. You were dead and now you're alive. I can't tell you how happy that makes me."

He smiled at her, then drew her deeper into the heart of his home. "Come into the salon, Maria. We can't talk standing out here in the foyer."

Sofía hastened down the stairs and followed them. She wouldn't give up easily. It was she who had brought Robert back to life, and she hadn't done it so this usurper could come along and claim the prize that belonged to her. Robert seemed unaware of her entry into the salon. She cleared her throat softly.

"Oh yes." He turned to her. "Doña Maria Ortega, may I present Doña Sofía, or as she is known everywhere, La Gitanita."

"We've met," Maria said easily. "In a manner of speaking. And shall I tell you what she's being called these days? *La emperatriz*. All Córdoba says that you are restoring the fortunes of the Mendozas, Doña Sofía, that you are the empress."

"All Córdoba loves gossip, however foolish it is." Sofía walked to the bell rope and tugged it. "Our guest must have some refreshments, Robert."

Robert didn't comment on her assumption of the role of hostess. "Indeed. I wish I had some of our new sherry to offer you, Maria. Remarkable stuff called *leche de Jerez*. You'll be hearing more of it."

"Will I? But surely you're making it to ship to England, Robert. That is if you can manage to get it there and the English can find the money to buy it."

He laughed softly. "You're as well informed and as clever as ever, Maria. And just as devastating. You know we're putting on a great show but things are not as they seem, don't you?"

"I imagined as much, yes."

Sofía felt hot blood rise to her cheeks. God, he was stupid to take this redheaded tart into his confidence. "It's only a matter of time," she said. "Wellington will soon finish Napoleon, and things will be as they were."

"Perhaps," Maria said.

One of Angelina's bevy of underlings came in. Sofía had issued no orders, but the maid carried a tray with a decanter of sherry and a plate of tiny cakes. From beneath downcast eyes she looked inquisitively at the stranger and at Sofía. Despite their retreat to the kitchen, the servants had already picked up the delicious fact that the hidalgo had a lady visitor, and that their mistress was furious.

Maria accepted a small glass of the oloroso and politely refused the cakes. Robert proposed a toast. "To happy reunions, Maria. And hopefully even happier meetings to come."

The sherry burned Sofía's throat. There would be no happier meetings to come. Somehow she was going to make very sure this vixen never entered the Palacio Mendoza again. She smiled sweetly at the other woman.

Maria Ortega wasn't paying attention to Sofía. She was looking intently at the hidalgo. "Robert, there's someone I want you
to meet. He's waiting outside in the carriage."

Robert's eyes flicked toward the door, as if he expected the
man to materialize because Maria had mentioned him. "If you
wish," he said. His unease was apparent in his tone. "But I still
prefer my privacy, Maria. I'm not yet up to dealing with
strangers. Is it something Doña Sofía can take care of? She's
remarkably competent."

Sofía wanted to fly at him, scratch his eyes out, no, the eyes
of the redheaded bitch. Competent! As if she were some hired
vassal. She'd show him competence. . . .

Maria Ortega was looking at her with a little half smile, as
if she could read her thoughts. "No," she said, watching the
effect of her words on Sofía. "This isn't her affair, Robert. I
want you to meet my husband."

The man was well wrapped against the weather. He wore a
black wool cloak and a muffler and a broad-brimmed sombrero
tipped forward over his face. He brought the cold in with him.
Sofía felt it eddy about him and reach out its tentacles to chill
her. She felt more—a sense of danger and mystery and fear.
She clasped her hands and stood very still, told herself she was
being foolish and fanciful. But the sensation increased when
the stranger removed his hat and unwound his muffler. He had
a long, livid scar stretching from the corner of his lip to his
right ear.

"Brother Elijah," Robert said softly. "Perhaps I should have
guessed. How long have you been masquerading as Maria's
husband?"

"It's no masquerade," Maria said. "He is my husband. We
were married sixteen years ago in Barcelona."

"But I know he's a monk."

"Was a monk," the man said.

He had removed his cloak now and he sat easily in one of
the gilt chairs of the salon. It was hard for Sofía to imagine
this dramatic figure, who seemed totally at home in the palace,

as a simple monk. His voice was low and vibrant. It compelled her attention, though his was directed entirely at Robert. "My name before you knew me was Ricardo de Maya. It is that again."

"I thought the vows of a monk were irrevocable," Robert said.

"Usually they are." He took the glass of sherry Sofía had poured for him. "*Gracias, señorita. Encantado de conocer La Gitanita. Todo el mundo sabe su valor.*" Sofía inclined her head in acknowledgment of the compliment. The man who called himself de Maya turned away from her and faced his wife. "Will you tell him, or shall I?"

Maria looked at Robert. "It's not a particularly long tale, nor a very remarkable one. Our marriage was arranged by our families. Ricardo and I met for the first time on our wedding day. I had rebelled at first, but when I saw him I decided it was not so bad an arrangement. Ricardo found it harder to obey, he'd wanted to be a priest. When after four years of marriage it became apparent that we would have no children, he applied to the Church for an annulment and decided to enter a monastery."

De Maya took up the story. "The annulment of the marriage was denied, but I was allowed to join the Monastery of the Precious Blood of the Savior and take temporary vows that were to last twelve years. The bishop promised to review my case at the end of that period. As it happened, the bonds between Maria and myself weren't severed entirely. They were kept alive by our — " He paused. "Our common interests. And by the time the twelve years were up . . . ." He shrugged. "The bishop was dead and all Spain was awash in blood."

"In a revolution you helped foment," Robert said softly.

He looked from Maria to de Maya, trying to imagine how much the man knew of his wife's activities while he was locked away in his cloister. All of it, he realized. De Maya knew of Maria's lovers. Doubtless he knew that Robert himself had been one of them. He was prepared to live with that knowledge because of the "cause" they'd both espoused. "I'd have thought

you might have a good reason for remaining in the monastery,"
Robert said. "It's supposed to be a place to do penance, isn't
it?"

De Maya leaned back in his chair, sipped his sherry, and
studied Robert over the rim of the glass. "I don't think you
understand, my friend. I feel no remorse for what I tried to
accomplish, only sadness that it failed because my countrymen
are too stupid and entrenched in their sins to see liberation
when it strikes them in the face."

Sofía gasped. She was beginning to understand the ramifications of this conversation. She knew nothing of the background of these three people, what had transpired between
them, but she suddenly realized that this man was somehow
responsible for the firestorm she'd witnessed in Spain. "A great
many brave men died, señor, in the North they are still dying.
They are protecting their country. I do not think they are
stupid."

De Maya turned to her. "I admire their courage, señorita, as
I admire yours. That does not make me approve of the ideals
or the program they're fighting for."

"Only your own ideals and your own program," Robert said.

De Maya shrugged. "Perhaps. That's human nature, isn't it,
Don Robert? But as it happens, the other side is winning and
mine is losing. There are powerful people, yourself among
them, who know my role in this business. The prior of my
monastery did not think it wise for me to remain. It seems I
put the entire community at risk. I went to my wife because
there was no place else for me to go. Fortunately, she was
prepared to take me back."

De Maya and Maria smiled at each other. Robert sensed some
peculiar intimacy between them, something unlike the bond
between ordinary men and women. He did not care to probe
those depths. "Why have you come to tell me all this?"

"We need your help," Maria said simply. "And we can offer
certain things in return."

"I have little help to give." Robert glanced at Sofía. She
seemed frozen by the revelations she'd heard. Of them all, she

was the true patriot, the one who had actually risked her own life for her ideals—no wonder these dark twistings and intrigues chilled her soul. Robert rose, took the decanter from the table, and refilled the empty glass she was clutching, managing to smile into her eyes as he did so. He gave Maria and de Maya more sherry as well, then took his seat again.

"As you guessed earlier, Maria," he said. "There's not much here but the shell of a grandeur that once was. The house of Mendoza is all but dead in Spain, I have reason to fear the same condition prevails in England. What possible help can I be to you?"

"England is the key," de Maya said quietly. "Whatever the condition of your family there at the moment, you have connections in London. We have none."

"Ah, I see," Robert said. "You want to go to England. Am I to provide a letter of introduction?"

"That and more," Maria said frankly. "Ricardo, tell him everything."

"Everything is a fairly brief history," the former monk said. "First, in Spain now there is no central government. As you know, local juntas rule each province. They mint their own coinage and raise their own armies. By the way, Don Robert, you have allowed Farola and the other dukes in Seville to function without you too long. They are carving things up to suit themselves, in hopes that they can get it all in place before the sleeping Mendoza giant wakes and gobbles them up. I suggest you see to it. But that's a digression, except insofar as it's this same Sevillano junta that wants my head."

He drank off his glass of wine before continuing. "The other part of the tale is in our so called colonies in America. For four centuries they have been raped by kings who claimed divine right for their greed. The people of America do not now intend to sit still and be raped by juntas made up of ordinary men like themselves. Rio de la Plata is virtually lost to us. In Buenos Aires they make their own laws and collect their own taxes."

De Maya leaned forward, fixing Robert with his dark stare. "I promise you that soon the same things will happen in Venezuela and Colombia and Peru. A new age is dawning, Robert. There will be new opportunities for men prepared to temper avarice with justice."

His eyes were as Robert had first seen them in the monastery garden; the light of fanaticism shone in their depths. Once he'd forfeited everything by siding with the monk. Was he now to make the same mistake with Ricardo de Maya? Was there any other way for a man to do more than survive? A sudden truth dawned on Robert in that moment in the salon; despite everything he'd been through, he was still not content merely to survive. The old fires still burned in his gut. He wanted power and wealth, not just for himself, for Rafael. Time, he needed time to assess the situation and the two hypnotic people sitting with him. "I note that you haven't mentioned the Philippines or the West Indies. Do you expect them to revolt as well?"

"Of the Philippines I know nothing, I've never had good intelligence from there. As to the West Indies, I think so. Perhaps Cuba and Puerto Rico will remain under Spain's rule, but Hispaniola is already part French. The Spanish half of the island is bound to give way. And there's Jamaica," he added slowly. "Jamaica has been British since 1655."

Robert heaved an inward sigh of relief. He saw it all now. He knew the way this monk-turned-revolutionary was thinking. His voice did not betray his sudden sense of mastery. "And that is what's behind the willingness of the British government to pour millions of pounds into Wellington's efforts to free Spain of Napoleon. The right to trade freely in the West Indies."

"Exactly," de Maya agreed. He sat back as if his case were made.

Maria cleared her throat delicately. Sofía and the two men turned to her. "Robert," Maria said. "You forfeited your right to colonial treasure to defeat Nelson and you lost. Without that constant influx of gold and silver your house is bankrupt despite its vast holdings here in Spain. But if you and your brother in England had preferred treatment in the new order to come—" She paused before adding, "The gold and the silver and the minerals are all still there, so are the people who crave luxuries

from Europe. America is as rich as ever it was. Only the be-
neficiaries of the wealth will change."

Robert waited a moment. "And in return?" he asked finally.
"What do you and your husband get from us in return?"

"We will be your agents," de Maya said. "You will give us
papers to establish that claim. They may be only empty documents now, but they will bear the name Mendoza and that
will swing enormous weight in the colonies. When independence comes, we will be real agents, and the presumed power
will become real power."

"And how will you use that power?" Robert asked.

"For good," de Maya said at once. "There will be new laws
to be made, a new order to be established. We will become
rich and we will make you rich again, but for our part we'll
use our wealth on the side of the angels."

Robert remembered when he'd heard that expression before.
Nonetheless, there was truth in what Ricardo de Maya said.
And great temptation. As things stood now, he had nothing,
no leverage to permit him to reestablish the ascendancy of the
Mendozas. If things happened as de Maya predicted and there
was revolution, it had to work. Whether the countries of the
Caribbean and Central and Southern America were colonies or
free states, they had to trade with Europe. If, on the other hand,
the old order did not pass away, he was dead. But he was dead
if he did nothing, and if his information was correct, Liam,
too, was dead.

Robert felt Sofía's eyes on him. He looked at her. He knew
she'd understood all the ramifications just as he had. He could
see that in her face. He waited for a sign, for an indication of
her thoughts. Sofía gave one short, sharp nod of her head.

"Have you means to get to England?" he asked de Maya.

"There is a ship leaving Cádiz harbor in ten days. The captain
has agreed to give us passage."

Robert stood up. "I need time to think. Come back here
tomorrow."

"We can't come back here," Maria said quickly. "We are in
hiding, Robert. We can't just repeat our movements and visits

and jog about the town as we please. You have to make up your mind now."

"I have to do nothing," Robert said softly. "I may do something, but I will take twenty-four hours to decide."

Maria dropped her eyes, chastened by his tone. De Maya watched him without comment. Only Sofía spoke. "The *cortijo* perhaps," she murmured.

Robert nodded. "Very good—an excellent idea." He turned to de Maya. "Listen, there is a small house on my land to the south. It's very simple, but more important, it's empty. You can trust your coachman?" De Maya nodded. "Good, I'll draw you a map. Go there, wait for me. I'll come tomorrow, or the next day at the latest, and tell you what I've decided. Whatever that is, you'll have lost nothing, it's on the way to Cádiz. I take it you're going, whatever I say?"

"We have no choice," Ricardo de Maya said as he stood up. "Come, my dear, we will avail ourselves of the hospitality of the hidalgo's simple country house." He turned to Sofía and bowed. "You've proved yourself a powerful ally to those you support, *Gitanita*. I hope and pray you will be our ally."

After the visitors left, Robert closeted himself in one of the small writing rooms of the palace. Sofía longed to talk to him, but she would not press. Robert's manhood was too fragile, too recently reborn. She wouldn't threaten that small spark, however great the stakes. Besides, she had something else to occupy her.

She was on her way to Rafael's room when a figure darted out from behind a corner and startled her. It was Puri. "Please, señorita, may I speak with you?"

"Does it have to be now, Puri? Shouldn't you be busy cooking?"

"The meal will be ready on time, señorita. But Angelina said you made me a promise."

Sofía was puzzled for a moment. Maria Ortega and Ricardo de Maya filled her thoughts, she had quite forgotten her conversation with Angelina. Then she remembered. "Oh, yes, you want to marry Enrique."

"*Sí*, señorita."

"And does Enrique want to marry you?"

"He takes pleasure with me, señorita."

Sofía looked at the woman. Yes, she would wager that Enrique took pleasure with her. Puri's body was magnificent, her breasts enormous, her waist tiny, her hips lusciously curved. It was startling to look from those endowments to the world-weary eyes and the iron-gray hair. But marriage, that was something else. And Puri was doubtless past childbearing age. "Have you been married before?" she asked the cook.

"*Sí*, señorita. Twice. Both my husbands are dead."

Worn out by their passions, no doubt. "Do you have any children, Puri?"

"Only two who are alive, señorita. A girl of seven and a boy of four. They live with my mother in the little pueblo of Santo Domingo."

Sofía was startled. She'd have expected Puri's children to be fully grown, and her mother to be long dead. Something she had not imagined was afoot here. "How old are you, *mi niña*?" she asked gently.

"I have thirty-one years, señorita." Puri hung her head as if the words shamed her. "It is the truth, I swear it. My hair turned this color when I was sixteen."

Thirty-one! Sofía cocked her head and studied the cook. Only three years older than she. Puri was telling the truth, she decided. "*Pobrecita*," she murmured. "We must put all this right."

"You will help me, señorita? Everyone says I am a witch, but I'm not. My temper is sometimes very bad, but it never lasts long. And you know that I can cook like an angel. And when a man—" She broke off, embarrassed. "I know how to please a man," she said. "And I love Enrique. He is younger than I am, but—"

"But not that much younger," Sofía interrupted. "I know Enrique's family. He has been with me for years. He is twenty-six. And if he has been pleasuring himself with you, then he can do the right thing and marry you. I will see to it, I promise you."

Puri grabbed Sofía's hands and kissed them, then she darted off toward the kitchen.

Dinner that day was superb. Puri had outdone herself. There was *sopa de gambas* with pink shrimp floating in a golden broth scented with saffron, and a huge sea bream stuffed with garlic and brought whole to the table. There were chick-peas stewed with onions, and potatoes fried in lard, and a whole kid that had been roasted on a spit, and green oranges bathed in honey, and loaves of bread made with a flour so finely milled they were almost pure white.

Sofía looked at the groaning table and smiled. This was Puri's way of saying thank-you, even before she had anything real to be thankful for. What would they be served once Sofía put her plans into operation? Whatever it was, she hoped Robert would be more inclined to enjoy the feast than he was today. He only picked at his food and drank three glasses of the rich and fruity *vino tinto* that came from the dark purple grapes of his vineyards near Ciudad Real.

In a few minutes he stood up. "Sofía, can you join me in the counting room when you've finished your meal?"

She nodded and watched him leave the dining hall. There were four braziers lit beneath the long ebony table, and their heat suffused the room, but she saw Robert shiver as he walked away. She turned back to Rafael. Since their return from Seville he had been served his meals on a tray in his room; today she had deemed him well enough to join them at the table. "Eat, *mi niño*," Sofía urged. "You must eat to regain your strength."

"*Sí, Mamacita*." He took another bite of the succulent kid.

Robert sat at the table in the counting room, where so many of his ancestors had sat, where doubtless they had made decisions like the one that faced him now. But were they the same? Did everything in both London and Córdoba ever hang so utterly on one turn of the cards? Probably, he told himself. Life was like that. A man came to a fork in the road and chose one turning rather than another and everything was changed.

Later, looking back on whatever the question had been, the answer seemed obvious and the decision made the only one that could have been made. But for the hidalgo of the time, it probably had never been so apparent, so clear.

Knowing that truth did not make his present choice any easier. He looked at the door to the palace proper and wished Sofía would hurry up and join him. Now, that was undoubtedly a truly new development. Had any of his ancestors sat where he sat and waited for a woman to give them counsel? Not likely. But maybe they had. Maybe there had often been strong wives of the hidalgos who behind the scenes advised their husbands. . . .

Another difference. Sofía was not his wife and he was not her husband. Still, they had a child. So perhaps he should marry her. What did he feel for her? Did he love her? How could he know? As far as he was aware, he'd never loved any woman. The other night though, when he thought the Gypsies might have harmed her, he was like a madman, capable of anything. But it wasn't because of Sofía that the blood lust had mounted in him and he'd done the things he had done to the Gypsy. It was for his son. And this decision was for his son. What he did now would have a profound effect on Rafael's future. And that was why it must be the right thing, and why he was not too proud to avail himself of Sofía's undoubted wisdom and good sense.

The door opened quietly on well-oiled hinges, and she entered the room. "You look very pensive, Robert."

"I am. Sit down, my dear. You know what I want to talk about, of course."

"Of course," she agreed. "And I think you know what I believe you should do."

"Yes, you gave me a signal when they were still here. I didn't miss that little nod of your head. But if it turns out to be the wrong choice, Sofía—"

"Can we be worse off than we are now?" she interrupted.

"Yes. That's the part I don't think you understand fully. That's what I wanted to talk to you about. Sofía, the junta that governs

Andalusia at the moment—the dukes in Seville that de Maya spoke of—they're bound to find out that I've thrown in my lot with the radicals once more."

"I see your point," she said slowly. "So if this Ortega woman and her husband are wrong, if there is no revolution in the colonies—at least not one that succeeds—you will be seen as a traitor to Spain."

"For the second time, perhaps. Though the situation with Nelson wasn't so clear because the Bourbons were still on the throne, and, theoretically at least, it was the king who had made common cause with Napoleon. This instance is different. Spain, or what's left of her, will fight to retain her colonies. One must be either for her or against her. So with that fact in clear view, my dear, do you still think I should give de Maya the authorization he wants?"

Sofía did not answer immediately. She leaned her elbows on the writing table, clasped her hands, and pressed her forehead to them. He could see the sweet curve of her neck and the way tendrils of hair escaped the thick bun she wore and curled at the nape. She was a beautiful woman, a luscious woman. And his if he wanted her, he knew. He knew, too, that he owed her everything. But was that love? Robert forced the thought away; time enough to settle that question later, when their future was clearer. He sat back and watched her and waited.

Finally Sofía lifted her head. "Robert, if we fail, you and I, if we make the wrong decision and back the losing side, it may be the end of us. It will surely be the end of the house of Mendoza here in Córdoba. None of that is unbearable. Life is always a risk, a gamble. I learned that years ago. If Carlos hadn't happened to take pity on me in that village in the mountains, I'd have been eaten alive by a cannibal. Have I ever told you the story?"

"No, I don't think you have."

"An outlaw named El Hambrero . . ." She shivered and waved her hand. "I'll tell you about it another time. But it's Rafael I'm thinking of now."

"It's Rafael I'm thinking of too," he agreed.

"I know. He's a little boy now, and what we do today will

determine his whole life." She paused for a moment, then took a deep breath and continued. "Robert, perhaps if we fail, Rafael will never be the hidalgo. Perhaps he will never be a wealthy man. I can accept that. What I can't bear is the thought that he'll be an orphan, an outcast, despised by those around him. I spent much of my life in that condition. I can't do it to my Rafi."

"I understand," Robert said softly. "But I think you have a plan. I can see it in those blue eyes of yours. What are you thinking, Sofía?"

"I'm thinking that if your brother Liam would take him in England, if he would raise him as his own, then we could afford to take this gamble."

He caught his breath. "You mean send Rafael away?"

"Not now, no. Not unless we have reason to believe that things are not going as we hope, as we've counted on. Then we must send Rafi to England. But I can consent to that only if we have your brother's solemn promise that he will raise Rafi as if he were his own. Would he give us that assurance? And if he did, would he keep it?"

"As to the last question, there is no doubt," Robert said quickly. "Liam is a man of honor, whatever else he may be. If he gave his word he would keep it if it meant the death of him. But whether he'll give it," Robert mused aloud. "Whether he'll consent to accept a bastard son of mine—" He stopped speaking and looked at her. "I'm sorry, Sofía, forgive me."

"There's no need. He is a bastard," she said calmly. "Now, you know he's your bastard, so it doesn't bother me when you say it. But I'll have no one else taunt Rafael with that. Is Liam the sort of man we can trust not to throw such a thing in Rafael's face?"

"Yes, I'm sure of it—if he agrees, but I can't be sure he will agree." He stood up, pacing the small room. "The thing is, we won't know what Liam says until after we've already committed ourselves to Maria and de Maya. I have to give them the letters of authority they want at the same time I give them a letter to deliver to Liam."

"So the gamble remains," Sofía said softly. "And it's double-edged. There's one other way," she added.

"What's that?"

"We take a solemn oath, the two of us. We swear that if things go badly for us, one or the other of us will escape to England with Rafael. Whatever the cost and whatever it means to the other one, or to the house of Mendoza. We put Rafael first, before any other consideration. Would you swear that, Robert?"

He looked at her for a moment. "Yes," he said finally.

"So will I," Sofía said. She looked around the room.

"You're looking for a Bible," Robert said. "But I'll swear no oath on a Christian Bible, Sofía. I remain too much of a Jew to do that." He went to a shelf in the corner and removed a few old ledgers and pressed the wooden upright that supported it in one corner. A drawer below the shelf opened.

"I never knew that was there," Sofía said.

"No one is meant to know it's here. It's a secret drawer. I discovered it years ago by accident. It was empty then, by the way. I put this in there." He withdrew the gold pendant and showed it to her.

Sofía looked at it, then pressed her hands to her eyes.

"What's the matter?"

"Nothing. For a moment I thought the lettering looked familiar. It doesn't, it was only my imagination. I have never been able to remember anything about my life before I was adopted by the Gypsies. Sometimes that blank time haunts me. What does this say?"

"It's a few words from one of the psalms. They're written in Hebrew. It's the most precious thing I own. Will you swear on this, Sofía?"

"If you will."

He nodded and held out his hand palm upward, with the pendant upon it. Sofía put her hand over his. "I swear before heaven that if there is reason to fear for Rafael's future in Spain, I will take him to England, whatever the cost," she said. "May God hear my words and damn me to everlasting hell if I break this oath." She looked expectantly at Robert.

"I swear the same," he said softly. "By the God of my father and his father and of all the Mendozas in time past. Rafael's future before all other considerations, so help me God."

Robert replaced the pendant in the secret drawer and put the ledgers back in place. "Leave me now," he said quietly. "I'll write to Liam and prepare the documents for de Maya."

"Yes." Sofía stood on her toes and kissed his cheek. "Robert, we've made the right choice. I'm sure of it. We won't go to England. Not you and not I and not Rafael. We're all going to stay in Córdoba, and the house of Mendoza will be greater than it's ever been."

He smiled at her. "I wish I had your confidence."

Sofía's blue eyes twinkled with merriment; the solemn woman of moments before had fled before the half-Gypsy gamin. "I have enough confidence for both of us. Do get busy and write those letters. And make very sure you don't give de Maya too much rope. Keep him on a short chain, Robert, or he'll gobble us alive."

Next day the weather changed again. Now it was gray and misty and incredibly warm. The roads turned to a sea of mud, and it took Robert six hours of hard riding to get to the little house on the *cortijo*.

For a moment he thought he'd come on a fool's errand. The carriage was nowhere to be seen and there was no sign of life. Not even a puff of smoke from the chimney. Then de Maya flung open the door.

"I thought you'd gone," Robert said, swinging out of the saddle. "Or perhaps never come. There wasn't even a hint of a cooking fire."

"We thought it best not to announce our presence," de Maya said. "Besides, there's no one here but us, and I assure you, whatever my wife's talents, cooking is not one of them," he added with a grin. "So there's no point in a cooking fire. We live on hard bread and dry cheese and hope for better times to come."

"Not an unusual diet for a monk, I imagine."

"No, but not one that tempts Maria. Does it, my dear?"

They had entered by the back door and were in the kitchen. Maria stood by the table looking at a moldy crust and the rind of a small piece of goat cheese. "This elegant food? No, not exactly."

"Well, I expect you'll fare better than this at my brother's table." Robert opened the leather satchel he carried and extracted a packet of letters and documents.

"I take it that means you accept our offer," de Maya said.

"I do." Robert held out the packet. The other man took it and shuffled through them eagerly.

"The two letters are personal, from me to my brother. You can read through the other documents later. The only one that matters now is this one." He extracted two folded sheets from the pile. De Maya looked at him questioningly. "A contract," Robert said. "Detailing exactly what is the agreement between us. A copy for you and one for me. We're both to sign."

De Maya nodded and began reading. After a moment he looked up. "This is very specific, Don Robert. And very limiting. According to this contract, we are to report to you the disposition of every real we keep for ourselves."

"Not for your personal use," Robert said. "I've made that quite clear. Your profits are yours to spend as you wish. But the business you do in the colonies is Mendoza business, and it must be fully reported to Córdoba."

"And agreed to in Córdoba?"

"Exactly."

"Unwieldy," de Maya commented. "That sort of leash has been the cause of many of the problems in the colonies. The person on the spot must make the decisions."

"Perhaps," Robert agreed. "Nonetheless, those are my conditions." He took a small vial of ink and a quill from the pouch and placed them on the table. "Do you care to sign?"

De Maya hesitated a moment, then nodded. He took up the quill and signed his name with a flourish. Robert looked at Maria Ortega. "And you, my dear. I think I'll feel happier if I have your signature on this document as well as your husband's."

Maria neither read nor wrote, but then, he didn't expect her to. Sofía's possession of those male skills was a miracle. Still, he held out the quill to Maria. She took it and made a mark where he indicated. Then she dipped her thumb in the vial of ink and impressed its print on the contract.

"Very good." Robert stood up and gathered his things. He took both copies of the contract and all his letters as well.

"I don't understand," de Maya protested. "Surely those things are for us."

"Yes, as soon as I know you're quit of Spain without being caught." Robert bundled the papers into his satchel. "I will meet you in Cádiz, Don Ricardo. Just before you sail. And presuming you have escaped the junta up to then, I will give you these documents."

"But, Robert, what if you don't get to Cádiz?" Maria pleaded. "What if you have an accident, or are waylaid by outlaws, or any of a thousand possible mishaps?"

"If any of them happen, you've lost a fine opportunity," Robert agreed. "My commiserations. But if the junta or any of its representatives catch you before you get aboard that ship in Cádiz, and these documents are discovered on your person, I'll have made my life forfeit along with yours. And for no good reason." He picked up his wide-brimmed sombrero and placed it on his head. "*Vaya con Dios, amigos.* I wish you Godspeed and a good journey. I'm sorry the cuisine isn't better, but stay here as long as you like. If you're caught, I need only say you broke in."

De Maya made one more try. "What if someone sees us meeting in Cádiz? If we go to your warehouse, that's yet one more risk."

"True," Robert agreed. He thought for a moment. "Do you know the Church of Santa Maria north of the port?"

Maria nodded. "I do."

"There's a hill behind it, and a grove of trees at the top. We'll meet there." They fixed a date and a time, then Robert waved and was gone.

"He is a very hard man," de Maya murmured.

"He is magnificent," Maria said. "I thought so years ago.

Then I believed he was a weakling and a coward. Now he's been transformed into even more of a man than I first thought him to be."

"I wonder what worked the change," her husband mused.

"That's no mystery. The woman. La Gitanita, took him apart and made him over. And she did a better job of it than God did the first time."

❧ 19 ❧

Four days later, on the morning Robert was to leave for Cádiz, the weather changed again. It became warm and humid and a hazy sunlight dappled the mid-November landscape. Rafael came to say goodbye to him, then Sofía sent him off to feed the cats. "I don't want you to go," Sofía said uneasily when the child was out of earshot.

"We agreed," he said brusquely. "We both decided that joining forces with de Maya and María was the right thing to do."

"I know, I still think it's the right thing. That's not the point."

"What, then?"

She shook her head. "I'm not sure. I have a feeling of doom, as if something terrible is going to happen. Don't go, Robert. Send Enrique, he can be trusted."

They were in the room off the Patio de los Naranjos that served as the library. Robert had the documents for de Maya and the letters for Liam in his hands. He'd read them again during the night, and decided they were as clear and persuasive as he could make them. He slipped them into a leather satchel and buckled it closed. "No, this is something I have to do myself." He picked up a pistol and eyed the barrel and spun the breech cylinder and checked the loading chambers.

"You're worried too," Sofía said, watching him. "You think there will be trouble."

"I don't, my dear. At least I've no reason to think so. But only a madman would travel the roads unarmed these days." He glanced up and smiled at her. "And I'm not a madman anymore."

"No, you're not."

"Thanks to you."

"It's not entirely my doing, Robert. I gave you the opportunity to return to life, but you had to decide for yourself to take it."

"And I have, and I don't intend that anything should push me back down the hole." He lay his hand against her cheek. Her skin was incredibly soft. He had a sudden sharp memory of the feel of her naked body, the musky smell of her passion. "Sofía . . ."

"Yes?"

He withdrew his hand. "Nothing, not now. Later, after I return." Sofía nodded, but he still read worry in her grave blue eyes. "Stop fretting, my girl," he said lightly. "Look, here's a whole room of books. Have a go at some of these while I'm away. There should be enough to occupy you for five days."

"I have read them. At least some of them."

Robert threw back his head and laughed. "You're always one step ahead of me. I'd give a lot to know who taught you to read and made you as you are, Doña Sofía."

"So would I," she said tartly. "But nothing in here is likely to tell me."

"It's a fascinating problem nonetheless. We must talk about it sometime." He tucked the pistols into his belt and picked up the satchel and started for the door.

"Robert, wait."

"Yes?"

She closed the space between them with a few steps and stretched to her full height and kissed his cheek. "God go with you."

Robert felt the place where her lips had brushed his skin— it tingled. He looked at her, at the tenderness and concern and intelligence in her face. She was somehow part of him, this woman, in a way no other female had ever been. Yet chasms separated them, whole cultures and lives and ways of looking at the world. "My God or yours?" he asked softly.

"Does it matter?"

With no further thought he pulled her into his arms and kissed her properly. It was the first time in six years, but it felt not at all strange. She tasted as she had tasted that afternoon at the little house of the *cortijo*—indescribably sweet, a mixture of honey and lemon and lavender. When he released her they were both breathing hard, and he saw the flush of desire that reddened her cheeks. Robert took her hand and pressed it to his lips. "We'll talk when I return," he promised. "I think we've still a lot to say to each other, you and I."

Robert's kiss haunted her. So much promise, as if the future she had dreamed about was almost within her grasp. And yet she wasn't happy. Sofía remained restless and anxious all morning. She paced the palace aimlessly and kept dashing out to one or another patio to look at the sky. It stayed as it had been, slightly overcast, and there was no wind. The temperature continued to rise. It was as hot as a day in July, but not with the dry, golden heat of summer. This was a damp, oppressive warmth that slicked the body with sweat and made it hard to breathe. Sofía returned gratefully to the cool stone-walled rooms of the palace.

Do something, she told herself. Anything to take her mind off Robert and his journey. Puri. Yes, this was the exact moment to deal with Puri's problem. She tugged on a nearby bell rope, and when a maid came she said she wanted to see the cook immediately.

Moments later the woman appeared. "You wish to speak with me, señorita?"

"Yes, Puri. I think it's time we did something about you."

"What, señorita?"

"We're going to make you look like a young girl again. Come with me." Sofía bustled off in the direction of her private quarters and Puri followed after, making the sign of the cross and praying that she was not in the hands of a Gypsy witch.

Sofía had discovered the instructions for making henna in one of the books in the library. She'd been puzzling about the problem for days before she happened on the solution. When she first promised to help Puri, it was because she remembered that Fanta knew a way to turn a woman's hair from gray to dark, but she couldn't remember exactly what Fanta used or how she proceeded. Then she found the old leather-bound herbal.

The book had been hand written by some former hidalgo or member of the family with an interest in medicine. He'd been a keen observer of nature besides. There were sketches and drawings of plants and herbs on each page, as well as directions for their decoction and use. Most of the recipes and formulae were against disease of every type, from ague to worms and something called fever of the brain, but one suited her needs exactly. Next to a carefully drawn picture of a plant with pairs of broad leaves along a thorny stem and clusters of white flowers were the words *Lawsonia Alba: Called in Arabic al-henneh. Moorish ladies make a powder of these leaves and mix it to a paste with water. This is used to stain the nails red and darken the hair.*

Sofía had studied the sketch. She'd seen the plant recently, she was certain of it. But where? After a few moments she remembered. It wasn't the plant she'd seen, it was a drawing exactly like this one. Done by the same hand, no doubt. And she'd seen it right here in the palace, in the *farmacia* cupboard near the kitchen. So her vague notion became a real possibility.

The mistress and her cook arrived at the splendid bedroom that once had been Doña Carmen's and was now Sofía's. Puri looked around her in astonishment. She had never even imagined such a room existed only for a woman to sleep in and adorn herself. Luxurious satin and velvet and tapestries were everywhere, even on the bed, and an entire table was devoted to a mirror and brushes and combs and varieties of bottles and jars and small marble pots. No wonder the mistress was so beautiful. But what was she doing here? This was no place for the likes of her. Puri shivered with apprehension.

"Take off your blouse and wrap yourself in this." Sofía produced a length of old linen from the drawer of a chest. The cook did as she was told, but with a look of terror in her eyes. "Stop being so frightened," Sofía said gently. "I'm not going to hurt you." She studied the woman as she spoke. Puri's skin was good, unscarred and healthy and taut, but there were rivulets of old dirt in each fold. And she smelled of sweat and the grease she used in the kitchen. "Puri," Sofía asked on impulse, "have you ever had a bath?"

"A bath, señorita? *Ay, mi madre,* I am not such a foolish woman as that. Every year before Easter I wash myself a little, but not so much as to get a fever. I swear it, señorita. I am careful and strong. I will make Enrique a good wife."

"Baths don't give you fever, Puri. They don't make you ill. They keep you well and make you smell sweet. Then no man can resist you."

The cook snorted. "I have no trouble to attract men, señorita."

"I know, but you want to marry Enrique, don't you?"

Two tears formed in the corner of the woman's dark eyes. "*Sí, señorita.* But I think he will only do it if you make him."

"I'm not going to make him, Puri. You are. You're going to show him that he can't live without you. Then the hidalgo will make a big fiesta in honor of your wedding. You can invite all your relatives and friends and you and Enrique will live happily ever after." Sofía hauled a brass hip tub forward, then tugged repeatedly on the bell rope.

The maid who answered the summons was Nieves, a young girl whom Sofía had trained as her personal servant. "Bring hot water," Sofía told her. "Three buckets of it—no, four. We need one for the hair."

"But you bathed only a few hours ago, señorita." The girl was becoming accustomed to her mistress's strange predilection for frequently immersing herself in water, but she'd never known her to do it twice in the same day.

"It's not for me, it's for Puri. Now, hurry and do what I say."

Puri had fallen to her knees in one corner of the splendid room. Her hands were clasped and she was weeping and praying to the Virgin to protect her. "Save your prayers for when they're needed," Sofía said. "Help me get this tub ready."

"Señorita, I will do whatever you say. I know you are wise and clever, and a Gypsy as well as a great lady. But I am a simple woman and I know nothing of these things. You have Gypsy spells to protect you. I will die if I put water all over myself."

"Nonsense. Now, do you want to marry Enrique or don't you?"

Wailing that she did, Puri allowed herself to be undressed and led to the brass bath.

Nieves returned with the steaming water and it was poured into the tub. Sofía added a handful of dried crushed lavender stems, and on second thought another one of jasmine petals. Then she rolled up the sleeves of her elegant silk gown and made a lather of some of the almond-scented soap Nieves made for her, and scrubbed the cook with her own hands.

"There, that's not so bad, is it?"

"No, señorita. I will be very calm and clean when they bury me."

"No one is going to bury you, Puri. You're going to be a beautiful young *chica* again. And you're going to get married. And if you're clever, you'll go on doing this at least once a week. It does calm you, and it makes you irresistible to your husband."

Puri wondered how La Gitanita could know that, since she didn't have a husband. But maybe she did once; she had a son, after all. Or maybe the señorita and the hidalgo . . . Yes, of course, they must be sharing a bed during the night, whatever the maids said about both sleeping rooms always being used. People said all manner of things. That the señorita was the reason the hidalgo was rich again, for instance. That she was like an empress who ruled the kingdom while the emperor only pretended to be in charge. But the people who said that had not seen the hidalgo in years. They didn't know what he was like now that his madness was cured. . . .

"Out with you, Puri. You're wonderfully clean. We're going to do your hair next. Do you have lice?"

"*¡Ay!* No, señorita. I kill them once a month with that terrible-smelling stuff Angelina said we must use."

"Good." Sofía parted the gray hair and studied the scalp nonetheless. The woman was telling the truth. She had used the mixture of coal and lamp oil that Sofía had ordered prepared when she first took charge of the household. "No lice," she pronounced. "So let's get this hair as clean as the rest of you."

Puri sobbed and Sofía scrubbed. In ten minutes it was done and the cook was led to a chair in front of the mirror over Sofía's dressing table. "Now, Puri, we're going to make a miracle." The servant was past asking what Sofía meant or what she planned to do. She kept her eyes closed and her lips moved in silent prayer. Clearly she did not expect to live through this experience.

Sofía put four large spoonfuls of the powdered henna leaves in a brown crockery bowl and poured in just enough hot water to make a paste. She pulled on gloves to keep her hands from being stained; she certainly didn't want hennaed nails like the Moorish ladies the old hidalgo had described, and began smearing the concoction into Puri's long thick hair. "I'm not sure how long to leave it on," she murmured. "That's the only problem." Puri wailed a little louder, but she said nothing.

They would wait half of one hour, Sofía decided, then wash it out. If nothing had happened she would try again with a thicker paste and leave it on for twice as long. Sofía sat down to wait, then heard a noise at the door of her bedroom. It was slightly ajar, and when she went to see if perhaps Rafael was looking for her, she found Angelina and a dozen maids standing in the corridor and trying to see into the chamber.

"What are you doing, gaping here like monkeys? Have you no work? Angelina, get them busy. Set them to scrubbing all the floors if they've nothing better to do."

"The floors are clean, *Gitanita*. I swear it on my mother's soul."

"Then scrub the walls. Why are you here?"

"Nieves said you were going to make a spell over Puri," Angelina whispered. "We came to see and to pray for her soul."

Sofía sighed resignedly. "For the love of heaven, aren't you convinced yet that I'm not a witch? Have you ever seen me do magic? I'm using an old recipe to color Puri's hair, that's all. It's just a plant, nothing more."

"*Sí*, Doña Sofía, I am sure you speak the truth, but . . ."

"But what?"

"But it's true you are a Gypsy."

"Gypsies aren't witches. There are no witches, you foolish old woman. There are only natural things we don't understand. Oh, there's no point in trying to explain. Get out of here, all of you. Go! Go!" She shooed them away and they scattered like a gaggle of geese.

Sofía returned to Puri. "That's it, we've waited twenty minutes. Back to the tub with you, my girl. Let's see what we've accomplished."

They had accomplished a good deal, a small miracle at least. Puri's gray hair had disappeared. In its place she had dark brown locks with a subtle hint of red. The change of color transformed her. Sofía stepped back to admire the results of her efforts. "You look beautiful, Puri. And at least ten years younger."

The cook studied herself in her mistress's mirror. Then she fell to her knees and took both Sofía's hands and kissed them repeatedly, murmuring benedictions on La Gitanita, her son, the hidalgo, and any relatives and friends whom she might not know.

"Back to the kitchen with you," Sofía said, laughing. "Take this." She removed a dress of yellow cotton and white lace from the cupboard and handed it to the cook. Then she looked at the dressing table and had another idea. She pressed a pot of beeswax into Puri's hands so the woman could sleek her hair back into a bun, and added two tortoiseshell combs so she could dress it in fashion. "Don't forget to wash your hair every week with soap and hot water, then you won't have to use that evil-smelling liquid to rid one of lice."

"But surely if I wash it, the color will change back," Puri protested.

"No, it won't. Not for a couple of months at least. When that happens I'll color it again. Better yet, I'll show you how to do it yourself."

The cook nodded, clutched the presents Sofía had given her, and started from the room.

"Let me know what Enrique says when he sees you," Sofía called after her. "If he doesn't propose marriage in the next week, I'll speak to him about it."

Poor Enrique. Sofía knew that he was in love with her. But it was better for him to make Puri a respectable woman than pine for something he could never have. Yes, much better, he'd have a wife willing and able to cook him delicious food and give him pleasure in bed. What more could he ask? So it had been a good afternoon's work, but the task was done and there were still eight long days before Robert would return. They stretched ahead of her as endless hours in which to worry.

These days of late autumn were short. The sun was dropping, and it would be dark within the hour, yet it was still hot. Sofía went out into the patios once more. She remembered the story about them: If one knew which paths and little doors to choose she could walk through all fourteen patios without ever once reentering the palace. So far she hadn't managed it. She'd try again; at least, it was something to occupy her mind.

From the Patio de los Naranjos to the Patio del Fuente was easy; she'd mastered that one. And she found her way from the Patio del Fuente to the one below Robert's bedroom, the Patio del Incienso, after only one false try. She looked at the spiral staircase that led to his balcony and his bedroom beyond. Oh, God, keep him, she prayed. Bring him safely back to Rafael and me. No, she mustn't stand here giving in to her worries and fears. She'd be weeping in a minute, and that would serve nothing. Which path? That one over there behind the rose-bushes. Yes, it led to a low door that she'd never before noticed.

The door opened on a walkway between two wings of the building. The walls were just far enough apart to accommodate the full skirt of Sofía's gown. Above her head were flat roofs whose parapets were pierced at frequent intervals with hollowed half circles of wood meant to carry off rainwater. Clearly this passage was purely utilitarian, intended for the gardeners and the servants, not the family.

She had to pick her way over moss-covered, uneven cobblestones that were slippery and precarious beneath her satin slippers, but she followed the passage all the way to the end.

It brought her to a large patio she'd seen only once before. What did they call it? Oh, yes, the Patio de la Reja, named for that barred gate set into the outcropping of rock on the far side. She started forward, intent on getting a better look at the gate. An ear-splitting clap of thunder stopped her progress.

Sofía lifted her head and stared at the sky. In the last few seconds it had turned ominously dark. Suddenly an east wind rose and thick, angry-looking clouds scudded overhead. While she watched, they parted, and there was a jagged flash of lightning accompanied by another burst of thunder. There was no countable pause between them; the storm was directly above her.

Sofía ran to a thick oak door that must lead back into the palace. She pushed at it—the door was locked. She had no idea where she was in relation to the rooms of the interior. She shouted and banged on the wood. No one came. The heavens opened, but not the door. Sheets of water poured out of the sky.

She ran back to the mouth of the passage that had brought her there. She was already soaked to the skin and in the few moments it had taken her to cross the patio the narrow walkway had become a rushing torrent. Water swirled over the cobblestones and eddied toward her. Sofía could not bring herself to step into the angry-looking flood. She turned and ran in the opposite direction, toward the cave.

The *reja* was locked with an enormous padlock she couldn't budge, but the hinges of the gate were rusted through. It came loose the moment Sofía tugged on it. It was too heavy for her to move. She jumped out of the way and let it fall to the ground. The hollow in the outcropping of granite was shallow, no more than twice the span of her arms, but it was tall enough for her to stand in. Sofía stepped into the shelter.

The storm raged immediately above her head. The sky was flushed with a strange glittering light that etched in silver the outline of the trees and shrubs in the patio, and gave them a new and somehow terrifying beauty. Sofía moved deeper into the small cave. There was another roll of thunder, this one so loud it threatened to burst her eardrums. *Madre de Dios,* what was happening? In all her life, in all the years of traveling the open road with the Gypsies, she had never experienced a tempest such as this. Terrified, Sofía dropped to her knees and pulled the dripping wet skirt of her gown over her head.

A slash of blue-white light split the sky; the bolt of lightning aimed itself directly at the cave. Then it struck. The world around her shattered.

Sofía felt a moment's searing heat and she smelled scorched flesh and knew it was her own. She heard a rumbling and groaning and the earth shuddered beneath her crouched form. Something was pouring down on her, striking her head beneath the thin covering of the silk of her gown. It wasn't rain, though she could still hear that beating down in the patio. It seemed to be an attack of small stones and stone dust, but whatever was happening, she was alive. After a few seconds the hail of falling rubble ended. Very slowly, tentatively, she lifted her head and uncovered her eyes, and looked around.

What she'd thought to be the solid rock behind her, the back wall of the little depression in the boulder, was gone. It lay in ruins all around her. She had to step over jagged lumps of granite to see into the hollow that had been exposed. The metallic light of the storm-thick sky pierced the gloom beyond, and she saw the cave.

Sofía put one hand to the side of her head. The lightning had singed her skin and seared a black mark in the skirt of her gown, but she was neither dead nor dreaming. She was truly looking at an interior made, or at least filled, by human hands. That much was apparent in the careful way the crockery urns and oaken kegs and barrels and the leather chests were stacked and arranged. Everything was neatly organized— smaller containers to the front, larger to the rear.

She took a hesitant step forward, then stopped and looked over her shoulder, as if fearing that some mythic character whose treasure chest this was would materialize and threaten her. But that was ridiculous. Whatever this was, it belonged to the Mendozas. It was their work that had made it. Why had Robert never said anything? Why did none of the old records explain? Because it was a secret so dark and so deep it was never discussed, perhaps it had even been forgotten. That reasoning reassured her. Besides, the storm was still raging a small distance from where she stood. No one would come and interrupt her, there would be no better moment to investigate.

She chose the smallest containers first because they were the easiest to shift. The urns and small barrels were the sort used to carry wine from the cellars to the kitchen. The covers of the barrels were nailed on, but only a kind of oiled cloth sealed the tops of the urns. Sofía lifted the first away and peered inside. Everything inside was wrapped in the same cloth. How carefully this had been stored; how precious the contents must be. She drew the first parcel from the urn, took a deep breath, and unwrapped it.

The glint of gold and the sheen of silver met her eyes—a flat golden plate divided into sections, another slightly smaller plate, also gold, and a silver goblet studded around the rim and the base with gemstones. There was engraving on each article, etched letters in some characters she could not read. But she knew them. Dear God, she did know them. Not individually, but she knew what they said.

She picked up the smaller gold plate and held it and closed her eyes. She heard a man's voice, old but strong and happy. It was a voice with laughter in it, even when he prayed the most solemn prayer. *This is the bread of affliction that our fathers ate in the land of Egypt. All who are hungry let them come and eat—all who are needy let them come and celebrate Passover with us. Now we are here: Next year may we be in Israel. Now we are slaves; in the year ahead may we be free men.*

She knew the prayer, she knew who was praying. It was her beloved grandfather, Benjamin Valon. She knew where she was, in Bordeaux at the home of her mother, Rachelle, and her father, León. She knew who she was, little Sophie of the long black curls and the big blue eyes—the much-loved and cosseted and spoiled child who had a voice like an angel and who, by age six, had learned to read and to count.

As if in a trance, she reached deeper into the urn and withdrew a folded length of silk. It was a large square striped blue and white, with fringes on the four corners. She stared at it for long moments, and her mind created a crosshatched shadow over the stripes. She saw them on the back of a man, swaying forward and back in prayer. The shadow was from the lattice screen and she was behind it in the synagogue. A melody came to her and she sang it softly. *"Micha mocha . . . who is like unto thee O Lord . . ."*

Sofía knew herself to be Sophie Valon, a Jewess, one of the Chosen, a daughter of the Covenant, as her grandfather had so often told her. She sat down on the cool earth floor, pressed her face to the silken prayer shawl, and wept torrents of tears while the rain beat down on the fourteen patios of the Palacio Mendoza in Córdoba.

For two weeks Cádiz had experienced the freak weather that plagued Andalusia, but the extreme cold and the heat and the lightning storms that ended it had all passed by ten o'clock of the night Robert was to meet Maria Ortega and her husband. The air was seasonably cool and dry when he climbed the hill behind the Church of Santa Maria north of the port.

By the light of the sliver of new moon, Robert could see three ships resting in the harbor. One of them was a merchantman—English by God, the red ensign flew aft. Forward he noted the courtesy flag that traditionally denoted the country of port. This one was blazoned with the arms of the Duke of Farola, a prominent member of the junta that had declared itself rulers of Andalusia.

"She's a fine ship, isn't she?" a voice said behind him.

Robert turned and saw de Maya. "Yes, she is. That's your passage to England, I presume." De Maya nodded. "Good, it looks as if you'll get away, then. I'm glad you've arrived safely, Don Ricardo. Where's Doña Maria?"

De Maya nodded toward the harbor. "Already aboard. It seemed the wisest course. Thank you for the use of your country house, by the way. We remained there quite peacefully until it was time to come here."

Robert murmured an acknowledgment and held out his leather satchel. "Everything is in here, exactly as we agreed."

De Maya took it. "I must say thank-you once again. We are

in your debt, hidalgo. But I suspect we'll find a way to repay it. That may take some time, you realize."

"I do. Any idea where you're headed? After London, I mean."

"Buenos Aires, I think. Though my wife favors Puerto Rico. We'll have to see what opportunities present themselves."

"The minerals of Rio de la Plata are tempting," Robert agreed. "But the sugar of Puerto Rico is also something Europe craves."

"You favor the island, then?"

"It occurs to me that islands present opportunities by the very nature of their limitations," Robert said thoughtfully. "But ultimately your decision must be based on politics, must it not?"

"Indeed. The real question is who will throw off Spain's yoke first, Buenos Aires or San Juan? If I knew that, the choice would be easy."

"Perhaps my brother will have some information for you. I don't know how things are now, but in the past the English Mendozas had active links with Jamaica. That was always a good source of intelligence about the rest of the Indies."

"Perhaps," de Maya agreed. "How will he receive us, your brother? Do you think he'll find the sudden appearance of two fugitive Spaniards an onerous burden?"

"That depends on how he reacts to hearing from me," Robert said frankly. "If he has any interest in the resurrection of the house in Córdoba, he'll treat you like the prodigal son and Doña Maria as the Queen of Sheba. If not . . ." He shrugged. "In any case, once you get to England you'll be seen as heroes, not fugitives. Liberal politics and reform quite suit the minds of Englishmen as long as they're not to be implemented on English soil."

De Maya looked grave. "That is my hope." He nodded toward the English ship lying in the harbor. Despite the late hour, men were scurrying over her decks loading cargo. "Is any of that yours?" he asked.

"Sadly no. I haven't progressed far enough out of the tomb to begin trading yet. But I fancy I will, Don Ricardo," Robert added softly. "I fancy I will."

"I don't doubt it." De Maya smiled a small smile. "And I have some information for you—you'll forgive my reminding you that Farola and the junta must be dealt with?" Robert nodded. "Good, then I'll be a bit bolder. Word is that the Cortés that has been chased around the country by the French now thinks to meet again."

Robert hadn't thought of the Spanish parliament, the Cortés, in years.

"Here in Cádiz. Thanks to the lack of any true king in Madrid, and Wellington and the English, they're feeling both safe and powerful. Each of the juntas ruling the country is to send representatives—they mean to write a constitution for Spain." De Maya waited to see what reaction this provoked.

"Are these would-be parliamentarians all liberals like yourself?"

"Many are. It's an opportunity, Don Robert—for the country and for you."

"Perhaps," Robert murmured. "If they speak for genuine reform."

"Would that recommend them to you?" de Maya asked.

"Yes. Does that surprise you? It shouldn't. Times are changing, whether I wish them to or not. The house of Mendoza will best thrive in a nation not always on the brink of civil war. A man doesn't need to be a visionary to see that."

"I agree," de Maya said. "So you must settle Farola and the junta, and influence this constitution, before you are truly Lazarus risen from the dead."

Robert nodded. "I'll see to it sooner or later." He took a paper-wrapped parcel from the deep pocket of his cloak. "Can you give this to my brother when you see him? I stopped at Jerez on my way here. This is that new sherry milk I was telling you about."

"If it pleases God, I will deliver it safely to the English señor," de Maya said solemnly.

Robert put out his hand. De Maya clasped it, then started down the hill. "Godspeed, my one-time monk," Robert called softly after him. "I will wait anxiously to learn what you find for us in the New World."

He watched until he could no longer see the other man's

departing form, then turned his attention back to the merchantman. There was less activity aboard the ship now; they
must have finished loading. Probably she'd sail as soon as the
tide turned. He thought of Rudi Graumann and the cargo of
bullion he'd brought—and all the consequences of asking for
and taking that shipment.

There was some new activity on the deck of the English ship.
Someone was climbing aboard. De Maya, no doubt. Robert
wished he'd thought to bring a spyglass. No matter, he could
recognize the swagger of the man without seeing his face. "Good
luck to you," he whispered into the night. "Good luck to us
both. If Liam is willing and able to help, then I fancy we'll be
glad of this night's work. If he isn't—well, that's something
else entirely." Robert was frowning as he descended the hill.

"Worst damned climate in the world," Liam muttered as he
stared out the window at the early December fog shrouding
Creechurch Lane.

He could not see the front door of the house from that
vantage point, but he heard someone pull on the bell, and soon
after he heard Joseph's voice. The boy seemed always to be
present if there was any activity at all, and he was much too
impatient to wait for a servant to open the front door. Liam
smiled when a few seconds later he heard his son bounding
up the stairs toward his study. Joseph knocked and burst into
the room before his father had a chance to invite him.

"It's a letter for you, Papa. A beggar brought it."

"Did you give him a penny?" Liam asked, taking the proffered
letter.

"I gave him two, Papa. He said that's what he'd been promised for safely delivering the letter. He was most grateful."

"There are plenty of people in London grateful for tuppence
these days," Liam murmured as he studied the wax seal on the
envelope. He didn't recognize it. He looked up at his son and
smiled. "Get along with you now, lad. I've work to do."

That was true. All the same he neither opened the letter nor
returned to his ledgers when Joseph left the room. His son
occupied his mind. The boy was almost thirteen. In a few weeks

he would be bar mitzvah. The observation of that old rite was not arranged at Liam's urging; it was Miriam, his wife, who had quietly found the rabbi and made arrangements for the Hebrew lessons and the ceremony that would follow. Miriam was far more aware of her Jewishness than Liam was of his, and she had made Joseph aware of it. Like calling his father papa, for instance. That custom, too, came from Miriam's side of the family. He and Robert had never called Benjamin papa.

The thought of Robert wiped the indulgent smile from Liam's face. He thought often of his brother in connection with his son. Maybe because his brother had no heir, and whatever ruins remained in Córdoba, there was no one to inherit them. Or maybe because Joseph looked very much like the uncle who had not seen the boy since he was very young. What a strange, divided family they'd become. Probably Robert would never meet the child Miriam was carrying now. He could know nothing of their joy that after so many barren years, Miriam was pregnant again. Liam sighed and told himself it was all spilled milk and there was no point in crying over it. Best see what this odd letter was about. He broke the seal on the envelope.

He read the brief note through once, then read it again. He might have examined the contents a third time except that his wife chose that moment to interrupt him. "Liam, the fishmonger is coming this afternoon. Can I have two shillings to pay him? Our bill is already two months old."

"Yes, my dear, of course." Liam reached into a drawer in his desk, took out two coins, and handed them to her casually, as if they weren't almost the last coins he had available for household expenses that week. He was trying very hard not to let Miriam worry about the shortage of cash they were enduring. She'd been very good about selling their new house in Richmond and moving here to Creechurch Lane after Benjamin and Bess died. Liam had told her it was so he could be closer to the business, but he knew she'd guessed the real reason, that he needed the money he could raise on the sale of the Richmond house, and that if Creechurch Lane had been worth more on the open market, he'd have sold it instead. It wasn't as it happened, so he was rearing his family in the heart of London's

East End, not in the country, as he and Miriam imagined when Benjamin gave them the house as a wedding present.

"Miriam," Liam said, glancing again at the letter he still held in his hand. "Can you arrange some refreshments for a guest later this evening. Some wine and biscuits and a bit of fruit perhaps. I expect that's all right for a Spaniard."

"A Spaniard?" Miriam's eyes widened. "Not your brother, surely?"

Liam shook his head. "Not Robert, of course. He's not a Spaniard for one thing, even though he acted like one the last time I saw him. And if he came to this house he certainly wouldn't be a guest. It's as much his as mine," he added softly.

"You miss him, don't you?" Miriam crossed to where he sat behind the writing table; she stroked Liam's hair back from his forehead. The hair was thinner now, and the forehead higher, but she still thought her husband looked like a lion. She was quite fond of him, really, which was extremely fortunate since for the past seven years theirs hadn't been an easy life. "It's too bad he's not here. That would comfort you in these hard times. Don't you think you might write to Robert and ask him to come home?" she asked.

Liam looked at his wife's swollen belly, then down at the folded piece of paper in his hands. "He's written to me. At least I have here a note from a man who says he wants to deliver a letter from Robert."

"The Spaniard who shall have wine and biscuits," she said smiling.

"Exactly. Send Joseph to me. I'll give him a note to bring round to this chap's rooms." He glanced at the address. "He's staying not far from here. Joseph won't have any difficulty finding him."

Liam was quite startled when Ricardo de Maya brought his wife along. "I know this isn't customary," the tall slim man said in his accented but clear English. "And my wife doesn't speak your tongue. But in light of what we're proposing, I thought it important that you meet her."

"Yes, of course." Liam looked at the red-haired woman. She

was disturbing, a sensual sort of female. Fine for a night's pleasure, but not for a wife. He hoped this Ricardo fellow didn't feel the same way. From what Robert had written, the two of them were to be deeply involved in this proposed venture. "She's a woman to be reckoned with" had been his brother's words.

Liam looked at the documents spread before him, then at his guests. "According to my understanding of these documents, you have Robert's authority to act as his agent in the New World. You are empowered to commit the house of Mendoza in Córdoba to the support of any new and independent governments the natives care to establish for themselves, is that correct?"

"Exactly correct, señor," de Maya agreed.

"Then pray, what do you want from me? Robert asks me to help you on your way to the Indies, and I'll do what I can, but he seems to imply that you want more. What might that be, Mr. de Maya?"

"The same authority from you as I have from your brother," de Maya said.

Liam sucked in his cheeks and stared into the air above his visitors' heads. No one said anything for some time. Finally the Englishman broke the silence. "I have connections in Kingston. Perhaps it might be as well if you took ship first for Jamaica."

"And from there?"

"From there you could go to any part of Spanish America that suited you."

"And what would we gain from this . . . er, this detour, señor? That is the correct word, I hope."

"It is. As to what you'd gain, that remains to be seen. The house of Mendoza has for some time been financing cargoes sailing from Jamaica. But I have considered establishing an actual bank with wider interests. Perhaps if in the future Jamaica had trading agreements with some independent country such as Cuba or Puerto Rico or Rio de la Plata, always presuming such places should become independent as you and Robert suggest"—he shrugged as if the matter were of only minor consequence—"well, perhaps this Mendoza bank which might come into existence on Jamaica might also come into existence in one of these newly established sovereign nations."

"Perhaps it might," de Maya agreed softly. "But they have been colonies of the Spanish Empire for many centuries, señor. They are likely to remain people who speak the Spanish tongue and think in a Spanish way, even after they break the links to the mother country and establish a more liberal and free way of life for themselves."

"Indeed," Liam agreed.

Extraordinary words for a Spaniard, but in the second letter Robert had written, the one dealing with business, he had warned Liam that this de Maya was a revolutionary and a fanatic. He'd also said he was trustworthy and brilliant. And doubtless Robert genuinely thought so. He'd certainly thrown in his lot with these two; the powers granted by the documents he'd given de Maya were wide-ranging and flexible. Of course, Robert admitted that Córdoba had "barely two farthings to rub together." He had little choice but to take risks. Liam picked up the business letter. "My brother is suggesting that in the future our two houses might once again be more closely united in our affairs. We've not been so for the past six years, but before that it was different."

"So I understand, señor. I have long observed the activities of the house of Mendoza."

"I'm pleased to hear it. Then you know that we can act in consort very well when it suits us. So you needn't worry about how the proposed Mendoza bank will deal with Spanish gentlemen of a Spanish set of mind, need you?"

De Maya smiled and stood up. "Not at all, señor." He turned to his wife and murmured a few words in Castilian. Maria Ortega rose and graciously inclined her head at Robert's brother. The good-byes of all three were cordial and polite. "I'll see what I can arrange about passage to Jamaica," Liam promised. "I'll send my son round to your rooms with word as soon as I know anything."

Later, lying in the hard, narrow bed in the cold English room that she'd hated on sight, Maria spoke her judgment on Liam Mendoza. "Not half the man his brother is. We could make any agreement we chose with him, then do whatever we wished. If it weren't for Robert."

"I'll not give my word and go back on it," her husband said. "That's a sin." He lay beside her with all his limbs rigid. He still could not accept the fact that he was sharing his bed with a woman, and that he was not damned to hell for so doing.

Maria turned, propped herself on one elbow, and drew a pointed finger along Ricardo's chest. "And we know you commit no sins, eh, *mi amor*?"

"Don't do that."

"Do what? This? But you're my husband, it's right and proper that I caress you. Aren't we joined in holy matrimony before God?"

"It can't be proper or right. There can never be any children. Carnal knowledge without children is pure lust, and lust is a sin."

She laughed softly. "You are holier than the pope, my Ricardo. Even he says that we are free to enjoy each other despite my barren womb. It's not my fault, after all. I did not ask for such a curse."

"I think maybe you did," he said between clenched teeth. "I think you're devil enough to have wanted the opportunity to whore with any man who took your fancy and pay no consequences."

"So you think me a whore," she whispered.

"I know you're a whore."

"Then you might as well use me, since I'm here and in your bed, Ricardo." She reached for the small bamboo cane lying on the nearby table. "Here, you can punish me for my whoredom, then make use of it. Go ahead, you know you want to."

She rolled over and lifted her nightdress, and he saw the two white half moons of her buttocks in the dim light that entered the window. He wanted to spring from the bed and break the little cane over his knee and tell her what he thought of her and all her perverted appetites, and sleep by himself on the floor, but he could not.

Some devil was inside him now, making him lift his arm and bring the stiff rod down on her flesh. And when he saw the

red weal he'd raised and heard her stifled moan of pain, he had
to do it again. And again and again and again. Until she was
sobbing and laughing at the same time and his manhood was
throbbing and enormous, and he thrust himself into her and
found the only release possible in these days since God had
rejected him.

On Creechurch Lane the master and the mistress were also
awake. They lay abed talking. Miriam wore a mobcap of ecru
linen that hid all her salt-and-pepper hair. Her nightdress was
also of ecru linen, and it had a high neck and long sleeves and
revealed no hint of provocative flesh. She was a modest, God-
fearing woman who knew her duty. Right now it was to induce
her husband to talk—and thus relieve his mind. "You're disturbed, Liam. Is it something Robert wrote? I'd have thought
you'd be quite happy to hear from him."

"I was, I am. It's just . . ." He moved restlessly beneath the
crewel-worked tester that canopied the four-poster; the feather
mattress that overlaid the one of straw shifted beneath him,
and he punched it into a new and more comfortable shape
before he continued speaking. "It's just that Robert's given this
de Maya fellow so much rope. What if he uses it to hang the
house?"

"But all these years you've been mourning the fact that there
was no longer a living house of Mendoza in Córdoba. And that
you had lost your brother as well as a business connection.
Now you know that neither one of those things is true. It's
enough, isn't it, Liam?"

"I suppose it should be. Besides, Robert's no fool. He's given
the two Spaniards plenty of freedom to make political alliances,
but he's kept a tight hold on the financial decisions."

"There, so what are you worried about?"

"Myself," Liam said softly. "My brother. Did I tell you he
sent two letters? The first one was written a few days before
the second. In it he told me how he'd been like a dead man
these past six years. But now he's come alive again, and discovered that he has a bastard son, of all things. The mother's
a Gypsy, or near enough as makes no difference."

"A Gypsy! He won't marry her, will he, Liam? He can't marry a Gypsy."

"He doesn't say what he means to do about the woman, but it's obvious he's quite fond of the boy and plans to make him his heir."

"Half Jew, half Gypsy," Miriam mused. "Heaven alone knows what that will produce."

"Half and half maybe, but completely a Mendoza, according to Robert. A Mendoza for Córdoba, and now we've a chance to unite the two houses again. The vineyards in Jerez are making some new sack. The Spaniard brought me a sample. Extraordinary stuff. Robert wants me to import it. He wants to ship it in bottles with a paper label stuck to them saying *Mendoza-Ruez*."

"Can you afford to import it?" Miriam asked quietly.

"Not a lot of it," Liam admitted. "But I'm going to write and tell him I'll take as much as I can. If nothing else, it will open the lines between us again."

"Good, a good decision, Liam. So I come back to my first question: what's worrying you?"

"The distance between us," he said after some thought. "Robert and I have grown apart. We've suffered separately where before we always suffered together. And our two sons, our Joseph and this Rafael lad of Robert's, won't even know each other." He patted her distended stomach. "And as for this one . . ."

Miriam put her hand over his, pressed his palm tighter to her flesh, and waited for him to go on speaking.

"My father dreamed that with me in London and Robert in Córdoba the house would be truly united, equals, not locked into the superior and inferior positions of the old days. But these children are absolute strangers from different worlds. If Robert and I renew the links between us, our sons are doomed to fight each other for dominance. It's written on the wall, Miriam. Like the prophecy that Solomon saw."

"Not Solomon," Miriam corrected him automatically, "Daniel." Her husband's ignorance of Torah and Talmud always astounded her. And he was a man and could read and write.

Naturally she could do neither, but all her life she had heard
her father telling stories from the Bible. To study the holy books
was the highest duty of a Jewish man; all study was a form of
prayer. But Liam—her thoughts broke off and took another
direction. After a few seconds she smiled. "Liam, answer me
two questions."

"What two questions? It's late, Miriam. We should go to
sleep. Nothing is going to get solved tonight while we talk
about it."

"Yes, something might. So two questions only. First, is what
everyone's saying true, that Wellington has driven the French
out of Spain?"

He looked at her in astonishment. "What in God's name has
Wellington to do with you?"

"Don't take the name of the Holy One in vain. And answer
me please. Is it true?"

"I think it's virtually true. The government says so, and
Robert claims that Napoleon's dragoons have all left Andalusia."

"Good. Now the second question. How long is this Spaniard
going to be in London?"

Liam shook his head. "I'm at a loss to know why it matters,
but not too long, I should think. A month or so. Why?"

"Never mind why. I'll tell you when I get everything worked
out."

Liam smiled indulgently and patted her hand. "You do
that, my dear." She was a foolish woman perhaps, but a good
wife. And talking to her always made him feel better. Liam
rolled over and managed at last to drift into peaceful
sleep.

Miriam lay awake a long time considering her plan. Yes, she
decided, it would work. Joseph was a smart boy, and even if
this tame Spaniard of Robert's wasn't going to be in London
long enough to teach him, there were other tutors who spoke
Spanish. She would find one. She would start looking tomorrow. But she would tell Joseph it was a surprise and he wasn't
to say anything to his papa until he could actually speak that
peculiar tongue. And when he did, and when there was peace,

why, what was to prevent Joseph from visiting Spain and meeting his uncle Robert and his cousin Rafael—and building some family feeling? Nothing, she decided, and she fell asleep, smiling.

❧ 20 ❧

Robert arrived back in Córdoba after midnight on the fourth of December. He'd been gone longer than he expected; he'd stopped at Jerez again on his return journey from Cádiz, and found Federico Ruez near death.

The young man had been almost crushed by one of the enormous oak trees near the house. To save on hired labor he'd been felling the trees needed for cooperage, and his inexperience had caused a disaster. Robert well remembered urging Federico to pare expenses to the bone. Because he felt guilty and responsible he stayed in Jerez until the surgeon assured him that though he'd had to amputate one of the young man's legs, Federico would live.

"Tell him that as far as I'm concerned, he's still chief steward here, and my partner," Robert had told Marisol. "He doesn't need two legs to make sack. And there's not a vintner anywhere can compare with him."

Federico's wife had been absurdly grateful. "*Gracias*, Don Robert. You are the kindest man in Andalusia."

"Nonsense, I know what's in my own best interests, that's all," Robert had insisted. "But now I must leave, I'm already three days overdue and there's someone in Córdoba who will worry about me."

Marisol had hidden her smile behind her fan, but Robert had read the look in her eyes. So even here in Jerez they knew about the woman they now called the empress. "I think there may be a wedding feast at the palacio someday soon," he said boldly. "I shall see that it doesn't occur until Federico is well enough to travel and you can both be my guests." There, let the gossips chew on that for a bit.

He'd ridden like a demon the rest of the journey, his blood singing with excitement because he'd made a decision, and his every instinct told him it was the right one. He would marry Sofía. She'd have him, he knew she would. She loved him. And he loved her. What else could this longing for her company be, or the burning in his loins when he thought of bedding her? Never mind that he'd been celibate for over six years, it wasn't just hunger for a woman that moved him. It was Sofía herself, the uniqueness of her, the beauty of her soul as well as her body.

The road melted behind him as his horse flew over the distance to Córdoba and he fancied he heard the fandango in the whistling of the wind, and that the waving trees danced in his honor. He laughed aloud with sheer joy.

He did not ring the bell at the gates of the Patio del Recibo. It was entirely unnecessary to wake the house servants at this hour; besides, he wanted to slip unheralded into the palace and make his way to Sofía's bed. She would be half asleep and he would take her in his arms and push up her silken nightdress and make love to her before he said a thing. They would seal their union with their bodies before they did so with their words. Perhaps tonight she might conceive another child. It would delight him if she did, but no one would take the place of Rafael, his firstborn and his heir.

Robert rode down the Calle Averroes and turned the corner into the Calle Judios. He stopped at the gate in the high wall that led to the stables. One short ring of the bell hanging outside roused the young groom. "¡Ay, hidalgo! I was not told to expect you." The lad rubbed the sleep from his eyes with one hand and reached for the reins with the other.

"No one knew I was coming," Robert said. "Take good care of this animal, *muchacho*. He's served me well." He relinquished the horse to the groom and flung his cloak over the top of a box stall. "Have you any clean water ready drawn?"

"In this barrel, hidalgo. I got it just this evening to give drink to the horses in the morning."

"That will do." Robert splashed the cool, fresh water on his neck and face and rubbed it over his hands. He couldn't wait for a real bath before he went to Sofía. This cursory cleaning would have to serve.

He left the stables, entered the palace proper and went upstairs by the narrow back steps the servants used. Everything was dark and silent, but that suited him exactly. He paused outside the door to Sofía's room and pulled off his boots. Godstruth! He couldn't very well climb into her bed in his muddy boots. Grinning, Robert opened the door and closed it carefully behind him, and padded softly across the Turkey carpets spread on the floor.

The curtains to the balcony were open and the room was lit by the moon, but the hangings were drawn around the bed. He parted them and lowered his head to kiss her. The bed was empty.

A sudden fear clutched at Robert's belly. Where could she be at this hour? He remembered the way he'd felt the last time he returned from Jerez, when Angelina had met him and told him that La Gitanita and Rafael were both gone. He'd had no difficulty believing then that she'd taken the child and left him as suddenly as she'd come. But that was before he knew Rafi was his son, before she admitted it, before he'd kissed her in the library and seen the way the blood of desire coursed in her as it did in him.

He told himself all that, but still he was gripped by the ache of loss. She wasn't there. What could that mean other than that she'd left him? And if she had gone, it was certain she had taken Rafael. Propelled by fear and rage, Robert ran across the room he'd entered with the eager joy of a lover. He sprinted along the passage to his son's room. A thin line of light shone beneath the door. He paused and pressed his ear to the door and listened. There was the distinct murmur of two voices, that of the boy and his mother.

Robert took a deep, calming breath. The two people he loved were both here. Perhaps the boy was ill, or plagued by bad dreams left over from his harrowing experience at the hands of the Gypsy. Whatever the crisis, it made no difference. He was there and so were they, and together they would deal with whatever threat presented itself. Robert opened the door without knocking.

An oil lamp shed soft light in the room. Rafael was not in his bed. He was standing in the middle of the floor with his back to Robert, looking at himself in a large gilt-framed mirror on the wall. Sofía stood behind him, her hands lightly on his shoulders. She wore her nightclothes, a gown and peignoir of pale yellow satin, and her hair hung loose to her shoulders and down her back. The exquisite beauty of her made Robert catch his breath and choked him past the point of murmuring a greeting to announce his presence. It was Sofía who raised her eyes and noticed Robert's reflection in the glass. She smiled at him and said nothing, but she moved aside so he could see their son. Robert took his eyes from her and stared at Rafael.

The boy was draped in a broad silk prayer shawl striped in blue and white and deeply fringed, and he wore a turban of woven gold cloth. The Moors had brought such headgear to Spain, and when they left, it was only Jews who continued to wear the turban. The sum of it was that Rafael was dressed in such a way as to make it apparent to the entire world that he was the son of a Jewish father.

"What in God's name are you doing?" Robert demanded. He had visions of some venomous Inquisitors bursting through the door, though of course, that was absurd.

"I'm showing Rafael his true heritage," Sofía said softly.

She turned and Robert saw something in her face that had not been there before. Sofía radiated a strange mystical glow. She reminded him of the man he'd watched taking ship for England, or of Harry Hawkins, perhaps. As for Rafael, he had not yet acknowledged Robert's arrival. The child seemed entranced by the vision of himself in the exotic gear. "Sofía, I realize you've done this for me, and I appreciate it but—"

"Not just for you," she interrupted. "For me as well, and for Rafi."

She wasn't making sense. But nothing in the room made sense. "Where did you get those things?" He gestured to the clothes his son was wearing.

"In the cave. They're very old, but still in perfect condition."

"The cave . . . what cave?"

"The one in the Patio de la Reja."

Hay un tesoro en la cueva. There is a treasure in the cave. Sweet God, he remembered the words, he'd never forgotten them. But there wasn't any cave or any treasure. "In the old strongroom? But I looked there any number of times. It was empty, and it's not big enough to be a cave."

"The cave is behind what you're calling the strongroom. There was a terrible storm and the back wall was hit by lightning. I was there. It missed me by hardly anything at all. Look." She lifted the hair that covered her left temple and he saw an ugly burn mark just beginning to heal.

"You must have that treated," he said at once. "Otherwise it will fester and cause a fever."

She shook her head impatiently. "I did treat it, that's not important now. The back wall of the old strongroom was destroyed. It wasn't a wall, just cleverly made to look like one. And behind it I found this tallith." She turned back to Rafael and fingered the silk of the striped stole.

"And you wanted to do something that would please me," Robert said softly. "Thank you, my dear, but—"

"I told you," she interrupted again. "It's not just for you. Rafi, where are your manners? You haven't yet said good evening to Robert."

The boy was finally distracted from the vision of himself in the mirror. He turned. "Good evening, Cousin Robert."

Robert hated when the child called him that, but they'd not yet told Rafael the truth. They hadn't figured out how to tell him the truth. "Good evening, *niño*," Robert said. "What have you been getting up to while I was gone?"

"*Mamacita* has taught me a song. Would you like to hear it?" Robert nodded. "*Micha mocha,*" the boy began. "Who is like unto Thee, O Lord . . ."

Robert listened to the words and he recognized them as Hebrew, though he didn't know what they meant. "Sofía, where did you learn that? How could you have taught it to Rafi?"

"I learned it at the synagogue in Bordeaux, where I was born," Sofía said quietly. "My grandfather used to take me with him to prayers every morning. My blood is Jewish blood. My name is Sophie Valon."

At last he understood. "You've remembered what happened before you went to live with the Gypsies," he whispered.

"Yes. I saw what was in the cave and I touched it—and I remembered."

"I had to trust someone," she explained as they walked through the night-shrouded patios. "I couldn't cover everything by myself, and I couldn't leave it exposed."

"Yes, I see that. Enrique?"

"He was the logical choice," she agreed. "I got him as soon as the storm abated and he did this."

They'd reached the Patio de la Reja, and Robert looked across it to where Sofía was pointing. He dropped Rafael's hand. "Stay with your mother, *mi niño,*" he murmured as he crossed the mosaic paving and approached the *reja.* It had been reerected, and the hinges and the padlock made secure. Behind the gate Robert saw at first only the shallow declivity that had always been there, but in the rear he could just make out a heavy tapestry curtain.

Sofía came up beside him. "We cleared away the rubble, hung the curtain, and put the gate back. There didn't seem anything else to do immediately. I thought of posting guards, but that could be provocative. What excuse would I give for them? And while I trust the servants, who knows which of them talk when they're not here, or what they say?"

"They say you're a witch and also an empress," Robert murmured. "And you were quite right—far better if they've nothing out of the ordinary to report. How do we get inside?"

Sofía took a chain with a small key from around her neck. "There was an old padlock but we couldn't find the key. Enrique had this one made by the locksmith the day after the storm."

Robert took the key and unlocked the padlock. The old gate swung open on newly oiled and repaired hinges. "A blessing on Enrique. We'll have to give him a suitable reward."

"We will," Sofía said. "He's getting married. I've promised him and his bride a big wedding fiesta."

Robert nodded, not much concerned with the private affairs of his servants. He turned to Rafi, standing silently beside them. They had removed the boy's religious finery before taking him down there; he was merely a young lad in his linen sleeping shift now. If Robert had his way, Rafael would be tucked up in his bed, but Sofía had insisted the boy come with them. It was his heritage, she'd argued, and he'd already had much of it explained to him.

"Have you been in here before?" Robert asked the child.

"Yes, Cousin Robert. Mama brought me. But I know that it's a very big secret and no one is to know what's inside except you and me and Mama. If they tear out my fingernails and gouge out my eyes, I'll never tell," he added dramatically.

Robert shivered. The childish voice piping those gruesome words was a grim reminder of vulnerability. Rafael was too young to realize how true they could become, or how much easier it was to stand up to torture when it was only imaginary. "No one's going to do anything to you, *mi niño*," he promised, "because no one is going to find out anything about this. Whatever it turns out to be." So far he had nothing but Sofía's description of what was in the cave, and she admitted she'd not yet explored all the way to the back.

They stepped behind the tapestry curtain and Robert turned up the wick of the lantern he carried. He raised it and looked around him. "Sweet God! What a hoard. It's beyond belief. No wonder you haven't examined all of it."

"It's not just that there's so much of it," she said. "Each time I come here I find some new treasure I hadn't seen before. Like this." Sofía picked up a miniature chest. It was small enough to fit in the palm of her hand, but it was worked in tooled red leather and embossed in gold. There was a tiny gold clasp and when she opened it and lifted the lid, she sighed with pleasure. "Look." She held up a tiny lace cap, obviously made for an infant. "I keep finding things like this and I can't stop marveling long enough to explore further. What baby wore it, do you think?"

Robert examined the scrap of lace. The pattern had been worked to form a single flower, a lily, repeated many times. "I've no idea, but whoever wore it is long dead. I'd wager a lot this little cap is many centuries old. I can't prove it, mind—it just looks that way."

"To me too," Sofía agreed. "Is there nothing you know about this cave, Robert? No old family stories or legends?"

He shook his head. "Only the vaguest kind of nonsense— at least I thought it was nonsense until now. Domingo hinted something years ago when I first met him, and as I told you, there is that inscription under the stone in the room with the mark on the wall."

"But no date," she said thoughtfully.

"None. What's in here?" Robert pried the lid off one of the small kegs. It was full of illuminated manuscripts written on vellum. He held one under the light of the lantern. "Godstruth! I'd never believe such things existed, that they could have survived the history of the Jews in Spain. Look at this."

The first page of the volume was bordered in russet and blue. There was an exquisitely drawn peacock top and bottom, and a lion either side. Below the topmost peacock were four men obviously debating. They sat on chairs covered with six-pointed Stars of David. The writing below was in Hebrew characters. "Can you read this?" Robert asked.

"No," Sofía said. "More's the pity. But Robert, look, there's a date here at the bottom."

Where her finger pointed he saw the Roman numerals *MCCLXXV*. Robert thought for a moment. "The year 1275," he said. "Incredible. That's over two hundred years before the Jews were expelled from Spain. And before the Mendozas of Córdoba decided it was most convenient to declare themselves Catholics."

"That's what my finding all this means," Sofía whispered. The tone of her voice told him he'd somehow touched her deepest thoughts. "You and I are to bring—"

"*Mamacita*, come look at this!" Rafael's voice interrupted his mother. He had wandered by himself to the rear of the cave and now he was beckoning Robert and Sofía. "I opened this big trunk in the back, and look what I found."

Robert carried the lantern to where his son was actually standing inside one of the huge chests. Rafi was knee-deep in coins. "Sweet holy God," Robert exclaimed softly. "It's not just religious goodies those wily old Mendozas stashed away." He swung the boy out of the chest and reached in and picked up one of the coins, but he didn't examine it immediately. Bound to be worthless, he told himself, bound to be some temporary currency long out of circulation and without value—unless it was from the same period as the manuscript. Because in those days . . .

He glanced down at the coin he held. A man's head decorated the center, but it was too well rubbed to tell him much. Around the rim was a Latin inscription. "'*Sit tibi, Christe*,'" he read aloud. "I can't make out the rest." He paused and thought through the translation. "'To thee, O Christ . . .' Sofía, God help me, I think that was the beginning of the inscription on the gold ducats minted by the Duke of Puglia. About seven hundred years ago."

He fingered the coin, then bit it. "It is gold," he whispered, his voice tinged with awe. "I'd stake my soul that these are genuine gold ducats." He turned to Sofía. "Have you any idea what it means if I'm right?"

"Are they the same as bullion?"

"The very same. There was a standard, rigidly adhered to. A ducat was fifty-four grains troy of pure gold. It never altered, and because of that they stayed in circulation for a very long time. So if these are from the thirteenth century, or even the fourteenth, that's what they have to be. They had no other currency. They didn't mint some base-metal coin and declare it to have a value based on a government promise of gold or silver to back it up. That's a modern heresy—the old boys wanted the precious metal itself, and nothing else. All the rest was barter."

He knelt beside the chest and plunged his arms up to the elbows into the horde. "It's crammed solid with the things. I need scales and a quill and some paper if I'm to figure out exactly what we have here, but it's a fortune, Sofía. A bloody fortune."

Rafael's voice piped into the silence with which Sofía greeted this announcement. "Cousin Robert, there's another chest over here with the same thing in it. And there are two more, but I can't open them because they're locked."

Robert felt faint for a moment. Then excitement exploded in him and burst forth in the form of one great chortle of laughter. "We're rich again, by God! Oh, Farola, you're in for it now, lad. I have you, as the saying goes, by the balls." He laughed a second time, then saw Sofía's puzzled face and realized he'd unwittingly spoken in English.

He jumped up and hugged Sofía to him. "Never mind, I'll explain it all to you later." He tipped back his head and looked at her. "And I'll explain other things as well." Rafael joined them and Robert reached out an arm and included his son in the embrace.

"*Como tu quieres,*" Sofía whispered. "As you wish, I'll wait for you to explain, but we must remain quiet and cautious, Robert. Now more than ever."

"I agree. I'm acting a fool." He dropped his voice, mindful again of the need for secrecy, and took his fob watch from the pocket of his waistcoat. "It's after two, but this is the best time for me to make a start. Sofía, you and Rafi must go up to bed. I'll see you safe there. Then I'll go to the counting room and get what I need and come back and begin making some kind of estimate of exactly what we have here in our treasure cave."

Sofía slept peacefully for the first time since Robert left for Cádiz. Not even the discovery of the cave and the revelations it waked had completely distracted her from her worry about Robert. But now he was here, he was safe. And they had gold again, enough to secure Rafael's future and implement the plan she'd been formulating since she held the tallith in her hands. She slept dreamlessly and deeply for four hours, and when she woke, it was because Robert was sitting on the edge of her bed and he'd taken her hand.

"Good morning," he said softly. "It's only just sunrise, but I couldn't wait."

"Good morning. You look tired." She lifted one hand and lay it aside his cheek.

"Perhaps, but I've never lost a night's sleep in a better cause. It's millions, my dear. I've not completed the weighing, there wasn't time, but it's many, many millions. We're safe again and we have a future—you and I and our son."

"And the junta in Seville has none," she said, smiling. "Or at least one less secure than before we found the treasure."

"How did you figure that out?" he asked, startled at her intuition.

"It wasn't very difficult. When you were babbling in that barbarian tongue you call English I recognized the name Farola. So I knew you had some plan for dealing with the junta." She laughed softly at his look of amazement.

"You're a marvel," he said. "A very beautiful marvel, I might add." She looked incredibly delicious, her face still flushed with sleep and her breasts nearly free of the delicate silk nightdress she wore. Robert bent his head and put his lips to the rise of creamy flesh.

The kiss took Sofía by surprise, and she gasped, then put her hands to his head and pressed his face closer. "Robert," she whispered softly. "Oh, Robert . . ."

He wanted to tell her what he'd decided on the road back from Jerez, before he knew that the future before them was truly marvelous. But he couldn't speak, his mouth craved only to be filled with the hard pink nipples of her breasts and then with her lips and her tongue. He ran his hands over her, caressing her through the sheer fabric of her gown until she wriggled out of it and tugged at the waistband of his breeches.

He had to break from her for a moment, just long enough to strip off his own clothes. Then he was in the bed beside her, holding her in his arms, feeling the moist warmth of her breath and the hot fire of her skin. "I want us to be married," he murmured into her hair as he crushed her to him. "I love you and I want us to be married."

"Shh. Don't talk now. Just love me."

"But you will marry me? Say you will."

"I will marry you, my love," Sofía whispered. "Somehow we will find a rabbi, and I will marry you and love you as long as I live."

With a moan of passion and triumph he rolled on top of her and possessed her, and knew he was making the future a part of himself.

The carriage moved steadily along the road. Robert watched Seville rising to meet him, becoming larger and more imposing with every beat of the horses' hooves. In a few moments Enrique reined in the horses in the Plaza del Triunfo. Robert climbed down from the carriage and walked toward the Alcazar, that fortress first erected by the Moors then confiscated by the Christian kings. He would enter by the Puerto del Lion, the Lion's Gate. It was he who had suggested this venue, but who was Daniel—Farola or himself?

The grandee was waiting for him. "Welcome, Don Robert, I have long wanted to see again the English hidalgo." The two men studied each other. "They said you were mad," Farola murmured after a few seconds. "You don't look like a madman."

"I'm not." Robert gestured to a stone seat in the corner. "Shall we sit?"

They walked together to the bench. Farola wasted no time "Whatever your state of mind, Don Robert, you remain English and a Jew, and a man with no resources but his lands. What business can we have to discuss?"

Robert smiled. The attack was too immediate, too head on. Farola must be very nervous indeed. "Whatever else I may be, I'm still the head of the house of Mendoza."

"I grant you that meant something once—now it means nothing."

Robert did not rise to the bait. "Tell me, have you been

carefully storing treasure to back the currency you and the junta have been issuing these past three years?"

"The currency is solid," the duke said. "To suggest anything else is ridiculous."

"No, it is not," Robert said. "But I have a proposition to put to you. I will back your coinage. With gold."

Farola gasped once before he recovered himself. "How can the bankrupt house of Mendoza have gold to offer the junta?"

"Bankruptcy is perhaps a state of mind. When a man is faced with a crisis, he sometimes convinces himself there is no point in going on. That does not necessarily mean he is right."

Farola tipped back his head and studied the Englishman. "You don't look like a lunatic, despite what they say. I suppose it is possible for a man to be insane, then recover his senses. I'm told anything is possible in these modern times. But how am I to know this offer of yours is genuine?"

"How much coinage did you put into circulation these past three months?" Robert countered.

"I'm not sure, the equivalent of a million reales, perhaps two million."

"Fine, by week's end you'll have the gold to back the equivalent of two million reales. In ducats," he added. He felt a flush of elation, a surge of pure delight that was the particular heady pleasure of business well concluded. He held all the straws, short and long, and he would deal them out to the grandee at his pleasure.

"Ducats, how quaint," Farola said. "Nonetheless, it's a noble offer. Let us presume for the sake of our discussion that your actions match your words. What do you ask in return?"

"First I wish to know the terms of this new constitution being proposed by the Cortés."

"The contents are secret. When and if it is promulgated, all Spain will know them."

"I am not all Spain," Robert said softly. "And had I not been as I was," he added frankly, "you'd have had no choice but to include me in the junta and in the deliberations thus far."

"True." The duke rose and paced the chamber. Robert

watched him and said nothing. The minutes ticked by. At last the other man returned to the bench. "The gold is available? You swear it?"

"I swear it."

Farola sighed. Clearly he needed that gold. Robert had guessed correctly. The junta's currency was without backing, it would collapse at the first challenge. "Very well," the duke said softly. "But if you betray me, I'll kill you, Don Robert."

"It is not in my interests to betray you."

Farola nodded. "No, I cannot see why it should be. So, the constitution . . ." He sat down beside Robert and spoke in a whisper. "We will outlaw torture and slavery and—" He paused and looked directly at Robert. "And the Tribunal of the Holy Inquisition is to be abolished."

Robert kept his face impassive. "Then there is to be religious freedom in this wondrous new Spain you mean to create?"

"I didn't say that."

"No, I did. Am I correct?"

Farola looked away. "We cannot make a new Spain, only bring the old one into the nineteenth century. The proposed constitution states that only Roman Catholicism is, and shall perpetually be, the faith of the Spanish nation. The exercise of all other religions will be prohibited by law."

Robert stood up. "I bid you good day, Grandee. We have nothing further to discuss."

He'd gone as far as the door when Farola's voice stopped him. "Don Robert, we are only men," the duke said softly. "We cannot make miracles. This is not France or Prussia or even England. This is Spain. Have you lived so long among us and understood our character so little?"

Robert paused but he didn't turn around. It was Domingo's voice he heard, the old hidalgo telling him more or less the same thing the very first day he'd ever set foot in the Palacio Mendoza. "Perhaps I have," he murmured, "but I see little in your brave new world that will be of personal benefit to me. For the amount of gold we're discussing, I want something more."

"I rather thought you did," Farola said mildly. "What?"

"The right to be the official bank of Andalusia, of all Spain, if that's possible."

"Ah, I see. There were those who said that was the prize offered you by Napoleon when you first made your unholy alliance. It seems they were right."

"Do you agree?"

The duke shrugged. "How can I agree? What you propose would give the house of Mendoza enormous power, more than they've ever had. And for all that you're the hidalgo, you're an Englishman. I can chew that, Don Robert, but I cannot swallow it."

"So my origins give you indigestion?" Robert smiled. "But I come from Spanish stock. In everything that matters I'm as much an Andalusian as you are."

"Not everything."

Robert nodded. "True, but my religion is not a subject for debate."

"Frankly, I don't give a damn about your religion. But there are those in the junta who are much more pious than I am. They will have difficulty making common cause with someone they perceive to be a Jew."

"I have already said the matter is not open to debate."

"Yes, but the Mendozas have a long history of compromise—a genius for finding ways of accommodation. Can you not emulate the sterling qualities of your ancestors?"

"In what way?"

"Only a small gesture or two. Your mistress, for instance . . ." Robert started forward, and Farola held up his hand. "No, no, you misunderstand me. I mean no disrespect to the lady. She is a heroine—besides, life hasn't been normal in these difficult times. But things are improving. The dragoons are gone. So if perhaps you should see fit to marry the woman whom all Spain admires and adores, and to do so in a Catholic ceremony that all Spain could see—why, then I think we might calm the fears of the junta and everyone else."

"And the bank?"

"I think it would be assured. After all, there must be an

institution to administer all this gold being supplied by the house of Mendoza."

Leaving Farola's palace Robert studied the magnificent edifice. In the Palacio Mendoza all the glories were hidden behind high faceless walls; this palace proclaimed its splendors to the world. It was never like that with the Mendozas, Robert mused. Because even when they were no longer Jews, they dared not flaunt their wealth. Jealousy made long memories, and provided their enemies with a cudgel they could always dust off and use. So be it. Generations of Mendozas had been patient, now it was his turn.

Robert leaned out the window. "Drive on Enrique. Take us home."

He had no idea how he would convince Sofía that they must be married in the cathedral by a priest, not now, when she was so fascinated by her newly remembered Jewish origins. It seemed less possible than ever when he returned and she met him in the Patio del Recibo. She had that same look of fanatic devotion he'd noticed before, that mystic glow. And she didn't spare a moment to ask him how things had gone in Seville.

"Robert, I have made the most wonderful discovery. You won't believe it. But you'll have to because you're going to see with your own eyes." She took his hand and led him into the palace.

"Sofía, where are we going? Can't it wait? I've a lot to talk to you about."

"No, this can't wait. I've been beside myself with impatience for three days. It's the most important event in the history of your family."

She led him to the Patio de las Mujeres, just outside the old room with the frieze of acanthus leaves. Robert stopped walking and did not allow her to tug him forward. "I think I can guess where you're taking me, and why."

Sofía looked at him and smiled and nodded her head. "Come see," she whispered. "I polished it myself and it's beautiful."

She'd found the plaque that had once hung in that room, the one that had made the mark on the wall. "I knew what it was as soon as I uncovered it in the back of the cave," she explained. "Because of its shape, and because of the pendant you showed me the day we swore to protect Rafael."

She had hung the plaque and it covered the mark exactly. It was exquisitely etched with birds and leaves and flowers; the Hebrew letters carved deep into its surface had darkened over the centuries, but that only made them stand out better against the gleaming brass face. "The words are exactly the same as on your pendant," Sofía said. "I got it and brought it in here and compared them."

"'If I forget thee, O Jerusalem, may my right hand forget her cunning...'" Robert quoted softly. He stood and stared for a long moment, then he turned to her and took her two hands and drew her toward him. "My dear, this can't remain here."

"Why not?"

"Sofía, have you forgotten where you are? This is Spain, not France. And you're a grown woman, not a child. The very thing that drove out your ancestors, the Inquisition, still exists and still hunts down Jews. It's to be abolished, but the practice of any religion but Catholicism will remain a crime. Who else has seen this?"

She hung her head. "No one. I locked the room and didn't let anyone in. But I hoped that when you returned, when you had made your arrangements with the junta, perhaps..."

"I was able to make arrangements, as you put it," he told her. "Good ones. But business dealings, my love, not a miracle. Sofía, you're obsessed by what you've remembered, and I understand that. But you mustn't forget that there's still Rafi to protect."

"I want him to be raised a Jew," she whispered. "Oh, Robert, I want that so much."

"I know. But he can't be. Not publicly, not if we mean to keep him with us."

"With us...? But where else would he be?"

"In England perhaps. It's easier to live quietly as a Jew in England."

"You mean send him to your brother?"

"If Liam feels kindly toward me, yes, it's a possibility."

"But you would not return to London?"

Robert shook his head. "My life is here, Sofía, my destiny. I promised my father that I'd take over the house in Córdoba and make it great. I have a second chance to keep that promise. I can't turn my back on it."

She clasped her hands and held them to her heart as if she were in mortal pain, and she turned and looked at the brass plaque. "'If I forget thee, O Jerusalem . . .'" she murmured. "But that's what you are suggesting we must do, isn't it? We have to forget that we're Jews. Or send our son away."

"Not exactly," Robert said softly. "My father once told me about this family motto. It was adopted centuries ago when the Mendozas were in exile in Africa. The man who originated it wanted his children to think of Córdoba as Jerusalem. It was Córdoba they were never to forget."

"And Rafael?" she asked in a hoarse whisper.

"Córdoba is Rafael's inheritance, my love. And he is our future. He belongs here with us. We can tell him of his Jewish heritage, even teach him about Judaism, though God knows how, since you and I know practically nothing about it, but whatever we do must be in secret. And we'll have to wall up the cave again, and leave all the religious things hidden for the time being. Rafi understands about secrets. He'll understand more as he grows older."

Sofía didn't say anything for a long moment, then she looked up at him. "Robert, I know something about Judaism, I've remembered it. You're not supposed to take the name of the Lord in vain. So if you promise to stop saying God this and God that and godstruth, maybe we can make a Jew out of Rafael. Now, will you put this plaque back in the cave, or shall I?"

"We'll do it together."

They removed the sheet of brass from the wall. "Can you get something to wrap it in?" Robert asked. "I don't think we should leave it as it is."

Sofía disappeared for a few minutes. When she returned she

carried the blue and white prayer shawl Rafael had worn the night Robert returned from Jerez. "Will this do?"

"It will do very well," Robert said solemnly. They wrapped the plaque in the tallith and carried it back to the cave.

"Not for always," Sofía said, looking around at the kegs and urns and chests that contained the heart and soul of what the Mendozas had once been, and what she prayed they would be again. "Just for now."

Robert saw the tears in her eyes. "Don't cry, my love. We're protecting our son, as we swore to do. Don't you remember?"

She nodded and managed a smile. Robert stroked her cheek with his finger. "The house of Mendoza will survive and flourish here in Córdoba, where it's meant to be—and not just for you and me, but for Rafael, and his sons after him. And someday things will be different."

"You're sure?"

"Very sure," he told her. "The winds of change are blowing, my little Gypsy, but they won't blow us away. We'll stand up to the wind, whether it brings storm or calm, and it will make us strong. And when the wind passes, Sofía, I give you my word, the Mendozas will still be here."

The History That Came After

In 1812 Napoleon invaded Russia, and was defeated by her vastness and her bitter cold winter. His fortunes waxed and waned after that, but he was never again seen as invincible. In 1815 Wellington delivered the coup de grâce at Waterloo, and Napoleon surrendered to the British and lived the rest of his life in exile on the barren South Atlantic island of St. Helena. He died there in 1821. In 1840 the French people brought his remains home and buried them with full pomp under the dome of Les Invalides.

Also in 1812, on March 19, in Cádiz, a Cortés made up of representatives of the various provincial juntas met and promulgated the Spanish constitution discussed in this story. In 1814 Ferdinand VII was restored to the throne, and proved a cruel and repressive absolutist. He repealed the constitution, but could not hold on to the Spanish colonies. In a short time only Puerto Rico, Cuba, and Manila swore allegiance to Spain. Andalusia had lost not just the wealth that had been hers by virtue of her role in the American trade; she lost, with all the rest of Spain, the opportunity to become part of modern

Europe. She became the poorest province of the nation, and the *guerrilleros* of one generation became the bandits of the next.

And the Mendozas? Ah, that is another story. . . .

Sweeping from Spain to England to the Americas in the last glory days of commerce on the high seas, FLAMES OF VENGEANCE is a thrilling tale of love, adventure, grand schemes . . . and revenge.

Heroine Lila Curran and her son Michael have suffered unspeakable brutality at the hands of Juan Luis Mendoza. . . .

Córdoba, Spain

1860. The darkness moved and breathed as if alive. It defined everything in Lila Curran's world. Sounds snaked through her black shroud, twisted around her, strangled her will to resist. She lived in perpetual night, the details of her captivity conveyed to her by all her senses—except sight. The metal collar around her neck was heavy; the marble floor cold, and the woven carpets she lay on rough. The sides of the enormous carved wooden bed to which she was chained were high—and the bed itself an almost unendurable torment, for it was placed just inches too far for her to climb on.

Lila could hear her child crying. Her six-month-old son was in the room adjacent to hers. He'd been christened Miguel in the Spanish fashion, but to her—always—he was Michael. Her baby boy, the sweet, tender infant born, she'd thought, of love and trust, had become as much an object of his father's hatred as she. Twice a day a wet nurse came and fed him and attended ·o his needs; the rest of the time Michael was alone and frightened, and he wept. And Lila tore at her chains and screamed out her fury and her pain.

Around her and Michael the household in the ancient and venerable Palacio Mendoza kept to its ordinary daily routine. Lila heard through her darkness the noises of servants going about their chores, of her husband, the mighty Juan Luis Mendoza, stomping along the passage outside her door or venting his insane rages in the patio below her balcony. Occasionally she heard the voice of Juan Luis's sister Beatriz or of her husband Francisco. Her in-laws knew she was a captive. But they, too, were Juan Luis's prisoners, incapable of breaking the bonds of his tyrannical rule—in thrall to the Mendoza legacy of power and wealth.

1861. They brought her food once a day, always the same, a kind of stew of vegetables and a bit of meat in a wooden bowl. No spoon was provided; to survive she must bury her face in the dish like an animal. Lila did it, she did whatever was necessary, because one thing she had determined in the thirteen months since Juan Luis had chained her. She would survive and she would be avenged.

Until the day when the voice of the child was silenced.

Lila listened for him, her heartbeats timed to his cries as they had been since her torment began, but there was nothing. She had thought there was no terror or fury she had not already plumbed, but the knowledge that Michael was gone— dead? murdered by his own father?—was a visitation from hell. Her pain and rage were beyond imagining. She could not scream; she hadn't the strength. All she could do was lie on the floor, her hands clasped to the metal collar around her neck.

Hours passed. And then she knew. Juan Luis had won. She was at last the victim of total despair.

"Lila, Lila, *puedes oír me, mi niña?*" The voice seemed to come from far away. It repeated the question a second time, in labored English, an urgent whisper. "Can you hear me? It is I, your sister-in-law, Beatriz. Lila, in God's name, are you alive?"

Her name, spoken in a human voice. In all the long days and weeks and months of her agony, she had not heard her name, the acknowledgment of her existence as a separate human being. "I . . . I am alive." Her lips cracked and began to bleed with the effort of making words. "Beatriz, my baby, my Michael—"

"Shh, do not talk, only listen. I am outside the door. I bribed the maid to unlock the corridor, but she would not dare to give me the key to this room. Juan Luis has terrified her, terrified all the servants." Beatriz's voice broke. "Terrified even us."

"Michael," Lila whispered. "My Michael . . ."

"That is what I have come to tell you. He is all right, *mi niña*, he is with me. Francisco and I have taken him to our apartments. I could live with it no longer, this wickedness. I prayed. I gathered courage. Then I told my crazy brother that if he did not give me the baby to look after, I would make a scandal even he could not survive. To torture a helpless infant, it is unthinkable. All Andalusia would treat him as a leper . . . Lila, do you understand? Your little Miguel, he is fine. He will be well, I will take care of him until Juan Luis comes to his senses." There was no reply. "Lila," Beatriz called again, "Lila, *puedes oír me?*"

The whispered response came after some seconds. "*Sí, oigo yo.* I hear you, I understand."

Her child was alive, well, cared for. It gave her courage. Lila knew she would survive.

1872. Sometimes Michael came to the balcony of her room. It was a difficult trick; he had to be quite certain that neither his father nor any of his father's spies would see him. He had to hoist himself up to the second story, using only the vines that grew on the stone walls of the palace as handholds, but he managed to do it sometimes.

Lila had been torn apart when the clandestine visits began. She longed to see her son, but she hated him to see her. True, things were somewhat better now. The metal collar and the chains had been removed, a gesture of munificence on the part of Juan Luis, some kind of relenting of his mad, unfound jealousy, but she was still a prisoner in this single room. Her hair, once flaming red, had turned to silver. She was as thin as a wraith—a shadow who dwelled among shadows, not a woman.

"Mama! Mama, are you there?" The boy pressed his face to the glass of the balcony doors. They were locked and he had never managed to find a key that would open them, but when his mother heard his voice, she usually came and parted the draperies a crack. Then they could peer at each other through the opening, separated, unable to touch, but with an illusion of closeness. "Mama," the boy called again. "Please answer me, it's important."

The curtains parted—only a hair, to open them wider might alert watching eyes. It was far too dangerous. "I'm here, darling. How are you?"

"I'm fine, Mama, fine."

Lila filled her being with the sight of him. He was a big child, enormous for thirteen, with her red hair and blue eyes. She pressed her fingertips to the glass. If only she could touch his face. Michael . . . Michael . . . the child of her agony, of her heart, the son she had not embraced since he was three months old. "Michael," she whispered, her mouth hovering near the panes as if her breath might kiss him though her lips could not.

"Mama, listen, I have something for you. It was wonderful luck that Tía Beatriz and I saw this letter before Papa did. She said I should bring it to you."

Lila looked at the envelope. It was large and thick. She had no idea where it had come from or how she could hope to put her hands on it. It was too fat for Michael to slide between the cracks. "Michael, you cannot give it to me. It won't fit. Besides, it's too dangerous. If your father finds out—"

"I don't care," the boy said. "It's important, I know it is. I'm going to break the glass." He held up something else. A large stone.

"Michael! No, you mustn't. Your father—"

"I don't care! I'm going to break the glass and get you out. We will run away from the Palacio Mendoza. We will run so far that Papa will never find us."

There was no place on this earth beyond the grasp of the enormous wealth and power of the Mendozas. Lila knew it even if her son didn't. Besides, she had no money, no family, nothing. Where could she take him? What would they do? "No," she whispered. "No."

"Mama, the letter is important. I know it is. I feel in my bones that it is."

Lila looked at the envelope. She felt something too. Something indescribable, something she had long ago thought was dead in her. Courage, the ability to do more than merely survive, a freshening of her will to triumph. She reached out a hand as if to take the document. It drew her with a mysterious power, a sense of absolute rightness, of destiny. "Yes," she whispered. "Yes, Michael, do it. Break the glass. Only enough to get the letter in, only one pane. I can cover the break so it won't be discovered for a while."

Juan Luis came to her that night. He often came these days. He would pace up and down the room that was her prison and rave at her, tell her of her crimes, of how she had cuckolded him. She'd long ago given up remonstrating, no arguments of hers could alter his insane fixation on imagined betrayals. Her only reply was silence. That night she listened for long minutes, aware of the stirring of air in the room from the broken glass as yet unnoticed. The letter weighed ominously heavy in the pocket of her gown. Finally she did what she had not done in months, she spoke.

"Juan Luis, listen to me."

He froze, startled by the voice he had not heard for so long. "So you deign to answer? To what do I owe the honor?"

"To the truth, Juan Luis. To knowledge. I have knowledge, and because of it you are going to set me free. Me and my son."

"What are you talking about?"

"Power," Lila said softly. "I am talking about power. And you are going to listen."

Two days after the letter was placed in Lila Curran's hands, she and her son, Michael, left the Palacio Mendoza. Their journey took mere weeks, but their odyssey would take many years and span two continents. They had embarked on a quest for that most elusive of all rewards; they wanted reparation for the lost years, the countless humiliations. They craved vengeance.

Fifteen years later, free and with her scheme for justice and revenge in motion, Lila has lunch with a much-changed Beatriz. . . .

A man wearing a tall white chef's toque appeared at their table and carved slices of beef from a huge joint on an elaborate silver trolley. Another waiter added roast potatoes and squares of Yorkshire pudding and asked the women if they would take gravy and horseradish cream. Lila refused the garnishes, Beatriz accepted both. The wine steward removed the Graves and filled fresh glasses with vibrant red claret.

"Will you hate it when Michael takes over?" Lila asked.

Beatriz paused, a forkful of meat halfway to her mouth. "Hate it? In heaven's name, why would I be cooperating if I were going to hate Michael taking over in Córdoba?"

"I'm not sure. He's bound to marry eventually. His wife will be mistress of the palacio."

"Thank God. For me, that is one of the bonuses." Beatriz leaned against the dusky green velvet banquette. She wore a burgundy silk dress, a bad choice because the color made her skin sallow, but she managed to look like a luxuriating cat as she relaxed her shoulders. "I shall travel. France, I think. Deauville and Biarritz. Perhaps Austria. I've always wanted to see Vienna and Salzburg."

"Without Francisco?"

"Of course without Francisco. If he does not have a stroke or commit suicide when he is ruined, I shall just insist on a quiet separation. You know what I told you about how he is in bed—bim-bang, like a rabbit. No more of that will be heaven."

"Beatriz, there's one thing still worrying me. . . . What if Francisco doesn't respond the way we think he will? What if he braves the storm and finds a brilliant solution of his own?"

"Francisco?" Beatriz giggled. The laughter bubbled until she pursed her lips and choked it back. "Believe me, dear Lila, it is impossible. He will run for help like a little boy who has fallen and hurt himself. You can be sure of it." She wiped tears of laughter from her eyes with a lacy handkerchief. "Like a rabbit. Bim-bang, he'll run down the hole."

"You're quite incredible, you know. Will you try some of those strawberries?"

Beatriz studied the dessert cart that had been wheeled to their table. "Perhaps just a few. And a little piece of that cake." She smiled at the waiter and agreed that he should bathe both treats in thick, heavy cream.

It was later, when they were sipping tiny cups of strong black coffee in the sitting room of Lila's suite, that Beatriz reiterated her single condition. "Michael will do what he has promised?"

"Take up the practice of Judaism, make his children Jews? Yes, he will. You have his word on it. He's already stopped eating pork," Lila added with a tinkling laugh.

Beatriz nodded approval and helped herself to a sugared almond from a silver dish. "Good. Because if he does not, I will bring him down. I do not know how, I'm not as clever at these things as you are. But I will find a way to ruin him."

The words were spoken so calmly Lila knew they were absolutely true. "There will be no need. Michael understands his obligations."

"Fine. Then everyone will be happy. And my poor dead parents can rest in peace."

"They indoctrinated you so thoroughly," Lila murmured. "How is it they failed with Juan Luis?"

"Who knows? It's doubly surprising because he was nine years old when my father died. I was an infant." Beatriz sighed. "Men are all a little stupid and heartless, are they not?"

"Juan Luis was many things, but not stupid."

"Still defending him, after what he did to you?"

"I'm not defending him," Lila said. "I'm simply stating a fact."

"Very well, but his son is different?"

"My son is wonderful."

Beatriz smiled. "Then we have no problems. Only Francisco has a problem." She giggled.

"I can think of a few others who aren't going to be thrilled with our activities," Lila said. "Jamie and Henry and Norman Mendoza for a start."

"They are all traitors pretending to be something they're not. Like their fathers before them." Beatriz dismissed the victims with a wave of her hand.

"What about you?" The wine at lunch had left a pleasant little buzz in Lila's head. It made it seem possible to ask such a question. "Haven't you been pretending to be something you're not all these years?"

"It seems like that, I know. But it is not the same. No one held a gun to Joseph's head and made him become a Christian. The family of my mother is from Madrid. They escaped to Italy in 1492 after the edict of banishment, but they returned about a hundred years later. Spaniards always return to Spain. It is in our blood."

"But they came back as Christians?"

"Only in public. The Caleros, my mother's people, were true Marranos, secret Jews. That's why Robert and Sofía chose Anna Calero to marry their Rafael."

Lila was trying to understand how a passion this deep and everlasting could be based on an unseen God. Her own motives were so different. She thought about the various other branches of the Mendoza clan in England. None of them had followed Joseph into Christianity; they quietly went on being Jews . . . after a fashion. Was that her sister-in-law's fashion as well? At lunch Beatriz had eaten her lobster with gusto. Little as she knew of Judaism, Lila did understand that the dietary laws prohibited lobster. "Do you consider yourself a Jew?"

"Of course." Beatriz pressed a hand to her heart. "Here I am a Jew. But that will not make my mother and father's dream come true. I have no children."

Lila nodded. Michael was, as she had always known, her greatest treasure.

"Everything is ready in Córdoba," Beatriz continued. "I made all the arrangements exactly as you instructed."

"You told them the code was minus twenty?"

"Yes. I did just what you told me to do. As soon as the cables are sent it will begin. I shall be well out of it, up at Westlake. Jamie has invited me to visit. He does not want me, of course, I'm not decorative enough. But he has to be gracious to a visiting cousin."

"Excellent, you can keep an eye on him." Lila poured more coffee and dropped three lumps of sugar into her sister-in-law's cup. It seemed as if they'd said everything they needed to say, but she could see at least one more question in the other woman's eyes. "What is it? Why are you looking at me like that?"

"Because I have always wanted to ask you something," Beatriz said, "and never have I had the nerve."

"Ask me now."

"Will you promise to answer?"

"You know me better than that. I'd never make such an open-ended promise."

"No, I suppose you wouldn't," Beatriz admitted. "You have always been too clever for me. But to ask costs nothing, does it?"

"Nothing."

"Very well, I will ask. How did you make Juan Luis let you go, how did you force him to give you so much money and his piece of the medallion? Most of all, how did you make him let Michael go?"

"I had information that he could not allow to become public."

Beatriz set down her cup with a clatter. "Lila, that is no answer at all. I know that. What information? How did you get it?"

Lila pursed her lips, thought for a moment, then smiled. "I won't tell you that, but I will tell you a story. . . .

* * *

Beverly Byrne's FLAMES OF VENGEANCE, a story packed with emotion and adventure, goes on sale in early November 1991. Look for this thrilling novel wherever Bantam Books are sold or ask your bookseller to reserve a copy for you.

<u>FANFARE</u>

Enter the marvelous new world of **Fanfare**!
From sweeping historicals set around the globe to
contemporary novels set in glamorous spots,
Fanfare means great reading.
Be sure to look for new **Fanfare** titles each month!

Coming Soon:

TEXAS! CHASE

By *New York Times* bestselling author, Sandra Brown

The reckless rodeo rider who'd lost everything he loved...
Bittersweet, sensual, riveting, TEXAS! CHASE will touch every heart.

THE MATCHMAKER

By Kay Hooper, author of STAR-CROSSED LOVERS

Sheer magic in a romance of forbidden love between rich and mysterious
Cyrus Fortune and the exquisite beauty he is bound to rescue.

RAINBOW

By Patricia Potter

A flirt without consequence ... a rogue without morals ... From a fierce,
stormy passion rose a love as magnificent as a rainbow.

FOLLOW THE SUN

By Deborah Smith, author of THE BELOVED WOMAN

Three women bound by the blood of their noble Cherokee ancestors ...
one glorious legacy of adventure, intrigue -- and passion!

THE SYMBOL OF GREAT WOMEN'S FICTION FROM BANTAM

Ask for these books at your local bookstore.

AN 293 - 7/91

From the bestselling author of
MONTANA WOMAN and EMBERS OF THE HEART

IN THE SHADOW OF THE MOUNTAINS

By Rosanne Bittner

IN THE SHADOW OF THE MOUNTAINS is
the breathtaking saga of a remarkable family who
endured tragedy and hardship to build a glorious
mountain empire. The Kirklands, from penniless settlers
to wealthy mine owners to Denver's regal first family,
together they pursued their dazzling dream of love and
glory.

David -- the brave mountain dreamer who risked his life
to stake a claim to a new life in the rugged Colorado
Rockies
Beatrice -- the ambitious, strong-willed matriarch who
sacrificed her girlish dreams for the perils and hardships
of an unknown, untamed wilderness
Irene -- the beautiful young woman who shared her
father's passion for the land and ached for the one man
she was forbidden to love
Elly -- the scheming daughter who vowed to possess the
family fortune and the man she worshipped above all
else
John -- the desperate son who struggled to escape his
mother's domination and carve out his own life.

**THE SYMBOL OF GREAT WOMEN'S
FICTION FROM BANTAM**
On sale now at your local bookstore.   AN 290 - 7/91

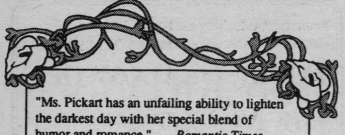

"Ms. Pickart has an unfailing ability to lighten the darkest day with her special blend of humor and romance." *--Romantic Times*

THE BONNIE BLUE
by Joan Elliott Pickart

Slade Ironbow was big, dark, and dangerous, a man any woman would want -- and the one rancher Becca Colten found impossible to resist!

Nobody could tame the rugged half-Apache with the devil's eyes, but when honor and a secret promise brought him to the Bonnie Blue ranch as her new foreman, Becca couldn't send him away. She needed his help to keep from losing her ranch to the man she suspected had murdered her father, but stubborn pride made her fight the mysterious loner whose body left her breathless and whose touch made her burn with needs she'd never understood.